From Within the Firebird's Nest

A Novel By
Sheldon Charles

This is a work of fiction. Names, characters, businesses, places, and incidents either are products of the author's imagination or are used fictitiously. Any resemblance to actual events or locales or persons, living or dead, is entirely coincidental.

From Within the Firebird's Nest by Sheldon Charles, Published by Valkyrie Spirit Publishing, PO Box 4357, Battle Creek, MI 49016-4357. http://www.valkyriespirit.com

ISBN: 978-1733958820 (Paperback)
       978-1733958813 (ePub)
Printed in the United States of America

Dedication

The Cold War was won by thousands of men and women who served during the years when the military was largely ignored by the American public. They received, no Veterans points, no parades, and no special medals*. It is to them that this book is dedicated with gratitude for maintaining world peace.

* The only exception was the Army of Occupation Medal, presented to military personnel assigned to Berlin.

Acknowledgements

Some think that an author sits alone in a room, at a desk, pouring words on to paper. That is true much of the time, but there are instances when an author needs to reach out for information or opinions that are just better coming from another human versus the internet or a reference book.

These folks were there when I reached out and made this book better because they took the time to lend a hand when needed. I thank them wholeheartedly, and I am glad I have people like these in my life. *Last names omitted to protect their privacy.*

Alan, Ann, Austynne, Beka, Brandy, Harry, Jay, Joe, Keith, Kelly, Lisa, Matt, Michael, Natalie, Pegi, Scott, Susie, Tammi, Tim, Tonya, and Valerie

Much gratitude to the folks at Maker's Mark Distillery in Loretto, Kentucky and at the Jim Beam American Stillhouse in Clermont. Kentucky for educating me about the making and aging of Bourbon.

Many thanks to my editor Jenny Grace for her advice and support and for my puppy MacBeth for being there when I needed to find my own *Satori.*

Finally, thank you Constance for your love, support, words of encouragement, advice, and putting up with me during this journey.

Table of Contents

Chapter One

Julian walked into the bank as he did most mornings, hoping for a bit of excitement but knowing the day would likely be extremely routine. He had gotten used to it over the years, accepting it as normal. At this point in Julian's life, *routine* had shifted from being monotonous to being a welcome situation, fewer demands meant he had the freedom to come and go as he needed for appointments or other personal business. After taking the last week off to move into his new home, he looked forward to returning to work for a change of pace and the chance for his aching muscles to recover. Maybe, for once, routine was exactly what he sought.

He had moved into his new workspace after his promotion in August, and one of the perks of the second-floor office was a large window with a view of The Square, a verdant and tree-filled park in the center of town surrounding the Woods County Courthouse. All he had to do was swivel his desk chair, lean back, and enjoy. At least once or twice a day, he found himself deep in thought as he stared at the trees and people walking by. Julian was at that age where people contemplated all three stages of life—past, present, and future.

Julian had no doubt that fortune had favored his life. When he first came to this country, he questioned everything about his destiny and fate. As the years slipped away, Julian gradually accepted what he was doing and just as he had made peace with it, the Soviet Union collapsed and the likelihood of his ever being called upon to perform his primary mission gradually faded. He was curious why he had never been told to formally stand down from his mission, but was more grateful no one had contacted him at all. He knew somewhere deep-down inside was a fierce loyalty to his Motherland and an absolute dedication to his assigned task, should he ever be called on to perform it. Even though

Julian had stopped doing the assigned readings several years ago, he still maintained the library of books. He also felt compelled to set aside time twice a week to listen for the radio broadcast that could call him into action.

As he was awaiting that transmission, life went on. He met and fell in love with a beautiful young lady while working on his bachelor's degree in Kansas-- Camille Robinson. From the first time he saw her expressive face and dazzling brown eyes from a distance, he was entranced. People with a life's mission like his are directed to avoid attention-getting situations such as interracial marriage, but he could not help but allow himself this indulgence.

After Camille and Julian were married in 1992, she convinced him to move to the small town in northern Oklahoma where her grandparents had lived. She had spent summers on their ranch enjoying days filled with 4H competitions, riding horses, and learning about cooking and canning from her grandmother. Julian's mission only imposed one geographic restriction on his choice of residence: it had to be within a twelve-hour drive of any of the states in the Midwest. A move to Alva met that requirement nicely, and after graduation, he went to work for the Ranchers & Farmers Bank.

His recent promotion was to Regional Manager. After two decades with the bank, he was well liked by the folks who worked for him and those customers important enough to deserve his personal attention. The job had proven to be the ideal cover for his mission by being stable and neither too visible or restrictive. The KGB had created an extensive manufactured background biography which resulted in a smooth bonding and background investigation when he was hired by the bank. With that requirement satisfied, no one ever questioned anything about his personal history.

Camille and Julian had three children -- two in the final stages of high school, and one just completing his sophomore year of college. Camille never questioned Julian's family history. Early on he explained the absence of parents was the result of an automobile accident when he was eighteen. She never pressed him as to why he had no relationship with any extended family since she had enough extended family to keep them both occupied. Their life together worked and Julian was wholly satisfied.

Julian's mind would wonder, at times, back to the day his father had dropped him off at the Academy. Papa was the only parent he ever knew; he was told that his mother had died in childbirth, so he had never met her. He loved his father deeply, but even at age six, he understood the sadness the man carried as the result of his mother's death. Almost forty years later, Julian's father leaving him at the school was still one of the most traumatic events of his life. He could still recall almost every detail.

His father had been both loving and caring, but he could also be brutally honest--not holding back anything from the young boy. If the boy asked a question, his father replied with the most truthful answer possible regardless of how harsh or seemingly inappropriate for his age. This included what took place that fateful day, which began with his Papa preparing breakfast in their Moscow apartment--sausages and eggs, young Dmitry's favorite. His father ate silently, which would happen from time to time when things were going on at work. Usually, they discussed school or his father would ask him riddles. On this day, there was none of that as they ate without saying a word.

After breakfast, rather than doing the dishes immediately, he took the Dmitry by the hand and led him into his bedroom. His father sat down on the bed and motioned for him to sit with him.

"Dmitry, as you know, I have worked for the government for a long time, and as a result, I find out when things are going to start changing in our country for the better or for worse." His father spoke in a calm voice, and Dmitry nodded as each point was being made. "This means that I, as your Papa, will sometimes know what is going on far enough in advance that I can do things that will help you because you are my son. Today, you will be receiving an opportunity to serve our nation in a brand new way and at the same time secure your future regardless of what happens here." Dmitry wanted to ask questions, but his father continued without pausing. "I am sending you to another school that will teach you a new language and new customs. If you study and work diligently, Dmitry, when you finish with the school, you will be sent to a brand-new land with many opportunities, and at the same time, you will be providing a vital service to our nation. I know you don't fully understand this right now, but do you hear my words?" The boy nodded. He had heard the words but didn't understand.

"Good. Now, we will pack a suitcase of clothes which will help you settle into your new school. They will give you clothes after you have been there for a few days and passed some initial tests." With that, Dmitry's father took a suitcase from the top shelf of the closet and began packing his son's clothes. Dmitry stood in the middle of the room not understanding what was happening. His father had tears flowing down his cheeks.

"Are you okay Papa?"

"Yes, yes – Dmitry, I am okay. I am just so happy that you are going to have this opportunity and I know you will do your best and will succeed."

"I promise to try very hard," the boy said, grabbing his father's leg.

Fyodor was doing his best to try to maintain some modicum of control over himself; he picked up the boy and held him in his arms close to his body. "I know you will my precious, precious boy."

The drive from their home to the Academy took the full day and was so long that the boy could not remember all the twists and turns it took to get from one place to the other. When they finally stopped, it was late at night, and Dmitry went from window to window inside trying to see his new school but was sorely disappointed. There was nothing. Peering through the windshield, he could only see a metal gate across the road.

Fyodor rolled down the window and handed a soldier an identification card he had taken from his wallet. After a few moments, the soldier returned from the roadside hut and gave the card back to his father. He delivered a snappy salute before opening the gate. Fyodor nodded and put the vehicle in gear. Dmitry had never seen his father treated like this before and realized he must be extremely important.

After they had driven a few kilometers, Fyodor pulled into a parking lot in front of a small, nondescript building. He motioned for the boy to get out and join him as he took the suitcase from the trunk. Dmitry sensed his father was greatly upset.

"The time has come, my son," his father murmured, as he knelt down. "Always remember that I did this because I love you and because I want you to have a fantastic future. Inside you-- no matter where you go from here-- always keep in your heart buried the fact that your mother and I love you. No matter what name your duty gives you --- you will always be Dmitry Fyodorevich Maldroski even though you will never use that name again." With that Fyodor wrapped his arms around his son and gave him a last embrace.

Upon entering the building, they were confronted by a rather stern-looking woman in uniform behind a large desk. His father and the woman spoke for several minutes before she handed him a piece of paper and a pen. When he was finished writing, he handed the paper back to the woman who glanced at it and nodded. The woman motioned for Dmitry. The boy looked up at his father confused and Fyodor motioned for his son to follow the matron. She led him into the formal training area for candidates assigned to the Crimson Firebird Initiative.

Dmitry never knew that his father maintained loose contact with the school to monitor and guide his progress. Dmitry never saw his father again, but Fyodor managed from time to time to see his son from afar. Fyodor did everything he could to distance himself from his son so no harm would come his way. Fyodor managed to expunge all records connecting them. Of course, Dmitry never learned of his father's actions and saw his absence as one more hardship that this particular assignment required of him.

Julian was almost to the point of dozing when the phone on his desk rang. He picked it up and tried to make his voice sound chipper rather than tired and more than a little sad. "Hey Dan, how are things down at Webster's Ornamental Iron and what can your favorite banker do for you today?"

After a conversation concerning the Webster company's need for additional capital, Julian hung up and checked his schedule for the day. Nothing of consequence--the Tri-County Business Group luncheon at the nearby Sandwich Shoppe. There was, of course, an item that was not on the calendar--listening to the twice weekly contact broadcast; Mondays, 9:15 in the morning, and Thursdays at 12:30 in the afternoon. Even though he had given up the required readings, he could not stop himself from listening for – what? An alert? A stand-down Message? Any Message? In all the years, he had only ever heard the standard Routine Message transmission.

He locked his office door. The antique 1958 *Blaupunkt* Console Stereo sat in the corner of the room. The console had been part of every space he had occupied since he was first provided a private office with the Ranchers & Farmers Bank. He lifted the console's lid and turned on the unit on, pausing to give the tubes a chance to come to life. He opened the door to the console where he had hidden a bottle of Pappy Van Winkle bourbon and a pair of rocks glasses. As static started to come through the speaker, he knelt down in front of the unit and pressed the *MW* button to access the correct frequency. Next, he spun the dial to the 930's MHz range and slowly twisted the dial back and forth between 900 and 1000, searching for the alerting notes that signaled the start of the broadcast.

The first sound after the six-note alert would identify the type of the transmission. The Message would be one of four types: Routine, Warning, Preparation, or Execution. Routine was signaled by any sound other than those expressly reserved for one of the other three types. As a result, the sound effect would normally be different with every single Message and the randomness would serve as a decoy for anyone listening to eventually ignore the constant change. A Routine Message could be ignored once the sound effect had been heard. It was just a way of periodically testing the system. The content sent after the sound effect was gibberish, consisting of random words and numbers to redirect attention.

Julian was listening for the sounds tied specifically to other

Message types. A phrase of classical solo piano indicated a Warning Message, a Preparation Message was preceded by the ringing of a church bell, and an Execution Message was signaled by the laughter of a child. When Julian learned this at the Academy, he and his fellow students were never told why those sounds were chosen or who had chosen this protocol, but these were questions that crossed his mind almost every time he prepared to listen.

The static was broken by a familiar and distinctive six-note alert tone. The set of tones played three times before the Message broadcast started, giving the listener time to locate the day's frequency and to copy the information. Julian grabbed his notepad and pen. He turned the volume down, placed his ear near the speaker, held his breath and waited. After the last tone played, there was a moment of silence and then the sound of an ape making grunting noises. Julian exhaled. *A Routine Message.* What he felt now was a mix of relief and disappointment. After all these years, the anxiety that Message might be a type other than Routine was still there.

This could go on for fifteen minutes. A woman's voice, with a British accent, reeled off randomly interspersed numbers, letters, and words. Even the presenter was random, over the years, he had heard, women, men, and children – with and without accents. The one thing that had not changed was the type of Message which was always Routine.

Julian pushed the FM button on the Blaupunkt and spun the tuning dial to 97.5 encountering the familiar voice of Austin Graves, reading a commercial. He turned up the volume a bit, unlocked his door and returned to his desk to contemplate his neat piles of paper.

"97.5 The Quake. Now Tommy TuTone – Jenny Don't Lose That Number...867-5309..." Graves' voice faded as the first few familiar notes of the electric guitar filled the office.

Routine was good... especially when you consider there was a more devastating alternative.

Highway 57D, which connects Mexico City and Piedras Negras, is often called the backbone of the Mexican highway system. In addition to cars, trucks, and other vehicles that are constantly transiting the road, another highway sits just alongside the blacktop, crisscrossing at points, and that highway carries electricity and telecommunications. The massive towers and thick cables running between them are ignored by most. Likewise, the small maintenance buildings that exist every 200 km or so along the route, fade into the scenery for those anxious to be on their journey. As a result, no one noticed when an additional maintenance building appeared just a few kilometers south of Matehuala. The building was identical to all the others throughout the entire country of Mexico, except that this one was neither built nor used by the government-run power company or any of its subsidiaries. The *Comisión Federal de Electricidad* itself missed the building's existence because it is not in the right location to be one of its own.

The cinder block and concrete exterior of the building were identical to the others which stood along Highway 57D, but there the similarity ended. Just like all of the other buildings, the exterior door was secured by a rather large padlock. Once that was opened, it revealed a sparse open room with a faux control panel with a multitude of dials and switches. By flipping the correct sequence of switches, a hidden panel would unlock and open.

When the building was initially constructed, a code needed to be entered on an electronic keypad hidden behind the panel. Over time, this was upgraded to a multifactor biometric entry system with a fingerprint and retina scanner. If all was correct, mechanical gears would whir as a 1,000-kilo concrete slab in the floor sank and slid out of the way, exposing a stairway leading down three levels. After proceeding 20 steps or so down the concrete slab closed automatically, and the room above ground returned to its dormant state. At the bottom of the stairs, the landing opened into a large control room. In the center of the chamber sat a desk with a newly acquired laptop used to monitor all activity within the numbers station. Mounted on one wall of the control room were three rows of reel to reel tape recorders, with four in each row. The recorders could be individually controlled by the switches, buttons, and dials on a banked panel which sat on a long desk immediately in front of the recorders. At the right of the recorders was a collection of floor to ceiling shelves which held a vast library of tapes and several wall lockers filled with equipment. To the left was a long, rectangular work counter with various radio transmitters and other telecommunication equipment. Unknown to the Comisión Federal de Electricidad, these receivers were connected to several antennas which sat on top of the cable tower located near the building.

On the opposite wall was a locked door which also required a secondary biometric confirmation, a retina scan, and led to a secure communications room. In that chamber, in addition to various encryption and decryption equipment, there were two large four-door safes each with dial locks. Scattered throughout the work area were five desk chairs, all of which were on rollers. The number of seats had been questioned by every worker in the facility since only two people were ever assigned to the station, with only one usually being present.

The sign on the outside of the building identified it as a power company maintenance facility belonging to the CFE, but to the staff and its owner, it was known as the Vodyanoy Transmission Station. It was one of the several numbers stations maintained and run by the KGB. In the first few years of the station's existence, any necessary communications were hand delivered by a secret courier from the Embassy, since the numbers station did not sit upon Soviet Embassy grounds. Over time, and with improvements to the technology at the station, that procedure transitioned to communique being sent via encrypted traffic to the station directly, and the station's contact with the Embassy was terminated and forgotten, which made it an ideal choice when the Crimson Firebird Initiative needed resources.

Once the Vodyanoy Transmission Station had been selected for

Crimson Firebird Initiative in 1981, it was removed from any and all records within the KGB except for personnel with clearance for the project. In a further bit of intrigue, nine years later all records of the station vanished from any KGB files outside of the CFI. This occurred just after the reassignment of two new officers to the location. Since that time, there had been several changes of personnel, with each pair of arrivals being trained by the departing staff. In each instance, both personnel were replaced at the same time, so there was minimal crosstalk between the old and new occupants of the station. The facility had become an island unto itself.

When the United States launched a new spy satellite in 2000, whose orbit would place it over the station, modifications were made at Vodyanoy. The station gained a paved driveway from the highway and a carport at the rear of the building. The concrete road prevented any tire tracks from ever appearing in the sand as the staff went to and from work. The carport prevented the satellite from observing vehicles. The commuting hours of the staff were also adjusted to avoid detection of their arrival or departure. Later, when the satellite shifted from espionage to DEA surveillance, the cloaking procedures put in place for the station did not change.

The two current occupants of the Vodyanoy Transmission Station had been in place for almost eight years. Neither Commander Nastia Zamurovich nor Major Yury Trechnikov had any idea of what had occurred in the numbers station's history, or how they had been selected for the assignment, by the mysterious arm of the clandestine services that had contacted them outside of normal channels. Both assumed they were part of the *Sluzhba Vneshnei Razvedki* -- the Foreign Intelligence Service. As with most personnel assigned within espionage services, both were private and close hold with personal information, and as a result, neither realized the other was also an orphan with no extended family. Neither had permanent relationships and were socially isolated so they would not be missed when they disappeared. They were also unaware the two people they replaced were buried within twenty-five kilometers of the numbers station, having met the same fate as their predecessors since the fall of the Soviet Union.

Nastia and Yury both regretted that their tenure in the numbers station was about to conclude. Nastia enjoyed the simplicity of her job. She had gotten comfortable in the mission and was able to accomplish it almost as a part-time occupation. There were various conflicts around the world and she could be reassigned to a more dangerous, front-line mission--something she did not desire. A desert city in Mexico was not what she was used to but it had grown on her after almost a decade.

When they first began working, they followed the *Daily Recipe*, using the massive library of reel to reel recordings to compose the new daily transmission. They first recorded the required Six-Tone alert onto a new tape, followed by the required sound effect from the media within the reel to reel library. Next, they began the arduous task of locating and transferring recordings of numbers, letters, and words (in called for voice or voices) from a myriad of sources to the day's recording to produce the Message as specified. The assembly of the Message could take hours as they searched through the individual reel to reel tapes for a particular word in the right voice.

A conclusion signal consisting of six zeros was added to the end of the recording once they had compiled all the sound bites into a single recording. They would take turns recording their own voice saying the zeros as a personal contribution since they were given no other specific guidance. Once the tape was complete, they used the transmission equipment to uplink it to the various repeaters and beacons across the United States. Twice a week, without fail, they would uplink and play the recording, at exactly 1523 UTC on Mondays and 1923 UTC on Thursdays.

Both Nastia and Yury were chosen for the positions at the Vodyanoy because they were technologists and the job required this skill. The station's first computer, a laptop, was acquired during their tenure. Therefore, as sound recording had transitioned into so many bits and bytes contained in computer files, Nastia decided to begin a project to record all of the speech snippets from reel to reel tapes into various subdirectories on a computer hard drive while using clear labeling for filenames. The file *banana.mp3*, in the subdirectory *German Woman*, was far easier to search for than a snippet of sound on 100 meters of recording tape. It took both of them several months to conclude this work but when they were finished life got much easier and their free time increased.

As time went on, they worked together to fine tune the daily assembly task until it was down to less than an hour, instead of four to five. The extra free time benefited them both. Nastia found great delight in making a comfortable home for herself as well as several pets she had rescued from the streets. Even though she was an attractive thirty-eight-year-old woman, she had no indepth relationships, taking the occasional lover when she felt the need and ending things when she was sated.

Yury, on the other hand, was kept busy with his discovery of dark-eyed Mexican women who were much more affectionate and easier to please than Russian women. His blonde hair served as a unique point of attraction for the local ladies, and his 6'4" athletic frame, along with his high cheekbones and more Western countenance, ensured many successful conquests. They had a cursory awareness of one another's off-duty activity, but they never pried for details, concentrating only on the exchange of work information when they were in the station together--which with few exceptions was a rare instance.

Nastia completed construction of the day's Message; she carried the laptop over to the work counter where Yury had spliced and soldered an input jack into the panel. Once the jack was securely in place, and all was ready, Nastia watched the digital clock until it was exactly 1523 UTC.

When the correct number appeared, she hit the play button on the laptop's MP3 player software. All forty-seven beacons played the same Message at the same time. By turning on and off specific switches, she could have narrowed the listening audience down to a single beacon or group of beacons.

Nastia first listened to the six alert tones and once she was sure all was good, she muted the speaker and leaned back in her chair watching as the progress bar moved from left to right while the Message played. From experience, she knew this one would take approximately ten minutes to transmit and then she would be free for the rest of the day. *Perhaps a trip to the farmers market this afternoon. I wonder if they will have any good citrus?*

Evan Davis rolled onto his back and then opened his eyes to find himself staring at the ceiling. He was alone in his bed. Marci was long gone, and his brief dalliance with Najila barely lasted until the end of his *human-interest* assignment in Kuwait. He found his mind taking him back to that place -- enjoying a sweetly vivid memory from so many years ago when he was serving with the Air Force in Berlin. Now, with his eyes open and a vague sense of his situation and surroundings, he felt his sense of satisfaction fading and his expression slowly turning to a pained grimace.

Life after his return from Afghanistan had been less normal than he had hoped. He and Marci were together for about three months before their similarities started to drive them both nuts. When she came in one day and told him she was leaving, Evan was relieved more than surprised. They both knew it wasn't working; they had built the other into someone neither found in their arms when daydream shifted into reality. After a month or so of the intense and burning passion for fantasy, things settled into the norm and both realized their error.

Evan also suffered from minor post-traumatic stress during this period, feeling ill at ease in some situations and experiencing nightmares from his worst times as an embed. Some counseling helped him cope and conversing online with others who were experiencing the same issues made it manageable and provided him with some needed tools. He could now sleep undisturbed, but tense situations could cause an almost unnatural state of awareness.

His novel had sold well, not a best-seller, but his place in the writing world was secure enough that publishers began approaching Arlen, his agent, with offers and advances. That accomplishment was augmented by his writings done in Kuwait, even though his full involvement in the events there was never fully known to the public. This made him restless, and he would not sign any deals Arlen brought in, as he did not want to feel beholding to anyone. It was a forced contractual obligation that had led Evan to Afghanistan and financial need that took him to Kuwait. He never wanted to be in that position again.

Evan embraced days like this one -- when nothing was either expected of him or supposed to happen. Now, rather than rising from the bed like millions of ordinary people, he closed his eyes and allowed himself to drift back into that state between awake and asleep where he found himself once again with Jodi.

His time with Jodi was the most sensual of his life. His friend Mark had introduced them while the two were dating but from the instant that Jodi and Evan met, they both knew something far more interesting lay ahead. Their connection began with stares that lasted a little too long and grew into accidental caresses that bordered on inappropriate. Then, one afternoon Evan answered a knock on his door and found Jodi standing there alone. He opened the door wider and stood to one side motioning for her to come in. Rather than walking into the room she paused, dropped her bag and coat onto the floor, and walked Evan backward as he closed the door. When the lock clicked shut, and Evan ran out of space, he felt her body pressed against his for the first time. She raised her face and looking into his eyes said, in a sultry voice, "Kiss me, you idiot--you know we both want it." He did exactly that.

He could not remember how much time passed between the first kiss they shared, as she pressed him against the door, and the point when they were both lying on the floor naked and entwined. What he did remember was that as he was anxiously exploring her with his hands and enjoying the feel of her mouth on his flesh, someone attempted to open the door without knocking and was prevented from doing so by Evan's head acting as a doorstop.

"Evan! Stop playing around, we need to get going," Mark said as he attempted again force the door open, this time running it into Evan's head with more force.

Evan pressed his hands against the door and forced it closed, pushing the button on the knob to lock it, just as Jodi took him deep into her mouth. A loud unstifled moan of pleasure escaped his lips followed by the muffled sound of snickering from the other side of the door, then footsteps walking away. Jodi and Evan began to pleasure each other in earnest, and as they did so lost all touch with any reality except for their own.

After, as they lay on the floor and Evan's breathing was returning to normal, Jodi slowly ran her finger over his chest and made some casual statement that the two of them needed to explain this to Mark at some point. She spun her body on top of his and kissed him again.

Evan had never felt a kiss quite like the one he shared with Jodi on that day or any other. Every kiss, caress, or even unexpected touch they shared could set his skin on fire. People often use the word soulmate to describe their perfect match--this was more like an explosion between gasoline and a lit match--they were perfect catalysts for each other.

A few weeks after this incident, Jodi was lying on top of him naked and as she caressed his face looked deeply into his eyes and said, "I love you, and all I want is to be your perfect fantasy. I'll do everything possible to make you feel loved, pleasured, and totally satisfied. That's the only thing on my mind -- to give you everything I am or can be. I'm seeking nothing at all for myself from you, all I want is to make you feel better than any woman ever has—heart, body, and soul." She stopped stroking his face for a moment, and while she continued to stare intensely into his eyes, she whispered, "I know you want to do the same for me. If we both succeed all that anyone will find in the morning is a large puddle."

With that, the terms were set for the balance of their time together.

Was that what it was supposed to feel like? Evan recalled the weight of her body on the day she made that declaration.

"Yes," he said out loud, jarring himself from his remembrance.

It was at that moment that Evan's Goldendoodle Zax pounced on the bed to remind him of the one responsibility that required him to get out of bed early in the morning. Yawning, Evan opened the front door to let the dog out and discovered an everyday standard manila envelope with no writing. There was no one around.

If there had been anyone there, Zax would have barked his head off. Naturally, the barking would've been followed by much tail wagging and begging the stranger for attention. After all, Zax was not a watchdog but a self-prescribed comfort and companion animal who had been with him since Marci's departure.

Sitting a coffee cup under the spigot of the Keurig, Evan turned the envelope over in his hands looking for some sort of clue.

No postage either. A cold chill ran through him as he remembered his IED training, but logic quickly took over, and he convinced himself that terrorists were not making paper-thin bombs quite yet. With that concern aside, he tore the envelope open to find a single sheet of tri-folded paper. He held the envelope open for a moment and peered inside to ensure he had left nothing behind before dropping it on the counter. Taking his coffee cup and the paper, he headed towards the living room and sat in his recliner. He unfolded the piece of paper and in the middle of the page found only a single typed line:

Wars are won or lost, but if the loser can still strike back from the ashes of defeat, it is never truly over. More? Call 555-279-3410.

He drank his coffee and reread the line which still made no sense.

"Nope, still a frigging mystery."

This was not the first piece of anonymous correspondence he had received since his tour in Afghanistan. He had received both fan and hate mail as the result of his articles. His novel also garnered a similar mixture of mail, but thankfully it was mostly from fans with only the occasional critic, delivered to his publisher. The occasional resourceful reader found his address and mailed a letter directly.

This was the first-ever personal delivery of an anonymous missive. He brewed another cup of coffee before letting Zax in. Evan decided to call the number out of curiosity, but the call would have to wait until he could pick up a burner phone that could be conveniently disposed of if the number he was calling belonged to some sort of psycho.

With that decision made, Evan showered and dressed. Zax jumped up on the bed and settled in and with a yawn went back to sleep. Apparently, Zax's agenda for the day was set as well.

Chapter Two

Maksim felt his fist make an impact with the side of Fyodor Ilyich Maldroski's jaw and forced his mind to slow the action into subdivided seconds so he could better control how the punch ended. As he felt the strain of bone and sinew, he knew if he allowed the punch to continue, he would break Fyodor's jaw. Since the goal was to hear the man speak, a broken jaw was an unacceptable outcome. So, with some reluctance, he pulled the punch. Maksim stepped back from where the old man was sitting and noted his subject had again lost consciousness. At sixty-seven, Fyodor Ilyich was a tough old bird.

Fyodor may have been tough, but his tormentor was a flawless professional who would eventually extract the secrets of a lifetime from the retired KGB bureaucrat. What Maksim did not know was the most important secret the old man carried was one he'd give his life to keep. So, after two hours of beating and mental torture, the old man remained silent.

The necessity of Maksim's assignment was the result of decades of KGB compartmentalization. The KGB kept its secrets by never allowing anyone to know the big picture. Every person held a bit of the plan, but only a few knew the larger scheme and fewer still knew the details of the whole project or its goal. When the walls fell and the central government went to pieces, it meant a lot of details were still in motion for which no one had any full oversight. Without oversight, many planned actions ran amuck. After several events came to pass that embarrassed the new democratic government, it was decided that a clean-up of past projects was needed to ensure the things still in motion were brought to a halt.

Maksim Fillyp Bondreovich was as much one of those forgotten details as he was its eventual solution. What brought Maksim into the espionage services was an SVR program known as Siberian Rime. Originally developed under the KGB, the program was an experiment to create ultra-effective solo assassins who were on the razor's edge of being uncontrolled sociopaths. Aside from normal spycraft, they were trained in hundreds of killing methods as well as basic human anatomy and morbidity for times when they needed to be inventive. The participant's existence footprint was entirely reduced to the point that except for DNA all other methods of identification were useless. Candidates were chosen for non-descript features, and average size and build so they could slip in and out of crowds unnoticed.

The program was abandoned by the SVR in 1998, only two years after going operational, when it was found it was difficult to control those permitted to kill at will and operate with individual autonomy. In late 1998 Zaslon was launched; it was a resurrection of Siberian Rime, but those agents were always working as a team and therefore under the watchful eye of someone on the team rather than operating independently. Trails of dead bodies were used to find and exterminate most of Siberian Rime's graduates once the decision to terminate the program was made. Maksim was an exception. He enjoyed killing to the point that it had become intently gratifying and he took great pride in completing assigned missions cleanly and efficiently. Since Maksim also derived extreme sadistic sexual pleasure from his violent actions, he was most anxious to move from one assignment to the next. The agency found him useful enough to ignore the occasional collateral damage or body of an overly curious prostitute whose removal he deemed necessary.

Maksim was smart enough to realize even though he had been given free rein in the past, it would come to an end when the last of the old projects were discovered and terminated. With no desire of becoming part of that mass unmarked grave, he would be ending his association with the KGB when this job was complete. Maksim had arranged an accident that was sufficiently violent to not raise an eyebrow when his body was not recovered. He had worked a freelance mission in

Kuwait, and he was attempting to line up more jobs under a new identity. Freelance missions paid better and gave more control over assignments. But this was the future--for now, he had to wait for his subject to regain consciousness so he could extract his deeply hidden secrets.

One bit of strategy he'd learned from his KGB instructors was to avoid harming a subject so badly he couldn't be released. Hitting someone repeatedly was okay, but not cutting off fingers or ears. With no hope of release, the subject would quietly await death rather than negotiate. But then there were cases like this one. Maksim was sure Fyodor had more to reveal, but nothing was working. Fyodor's file depicted a lifelong, desk-bound, bureaucrat, but his resistance was that of a trained field agent.

Fyodor did not open his eyes; he kept his body as still as possible so he could gather his thoughts. Fyodor's training had served him well, but at its core was one basic tactic —keep your wits about you and not allow pain to ever make you lose mental control. This had served him well when he was an operative in France and found himself captured by the intelligence services, and it had served him well thus far tonight. Fyodor had to maintain control, and then at the last possible moment plant an alternative truth to misdirect his tormentor. This was the only way to ensure Dmitry's safety.

As his mind began to clear, and he reflected on how he'd gotten here and cataloged his surroundings. Fyodor had been playing chess in the park and was walking back home to fix himself a bit of lunch. He heard a noise from behind, but before he could react, a large hand covered his mouth. Then Fyodor felt the sting of a hypodermic needle on the side of his neck. He was unsure how long he had been unconscious and since the empty room had no windows, Fyodor had no way of telling if it were day or night – – he may have even been there for days. *No, not days. My stomach would be empty and I'd be hungry if it had been days*, he thought.

The inventory of his surroundings led to the following determinations: Fyodor was bound to a sturdy high-backed wooden armchair. His legs were attached to the chair legs. He slowly parted his eyes just enough to see his arms were tied to the chair's arms by several layers of fabric tape. Closing his eyes, he tried to determine where he was based on what he could hear. There was some street noise resonating from below – – so he was on an upper floor. There was a bit of echoing when his tormentor spoke which meant the space was devoid of furniture and carpeting. The building must be private since there was no concern for his screams. The room was somewhat chilly, but not frigid…perhaps the heat from the city was keeping the building warm.

He assumed the kidnapper was also questioning him. Up to this point, he was not told who had taken him or why. There was little concern for Fyodor's answers as he was struck almost immediately after being asked a question. Fyodor felt he didn't know the man, but that didn't mean he was part of a governmental agency that had been formed after the fall of the Soviet Union. Oligarchs within the country had started creating their own intelligence functions and gathering information needed to protect their fortunes. There was just no telling who had sent this man. Perhaps he was part of the new KGB.

The new KGB? What else could it be called? Fyodor had watched it all change so quickly and he had known it was coming. As a trusted operative and later an office rat with the ability to interpret data and piece together truths, he watched Communism stall, then fail as the Soviet Union collapsed upon itself along with the KGB which dissolved in 1993. Fyodor had predicted the failure a decade before it happened; there was no alternative. He placed his own son Dmitry into a program that would take him to the United States and ensure that he was long gone before the collapse. The Crimson Firebird Initiative provided his son with a new life in a country with a future.

When Crimson Firebird was started in 1972, he had been pulled into the project by Sergei Kirill Mikhailov, a former colleague. It was all a bit of chance that turned to fortune when Sergei happened to notice Fyodor while passing through the halls of Lubyanka, the KGB administrative building in Moscow. He hadn't spoken to Fyodor that day, but as the founder of the KGB's Strategic Intelligence program, Sergei was able to reach out to certain parties to discover where Fyodor was working and to have him transferred to his program the next day.

A strained, confused, and wary Fyodor reported to the Office of Strategic Intelligence in one of the sub-basements of Lubyanka the next morning, where he explained to the secretary that he had no idea why he had been summoned. It was a running joke that Lubyanka was the tallest building in Moscow, as you could see the Gulags of Siberia from its basements. That joke did little to calm Fyodor's fears as he was ushered into the Director's office and told to wait. Like all the offices in the building, the door placard only listed the office holder's title and not the occupant's name. The KGB had discovered that omitting names made immediate reassignments and terminations much easier. So, as Fyodor sat in the large office, he found himself discreetly examining and inventorying the office to figure out who had summoned him.

The door behind him burst open as a familiar voice called, "Fy! So happy to see you, Comrade," Sergei said smiling earnestly as he greeted his old colleague. He walked to Fyodor and hugged him like a long-lost relative. "Please, sit – sit," he said upon releasing him, "we have much to discuss, and I have the job of a lifetime to offer you. First, tell me -- why did you leave the field service? You were so good at it."

Sergei took a seat next to Fyodor rather than behind his desk. This was to be an intimate conversation, and Sergei was carefully laying the groundwork. He was hoping proximity would also rekindle their friendship from years ago.

Sergei and Fyodor had met, become friends, and worked together -- somewhat -- during the Prague Spring. Each was working a different angle of Czechoslovakia's brief dalliance with democracy. Fyodor was on the streets working undercover with the youth movements that were supporting the democratic change. He was also working several sources within the movement, and as a result, the Soviets had an almost clairvoyant view into the future plans and actions of the youth movement and were able to effectively counter action after action. While his espionage activities were top rate, Fyodor's fame for those successes was known to only a handful; this guaranteed his anonymity and career stagnation.

Sergei, on the other hand, was working the plum assignment of Political Office in Charge of Propaganda and Alliance Development. He spent his evenings at glorious parties and mass meetings for those Czechs who supported continued communism and a strong alliance with the USSR. As a result of his personal charisma and inside information supplied by Fyodor, he made many friendships and contacts within the future Czech government, the Soviet military, and the Politburo in his home country. Over the years, he had used those associations to move up within the KGB and to wiggle his way into a leadership role that allowed him a lavish lifestyle and freedom of motion to develop his own pet projects.

With Normalization in full swing in early 1969, the two men parted ways, and they did so in the best of terms and with an appreciation of the other's talents and abilities. Each also had loyalty and love for the other as a result of working closely and relying on the other man to have his back. Such friendships were exceedingly rare within the KGB and were automatically suspect because of the possibility of compromising information. However, because the two worked in different sections and were never formally aligned, no one knew about their closeness except them.

Fyodor spoke freely about his assignment observing and reporting on the evolution of communism within the unions operating in northern France and southern Germany following the Prague Spring. It was those actions that eventually led to his capture by the French as he was preparing to cross the border into West Germany in late 1969. He did not have to specifically mention his questioning and torture, he knew Sergei was well aware of what happened to captured spies during the Cold War. With great detail and pride, Fyodor related how he was eventually traded for five French Iberian radicals who were arrested trying to stir discontent inside the Soviet Union. The exchange had occurred on a foggy October night, utilizing the famed Glienicker Brücke in Berlin as a neutral transfer point. The five radicals approached him as he walked back into the Soviet-controlled part of the world. After several weeks of debriefing by both the KGB and the East German Stasi,

Fyodor was allowed to return home to his wife for a month of rest and recuperation. It was during this period of being reunited that his wife became pregnant.

As a recently returned spy, it was not uncommon or degrading for him to be reassigned to desk work for a year or two to allow time to pass and his notoriety to fade with the West. With his wife bearing what would be his only child, Fyodor was not unhappy with the temporary assignment as it kept him at home. Their apartment was adequate and comfortable. All appeared to be going well for Fyodor's fledgling family, but in the seventh month of his wife's pregnancy things tragically changed.

Moscow, Russia

Fyodor was providing a matter-of-fact version of his past since he and Sergei worked together in Prague. He was guarded knowing that Sergei would be aware of all of the details about his life but might be waiting to see which ones Fyodor lied about.

"Ah, my friend would, at last, become a father. Congratulations!" interjected Sergei, who felt a need to take control of the conversation.

"Alas, it was not to be the expected joyous event. At the end of the seventh month of my wife's pregnancy, I came home one evening to find Svetlana sitting in a bathtub of cold water, barely breathing, having slashed her wrists. I called an ambulance, and they rushed her to the hospital, where they were able to save her body but not rescue her mind." Fyodor paused as he reflected on the depth of this loss again, "For a month, she existed on a ventilator while the young one inside of her was given time to further develop. Then, the doctors told me there was a risk of harm to the baby if allowed to remain in her womb any longer, I agreed to let them retrieve the child using the cesarean section technique. Shortly after that, Svetlana passed away leaving me with our son, Dmitry. She never gave any indication that she was suicidal or even depressed. It was just sudden and then over." *A mystery that still remains to haunt me every time I look at Dmitry.*

Even though Sergei was well aware of the story, hearing Fyodor say it aloud was sobering. "Tsk, so sad, but at least the young one was saved," Sergei finally said filling the silence.

"Yes, and Dmitry is growing into quite the little boy. He turned two about six months ago and is getting smarter every day. My sister has come to reside with me until he gets old enough to be a little more self-reliant and I get a little bit better at being both father and mother." Fyodor found himself grinning when he thought of several instances when he humorously failed at one role or the other. "Anyway, due to those new responsibilities, I gave up the excitement of fieldwork for the rather mundane but joyful existence of being a father. My last assignment was just completed, and I was on my way to Personnel when I was instructed to report here instead." Fyodor hoped Sergei would reveal his new assignment.

"Well, my friend, this is indeed fortuitous because I have an unusual and challenging assignment for you, that will allow you to remain at home indefinitely until the project is done. Given the timeline from planning to full fielding and continual supporting resources -- this assignment will probably last the rest of your career. However, I promise you that some of the excitement you crave will return to you through your daily duties. After we parted ways in Prague, I went on to several assignments, to include a few years as Rezident in the Middle East, dealing with the assets that we had assigned to the region to track actions being taken by the United States that might endanger the interests of the Soviet Union. As…"

"Pardon me, but I am not familiar with the term *Rezident*," Fyodor interrupted.

"Of course, when we were last together the term used was the less colorful *Station Chief*. The duties are the same, to control any and all espionage activities within a station located in another country. These stations are now referred to as *Rezidenturas*. My primary function was to run various intelligence assets and gather all information that was possible. I found the work interesting--particularly the finesse necessary to successfully utilize illegals - those spies who were in the country with no diplomatic cover or other legal reason for being there. The full-time espionage activities of these personnel could be quite exciting…." Sergei realized that he had gone off on a tangent and stifled himself.

"Anyway, as you may recall my Czech was not the best, but I seemed to pick up Arabic much more quickly, and by the end of my tour, I could almost pass as a native speaker. After that, I was brought back to Moscow and allowed to pursue what has proven to be my real forte: strategic intelligence. I was first approved to establish and then lead the KGB's Strategic Intelligence Program, and as a result, I have been able to get many of my ideas not only approved but fielded. Do you know what the purpose of strategic intelligence is?" Sergei did not wait for a response because he was not prepared to give up the floor. "We look at those long-range targets that don't even exist yet, to establish a response for when they do appear. One thing that has always troubled me is the concept of mutually assured destruction, the fact that the West would never launch solely because we would launch a counterattack and then the entire world would be destroyed. But what if the West launched first, in such a way that they destroyed our capability to respond to their aggression?" This time Sergei paused allowing Fyodor to consider his question.

"I would suppose, they would win by default," Fyodor said flatly.

"Exactly! Therefore, we must be prepared to answer for that possibility. We must have a way to strike back even if all of our nuclear capabilities are completely destroyed. The Soviet Union must be prepared to hit back decisively and permanently regardless of the status of our own nation because of a dastardly act of aggression by the West."

"But, if we do not have any weapons left, and they have already launched against us and presumably have destroyed much of our military infrastructure and personnel. How could we hope to lash out at them in any sort of decisive manner?"

Sergei's emotion was beginning to become infectious, and he could feel his excitement starting to rise. "While pondering this question almost a year ago, I came to the conclusion that only one thing would save us from total annihilation. The Crimson Firebird." Sergei picked up a stack of folders.

Fyodor was familiar with the Slavic legend of the Firebird and its symbolism. The Firebird was always pictured as a rather large bird, similar in appearance to a peacock, with feathers of red, orange, and yellow giving the bird a resemblance to a raging fire. Among the Firebird's most important mythical powers was its ability to continually be reborn from its own nest of fire. Not unlike the West's Phoenix, it would rise out of the fire of his own destruction to be reborn and renewed. It became apparent to Fyodor how that symbolism was going to be captured and used by Sergei.

Fyodor knew he was pushing his limits, but he wanted more serious answers and less hyperbole from Sergei. "So where are you keeping these trained Firebirds that are going to restore us should the West decide to be preemptive? Perhaps, in a giant birdcage on the roof?"

Sergei pushed the question aside with ease and proceeded with his explanation at his own pace. He had been waiting too long to share his idea and bask in the glory of its ingenuity. "Tsh, you know I mean the bird as a symbol, a symbol of how our country is continually reborn and renewed – – and this time avenged as well. The Crimson Firebird Initiative will be the greatest strategic plan ever developed from within the walls of the S Directorate. I have slated it to be parented by myself and you." Sergei realized for the first time he was revealing how all of this was going to work to anyone other than himself. "We will scour the country and recruit young people, progeny who we will train, educate, and then release as a force within the borders of our principal enemy the United States of America. Once these young people are there, they will remain hidden but ready to spring into action should anything disastrous ever befall our beloved nation, leaving it unable to retaliate. Then if the West were ever so bold as to launch a first strike against the Soviet Union, they would discover they had been harboring a viper close to their heart that was ready to deliver a fatal bite. We both know it would serve them right to be struck down in the midst of their celebratory victory party." Sergei's eyes were wild as he was in the throes of describing devastation against an enemy he had been taught to wish annihilation for since becoming part of the KGB.

"To what end?" Fyodor asked, sincerely wondering what good it would do to destroy all those who had just destroyed you. "We would destroy humanity for pure revenge?"

"No, of course not. Don't be so flippant. We would not destroy the United States… we would simply remove the people who were there so that those who survived from our country would have a new, undamaged home to occupy almost immediately. The details are all there in the plan. It includes how the agents would be stood up and activated as well as the limited number of people within the Soviet Union who would know the full scope of the CFI." Sergei dropped folders on Fyodor's lap one at a time.

"What type of weapon would kill people without destroying any property?" Fyodor asked. This was one of many questions the two of them would spend the next several hours discussing and it was the one that weighed heaviest. How could this be anything less than the extermination of humanity?

"Bioweapons. Of course, the one that is truly needed has not been developed yet, but it will be and soon. When that weapon comes into existence, it will be primarily for the benefit of this program."

Fyodor and Sergei spent most of the day discussing the plan in broad terms. Fyodor discovered, among other things, that only four people would ever be acutely aware of the program at one time: The General Secretary of the USSR, the Director of the KGB, and the two of them. They had an unlimited amount of money to work with, and that money had already been block allocated to the program so it would never be caught by some politician. Sergei had seen to it that the money was transferred to a numbered Swiss account with funding moving out as necessary, but the initial currency infusion was also being used to produce even more funds through investment.

At the end of their discussion, Sergei explained that Fyodor's role was to run the day-to-day operation of the CFI as it went from concept to being fully viable and mission-capable. Aside from that, he would cover his activities by working as a coordinator with the various Rezidents in foreign countries to help support logistics operations for their illegals. It was an incredibly effective cover since it would provide Fyodor with the reason and need for specific access and information that would conceal his activities for the Crimson Firebird Initiative.

Fyodor left Sergei's office at the end of the day sharing his excitement. They were not merely going to destroy the enemy but they were going to exterminate and then overtake him entirely. The one loose end to their entire project did not come to a culmination until mid-1986 when the *Chimera Project* produced the first vials of *Chimera K629*. The *Chimera Project* was the latest iteration of Vladimir Ilyich Lenin's poison development project formerly known as the *Special Room*. Lenin established the Special Room after it was discovered that a bullet used in an unsuccessful assassination attempt against him had been dipped in poison. Over time, the Special Room evolved from organic toxins to man-made compounds and various radioactive isotopes. The latest iteration of the Special Room, the *Chimera Project*, had moved on to the development of viruses and other biologicals that could be used to kill.

Chimera K629 was a perfect destroyer, with the capability to sit on the shelf for decades before being called into action, and then once called, having an exponential destructive capacity that would wipe an entire country clean within thirty days. *K629* was a combination of viruses which formed a hard-to-detect and destroy-hybrid that would eventually self-destruct over multiple generations, and then leave the targeted environment clean and livable within weeks.

Should a firestorm ever destroy the home nest of the Crimson Firebird, the Firebird was prepared to be reborn and to return in glorious victory upon the nest of the one who had attempted to destroy it.

The loud squeal of a data burst filled the air, causing Abdul-Maleek

Kaseem to lunge forward and turn down the volume on the external speaker connected to the shortwave radio. He leaned back in the folding chair. Typically, Abi used headphones, but tonight he had another person in his lair and wanted him to hear the radio broadcast.

The shortwave radio and speaker sat on a small folding table along with the sole light source, a gooseneck desk lamp. The radio was an older model housed in a large metal case that was about 60 centimeters long by 50 centimeters deep. Even though the radio was tubeless, it took several seconds to power on and became extremely hot if left on too long. The microphone was disconnected and hidden behind it, as Abi never had cause to transmit, only to listen. A spiral notebook and pen sat in front of the radio.

The space was not really a room but the result of removing the shelving from a small pantry in Abi's kitchen. It was completely without frills, and the only purpose it served was to provide a private area for the radio and one listener. Tonight, since there were two listeners, the barren room felt crowded.

"This noise will stop, and then the numbers will begin," Abi said, without turning toward the figure who skulked in the shadows behind him. Over the sound of audible data, he could hear his guest's feet shuffle impatiently on the linoleum floor.

The noise from the data transmission abruptly stopped and was replaced by silence. There was an absence of static, and then a female child's voice spoke.

"Ready? Ready."

"A child?" asked the person behind Abi.

"Sometimes, it varies."

The child's voice continued, "Twenty-Eight Alpha, thirty-three Oscar. Five – five – five – nine- twenty-three – eight. The horse will not be found here. Twenty-nine, niner, three, zero, zero, seven, zero, Five. Repeat two and five. Sum all…"

After a minute or so of this monolog, Abi leaned forward again, this time decreasing the volume to a point where he could converse comfortably with his guest. The string of numbers continued in the background.

"It continues like that for several minutes. Sometimes it goes on for as long as twenty minutes but usually not less than three minutes or so." Seeing his guest was unimpressed he added, "Also, the voices vary from child to adult, male or female, and several broadcasts have been in a variety of languages, not just English."

"Well, my young friend, what does it all mean – or does it mean anything at all?" An older man, wearing crumpled clothing and possessing a long beard, stepped from the shadows into the light.

Abi was perplexed that Qa'id did not understand the significance. "Don't you understand? It is some kind of code. Some sort of *spy* code." Abi was visibly excited at the prospect and hoped Qa'id Al-Abidin would be drawn into his cause.

"And have you broken this code, my son?" Qa'id said suppressing his smirk as he removed a pack of cigarettes from his shirt pocket, shook one out and lit it. He inhaled the acrid smoke briefly and exhaled it into the cramped space.

Even though he tried to hide it, Abi winced when he heard the word "*son.*" Since the death of his father a decade before, he had not been anyone's son. Even though he had great respect and felt indebted to the older man, he was not and would never be his family. Abi arose and sliding past the older man, he opened the door to the apartment so the smoke would not engulf the tiny room.

"I don't know yet, Qa'id, but I will figure it all out in due time. I know it is some sort of one-time cipher, or more likely a book code."

"Book code?" Qa'id asked raising an eyebrow. This book code system was new to him. He was familiar with one-time ciphers, a pad of code sheets used in tandem with the sender and receiver using the same sheet of words and numbers as a key to encrypt and decrypt a transmittal. One-time pads were extremely secure because without the proper pairing of sheets it was impossible to break the encryption and even if the code was broken, the cipher formula changed with the next one-time sheet. The greatest danger with the one-time method was the sheets themselves--since multiple sheets had to be carried and secured by various people. If the authorities discovered these sheets among a person's effects, the holder was instantly incriminated and the code compromised perhaps for an extended period of time. Qa'id had heard of such incriminations and their deadly ramifications.

"Book codes are ingenious," Abi said becoming emboldened to express his ideas, "Any book or written page becomes the code key for the sender and receiver. The sender need only transmit a set of coordinates for each word as the transmission."

"Coordinates?" Qa'id was becoming interested and sat down to listen.

Abi continued, "Yes, the page, line, and number of the word within the line. So, twelve, thirty-four, eighteen would mean page twelve, line thirty-four and word number eighteen within that line—within that book. The beauty of the code is without the correct key the system is almost impossible to break, because of the sheer number of possibilities being used as a key. The only drawback is that both the sender and receiver must have the exact same copy of the publication; the simple variation of a few words between versions of a book could make the key useless and the result gibberish."

Qa'id raised his bushy eyebrows, nodding slowly. "And since any book can be used, they could pick a book that would not be suspicious for either of the two correspondents. A simple travel guide, famous novel or book of scripture would easily be ignored. Ingenious,"

"Exactly," Abi wanted to expand on this and capture Qa'id's imagination, "the key– a normal book-- could be openly carried or even acquired when needed then disposed of by dropping it into a rubbish bin. Best yet, all of this could be done in the open without wasting time and resources attempting to conceal what is actually going on. Hidden in plain view."

Abi felt satisfied he had made an inroad into the mind and imagination of his mentor. Suddenly the room went silent, and both men turned towards the speaker. Abi turned up the volume in time to hear a different voice conclude the transmission:

"Complete. Complete."

When the voice finished speaking, there was the brief sound of bells, and then a piano chord was struck and left to fade to silence. After a second or two the silence was replaced by static.

"And so, our spy now has his information and can go off on his clandestine mission?" Qa'id raised his eyebrows.

"Quite possibly, but suppose we were able to decrypt those missives and use them to our advantage? Suppose those communiqués were from the American CIA? Or even the Mossad?"

"Hush now!" Qa'id's stood quickly and his eyes darted around the apartment as if some authority would suddenly appear and seize them for speaking such words out loud. "Abi, you can never be safer than when you are silent." Qa'id took a breath to calm himself. "These broadcasts may serve some passing interest for you, a bit of entertainment to pass the time; however, even if you were able to somehow find the key and break the code, individual notes sent to some lone spy would probably have little value for us or our friends who are fighting for our future and our homeland. Besides, why would any powerful nation use such a simplistic method to communicate sensitive information when there are better gadgets available to do such things?"

Abi was crestfallen, but he was not defeated. His defiance shone through as he responded. "You said the best reason why: it is all being done in the open – in plain view. Because of that, the broadcast is ignored as being too illogical to be a serious method of communication. But these transmissions have existed since after World War I. They originate from broadcast points called numbers stations, and there are literally hundreds of them that send out broadcasts around the world using the most primitive of technologies to maybe transmit the most complex and secret data. All it takes to listen is a shortwave radio, which can be bought anywhere, and in most locales possession of one, will not even cause a second glance. These receivers have gone from being a tool for governmental spies to being a late-night hobby for introverts in their mother's basement."

Qa'id lowered himself into the chair, and stared at the shortwave radio, as he listened to Abi's argument as to why this meaningless bit of minutiae should matter.

"There are also numbers stations which have been repeating the same script over and over for decades. Most of these have become urban legends to the amateur radio crowd. For example, somewhere in the middle of the desert in the United States is a broadcast that has been repeating since December 2004."

"Really? Differing words?"

"No, the same words, the words themselves are nonsense, but except for a short period when it stopped, it has been broadcast continually, at the same time of day, and on the same frequency for years." Abi began pacing to control his rising passion on the subject. "No one knows why they exist or who is making the broadcast – even with sophisticated equipment they can't figure out the transmission's origin or who's receiving it."

"Hmm" Qa'id nodded, not a sign of agreement but one of understanding.

"Because of things like that, and the types of people who typically spend their nights listening to shortwave radio, these numbers stations are widely ignored. Occasionally they get minor attention here and there -- then the interest is quickly dismissed as an absurd conspiracy theory."

"Nonsense with no purpose. Meh." Qa'id thrust his palms into the air in resignation.

Rather than being discouraged, Abi felt like the time was right to proceed to the deeper part of this demonstration.

"I believe these numbers stations are not broadcasting using one-time sheets but using book codes. Some of these stations have been broadcasting since the Cold War, bypassing the need for maintaining pads of one-time sheets also means avoiding risk for operatives in the unfriendly territory; therefore, the use of a book code is even more likely."

Abi moved a chair from the kitchen table to where Qa'id sat to draw Qa'id's focus directly on him and what he was saying.

"Over the past few years, terrific progress has been made with the digitization of books. Of course, this started with older books and as it moved forward vast swaths of literature are now available online thanks to things like *Project Gutenberg. Project Gutenberg* took on digitizing much of what they regarded as great literature since various copyrights on the material had expired."

"Wonderful," Qa'id said flatly, "so now the spies do not have to carry a printed copy of the book around with them as long as they have access to the internet thanks to a group choosing to name themselves after a forgotten German printer. How does this help you with breaking the codes?"

Abi held his hands up. "One of the things that made book codes so hard to break was the need for both parties to have the exact same version of the exact same book to encrypt and decrypt any given transmittal. Without that book, an eavesdropper had no key to help them figure out what the broadcast text meant all they had was a bunch of seemingly random numbers. The only way to find the key was to look through millions of possible choices."

Abi dropped his hands, and carefully watched Qa'id's expression as he came to the point of the evening "What if I could take those numbers, and use the coordinates to extract the target words from thousands of books at once rather than having to do it one publication at a time?"

Qa'id shifted in the chair. "Then, you would end up with hundreds of documents that are meaningless and maybe one that has some sort of meaning. The Allies tried the same during World War II when they had huge rooms of people trying to decipher the same transmittal with the hope that one out of the group might be able to come up with something that made sense. Most often, the information was useless by the time they were able to decipher the document's text" Qa'id shook his finger at Abi, "What good is it to decrypt an instruction for action if that action took place two weeks before you are able to figure out the transmittal that ordered it. By the time they broke that key hundreds of new keys would be in use." Qa'id was beginning to lose patience, and if Abi could not sway him, the evening would be wasted.

"But Qa'id, what I'm telling you is that I can run an extraction of the coordinate words from 1,000 books in my database at once and in under a minute. Then, using a fuzzy logic program, I can ignore all of the nonsense responses and keep only those that seem to make some sort of sense. After the comparison has been run against all the books in the database, I am left with a page or so of possible text results that can be quickly scanned to determine whether a sensible script was transmitted." Abi let this sink in for a moment before he continued. "The book code might have seemed safe to use during the Cold War because even with a room full of people with each using a different book to run the decrypted cipher, it would've taken years to examine all the possibilities." Noticing the glimmer in Qa'id's eyes he knew he was making an impact, so he pushed the example further. "In fact, it would've required multiple warehouses to store all the possible books that might have been used. Technology has obliterated the need to perform such tasks manually. It has compressed those warehouses full of books into so many gigabytes on a hard drive inside of a notebook computer. Those numbers stations that are still broadcasting have not kept up with technology and remain unchanged because their owners have been left with a false sense of security. We can use that to our advantage, and they will be unaware until it is too late."

Qa'id's stern look faded as he began to imagine the possibilities. "You have successfully done this?"

"Yes. Well, at least I think so. I've been able to come up with text that makes sense out of these numbers, but there are still things I don't understand fully – things that may come into play during the decryption. During the transmission we just heard, what's the significance of 'The horse will not be found here'?" Abi allowed his thoughts to freely associate as he continued. "Is it a code inside of a code or something that only relates to a specific receiver? Maybe it's a phrase that would only be understood by one person – – a private joke or some means of validation. Some of the broadcasts I've intercepted contain data bursts, music, bells, and other sounds-- I'm not sure what the possible meaning is…if they mean anything at all. They could just be scruff hiding the correct path."

Qa'id now saw the value in this and began to formulate a plan to use this discovery of Abi's. "Yes. Don't waste your time with that – – at least not now. Concentrate on figuring out transmittals we can confirm against some sort of immediate action. Perhaps an order for a particular action that then happens. As the Quran teaches us *'Muslims must muster all weapons to terrorize the infidel,'* this could be a powerful weapon." Qa'id began to stand, so Abi did the same. He took the younger man by the shoulders and looking into his eyes, Qa'id expression brightened and at Abi and nodded as if to say well done. Pulling Abi towards him, he kissed him on both cheeks in a show of fatherly affection. Releasing Abi, he proceeded to the front door with the young man following closely behind. Qa'id grasped the doorknob but then turned to face Abi. "The broadcast that you spoke about, the one from the desert in the United States. What does that transmission say?"

Abi felt deep satisfaction in knowing that Qa'id had been paying attention to all he had said. "It's a clip from a 1949 animated cartoon that featured a character called, Yosemite Sam. He says: *'Varmint, I'm a-gonna b-b-bloooow yah ta smithereenies!'*"

Qa'id's expression did not conceal that he was puzzled and then in a rare reaction to humor he was soon overtaken by laughter. "Indeed," Qa'id finally said as he opened the door and departed.

As Julian Shepherd placed the books onto the shelf, he recalled it had been almost a decade since he'd given up his assignment of reading through the collection every few years. The assignment had an easy methodology; there was a total of 102 books in the leather-bound collection of literature, and he had been directed to read thirty-four of them every calendar year. This amounted to completing a little over three books per month--which in the end resulted in touching every single book in the collection at least once every three years. This exercise served two purposes: first, it made him familiar with the books, making the books' primary objective somewhat easier should he ever be called upon to use them; and secondly, it caused the books to become uniformly worn over a period of time. No one gave a second look at the collection of books, on a board and cinderblock bookcase in the living room of his first apartment, or now on the built-in oak bookcase in his office. With a slightly more worn appearance after several years of repeated readings and relocations, they just appeared to be so much furniture rather than something of which to make note.

Three shelves containing the full 102 volume set of *Brandt's Compleat Collection of Great World Literature* were on display in his home, their gold embossed lettering had faded a bit. Julian had always felt that Brandt was a bit presumptive in assuming this collection was at all complete; it might be the start of an excellent collection of English language works, but it failed to include anything beyond the Western half of the globe. Marking the completion of the last task off the to-do list in his mind, Julian first broke down the empty boxes that were scattered about the floor and carried the flattened cardboard outside to his recyclables bin. He deserved a liquid reward, and upon taking a cold beer from the refrigerator, he lounged on his brand-new brown leather La-Z-Boy recliner to watch TV.

Camille, without saying a word, abruptly climbed into the chair and plopped onto his lap. She spent a moment or two repositioning herself and stretching her legs out between his until the length of her body was pressed against his with her head resting on his chest with her arm draped over him. If the kids had been home, some comment might have been made, but as it was just the two of them, the intimacy was welcome. Both of them had chosen T-shirts and shorts for a day spent unpacking. He loved the feel of her smooth legs as they rubbed against his.

Ever since he had told Camille that he genuinely enjoyed the look of her legs and ass in denim cutoffs, she always wore them for Julian, at least when they were home alone. As she began to glide her bare legs against his, Julian reached down and stroked her ass through the denim, his fingertips reaching the frayed edge at the leg opening. He gently caressed the flesh at the top of her leg where it met the curve of her ass. A hungry moan escaped Camille's lips and she raised her head to kiss him.

Life in rural American does have its privileges, thought Julian as he felt her hand glide across his chest, down his stomach, under the waistband of his shorts and at last grasp his erection, *Mmm, yes.*

Chapter Three

Dieter had started working on the task his friend, Fyodor, had requested of him because he could operate on his own. Now, however, Dieter was concerned because he had been unable to get in touch with Fyodor for the last two weeks to pass on progress details and verify any last-minute instructions. Historically, years had passed with no communications between them. Having met in the early sixties when he was working with the Stasi in Prague, to their Berlin reunion, and finally the dissolution of their respective countries, years passed with only widely-spaced letters and no telephone calls. That was before Fyodor reinitiated contact a month ago to make an urgent request.

Spending time pondering how Fyodor had found him after all these years was not worth the effort. Fyodor was a skilled KGB agent, and when they had last seen each other in Berlin, he was headed toward a career as an intelligence bureaucrat. Fyodor's continued trajectory would have left him with assets and resources providing him with his own source of back-channel information. Even Dieter still maintained a small network of people he could contact in a pinch.

When the breakup of the USSR was in full swing, the German Democratic Republic led the way by disintegrating in 1990, a full year ahead of their primary supporter. Dieter was one of a few Stasi agents who were fortunate enough to be out of the country when it broke apart. Because he had been an agent rather than a standard officer, any files on him were held in only one location far away from the physical Stasi headquarters in Berlin. Dieter was never quite sure who was responsible for doing so, but someone during the middle of the upheaval saw fit to destroy all his records and any of his operations. The second stroke of luck occurred when Dieter's Spymaster, upon reflection of his managing role during missions he had directed over the years, decided that suicide was better than going through a disgraceful public trial.

With no one needing to exchange Dieter's identity for his own freedom in some sort of plea bargain and his historical records destroyed, Dieter found himself in the most fortunate of circumstances for a man who had spent his life performing morally sketchy acts on behalf of a government that no longer existed. All of that coupled with his having been on assignment in Poland with an ironclad cover story and identity, allowed his transition into post-Cold War life to be instantaneous and without fear of being tracked down and put on trial. Things worked out surprisingly well for him during that transition indeed.

In the years that had passed, Dieter had not been contacted by any of his old friends from the espionage business outside of the small circle he maintained in case of emergency. He eventually left Poland and relocated to Bavaria in southwestern Germany. Dieter remained unmarried but had an abundantly fulfilling social life with the local people of his village. Life was good and quiet until six weeks ago when he received a phone call on his handy from Unbekannt Nummer -- Unknown Number.

Even though decades had passed since their last contact, the voice was instantly recognizable and rather than causing fear -- which some voices from his past could -- he found himself feeling oddly nostalgic and drawn into the yet unrevealed favor being asked of him. Fyodor gave away no details during the phone call but requested a meeting in Munich a few weeks later. Dieter agreed without hesitation, and his friend provided a destination and time. Fyodor, sensing Dieter's jovial mood over the phone, attempted to quash any perception that this was solely a friendly reunion, ending the phone call by saying, "This is about unfinished business and our responsibility to the future. See you next month, my old friend. Tschüss." With that, Fyodor had hung up leaving Dieter to fill the time between the call and the eventual meeting, wondering what this could possibly be about.

When the appointed day came, Dieter boarded the train from his little town into the city of Munich. It was not that he disliked Munich, he just did not like being in crowds anymore. There was a special alert and on-edge feeling Dieter got in crowds that had been part of his life for so long it was hard to suppress as he got older. His time in the München Hauptbahnhof was brief, only long enough for him to debark from the intercity train and board the U2 subway car a few tracks over. Once on the subway car, Dieter counted stops until coming to Sheidplatz, where there was a short wait until the U3 train arrived to take him to his final destination on the subway at Olympia-Zentrum. From there, he took a short walk through Olympia Park. The 1972 games had been a disaster for the city because of the massacre of Israeli Olympians by Palestinian terrorists. The only upside was the city had fantastic venues for sporting events as well as excellent transportation to and from the park located just outside the city center. On days like today, when no events were scheduled, it became an ideal place to meet without drawing attention.

As Dieter walked, his spy senses came back in full force. They had never actually left him, but some of the constant paranoia had lowered its volume in the intervening years since the fall of the GDR. He spent his time while walking, looking around at the grounds with which he was thoroughly familiar, but because of his purpose on that day they held here had an air of mystery – leaving the familiar tainted with an undercurrent of anxiety. The lush green landscape, smattering of benches, and other features held shadows that might contain a threat – the normal camouflaging something beyond a foraging squirrel. All of this made it easier for him to keep his awareness peaked for the unusual.

His cover for the day was that of a German tourist which did not require much beyond seeming curious, slightly confused, and asking for directions from a willing local; the cover allowed him to conceal his slight anxiety within the disguise. Nothing unusual about a tourist taking time to more closely observe a stand of abstract shaped topiaries as it provides a cover for a well-trained espionage agent searching for that which was out of place within the stand to aid in identifying threats or perhaps a hidden communication.

There was a small squiggly mark upon the wooden park bench just ahead. It was less than fifteen millimeters long – barely noticeable. It would not arouse any suspicion, and because it had been made with chalk, it would quickly disappear as soon the next rainfall. The mark had served its purpose, and the meaning was received-- Fyodor had made it to the city without incident, and he would be waiting for Dieter at their prearranged restaurant.

Dieter's pace picked up, but he continued to look around to embellish his air of German tourist. Occasionally, he would pause and remove the small Kodak from his pocket to take photos of this or that – knowing all the while there was no film in the camera. The walk was just over a kilometer; he could have easily come up at the subway station nearer to Hofbräu am Oberwiesenfeld, but there was a method to throwing people off your trail if you were being followed. Soon, Dieter turned onto Winzerer Strasse and could see the restaurant just ahead.

The Oberwiesenfeld was selected by Fyodor since the restaurant was small and off the beaten path but frequented by enough tourists so a stranger would not be out of place. The specialty was Bavarian food which was a favorite of Fyodor's. You don't get a lot of good Bavarian food in Moscow or Minsk. In the August heat, most patrons chose the outside tables in an attempt to catch a breeze, leaving the interior of the restaurant almost empty. Fyodor waved to Dieter from one of the back tables and then stood to greet his old friend with a firm handshake and warm embrace. Dieter removed his hat, dropped it into an empty chair, and then sat down at the table with his friend.

"So, the years have been kind to you; I can hardly tell the difference between now and when we last saw each other the night I departed Berlin," Fyodor said.

"Phffft! I thought we were friends; how can you lie to me like that. In the last three decades, I have put on at least fifty pounds and what used to be a crown of dark brown hair has now turned into a ring of gray hair with a bald head poking through the middle." Dieter made a circular motion with his finger over the top of his head; his voice was filled with the playfulness of long-lost friends finally reuniting.

What followed next were brief pleasantries back and forth, as they compared life notes spanning the years since the seventies. As often happens with old friends their conversation seemed to pick up seamlessly as if the last conversation was minutes ago rather than decades. Each man took turns speaking and listening intently with a true interest and concern that only people who had shared deep life events would have for each other.

After receiving their drinks and ensuring no one was paying them attention, Dieter leaned forward and spoke in a soft voice, "So old friend, while it's nice to finally see you after all these many years, I need to know why have you suddenly contacted me with such an urgent request that we meet."

Fyodor sighed, and began to tell the tale of the Crimson Firebird Initiative in detail. Crimson Firebird should've met the same demise as many other operations with the release of all personnel to either new jobs within the forming Federal Security Service or the Foreign Intelligence Service of the Russian Federation. Those with too dark a past due to wet work, or those having no skills needed by either of the new agencies, found themselves suddenly disavowed, unemployed, and left to their own devices. This led to a glut of highly-skilled intelligence operatives becoming freelance operators to the highest bidder. However, in a handful of instances, like Crimson Firebird, with agents under deep cover in foreign countries, formal ties were just simply cut, and they were left to continue on in the role in which they had been placed.

"Unlike the others, those with the Crimson Firebird Initiative were not directly released. They were left sleeping."

Dieter was confused, "What do you mean by that? Left *sleeping*? -- How?"

"They were never given any instructions to stand down, they were left in the same alert status that the sleepers had been in since they were launched into the field and became operational. This means anyone with the proper codes and the appropriate methods of contacting them could make them active once again. The sleepers could be directed to carry out the directives of their mission, and since they remained active foreign agents operating covertly in America, they were still at risk of arrest." Fyodor did not yet reveal the details of Crimson Firebird's primary mission--the real reason for asking Dieter to meet.

Their food arrived, and their conversation turned to how their favorite football teams would perform in this year's World Cup. Fyodor enjoyed the ultimate in Bavarian cuisine: the Schweinshaxe, a pig's knuckle roasted till crispy on the outside and fork-tender on the inside. Dieter had opted for the more universally known Jagerschnitzel, a deep-fried, breaded pork tenderloin covered in brown gravy. Neither man showed a lack of appetite, but only one was conscious of the gravity of the situation.

Dieter was the first to push his plate back and lay his utensils down. The meal was quite filling and more than he was used to eating. He made a mental note that he would have to work off the extra calories. Fyodor sucked the last of the flavor from the bare knucklebone and wiped his lips with his linen napkin. They withheld their deeper conversation until the waiter cleared and brought coffee.

After taking a deep drink from his cup, Fyodor leaned towards Dieter once again. "You remember that I told you about my divorce, when you debriefed me in Berlin, the morning after you picked me up from the Potsdam side of Glienicke Bridge?"

"Yes, of course. 1969, it was the beginning of an arduously long month, and I like to think of it as what solidified our friendship."

Fyodor nodded in agreement, it was a time when he really needed a friend and Dieter had proven to be one. Fyodor had been held by the French government for what seemed like an eternity but in reality just under six weeks. The French had spent time torturing him both physically and mentally. Fyodor had never mentioned to anyone he was on the verge of breaking, especially when the physical torture involved the use of pliers. He heard rumors about his exchange for Iberian dissidents in East Germany. He was leery, but after a few more days the physical torture had stopped. It was standard procedure before releasing a prisoner to stop physical abuse and allow the wounds time to heal before an exchange.

After another two weeks or so passed with regular meals, opportunities to sleep, and no further interrogations, Fyodor was handcuffed and put into a series of cars, traveling from the French prison to a small safe house in the Wannsee district of Berlin. During the journey, there was no effort made to prevent Fyodor from knowing his whereabouts. They wanted him to know an exchange was imminent. Fyodor knew he should be taken to the Glienicker Brücke at some point, a bridge over the Havel River between East and West Berlin, and then exchanged for something the French wanted of equal value to him. Of course, he remained suspicious since Western intelligence was known to use the possibility of exchange to extract further information from a prisoner who would let his guard down at the prospect of release. After obtaining additional data, they would take the prisoner back to his cell rather than to the bridge.

The men guarding him said nothing, but he could hear voices speaking in both French and German in the next room, as well as the occasional phone ringing and being answered. Since he remained handcuffed and was continually guarded, he was unable to reposition himself to hear what the voices were saying. In the middle of the third night, he was awoken and told to dress without reason. The handcuffs were removed, and a new gray suit was placed on the bed. After dressing, he was handcuffed again and loaded into a windowless gray Mercedes delivery van. This caused Fyodor to feel panicked that he was about to be taken back to his prison cell rather for an exchange. This panic caused him to misperceive time, believing they'd been on the road for over an hour instead of the fifteen minutes it took for the van to reach its destination.

The rear doors of the van opened and he was prompted to exit. Off to one side of the road that led across a bridge, there was a crossing gate manned by a soldier with an automatic weapon. Further down the road, across the bridge, was another crossing gate guarded by a soldier wearing a different style uniform. He was at the Glienicke Bridge. One of the men guarding him motioned for him to stand still, withdrew a pack of American cigarettes from his coat pocket, and shaking one out offered it to Fyodor. Fyodor placed it between his lips and accepted the offer of a light from a second guard.

"They're not quite ready," said the guard. "Just relax and in a few minutes, you can take a short walk towards home."

But it was not home to Fyodor--just another country that wasn't the Soviet Union and left him feeling at risk. After he had taken a final drag on the cigarette, Fyodor dropped it to the ground and stepped on it. At that moment, motions on the opposite side of the bridge drew his attention. A van similar to the one he had arrived in pulled up on the opposite end of the bridge and men were getting out. Fyodor's guard placed a hand upon his shoulder and pushed him towards the crossing arm on the side of the bridge. The soldier made no move to open the crossing arm but stepped back so Fyodor and his guard could position themselves in front of the barrier. Movement on the other side ended when five men were similarly positioned in front of the East side's crossing gate, accompanied by two guards, one who raised his arm and waved.

The guard standing next to Fyodor also raised his arm and then turned to him, removed the handcuffs, and said, "Slowly, walk towards the other side. The idea is for them to reach this point at the same time you reach the other side. Even though you might be tempted, do not run. That could end this entire exercise in a hail of bullets."

Fyodor nodded. The guard had no concept of reality, why would a KGB agent who had been captured ever run towards what was awaiting him on the other side? He slowly stepped forward to journey across the bridge. In the middle of the bridge, he passed five Iberian men who were headed in the opposite direction. All of them were smiling, assured that freedom awaited them on the other side. Fyodor, on the other hand, knew that another ordeal was to begin once he reached the Potsdam side. Upon negotiating his way around the crossing barrier, he was greeted by Dieter Seig, a familiar face from his time in Prague.

Since no one other than the two men knew the depth of their previous association, Dieter's selection for this duty was kismet. Neither man showed their familiarity, even though there was a particular joy at seeing each other again. Outsiders only saw a handshake and an emotionless brief nod as they greeted each other.

"Comrade Commander Maldroski, I am Capitan Dieter Sieg with the German Democratic Republic's Ministry for State Security," Dieter said, extending his hand. "Welcome to the DDR."

Fyodor was put into a large black sedan and moments later arrived at the Ministerium für Staatssicherheit, the headquarters of the Stasi. Upon entering the building Dieter departed without speaking, and another agent took him down a maze of corridors that eventually ended in a small, simple room with a bed and chair. He was told to get some sleep and upon departing the agent closed the door behind him. Before going to sleep, Fyodor attempted to open the door to the hall. It was locked.

The next morning, Fyodor was woken by a knock. He was led to a bathroom and given a chance to bathe, shave, and get dressed in a rather plain shirt and pants; Fyodor was felt mildly reassured since it was not a prisoner's jumpsuit. He was led to an interrogation room. While it was unusual for a KGB agent to be debriefed by any agency other than the KGB itself, it was allowed because the East Germans had provided the five Iberians who were exchanged.

The act of a standard debriefing is to gather information from the person who had just gone through a rather traumatic event to prevent that event from occurring again. Quite often, pilots who have been shot down or hostages who have been released are debriefed so their experiences can be cataloged and documented for future use. The debriefing of a Soviet spy during the Cold War was anything but an exercise in documenting things beyond the control of the subject. All the details of how the spy was caught, and intelligence regarding the agency that held and questioned the spy, were just the surface layer. Next came a deep dive into why the spy had been caught and what things the spy had done wrong. Unlike the level of forgiveness that may have been practiced in the West, these mistakes could lead to a seasoned KGB agent being sent to the gulags or executed. The assumption from the outset of the debriefing was that the spy was at fault and wholly responsible for the situation.

As Fyodor was sitting in the interrogation room the morning after the bridge exchange, he noted his surroundings. The room was sparse, containing only a table and two chairs. Along one wall was a large mirror, which Fyodor assumed was a two-way device and there was probably a group of people observing. There was a video camera on a tripod sitting in the corner, but there was no cameraman present. This was long before you simply pressed a button on a camera to record events, so a cameraman would be needed in the event of a confession.

A short while later the door opened, Dieter entered the room and nodded acknowledging Fyodor. "Comrade Commander, is there anything I can get you? Coffee perhaps, a cigarette?"

Fyodor was guarded. His own KGB training told him not to accept anything from an interrogator since he would be indebted and weak. But his training had not prepared him to be debriefed by a friendly acquaintance -- an acquaintanceship neither party was acknowledging. What Fyodor did know was that he was starving and a cigarette and a cup of coffee sounded like heaven.

"Yes, I would appreciate both, milk with the coffee please," Fyodor said in a calm voice. Dieter looked into the mirror and nodded and then sat down in the chair on the opposite side of the table.

Neither man spoke, and after a moment of silence the door opened, and a uniformed guard set a small wooden tray on the table before leaving. The tray contained a pack of East German cigarettes, two coffee cups with saucers, milk and sugar, and an ashtray. Dieter divvied up the items before opening the pack of cigarettes and shaking it so a single cigarette protruded from the end. He offered it to Fyodor who pulled the cigarette out and put it in his mouth. Dieter reached into his pocket and withdrew a Zippo lighter, holding the flame steady for Fyodor.

After taking in a deep breath of smoke, Fyodor exhaled with a sigh. "Thank you. Amazingly enough, for a population that seems to smoke everywhere, including hospitals, the French were vehemently opposed to providing me with cigarettes while I was their guest."

The statement drew a slight grin from Dieter who withdrew a small notebook and pen from his pocket. With minor pleasantries out of the way, he glanced over at the mirror and nodded, this time to signal the formal start of the debriefing.

"Now Fyodor – may I call you Fyodor, Comrade Commander Maldroski?" Dieter paused and waited for Fyodor to nod his approval. "Fine, Fyodor, this is an informal debriefing to gather information about your capture and false imprisonment in France. Let's start with the week before the French security service picked you up at your apartment. No need for excruciating detail, we will get into more depth later. I just want to capture an outline of the events as they occurred."

So, the method of interrogation was to be a phased interview. Fyodor would be required to tell the story over and over again with increasing layers of detail until such time that one of the details didn't match, and he was taken away, or until they were satisfied there was no more to be told and he was released. Fyodor related all that had happened the week before his capture and about the capture itself. The week was actually fairly low-key. He had made his usual rounds picking up information from various dead drops and maintaining contact with those in town who acted as his underground grapevine of gossip. He had no inkling anything was amiss until Thursday afternoon when he was out for a casual stroll and noticed the pickup signal for one of his dead drops was unexpectedly missing.

"A dead drop exchange is a remarkably simple method for information to be passed between two people covertly," Fyodor started to explain.

"Yes, yes –" Dieter interrupted, "I am familiar with this methodology; no need to go into detail. As an experienced intelligence operative, you were using this technique when you realized something was wrong?"

Fyodor nodded, he had hoped to drag out his recollections of events by explaining in minute detail, but whereas Deiter seemed to be trying to help him – he could not make it look too easy. He began again without the in-depth explanation; Fyodor had not been given a signal that a communiqué had been left in the dead drop by one of his sources when it was expected. There could've been many reasons for this, the provider of the communiqué could have been sick or delayed, but the primary cause for a missing signal is to tell the receiver to stay away from the dead drop because nothing is there. It is intended to minimize the risk of using this type of information transportation system.

Fyodor's mistake that he couldn't admit, was that even though there had been no signal, he still went to the pickup site. His reason for going there without a signal was something he couldn't admit either; Fyodor had been concerned for the provider because he had been on the verge of becoming sexually involved with her. Knowing full well the risk of getting involved in the field, Fyodor made his first mistake in the chain that led to his arrest. He assumed the woman was truthful and was not a spy sent to entrap him.

What Fyodor had not realized was that by going to the drop site, where he was not supposed to be, at a time when he was not expected to be there, the French government would launch into action against him. Fortunately, they had not yet gathered any useful information about his activities. Unbeknownst to Fyodor, the French had been aware of his activities for some time and were using him to trace information through the KGB intelligence chain.

Several months earlier, when Fyodor had been recruiting various contacts in the area, one of them went directly to the French intelligence service. They, in turn, placed Agent Monique Bernard in a low-level clerical position within the local constabulary. The French waited for Fyodor to make contact with her and then recruited her as a source of information. After about a year of Monique supplying Fyodor with relatively trivial bits of information, the French raised the stakes by having her provide false information that would be seen as vital to the KGB. Doing so allowed the French to monitor how the data was moved from France to the KGB and onwards within the Soviet government. The first part of this was to plant a red herring by having Monique provide information about the resurrection of the *Guarde Nationale France* to assist with the local labor unrest Fyodor was responsible for fomenting.

The French National Guard had not existed since 1872, and such a step might upset the balance of power in Europe as it would supply more immediately available forces to NATO; therefore, it would be of great interest to the KGB. Of course, no such move was under consideration, but the information was valuable enough that Fyodor would immediately report it as quickly as possible. By tracing how this information was transferred, the French could find out their intelligence vulnerabilities. While this was ongoing, a bit of captured information changed their action against Fyodor from passively providing information to him to an active counterintelligence operation against him.

The French had intercepted a dispatch bound for the local Rezident who was to inform Fyodor that his wife, Svetlana, was filing for divorce. This type of tenuous circumstance was ideal for the French as it left Fyodor vulnerable and easy to exploit. It always surprised Western intelligence sources that the Soviets would be so casual in informing their field agents about the loss of their home stability. However, the Soviets believed their agents were much better off without the distraction of wives and children. Many in the Soviet hierarchy saw a pending divorce as a way of actually focusing the attention of an agent in the field.

The action of his wife left Fyodor open to a type of exploitation that the French had raised to a near art form – – the honeypot. Put a beautiful, flirtatious, and interested woman in the vicinity of the subject, allow him to fall for the woman and then use her as motivation to get the subject to do whatever you needed. Variations of this exploit included using the affair as blackmail or using a handsome man instead of a woman if the subject's proclivities were such. Over time this exploit was employed by both sides; however, because of Russia's own misogyny, they had few female agents in the field and therefore could not utilize this method as effectively as the West. An additional shortfall for the Soviets was that most of their female agents were unattractive.

When the leak came in about Fyodor's divorce, the French State Security Service decided that a better use of Monique might be for her to become romantically entangled with Fyodor to turn him into a double agent. By doing this, the French could expose and gather information on Soviet espionage capabilities not only in France but also throughout Europe. This tactic resulted in Monique paying more attention to Fyodor and then openly flirting. They had begun meeting for the occasional drink, which turned into dinner and was poised to turn into more. As a result of that development, French intelligence decided it was time to gather solid evidence against Fyodor by setting up film and audio surveillance of both his dead drop point and his apartment. The easiest way to ensure that Fyodor would not be near the drop point on a particular day was to have Monique not to give the signal that any intelligence was available for pickup. Without the signal, Fyodor would not need to go near the dead drop point on the normally scheduled day. An excuse could be given later as to why she had not provided the signal.

All of this led to the fateful Thursday when Fyodor went to the drop point where he was not supposed to be, at a time when he was not expected to be there. In actuality, he never got close to the drop site because some distance away he noticed activity. Upon seeing this, he ducked behind a stand of trees and using binoculars witnessed French intelligence personnel installing cameras and other surveillance equipment at the drop site. The first thing that ran through his mind was the KGB could not afford the technology and would've been forced to put real agents on site to manually perform the surveillance. The second thought was that his cover had been blown and he needed to extricate himself as quickly as possible. Fyodor then made his first mistake much worse--he returned to his apartment rather than immediately fleeing across the French border.

Usually, an agent would not return to his apartment after finding out his cover had been blown; this was a fundamental rule for all spies. But he deduced that since they had not arrested him up to this point, they were still in information-gathering mode. Therefore, he should be able to return to his apartment with relative safety. Once there he could destroy any evidence, gather necessary items, including a German passport and money for his trip back to the Soviet Union. What he did not know, was that at that precise moment two French agents were inside his apartment installing listening devices. Based on his routine, Fyodor was not supposed to be back at the apartment for several hours. When he unexpectedly walked in and caught the two agents inside his place, they had no option but to immediately arrest him. If this had occurred in the dark of night, the French officials might've been able to quietly take him downtown and before dawn convince him to spy for their side as a double agent. However, this happened in a relatively small town, during the late afternoon, and there were far too many witnesses to hope that Fyodor's capture would remain secret.

The version Fyodor provided to Dieter omitted the details of the missing dead drop signal, his trip out to the dead drop site, and instead began with him surprising the agents inside his apartment -- having no prior knowledge that the French security service was aware of his presence. Since he had never become romantically entangled with Monique, and he knew the French Secret Service would never allow her status as an agent to become known, he only admitted her role as a source. The fact that her information was false was no reflection on him since it was his job to gather the information and send it in rather than verify.

As Fyodor's mentor once told him, it was the small details that could get you in trouble one moment, then in another moment, those same little details could help set you free. All he had to do was remember the details and repeat them identically each time. Luckily, Fyodor was excellent at compartmentalizing to avoid lapses and crossovers that would trip upmost. Also, Dieter's demeanor and leading style of questioning were giving Fyodor a chance to create the story as he went. Since the situation was unrushed and not contrarian, Fyodor's created version had enough detail to seem plausible.

"That's fine, Fyodor," Dieter said nodding towards the window as if to signal the session was over. "How about some lunch?"

Rather than having his lunch brought into the small interrogation room, Dieter walked with Fyodor down to the public cafeteria on the first floor of the building. Fyodor assumed that the *Stasi* version of this type of interrogation was entirely different than the KGB methodology. The KGB would never have allowed him to leave the room until the debrief was complete; in fact, they would've provided a small bucket in the corner to use as a bathroom.

The two men took bread, cheese, and cold cuts from a small buffet that was set up in the corner of the room, then Dieter led them to a private dining area off to one side of the cafeteria where they sat down and started to manufacture sandwiches from the items they had gathered.

"By the way, old friend, this is not the usual way you have lunch during a *Stasi* debriefing. I was able to pull a few strings and get them to agree to allow this on the basis that a friendly encounter might help loosen any deeply hidden and covered details…" Fyodor started to object, but Dieter laid his hand on his shoulder, leaned toward him, and continued in a low voice. "Shhh. I know you are an honorable man like me and you will do only those things that are necessary to carry out your mission to protect your Motherland. I truly think it's disgraceful that they're treating you this way when they should be awarding you a medal. Since they are not, I will do my best to help make this less painful for you, so that you can get out of here as quickly as possible without any scars. Either physical or mental."

Dieter removed his hand from Fyodor's shoulder and sat back in his chair. "Planning a fishing trip once you get back to Minsk?"

Fyodor felt a huge weight had been removed from his shoulders. He took a deep breath and began to tell Dieter about his wife and possible plans for the future. Fyodor felt sure he could convince Svetlana not to divorce him but instead start a family since he would give up fieldwork and remain at home as was her desire.

The debrief by Dieter took six days, because he did not attempt to trip up or trick Fyodor, the follow-up debriefs by the KGB were a simple matter of remembering everything he had told Dieter and regurgitating it. In another break from standard protocol, the KGB debrief was conducted inside the *Stasi* headquarters rather than back at Lubyanka. Fyodor felt comforted knowing Dieter was behind the two-way mirror through the rest of this interrogation. Following another five days, which included him providing all the information he had on Union activity in the area and any other intelligence that may be useful to the next agent on the ground, he was released without charges or condemnation.

Before he left, Fyodor spent an evening out with his friend enjoying the last German beer he would have for a while and trying to in some small way express gratitude for what Dieter had done for him. Since they had endured a debriefing, any observer would assume the cordiality between them was born there rather than in joint service in Prague years before. They exchanged addresses and other contact information, but aside from the occasional letter they did not speak over the telephone or meet each other in person again – – until today.

Leaning close to Dieter, Fyodor spoke in a calm, matter-of-fact, whisper. "The purpose for the existence of the Crimson Firebird Initiative was to provide the Soviet Union a way to retaliate against the United States should they ever initiate a nuclear first strike. It was thought that such an attack would likely destroy the Soviet nuclear arsenal before the USSR launched. So, the CFI provides the retaliatory capability." Fyodor leaned back in his chair and watched Dieter's expression betray him with surprise.

Dieter was deep in thought trying to figure out how such a thing could possibly operate. He had questions that Fyodor must answer before asking him to take action on his behalf. "Putting aside for the moment, that a retaliatory strike after a war is lost serves no purpose, what type of attack will the Soviet Union possibly launch against the United States if their nuclear arsenal had been destroyed?" Dieter tried to keep his voice calm and low.

"A devastating counter home-based strike, of course."

"But how? If the Soviet nuclear arsenal had been destroyed and the Supreme Soviet no longer existed to give such an order, how would any type of retaliation be possible?"

"Using biological weapons packages that had already been placed within the United States near various population centers." Fyodor repeated the same answers that had been given to him by Sergei over forty years ago, almost verbatim.

"Forgetting for a moment how the weapons got there, who could possibly direct usage and who could actually set them off? If things were in shambles within the Soviet Union there would be no one left." Dieter did what he could to try and calm down. The thought that these weapons actually existed and might still exist worried him greatly.

"The Crimson Firebird Initiative included various sleeper agents who were put in place near where arms had been hidden. These sleeper agents would be alerted and in stages or all at once perform final assembly of the weapon system, bring it online for launch, and then finally detonate it. Since any normal methods of communication may have been compromised or destroyed, and the Supreme Soviet may not be in the position to give such an order, a network of numbers stations was put into operation to provide a reliable way of communicating with the sleeper agents in the field. Also, the authorization codes were not only held by the Supreme Soviet but also by a few people within the upper echelons of the KGB S-Directorate. At any point, these KGB appointees could begin the sequence of events necessary to allow the weapons to be detonated, without intercession or permission from anyone within the government."

Dieter gave a low whistle. "And you say, that this Crimson Firebird is still fully active?"

"Well, parts of it are. I have no way of knowing if anyone has been in contact with the sleeper agents. It is likely that the sleepers have forgotten to continue monitoring the directed frequencies and have just assumed their individual lives within the covers provided. As for the biological weapon devices, part of the original Crimson Firebird plan called for the weapons to be taken to Canada, disassembled, and left inert when the program was deactivated. I had assumed that those directives would have been carried out and they were now no more than so much low-level hazardous waste." This was the first time he had ever said any of this aloud and he was enjoying finally confessing all that he knew.

"However, I now have information that leads me to believe the weapons were never removed and there is a risk that multiple biological weapons could be detonated inside the United States, throwing the entire world into chaos."

Dieter was silent for a moment and then asked, "Why come to me and why now? I will do all I can to help you, my friend, but I am not sure exactly what you could expect of me. I know nothing about these sleepers, and I am not a biologist or engineer."

"I need your assistance to disarm all the weapons and ensure they are left inert. Also, and most importantly, I need you to ensure none of this is traceable to my son." Fyodor finally stated why he had called Dieter in the first place.

Fyodor gave Dieter a brief summary of the actions required. Mostly to coordinate with other people who were already in place. Dieter would provide full information on the program to include specific codes of authorization to complete specific tasks in order to ensure the weapons had been neutralized. The rescue of Fyodor's son was a bit more complicated as he would have to actually meet with him face-to-face, provide him with some required documents and currency, and then assist his son in obliterating the final bits of evidence that would link him back to the Crimson Firebird Initiative.

They stood by the door of the restaurant preparing to go their separate ways.

"I will send you all of the additional information we discussed in the next day or so. I will include a phone we can use to communicate as needed." Fyodor watched Dieter nod at his words, and then he paused to wait for Dieter's eyes to meet his. "You will have enough information to complete this without me. I know that soon enough of my past will be pieced together for them to find it necessary to silence me permanently."

"No. If things are this dire, Fyodor, let me help you escape."

"Alas, my friend, I have made the bed that I now lay upon. Anything I do to help myself would only expose more risk to my son. I can accept my fate, but I don't want my sins to be laid at my son's feet. Help me by helping him separate himself from all of this."

They parted with no more than a handshake, Fyodor knowing full well the gravity of the favor he was asking of his old friend. Any joy at their reacquaintance had been taken away by the required actions in the path ahead.

As Dieter sat quietly on the train from Munich, the information kept turning around in his head. After several years, the Cold War had become so much hyperbole. Dieter knew enough people in high places to realize most knew an all-out war between the two superpowers would never come to reality. The thought of mutually assured destruction was so horrific it prevented anyone in the highest offices from ever being insane enough to think it would ever be justified. He rightly believed that the public admission that such capabilities existed was a defense strategy all its own, preventing the other side from ever considering a first strike. But what Fyodor had told him was a different level of insanity – – assured destruction not for any kind of gain but strictly for revenge, and because it was a secret, it would never play any preventative role in decision-making. The concept was pure destruction for destruction's sake.

As he stood to exit the train, Dieter shook his head and thought to himself *Gott erbarme dich* – God have mercy on us.

A week later, Dieter found a courier standing at his door with a box in his arms that contained folders regarding the Crimson Firebird Initiative, a specialized cell phone capable of encrypted transmission, and €100,000 in cash. *It appears we have begun.* Dieter started reading the first folder. Planning had been one of Dieter's skills, so he only needed to talk to Fyodor once after receiving the box and before beginning the mission to clean up this forgotten detail.

Now, Dieter was unable to contact Fyodor at all. Looking down at the phone to locate and press the button to end the call, Dieter closed his eyes and feeling the full weight of the realization that he would never speak to his friend Fyodor again. The only thing he could do at this point was to guarantee the success of the favor that was asked of him.

As Evan stood before the display of pay-as-you-go cell phones, he flashed back to various police dramas and how they tracked people down who were using burner cell phones. He was doing nothing illegal; Evan just did not want to have a traceable phone number. His phone could block his identity, but he wanted a little extra security because he wasn't really sure who he was dealing with or what they could possibly want. His experience with fans up to this point had been relatively positive, but he knew from his agent and from other writers that the *psycho-fan* was out there somewhere. Evan had just not met that fan thus far.

He grabbed a phone in a bright green box with 200 free minutes and paid using cash--another of the *hide my trail* tricks he had learned from television. Getting a glimpse of himself in the glass of the door, he thought he might drive the short distance to Houstynne's salon to see if she could fit him in for a haircut since he was looking a little shaggy.

"Long time no see," she said while cutting a client's hair. "You been cheating on me?"

"Me? Cheat on you? How dare you accuse me of such a thing. You know you are the only artiste I ever let touch my hair so intimately," Evan said, helping himself to one of the empty chairs along the wall.

"Oh sure, that's what they all say. Then some lonely night, in another town -- when you've had one too many drinks -- you allow yourself to fall into some other stylist's chair and let them have their way with your hair." She was smiling as she said all this; however, her client was not quite sure what was going on.

"But baby, you know I couldn't do that. It just wouldn't be the same letting some stranger have their way with my hair. You are the only one for me." Evan had picked up a magazine and was thumbing through it, looking up long enough to respond to Houstynne's latest remark. "So, what do you say? Can you fit me in and remind me of why you're the only one for me?"

At this point, Houstynne dropped the pretense of being angry and assumed the usual happy persona that Evan had come to welcome and enjoy.

"Fine. But if you ever let another pair of scissors near you…"

"I know, I know – but you realize my head is really the wrong shape for a Mohawk."

Houstynne looked up at Evan for the first time and pointed her scissors towards him making several quick cutting motions for effect before returning to her client.

Evan might've been holding a magazine but he was not reading it. He kept thinking back to the envelope he found on his porch this morning. There had to be some meaning to the phrase, but Evan couldn't connect it to anything. One of the ways that he maintained control over his memories was to keep control over the individual elements in his life. This interruption cost him, and he was not sure how to recover.

Houstynne invited Evan to have a seat, tied the smock around his neck and began combing his hair. Evan watched her in the mirror as she went about her work and made various faces at the end results of her battles between his hair and her comb.

"Nothing unusual or crazy? Just keep you looking like the handsome guy you are?"

"Sure, don't stop until you're overcome with lust, drop your scissors, and run away with me for a weekend," he said, adding a wink.

"Ooh baby, the things I'm going to do to your hair."

Anyone seeing this exchange from the outside might not understand the unique relationship Houstynne and Evan shared. But that was quite all right, as long as they understood each other that was all that mattered. As she cut his hair, Evan quizzed her about the status of her daughter Ellie-- "Awesome as always,"—boyfriend--"Not so much a boyfriend; just someone who fits my present,"-- and her business--"After a year, growing but wished it would grow faster."

She likewise asked what was happening in Evan's life, how his latest book was coming along, and of course, about Zax. Even though she had only met the floppy-eared brown-eyed dog once, Evan talked about the animal a great deal, and she appreciated the animal's many attributes and persona. Evan was never quite sure how he and Houstynne related, but she gained a foothold with him early on by having an artist's personality that reminded him of so many people he had known and loved when he was younger. Evan saw her as a warm escape as much as a provider of an essential service.

She finished off his hair then trimmed his mustache and goatee. A quick once around with a blow dryer and brush – – then she stood back.

"You came really close to messing up again," Evan said as he examined her work in the mirror. "I keep telling you if you make me too sexy, I won't be able to get my book finished."

"*Mea Culpa*, my *Lord of Words*, I shall be more cautious next time." Houstynne performed an exaggerated curtsy and removed the smock from around his neck.

As Evan stood up, he withdrew the wallet from his back pocket and took out enough money to cover the haircut and tip. Upon handing it to her, he bowed deeply. "Forgiven, my *Hair Artiste*."

They both laughed at the shared joke, and he headed out to his car. Along the way home, he hit a local fast food eatery and managed to devour the meal while driving.

Zax greeted him at the door with a wagging tail and several nuzzles that let Evan know he was missed even though he was only gone a brief time. It was either that or the aroma of the just devoured hamburger. After letting the dog outside, Evan sat down at his dining table and tore open the cell phone package.

Reading through the instructions he was surprised to find that to activate the phone he would have to have a credit card. So much for anonymity. Recalling he had a twenty-five-dollar Visa gift card, he put the battery into the phone, plugged it into charge, and went to retrieve the credit card. He did not wait for the phone to fully charge before activating it. He was asked what area code the service should be tied to, and he decided to use 773. After all, Chicago should have thousands of numbers -- it would be as good a place as any to hide his.

Evan sat for a moment staring at the device. It was not long before this time of solace was interrupted by Zax pawing at the door. After letting the dog in and providing him with a treat, he picked up the letter that had been dropped on his porch earlier and reread its text.

Not all wars end when the shooting stops. More? Call 555-279-3410.

Evan's own experience with war thus far was that it never ends, it just calms down to a low roar in your mind that you try to control as best you can. Somehow, he knew this note was not about mental anguish and haunting memories; it seemed to relate more to Plato's statement about only the dead seeing the end of war. The world's history suggested that peace was sometimes just that uneasy calm between the last war and the next. Evan's deep pondering about the nature of war and peace was interrupted when his new phone vibrated. An SMS had been received:

```
>Your device is now registered with the network.
```

His brain went into an anxious overdrive as he ran his fingers over the keypad and considered when he should make that call to find out *more*.

Abi closed and locked the door behind Qa'id. He returned to the small closet that contained his shortwave radio and switched the unit off. Abi then unplugged the radio as well, even though no technology existed that could turn on such an archaic radio remotely to use it as a listening device. Qa'id had instilled in him a high degree of paranoia, so his fear over the possibility of hacking extended to everything electronic whether it made sense or not. Finally, he switched off the small desk lamp and closed the door to the closet, withdrawing a key from his pocket to lock the door that utilized a deadbolt.

Abi allowed himself to feel a level of a personal victory for the evening. Qa'id had listened and responded positively--even asking him to research his theory further. It was a good day all in all; he would have to go to Areef's shop the next day to tell him — *tell him what?* There was nothing that Abi could tell Areef about his meeting. That was too bad, Abi really wanted to share his victory--as it was Areef who got him listening to the shortwave radio just a few months prior. It was also Areef who gave Abi a stack of amateur radio magazines that led to Abi's discovery of numbers stations and helped guide his research about the stations. He was a good friend, but this was one secret that he could not share.

Abi's friendship with Areef had begun when he was just thirteen and happened to wander into Areef's *dekkan*, a small Arab convenience grocery and whatnot shop, called Oasis Mart. Oasis Mart served a growing immigrant population that chose to live in and near West Midlands, England. Abi had walked past the shop many times before actually going in, but once he stepped into the store, it was like entering a different world. The smell of Middle Eastern spices and the brass bell chime that sounded were unlike any British store. The shop was long and narrow, with shelves from floor to ceiling on both walls; the center of the store was divided into three cramped aisles with additional shelving units as dividers. The shelves were stuffed full of food items and spices from the Middle East and Arabia. Canned and packaged goods had Arabic labels to which Areef had dutifully added stickers, providing English for those second and third-generation immigrants who had not been brought up speaking and reading Arabic. Past the shelves of food was a small magazine rack which held both local newspapers and magazines in Arabic and English. Beside these racks were a few chairs and a small table where one might sit and read.

Along the back wall of the store were shelves that displayed small electric appliances, and other miscellaneous goods that Areef sold on consignment or had purchased for resale at various garage sales. Areef usually positioned himself behind the glass-topped counter near the front door where a large mechanical cash register stood guard over the only entrance or exit, depending on which way you were headed.

On that first day, Abi wandered through the store with the utmost of caution. He kept his arms to his side and his hands in his pockets as he looked wide-eyed at all the items that he discovered. Rather than exploring every detail of the store on this first visit, he took a circuitous route, snaking through all the aisles in the front, making a quick pass past the news racks, and then slowly past the shelves in the back while taking the time to catalog the shelves from ceiling to floor. When he came to the door marked Private, at the furthest end, he turned around and proceeded directly back toward the front of the shop. He walked past the counter at a quick pace towards the exit. Areef did not say a word to him but only smiled and nodded to the boy as he left his shop.

It would take many visits to Oasis Mart before Abi dared to speak to Areef. During those visits, Abi carefully inventoried everything that could be found in the shop. He took such care, it was surprising he had missed what would normally be of great interest to a thirteen-year-old: the glass counter at the front of the store, upon which the sizeable cash register sat, contained a myriad of candy and other inviting sweet treats. Once he noticed the treats, he took his time entering the store to gaze upon the sweet goodness that was just beyond his reach. Unlike the items in the rest of the store, he would have to deal with Areef if he decided to purchase anything inside that display case. This may never have been an issue since it was rare he had more than a few pence, until the day he found a one-pound coin on his way to school and the day he and Areef would first speak to each other.

On that day, Abi ran into the store and paused at the massive glass display case and to make a shopping list while adding and subtracting from the coin that was in his pocket. At one point, he decided to get more than one *Aero* bar but then wondered if it might be better to use some of that money to get the chocolate coconut *Bounty* instead. Areef stood behind the counter silently and watched Abi. He knew what the boy was doing as he had seen many young boys and girls do exactly the same thing when they finally had enough money to buy more than one item. The shifting expressions on the boy's face indicated a decision had been reached, only to disappear seconds later.

"Perhaps," the old man said as he placed his hands on the countertop and leaned forward towards Abi, "you should allow me to take out everything you are thinking about and put it here on the counter. That way, you can move the items that you have decided to buy to one side, and it will be easier for you to see exactly what has been chosen and what items you still have under consideration. Sometimes looking at all the possibilities through a pane of glass can be mind-boggling."

Abi looked up at the man as he spoke. In all the times he had been to the shop, this was the first time he had ever heard Areef speak. Most of the people Abi knew spoke English with some sort of accent, but this man had something of a strange lilt he had never heard.

"I think," said Abi while considering this new method for making candy decisions, "that might be a perfect idea."

Areef opened the back of the display case and spread out a full assortment of candy he thought the boy might like. Once this chore was complete, he stood back up and said, "Voila!" motioning with his hands.

Abi moved the candy he was seriously considering off to the left. As an afterthought, he took a *Lion* bar from the selection that remained then his facial expression looked puzzled for a moment, and he returned the candy to its original place. He was a few pence short to get the *Lion*.

Areef took out a small paper bag for Abi's candy. He did not bother to tell Abi the total amount due. Areef held out his open hand for the pound coin. The old man turned to the cash register, and after pushing several keys, a bell rang, and the drawer on the machine opened. He dropped the coin into it and took out several pennies handing them directly to Abi as he shut the drawer on the register. Areef then picked up the paper bag and started to roll the top down to close it before handing it on to Abi, but he stopped and set the bag back on the counter allowing it to reopen. He then held up his index finger as if he were about to say something crucial. After a moment, he reached down, picked up the *Lion* bar, dropped it into the bag, and quickly rolled the top shut.

"A gift for a new friend," Areef said while giving the young boy a reaffirming nod.

"Thank you. Thank you very much." Abi held the bag tight against his body as if it were the greatest treasure in the world.

After exiting Oasis Mart, Abi immediately turned toward home, running as quickly as he could. When he entered the apartment where he and his mother, Fakhriya, lived with several other relatives, Abi hid the bag off to one side of his body as he walked past the adults who were sitting around the dining room table carrying on a heated discussion in Arabic. Once he was safely in the small bedchamber he shared with several cousins, he went to the corner where his mattress sat on the floor. Abi lifted the mattress and hid the candy. He lay down on the bed trying not to let his extreme joy show itself outwardly, knowing his own private treasure was safe and awaiting a time when he could enjoy it all by himself.

That incident led to one of the most stable relationships in Abi's life, and it was also one of his warmest childhood memories. Areef became a mentor for Abi, guiding him through a problematic puberty as well as focusing his attention on science and developing computer skills while his contemporaries were busy playing video games and discovering music. Areef also helped him learn to cope with his anger over the killing of his father, his anger toward the Mossad, who was responsible, and Israel in general. Abi saw all this as the cause of everything bad in his life--from the loss of his father to living in a shared flat in England with his mother rather than in their homeland.

Areef had not taught him to completely dispose of his negative emotions or his desire to somehow strike back at the faceless haunting enemy. Abi would not meet Qa'id, who would guide him towards a means of lashing out, until just after his seventeenth birthday. At that point, with nine years of bottled up anger and frustration, Abi was the perfect weapon to be used against his own enemy as well as a greater one.

Chapter Four

Western, Michigan

As he pressed the phone to his ear after dialing the mystery number, Evan wondered why he was even bothering to call to someone unknown about – – something. Too late for such thoughts now, as he had already put things in motion. He heard the phone ring once and then silence.

"Hello?"

"Mr. Davis, so good of you to take the time to call," was the response from the accented voice. "I hope we can meet to discuss things face-to-face; are you in Chicago?"

"Um, no. This is just the phone I use when I'm traveling. Who are you?"

"For now, just call me Heinrich, and if you are done traveling and will be home for a bit, I could come by there in a week or so, when I return to the area. I have other appointments. If you would prefer we could meet while I am on the road instead, to expedite things," the voice said calmly.

Evan could not place the accent-- Eastern or Western European. It had been too long since he had traveled through that region of the world. "What do you mean by meeting with you on the road? Why can't you just tell me about this now and let's be done with it?" Evan's slight anxiety shone through.

"In a few days I will be in the Atlanta airport for an extended period while I change planes. We could meet there at the airport. I would be more than happy to arrange a round-trip ticket for you. I am sorry to seem so mysterious, but doing this over the phone is just too *exposed* for the information that I need to pass on. I promise you that this will be well worth your while; surely, you still have the curiosity of the journalist who wrote dispatches while an embed in Afghanistan, don't you?"

"I am not really a journalist, that was just something I did as a one-time gig. Perhaps I'm not the right person to talk to about this, I don't have a regular column or any way to provide publicity for your information."

"Publicity is not at all what is needed or wanted. I assure you; you are exactly the person who is needed in the situation, and in the end, you will be glad that you have been afforded this opportunity. I know the unpublished details of what took place in Kuwait, so let's say I know your other capabilities as well. Let me do this to expedite matters... I will send you a sample of the information that I need to discuss with you along with an airline ticket to Atlanta for this Friday morning. I will also include a cashier's check for $5000. Take a day or so to review the information and if you decide your curiosity is aroused, you will board the plane on Friday so we can talk further. If not, you securely dispose of the information that I sent you, along with the airline ticket, and you keep the $5000 for your time and trouble."

"$5000--just to take a look at something? I am not sure if I will take this on or not, but you do have a way of getting someone's attention. You haven't even told me what would be required of me; if I do decide to listen to the rest of what you have to say," Evan responded.

"If things go as I expect them to, you will have an opportunity to stop an exceptionally diabolical plan that was set in motion decades ago – a plan that now appears to be on the verge of going off the rails. I will make the necessary arrangements, and some material will arrive at your door tomorrow morning... have an enjoyable afternoon, Mr. Davis." With that, the line went dead.

Evan stared at the phone as if it contained some answer to this mystery or at least why the phone conversation had been terminated while he still had questions. "ARRGHH!" he screamed into the receiver, knowing full well no one was on the other end to hear his frustration.

Dieter Sieg pressed the end button on his cell phone and then slipped it into his briefcase. As he sat in the sedan at the end of the street looking at Evan's house, he was sure some sort of reaction was taking place inside but apparently not volatile enough to be seen from this distance. That was good. He knew the information that he was about to send to Evan regarding the Crimson Firebird Initiative would be enough to interest the writer and to spur his involvement in Dieter's mission to disarm the program. With that settled, he started his car and proceeded out of town. He had done what he needed to do from this locale, and it was time to move to the next stage of the plan.

Evan's night was anything but relaxing. Much of the evening before going to bed was spent pacing, peering into the refrigerator, and flipping aimlessly from channel to channel on his TV as he pondered the entire situation. He was not a fan of mysteries, and Heinrich had given him a rather large one. What he knew at this point was that someone from somewhere in Europe, with full command of spoken English, wanted him to do something for him based on Evan's journalism. He was told he would be glad that he had participated in whatever this was…oh, and this was to fight something diabolical that had been in the works for decades. *What the hell did all that mean?*

When he finally forced himself to go to bed, he lay there awake. Every ten minutes or so, he would open his eyes and glance over at the clock as he watched the night crawl by. Using relaxation techniques, he was able to remain on this side of anxious, but his mind kept running through the sparse details of what he did know about the situation. Philosophical questions also crept into his consciousness. *Why me?* Was foremost and that thought kept turning over and over in his head without any answer that made sense. The last time he remembered looking at the clock it was after three when a new mystery occurred to him—why was this Heinrich person placing such an extremely high value on his services? After all, he was offering to pay him $5000 just to review some papers. Evan did not know if he was awake, asleep, or someplace in-between when his train of thought was interrupted by the sound of a slight plop followed quickly by Zax's barking.

Instinctively he realized this must be the promised envelope from Heinrich. Evan threw back the covers and ran to the front door where Zax continued barking. He threw the door open and saw a FedEx truck pulling away from his house. Zax raced to the edge of the yard.

This time Heinrich had relied on FedEx-- so much for possibly getting a look at him. He leaned over and picked up the envelope. Evan whistled for Zax who ignored him as the dog proceeded on his morning rounds, so he headed inside for a cup of coffee to face the new enigmas inside the mystery envelope that greeted him today.

He gave the delivery only a cursory look, as this was a standard FedEx style and not a blank manila envelope. There was a return address, but no return name. Evan would look the address up later to see if there was more information to be found, but he seriously doubted it. Whoever Heinrich was, the man did a better job than Evan of hiding himself. He shook the contents out on the table and three items fell out: Two white, business-sized envelopes and a folder with some strange writing. He spread the contents in an arc on the table.

Upon opening both envelopes, he found that one contained a cashier's check for $5000 with his name as payee, and the other held a first-class round-trip to Atlanta from Detroit. Well, what Heinrich promised was delivered. The folder had a strange logo at the top and Cyrillic writing. As he sipped his coffee, he noticed an English translation of each line.

Evan's memory of the Cold War, while still vivid, was not comprehensive. He lacked specific knowledge of how alliances and espionage were handled by either the Soviets or the United States. While he had seen military plans, he was unaware that there were differences as to how the two nations handled them as well. The United States, unlike the Soviets, produced most documents in multiple languages to make things more commonly accessible to their own people as well as any allies who might need access to a document. Due to NATO ties, the United States typically produced documents in English, French, and German; the Soviets used only Russian and English. The Soviets chose to use only two languages, ignoring the multiple dialects and languages used within their own federation. English was an accommodation to Soviet Bloc allies were outside, such as the Chinese and Cubans, who were more adept in English than the less universal Russian.

Evan was holding a standard cover sheet for a classified Russian document, this one produced by the S Directorate of the KGB. It gave the basic classification of the information, additional details as to what the document was about, and who was allowed access to the document. This way, anyone coming upon the material could clearly see who was authorized to read the information. Since the document would usually be stored in a vault or safe, it was assumed anyone with access to the material up to this point would be bound by and follow the directives and limitations on the cover sheet.

Совершенно секретно/особой
Particularly Important

Особая папка en Инициатива Малинового Феникса
Special Folder: Crimson Firebird Initiative

Отдельный проект - Доступ к полной информации ограничен:
Compartmentalized Project - Access to full information limited:

Премьер-министр СССР
Soviet Prime Minister

Комитет по государственной безопасности (КГБ) Директор
Committee for State Security (KGB) Director

Инициатива Малинового Феникса - S Директор Директора и Заместитель Директора
Crimson Firebird Initiative (S Directorate) Director & Deputy Director

Evan read the sheet twice, just to make sure he understood. This was limited to only four people – *and now I have it.* Research on the Internet informed Evan that *Particularly Important* was equivalent to the West's *Top-Secret* level. This meant compartmentalization with people working on the project only being given the information that related to their piece of the project.

What the hell have I gotten myself into? He stared almost fearfully at the cover sheet. Evan considered that the document could be fraudulent and was being used somehow to manipulate him. Whatever was on those pages would have to be verified before he would accept them as fact. Two things kept running through his mind--the note in the first envelope and Heinrich's words on the phone. "Wars are won or lost, but if the loser can still strike back from the ashes of defeat it is never truly over," and "an opportunity to stop an exceptionally diabolical plan."

"Time to dive into the rabbit hole," he said as he picked up the document and flipped the cover sheet open to reveal the first page. The page was entirely in English. Before reading the document in earnest, he flipped through the pages and glanced over the section headings in the table of contents: Abstract, Assumptions, Preparation, Authority, Execution, and several more. The Soviets followed a format similar to what he had seen in Afghanistan. The plan provides a bottom-line upfront – then solidifies the current status of things along with the change that is intended and provides the details on how to get ready to make it happen. Most importantly, the plan provides details on who makes *Go/No Go* decisions and how it will all happen. This is a format works quite well in passing necessary information more or less objectively without a lot of added fluff.

Evan let Zax back inside and brewed another cup of coffee before diving into the rest of the document. As soon as he sat down in his recliner, Zax made himself at home beside the chair easily within Evan's reach for the occasional head rub.

Abstract

The Crimson Firebird Initiative (CFI) is designed to be a self-contained action project that will allow the Soviet Union to react offensively should the homeland, and sea-based thermonuclear missile arsenal be completely destroyed or lose 75% of its capability. The project places standalone weapons of mass destruction at various strategic locations within the borders of the United States of America that will be activated and released by a force of deep-cover agents also placed within that country by this plan. The CFI operatives will receive extensive education, indoctrination, and cultural training which will allow them to spend their lives well-hidden at various locations near where the Launch Preparation Assembly Kits (L-PAKs) are based. Periodic and ongoing communication with the CFI Agents will be strictly unidirectional using rudimentary versus high-tech methods to prevent the chance of loss of connectivity. Upon being alerted, CFI Agents will have the independent capability of arming the previously placed devices and setting their final detonation in motion. It is likely all CFI Agents will be lost should actual implementation be necessary. Because this initiative is designed to go into effect after massive destruction within the Soviet Union, authorization to activate the CFI rests solely with the General Secretary or the Committee for State Security (KGB) Director who will be kept apprised of the program personally by the Crimson Firebird Initiative (S Directorate) Director or Deputy Director.

Evan pet his dog as he contemplated what he just read. *The bastards really were crazy.* Growing up, the Soviets had always been the evil villain from every *James Bond* movie Evan had ever seen to *Bullwinkle* cartoons he enjoyed every Sunday. As he grew older and started to develop his own opinions and perceptions of the world, Evan could not allow himself that absolute. It simply was not possible that all Russians were evil and bent on destroying the United States. After what he just read, he had to add a codicil that allowed for a Soviet leadership crazy enough to want to destroy the United States even after they lost the war for no other reason than some sort of ultimate payback for their own destruction.

As he read the Assumptions section, he was amazed at the detail, including percentages of the Soviet population killed, numbers of Soviet missiles destroyed versus launched, survivability of the Soviet nuclear submarine fleet, and the possible annihilation of the Supreme Soviet during the initial exchange. Evan could not believe the matter-of-fact and unemotional description of the post-apocalyptic Soviet Union following the devastating attack. One of the assumptions was the United States launching first against the Soviet Union; in other words, this entire scenario was fundamentally based on a nuclear attack, not a nuclear exchange. Unlike many of his generation who had lost faith in American institutions, Evan could not believe his government would intentionally launch a civilization-ending war on purpose. But having been a child of Hollywood as well, he had seen instances where such an attack took place accidentally. If that was possible, the actual implementation of this plan was also plausible. The thought made him shudder.

Evan noticed as he turned the page that what he had was incomplete; the document skipped from page one to page eight. *I should've known that Heinrich was not going to give me a complete report -- just enough to whet my appetite and make me curious enough to meet.* Heinrich understood human nature entirely as Evan was almost convinced.

Expected Devastation

The biological warfare devices which will be utilized for this program are described in greater detail in Appendix R. Basic information regarding the virus variant used, as supplied by the *Chimera Project*, is as follows:

The virus provided is known as *Chimera K629*. *K629* is a genetically modified version and the combination of Bacillus Anthracis (Anthrax) and Ebolavirus (Ebola hemorrhagic fever). This combination will allow *K629* to lay dormant for up to 50 years or beyond when maintained at a storage temperature between -21 and 52°C (-5 and 125°F) and have quick and devastating effects when activated. *K629* can benefit from a concentrated oxidizer which acts as a catalyst to accelerate the end of dormancy and the viruses spread.

Once active, the spores will begin to multiply at an exponential rate, doubling every 12 hours. Effective geographic dispersal information is contained within specific tables, as is the multi-generational mutation variable which will cause the root virus to self-destruct over a period of time due to the insertion of specific genetic traits. Human to human transmission of the virus halts the multi-generational mutation factor. Therefore, as long as the virus lives within a single human, the transmission will continue regardless of what happens to the virus spores outside of human hosts. Once it has infected its host, *K629* shows no visible symptoms for a gestation period of 96 to 120 hours but is highly contagious during that time. This allows the virus to spread before any realization an infection has occurred. Once the virus goes active within a human host, 97% assured fatality occurs within 72 hours.

Ignoring factors such as the wind, dispersal altitude/height, and obstacles that may lie in the direct path of the spread radius (affecting its optimal distribution), each weapon should be expected to initially become active and infectious within a 10-25 km area. Due to the exponential growth pattern of *K629*, the area affected will double every 12 hours. It is expected that all humans within a 100km radius will be infected within 36 hours while showing no external signs of distress.

Chimera K629 has no physical, explosive effects. Therefore, infrastructure damage will be limited to unknown factors that may arise due to civil unrest due to panic during the period between identification of the virus as a factor and the tipping point between a majority of the population being initially infected and total population mortality. Migration and repopulation could occur within the affected area in 90 to 120 days.

"Oh shit," Evan said in a quiet voice. The gravity of the situation hit him like a body blow. Scenarios played out within his mind. If the target were Chicago, the wind could carry the virus all the way into Indiana and Michigan; if they targeted New York or San Francisco, it would affect huge population centers. *My God, what were these lunatics thinking?* Then, not unlike Scrooge, he realized what he had been presented with was a possibility and necessarily what would come to pass. The original start date for this project was 1972--a long time past; *was any of this actually done? If so, did any of it still exist after the fall of the Soviet Union in 1991?*

Instinctively, he flipped to the back of the document to look for the appendix but instead found a list of various credits for the pages of the report. *The bastards went so far as to footnote the damn report*, – the revelation caused an involuntary sneer. At the bottommost position on the last page, was the following in bold print:

The personnel responsible for the content and execution of this plan: Director and Deputy Director,   Crimson   Firebird   Initiative   (S Directorate), Sergei Kirill Mikhailov and Fyodor Ilyich Maldroski, respectively.

Well, at least now Evan had the names of the architects of this madness: Sergei and Fyodor. But what would he do with that information? There were references to using something called numbers stations for communication but no detail on what they were or how they would be employed. Also, missing from this extract of the document was any the information about where the devices were hidden, how they got into the country, and who was going to set them off. He was given just enough information for panic but not for action. *Not good…this is exactly where Heinrich wants me*. He had no choice. Evan would have to meet with Heinrich to find out what this was all about. Then the second wave of realization hit, even when he knew what all this was about – – what the hell was he supposed to do about any of it?

The nocturnal vision was a familiar one, but that did not mean the thoughts were comforting or welcome. In fact, the movie playing in Abi's mind was a combination of memories of his last night home in Palestine augmented by his thoughts and fears. What was real or created didn't matter since every detail was now accepted as indisputable fact. The vision had evolved over the years from one that played out in first person to one he watched as a silent bystander. Perhaps it was this shift that added an authentic feel.

"Mum?" the young boy said as he walked from the dark of his bedroom into the well-lit living room. The room was simple and typically kept neat and well organized. However, what the boy found was broken glass and overturned furniture; the noise of the upheaval must've been what had woken him. His mother, Fakhriya, sat on the couch, hunched over and sobbing. Upon hearing Abi, she sat upright and extended her arms. The boy started to run towards her, but a shadowy figure by the open front door was menacing; Abi slowed his pace as he tried to make sense out of the scene. Just before he reached his mother, he saw a second figure standing in the doorway between the living room and kitchen.

When he reached his Fakhriya's outstretched arms, Abi first felt her fingertips grab for him and then she leaned forward scooping him up and placing him in her lap where she held him tightly. As his eyes adjusted, Abi stole sideways glances at the two figures. Both were dressed in black, the one near the front door sported a huge beard while the one in the door of the kitchen was cleanly shaven; each cradled an AK-47 in his arms. Neither man appeared to be overly hostile at the moment, but they were visibly vigilant.

Abi could hear men's voices outside arguing through the open door. Fakhriya rocked him gently while she held his head against her breast. He could feel her body quivering as she tried to stifle her own fear to comfort the boy. He heard someone enter the house speaking at a fast pace to the two men. The one with the beard turned and immediately exited the house, but the clean-shaven one blocking the doorway to the kitchen walked towards Abi and his mother and without saying a word grabbed the boy by his arm and proceeded to pull him towards the front door.

Abi screamed for his mother as she pulled on his opposite arm to prevent him from being taken outside. Another large man entered the house, this one wearing a beret; he quickly surveyed the situation before walking directly over to her. The man took Abi's mother by her shoulders, threw her back onto the couch, and then pointed the finger at her while shaking his head. With that, Fakhriya turned her face towards the sofa sobbing loudly, and the man that had hold of Abi's arm dragged him through the door and into the front yard.

There was not a full moon that night, but somehow Abi managed to see the group of men in his front yard circled around his father who was down on his knees in the sand, his shoulders slumped. There were eight men total and all were wearing similar dark clothes. Abi would learn later that these were a form of military uniform. The boy tried to pull away from the clean-shaven man so he could run to his father. Part of him wanted to be comforted by his father, the other to bring him comfort. He could hear the voices of the men as they argued back and forth in Arabic. Abi was puzzled by his English speech and thoughts in this vision. This confusion was only momentary because the vision's pace gained speed from this point forward.

The men continued to argue back and forth, while one occasionally hit or pushed his father who remained silent. Whenever his father was struck, he cried out, and this caused the assaulter to glance Abi's way before withdrawing to his former position in the circle. Abi could not see his father's face clearly but could tell there was a streak of blood on one side. In a child's mind, anything that caused you to bleed was fatal. His father's wounds were superficial up to this point, but they were part of the sequence of events that would include his father's eventual death.

There were several more minutes of arguing. One of the men had three long scars on the left side his face that ran from just below his eye and disappeared below the collar of his shirt. He appeared to be the leader of the group and withdrew a pistol from its holster, then held it up in the air. This action caused the rest of the men to become silent, and it was in that silence that the leader lowered the pistol and pulled back the slide on the weapon, chambering a round and preparing it to fire. With all of the men now silent, that metallic sound echoed in the stillness. The leader pointed the pistol towards Abi's father, taking a step forward, so the barrel was actually in contact with the side of his father's head.

The man spoke, and try as Abi might he could never remember the words after waking from the vision. It was just so much background noise in a scene that would affect the rest of his life. At one point, near the end of his speech, the scarred man motioned with his head towards Abi and then spoke directly to him in curt and angry tones. The leader shifted his attention to the man who was kneeling before him, and while standing there in silence, his scarred face turned from anger to cold contempt.

There was a noise from inside the house, which caused Abi to turn his attention from his father's plight to the location where he had last seen his mother. As he watched the open front door, he saw his mother come bursting through it only to be pulled back by an unseen force. A man's voice was yelling while he heard his mother screaming -- then in the middle of that cacophony there was a single gunshot.

Abi's head snapped back to where his father had been kneeling, and he watched as the man slowly crumpled to one side in the sand. Once the body came to rest, a blood pool started to form around the man's head and spread outward. Abi was in shock for a moment and then tried to run to his father only to be prevented by the clean-shaven man who had dragged him outside. Rather than putting up with the boy's struggles, the man picked him up and carried him back into the house, then threw him down on the couch, knocking the wind out of Abi.

As Abi struggled to inhale, he looked up to see his mother being held back by yet another one of the invading force, this one with a mustache. She was fighting against the man mightily and eventually broke free and ran over to the boy, taking him into her arms to comfort and calm him so he could breathe once again. The invaders glanced at each other and nodded, then one at a time they left through the front door, the last one closing it behind them. No word of explanation, no apologies for the actions taken, no promise not to return later for further violence directed at Abi or Fakhriya.

Abi would never forget the quaking of his mother's body as she cried over the death of her husband while she sat holding her son. He could hear voices outside arguing again and additional gunshots. This caused Fakhriya to stop sobbing and with great strength maintain her silence as she picked the boy up and carried him through the kitchen and then through the back door into the alley that ran behind their home. Once they were outside, Abi could hear more gunshots, more yelling, and the sound of vehicle engines. It was the last time Abi would ever see their home in Palestine.

Abi slowly opened his eyes, and even though he was surrounded by darkness, he realized he was again safe in his small apartment rather than back in the Middle East. As occurred each time he had this vision, tears flowed freely from the corners of his eyes, but it was no longer accompanied by the body-racking sobs that were part of the vision when he was younger. The sadness he felt was most intense at this moment, but it was the same familiar sorrow he felt on some level every day since the event that was his constant companion. It was almost a decade after that tragic night that he found out the details of what had occurred.

Shortly after meeting Qa'id, Abi shared his personal history. Qa'id offered to research the events of that evening. It was a few weeks later when Qa'id returned with this story: The Israeli army had dispatched a team of commandos to assassinate his father because he had been working with the Palestinian Liberation Organization to stir up discontent among the Arabs in Israel who deserved to be treated more fairly. The chaos of noise that Abi heard as he and his mother fled was the PLO attacking and killing those soldiers to avenge the death of his father.

But Abi swore that those few lives were in no way equal to what had been taken from him, and he vowed revenge against the State of Israel at some point during his life. After Qa'id had told him in broad terms about the traumatic events, he set about indoctrinating young Abi with many skewed truths about who was ultimately responsible for the actions that night as well as those that had been occurring since the rise of Israel after World War II.

"Without the United States, Israel would not exist. If Israel did not exist, your father would still be alive, and your family would still be whole. This applies to many of our brothers in Palestine, and why we must never let the battle end until we have avenged them all." The first time Qa'id had told him this, he did so while looking him directly in the eye, with a reassuring hand on his shoulder. The sincerity of that moment carried on every time Qa'id spoke to Abi about the larger connections and responsibility for the pain his people felt.

Near Smolensk, Russia

The silence told Fyodor that Maksim had left the room at least momentarily, but he would be on him again, so he needed to mentally prepare. His goal was to last long enough to convince his captor that he had secrets, and then eventually let go a flood of information before being permanently dispatched by his opponent. He had lost track of time but prevented himself from wasting time overthinking that mistake.

All the tricks of the craft he had learned over the years of being a spy and working for the KGB were failing him as physical pain took over. When this occurred, the subject of an interrogation was most likely to give away the most deeply held information, and a flood followed with no hope of being able to withhold anything. The only thing that was clear in his mind at the moment was the necessity to protect the only person he cared about in the world.

Sand and other debris on the bottom of Maksim's boots grinding against the concrete floor announced his return. Maksim was deliberate in his approach. He knew anticipation was a double-edged sword; when the end result was happiness, it served to maximize the pleasure of the moment; when the final result was to be pain, anticipation caused fear and dread. Maksim wanted Fyodor anxious and scared.

"So, my friend, you are again awake. Don't bother trying to pretend you are not... the change in your breathing gives you away." Maksim took hold of a straight-backed chair and tilting it forward, allowed the front legs to slowly drag, screeching along the floor as he pulled it toward Fyodor. Eventually, he dropped the chair directly in front of Fyodor with a loud bang that echoed throughout the empty building.

"Why don't we make this easy so we can both go home? My purpose here is simple, I am gathering information about covert operations that may have existed within the old KGB; my employer wants to be able to use that information as a bargaining tool should he need to negotiate with the government in the future. As you must realize, information is a commodity of great value. You are not any sort of target; you are just merely a repository of information – a possible ally to my mission. Once I have all you know, and I can verify that which you have told me, I will cross your name off the list of information resources. I will let you go back to your *dacha* in Minsk where you can continue to draw your pension and play chess with your friends in the park. Otherwise..."

Rather than using words alone to make his point, Maksim drove his fist again into Fyodor's jaw. Maksim allowed his fist to travel slightly further this time, ensuring the pain resonated in the sinew and bone of Fyodor's mouth. Still, he did not take it so far as to break any bones or teeth. When Fyodor's head returned to its starting position, it fell forward, and blood dribbled from his mouth.

"You see my friend, talking to me would be much easier than continuing with that sort of *motivation*."

The last punch had almost caused Fyodor to blackout; it was

time.

"If I tell you of all the projects that I was involved with, then you will let me go home?" Fyodor knew full well that any response was going to be a lie. But then, everything Fyodor was about to say was a lie. In the end, it all balanced out.

"Why of course," Maksim said smiling. "After I verify the information. Let's speed this along, and I will tell you what I know about you already-- you used to work for the KGB. As such, you handled various projects for the leadership there. So, that part is over – – why don't you tell me the rest of what you know so we can move this process along?" Maksim reached forward and patted Fyodor on the shoulder. He poured some bottled water into a glass and returned to Fyodor, raising it to his lips. Tilting the glass, Maksim allowed Fyodor to drink.

The cold water that flowed into Fyodor's mouth caused him pain since he had bitten his tongue while being hit. Belaying that bit of discomfort, he swallowed the first drops of liquid. Maksim lifted and spun the back of the chair in front of his subject and straddled it.

"Now, you see? You start to be cooperative, and I can be much nicer." Maksim raised his hands, much as a magician would at the end of a trick.

"As you say, I was a Commander with the KGB," Fyodor stated in a low voice, through the pain of the recent attack on his jaw. "As such, I worked in the S Directorate, and my primary function was to act as a liaison to the various Rezidentura in the West to assist them with their illegal's operations." As he heard the words come out of his mouth, he knew full well that admitting what he had said in that one sentence alone was enough to justify the death penalty for treason. It was the beginning of the end.

Chapter Five

Atlanta, Georgia

As the other passengers rushed to deplane, Evan remained in his seat. He was anxious to get the meeting over with Heinrich but knew it wouldn't be that easy. The document he had seen was beyond scary, it was utterly terrifying. Based on everything that had occurred up to this point, Evan had no reason to doubt the validity of the documents plan. The Cold War he believed was in the past had unexpectedly reappeared.

When the rush of people had quieted a bit, Evan pulled his backpack from underneath the seat. This bag was almost identical to the Swiss Go-bag that had served him well through his tour in Afghanistan and his adventure in Kuwait. The only significant changes were the bag itself, which was replaced because of permanent bloodstains, and his ten-inch Buck knife, which was removed due to TSA rules regarding weapons. The Go-bag's many zippered pockets were full of useful and comforting items--chargers, aspirin, computer cables, fingernail clippers, wet wipes, and a spare toothbrush. The backpack remained ready at the top of his closet for his next call to duty. All Evan needed to do was to unzip the back compartment and drop in his laptop.

Slinging the backpack over his right shoulder, he made his way to the front of the plane and past the gauntlet of flight attendants who thanked him for choosing Delta. While walking down the jet tube, his imagination caught hold of him again, and he found himself suddenly gripped by anxiety. *What the hell am I doing? Why the hell am I doing it?* He had no answers.

He had no instructions to follow upon arrival. His burner phone rang several times before Evan realized the cause and answered it. He noted the screen showed Unknown Number for the identity of the caller before raising it to his ear.

"Heinrich?"

"Yes, Mr. Davis, it is I. I trust you had a safe and uneventful flight," the accented voice was polite.

"The flight was fine. Can we get on with this? Where are you?"

"I am so glad to hear it; I have arranged a small cordial space for us to speak privately. If you will proceed to the main international concourse and find The Club at ATL, you will be met at its entrance so that you can gain admittance."

Evan was growing tired of Heinrich's calm demeanor. "Fine, I will be there as quickly as I can." Evan looked for signs to guide him to the international concourse.

"No rush, feel free to take your time. See you shortly."

There were few places further apart than the T Concourse where he had just landed and Concourse F at the other end of the world. Taking the escalator down, he headed for the tram.

❧

Inside the Kerzhenskiy Nature Preserve, Russia

The Academy's formal name was The Gamayun Education Centre, but it would be wrong to refer to the Academy as just a school, it was so much more than that--it was its own world. Since its founding in 1975, the facility only had one goal: to produce superior agents capable of being placed in independent, deep undercover in the United States in support of the Crimson Firebird Initiative. No one at the school knew the CFI's formal name, in keeping with its highly classified status, it was only referred to as *the mission*.

Dmitry was taken to the processing center in the central campus after leaving his father at the registration area. First, a basic physical exam was performed then he was assigned to a house on the grounds where he would live for the next few years. He was given an American name, Julian Shepherd, as part of the transition and also received a new birthday, 23 September 1969. All of this was part of the gradual indoctrination to a new personal history. After entering the area beyond the registration desk, no Russian was spoken as everything was done in English. Dmitry had a rudimentary knowledge of the language he had picked up from his father, but it took several weeks before he could communicate effectively. He and the 143 other prospective agents were sternly chastised and corrected for words they mispronounced or pronounced with any sort of accent. The goal was to have them all fluent in their new language and sounding like Americans.

The first five years of training concentrated on the pupil forgetting everything Russian. The children lived in homes with designated adult couples acting as if they were American parents, going to an American-style school, playing American games, and watching American TV. The KGB had spent massive amounts of money to recreate a typical American city within their own borders to train the agent selectees who would eventually be used for the CFI. The environment utilized at the Academy was totally immersive and continually updated with new information from agents currently in the United States. Consumer products and videotapes of American TV were already being routinely shipped from the Soviet Embassy in America. Those items of contraband were diverted on arrival from their original destination, from people in the Soviet hierarchy to the Academy.

Dmitry was gradually changing into Julian. He never would forget his father completely, but he allowed what was happening to him to be accepted as part of what his father wanted. Fyodor's words kept ringing through his head that what was going on would eventually benefit him for the rest of his life. So, unlike the other students, Dmitry was among the few who never questioned why they were learning these lessons. The reward would be at the end.

As with everything else that the KGB did, the program was so compartmentalized no part knew with the other part was doing. At this point, only four people knew the ultimate goal of the Crimson Firebird Initiative and how the program was functioning on a day-to-day basis. The Soviet General Secretary and the KGB Director were merely observers of the program; Sergei Kirill and Fyodor Ilyich were the program's proud parents, but due to its secrecy they could brag to no one about their successes.

The second five years took each of the candidates, who had just spent the previous five years being Americanized, to indoctrinate them with Communist ideals and a sense of mission focus. One of the goals was to ensure each of the sleeper agents, could be counted upon in the United States to perform reliably. There could be no greater failure for the program than having an agent suddenly rethink his entire motivation when told to proceed or worse while in the middle of performing. As it was, trust was a new concept within the KGB. Historically, the USSR had spent more time and money spying on their own citizens than they ever did looking outward. The Crimson Firebird Initiative required the KGB to stop that routine surveillance and place trust within this select group to accomplish their mission exactly as instructed.

The final few years at the Academy were spent assuming the identities they had been provided, which included the ability to flawlessly remember all parts of the manufactured back story. Names, dates, places, events, and experiences were all part of the vast catalog of information that required memorizing and embracing as their own personal history. Also, many of the candidates learned trades in the context of their roles in the field. Dmitry was lucky to be selected to attend a university and assume a career in the financial industry. Even though his academic testing would have led to this end, his father had ensured his boy was placed on this career path versus one of manual labor.

Periodically, during the training process, it was necessary to remove students who either were not performing up to standards or whose behavior was deemed to be unstable. These students were removed from the facility, never to be seen by anyone again. It was an institutionally supported rumor that they were transitioned to less demanding foreign service roles within the government. The personnel who made these decisions and carried out the removal operation, appropriately called the process *culling the unfit*. Anyone removed after the first two years was terminated and quietly disposed of to prevent any risk of a security breach. Because of the extensive screening process, before selection, the cull rate was less than 10%, which was lower than forecast.

In 1986, the last year of training was focused on a single learning objective – flawlessly performing the primary mission. Each student was presented with the full 102 volume set of *Brandt's Compleat Collection of Great World Literature*. As a cost-saving measure, the volumes they worked with at the Academy were not leather-bound, nor gold-edged; other than that, they were identical to the ones that would be provided to them at their eventual destination. They also began the assignment of reading the first thirty-four volumes, which would eventually lead to reading the entire collection every three years.

Part of the logic behind the assignment was to get them familiar with the volumes and to ensure that the books became gradually worn over time. However, the assignment was primarily meant as a mental exercise in obedience. Almost every day, they were expected to accomplish some of the reading – – but in the strictest sense nearly every day they were called upon to fulfill a mission they had been directed to perform. It was hoped that this continued obedience would have positive impacts should the day come when they were required to carry out a much larger mission.

During that final year, there were lessons on how to retrieve and decode transmissions that were going to be provided to them via the numbers stations which were already in operation within the United States. The KGB had managed to reassign several existing numbers stations from their current missions to the CFI. The numbers of stations selected were scattered across the United States and had been in operation for many years – – the stations had been around so long they were being ignored.

The method of Message retrieval varied, so each student was required to learn about several different devices that could be utilized. Most of these devices were available at the local neighborhood *RadioShack* or via any number of amateur radio supply houses. There were also lessons in how to repair the more standard devices, should the need arise.

The students were also taught about the four different kinds of

Messages that could possibly be sent: Routine, Warning, Preparation, and Execution. Except for Routine, which was used simply as a validation that the transmission source was working, each type of Message required some sort of action on the part of the agent in the field.

Breaking down the Message into something usable was more complicated. Each Message had a similar format but with shifting variables, depending on the type of Message. All Messages had Type and Text data, Execution Messages also included a Validation section. These sections were sandwiched between an alert tone, which was a sequence of six notes played three times before the Message started, and a suffix which was a voice saying the number *zero*, six times.

Once all of the students could successfully break down the Messages and had memorized the necessary formulas to perform the decryption, their instruction moved on to learning spycraft. Even though these were deep cover agents and not active spies, it was necessary they know and understand how to use specific espionage techniques to cover their tracks on a daily basis as well as when they moved to the execution phase of their mission, should it be required. Dmitry, as well as the majority of the other students, thoroughly enjoyed this portion of their education because it was active and there was a chance to do something more creative than rote memorization.

Aside from the formal codes that were being used by the program, the students learned how to create their own systems on the fly, should it prove necessary. One of the techniques learned was a simple *skip code*.

"The use of this code requires that you know something personal about the subject with whom you are communicating to call their attention to the beginning of the communiqué." Professor Zheleznova dimmed the lights in the room so the students could see the display screen more easily. "In preparing the code, you will decide on the text that you want to transmit, and then you will build a paragraph as camouflage around the communication you're hiding. In this example, the important text is *Subject discovered identity, you must leave before found.*

Since it is never a good thing to have a subject determine your true identity, we must let our fellow agent know of the discovery and his need to depart as quickly as possible."

Professor Zheleznova looked around the room to ensure the students understood the lesson. He then changed the material displayed on the screen to the completed letter, with the desired content in bold:

> Dave,
>
> You may have noticed the dent on the fuel tank of your motorcycle. Wasn't sure how to approach the **subject**, but knew eventually I might be **discovered** and you'd come to realize the **identity** of the one who did it. **You** do not need to fret, I **must** take responsibility and will pay to **leave** the bike just as it was **before** I damaged it. Sorry, you **found** out about it this way.

"As you can see here, we have worked the desired communication into the text of this letter which could be sent in the open. The word *motorcycle* is a keyword to tell Dave the communication is about to begin. It will require some actual thought on Dave's part to find the communication start, but once he discovers that, it is easy to figure out that the words of the communication require him to skip six words in between each pertinent bit of text. Keep in mind, this is not ideal and is meant to be used only in emergency circumstances-- as it is almost the least secure method of information transmission. By the way, once you have decided upon this text, you would need to find a way to dent Dave's motorcycle fuel tank to make the letter valid. Don't worry, Dave would rather have a dented motorcycle than being arrested for espionage."

Even the simplest spycraft techniques received considerable interest from Dmitry. When learning about dead drops, a technique which had almost cost his father his life, he was entertained by the myriad of devices that could be used to hide the dropped communication.

"When performing a dead drop, you should always select an object that would naturally be seen in the environment in which you are operating." As Professor Zheleznova spoke, the display showed examples such as fake rocks, which had secret compartments, miscellaneous trash items with hiding spaces, and a dead bird. The professor continued, "Yes, even a dead animal carcass can serve as an effective dead drop. Better to utilize a dead bird, then end up dead yourself."

During the final year, the students also learned how to handle firearms. Since it was understood that firearms would be available to them within the United States, their training involved the use of a variety of standard weapon makes, types, and calibers. Dmitry excelled at this, in particular, 9mm pistols, which led to him earning the kudos of the class champion with the weapon beating out a female candidate, Tricia Le Clair, by a single point.

In the end, 114 of the students were selected to go directly into deep cover assignments related to the prime mission of the Crimson Firebird Initiative. The balance of the class would also be under deep cover but would perform maintenance and other tasks as needed during the CFI lifecycle. Julian, of course, was one of the 114 selected, eventually departing the Academy for the United States by way of Europe, finally landing at the University of Kansas to study finance. Some students found themselves at various colleges while others went directly into trades.

A few hours after the last student departed the Academy in 1987, all of the faculty and staff were called to meet in the auditorium. Once attendance had been taken, Maksim Fillyp Bondreovich gave a short speech congratulating the successful team.

"The students who have departed today represent the most ideal outcome for the Academy. These most select graduates are now heading to their assignments across the United States prepared to take on missions that are vital to the survival of the Soviet Union. You are to be congratulated and appreciated." Maksim paused to allow the reaction of tremendous applause by the staff and faculty to quiet down as they congratulated themselves and basked in Maksim's praise.

"Shortly, you will all receive your new assignments for instructional posts within the Soviet Union. All of you will be proceeding to more challenging and high-paying assignments that are worthy of both your talent and expertise. But first, I bring a special treat from Director Sergei Kirill Mikhailov, a just-released film of the Soviet Army's Men's Choir's recent performance in Red Square." Maksim knew no one would dare attempt to leave during the film due to its content and the high regard for Sergei.

Maksim quickly exited after the lights had dimmed. Once outside, he walked briskly, removing a remote-control device from his pocket. He pushed its single-button that activated the dispersal mechanism attached to a tank of sarin gas which released the toxic and fatal chemical into the ventilation system of the auditorium. When he reached a safe distance, he paused, without turning back. Maksim held his breath and remained still as he listened until he could hear and enjoy the screams of the people condemned to death accompanied by the frantic banging on the doors of the theater. He had made sure all the exit doors were securely locked.

Maksim stood still for almost fifteen minutes until all sound from the theater stopped except for the music from the film. He was the only remaining living person at the site which brought him an extreme level of satisfaction. As often happened during operations like this, he found himself sexually aroused; he would need to find an outlet. He raced out of the Academy grounds and through the registration building to his parked car. Picking up a field walkie-talkie, he made contact with those responsible for the next phase of the clean-up and with a few brief commands he passed orders to the five pilots who were loitering in MiG-29B's high above the site. He instructed them to proceed with the mission in exactly five minutes. This would give him more than enough time to exit the area before they completely destroyed all of the buildings and created an inferno that would remove any evidence of the Academy and its personnel.

As Maksim's car pulled onto the highway from a side road, he could see a giant fireball growing in his rearview mirror as each of the five MiG aircraft dropped their high incendiary ordinance. When completed, the MiG's would return to their home airfield, having completed a routine, nighttime, live ordinance training mission. Tomorrow's *Pravda* would include a short story explaining a factory used to produce highly volatile chemicals had blown up overnight due to an accident. As a result of toxic fumes, the entire area would be cordoned off for a lengthy period of time.

Maksim dialed a familiar number on his car phone. He spoke a single word: "Polnyy" – Complete. No verbal acknowledgement was expected and the line immediately went dead. Maksim floored the accelerator, wondering how long it would take him to get to the nearest Tochka – whorehouse. If it took too long, he would simply target any lone woman to prey upon.

Five hundred kilometers away, Sergei dropped the phone into its cradle feeling a blend of relief and satisfaction having heard Maksim's one-word report. He spun his chair around and opened the cabinet behind his desk, revealing a Sony hi-fi system. The superior quality import was one of the benefits of being a bureaucrat of his stature. The album of classical Spanish guitar music he placed on the turntable, which was forbidden by the Gosteleradio, was further evidence of his position within the KGB's nomenklatura. As the music began to fill his office, he leaned back in his chair and closed his eyes— allowing Emili Pujol's guitar to surround him in tranquil tones.

The first stage was complete, and it was time to bring the CFI online as a viable and capable weapon. Not only that, he had managed to keep the entire program hidden from the Supreme Soviet since the death of Yury Vladimirovich Andropov. Andropov had previously been in charge of the KGB and was well aware of the Crimson Firebird Initiative, so when he took over as General Secretary, Sergei was able to convince him not to inform his successor about the program as a matter of paranoid caution. When Andropov died of kidney failure, and Mikhail Sergeyevich Gorbachev was named the new General Secretary, the number of people who knew the complete story of the CFI were reduced to two and Sergei kept it that way. He was openly suspicious of Gorbachev, and his program of *glasnost*, which he was sure would lead to the demise of the USSR.

Eventually, Sergei would have to deal with Fyodor but not tonight. Tonight was a success, and he would celebrate it in his own way. First, he called his mistress and told her to be waiting at his home when he arrived in approximately an hour. Next, he called Fyodor to let him know the preparation phase of the CFI was complete and the deployment phase was underway. Such news called for a celebratory libation, so Sergei invited him to his office for a drink. He knew full well that Fyodor would turn him down, in fact, Fyodor had become more and more distant. Yes, he would need to deal with Fyodor at some point, and it would probably be sooner rather than later. But now, Galina was waiting.

The Gamayun Education Centre had served its purpose, and now it's only class of 131 were deployed and would shortly be operational. It was a complete success by any measure, but there were only two people who now knew what that success actually meant: Sergei Kirill Mikhailov and Fyodor Ilyich Maldroski.

The Club at ATL was designed to replace private first-class lounges for several airlines as well as other travelers with the right combination of credit card ownership and privilege. The result was a pleasant lounge that lacked higher-end amenities.

The sliding glass doors opened allowing Evan to step inside The Club at ATL. He was immediately faced with an entry control desk at which sat two staff members eager to help. Evan paused a moment to orient himself.

"Mister Davis?" a striking blonde in an unfamiliar airline uniform greeted him with an accent.

"Um, yes. That's me."

"Follow me, please. Herr Sieg has arranged for a private room in which the two of you can meet."

Evan adjusted his backpack and followed the woman first down the walkway, through several doors opened with an electronic key card, and finally down a stairway which led to a large double door where she punched in a code.

"Thank you for allowing me to be of service, I will leave you now." He did not say a word before heading down a paneled wood corridor that opened into a rather large room with several large easy chairs. There were a small buffet and a liquor collection all laid out. A silhouetted man was staring out a large bay window down upon the flight line. An aircraft was taking off down the runway, and he acknowledged Evan's presence by holding up a single finger as if to tell him to wait just a moment. Evan began gathering information about the man who was standing in front of him; he noticed the black suit the man wore was freshly pressed and his shoes were highly polished. *Concerned with his appearance-- either his ego or an aura of professionalism.* When the aircraft successfully made it to the end of the runway and clawed its way skyward, the man turned around.

"Ah, at last, we meet, Mr. Davis. I am glad you decided to take me up on my offer, and I look forward to speaking to you today. Thank you so much for coming," Dieter looked directly into Evan's blue eyes and extended a hand which Evan took and shook rather halfheartedly.

"Um yeah, there are a few things I would like to hear about and get straight. As I've said from the beginning, I'm not sure why you chose me for whatever this is. I honestly believe you have the wrong man." Evan shrugged the backpack off his shoulder.

Dieter motioned for Evan to take a seat and offered a drink. Even though it was still relatively early in the day, Evan opted for a Makers Mark 46 and Diet Coke, which Dieter prepared for him, a little on the strong side. Dieter poured himself a healthy portion of single malt scotch over ice and sat down in the chair closest to Evan.

Dieter was taller than expected, probably just over six feet, and was clean shaven. Evan had imagined he would be thinner or more muscular--*too many Hollywood movies.* Dieter's face did not show his sixty-five years but rather had a youthful determination. He was balding with the common laurel of shiny silver hair on the sides and back that accompanies male pattern baldness. His eyes were a light blue or gray, but without any coldness. His expression was more pleasant and friendly than he expected as well, with lips that had a slight upturn rather than being sour or stern.

"Mr. Davis, or may I call you Evan?" Evan nodded. "Evan, I think you are the exact person needed for this particular assignment--not only because of what you've written but because of the many good and empathetic things I've heard from those who know you. You also can be counted upon to maintain confidences and perform in the most ethical manner possible."

"Look, Heinrich, I don't know what you expect me to do with the information you've given me thus far – – I can't even begin to contemplate what service you have in mind. Afghanistan was a one-time thing... to be honest, I needed the money. As for Kuwait, I was overcome by events and reacted to prevent disaster. You can find hundreds of men with better skills to do whatever it is you need." Evan wanted to attempt extricating himself from this situation.

"I know all the details of what happened in Kuwait," when he said this, he emphasized the word *all* letting Evan know he had inside knowledge of what had transpired. "and I understand the dangerous situation in which you found yourself in Afghanistan. What I'm proposing is not as openly dangerous but every bit as important. Also, rather than reacting, you will have a chance to plan your actions and prepare for them rather than being thrust into – – what was the descriptor you used at the time? The inferno at hell's gates?" Dieter tilted his head back, recalling the article.

"Well, I do have a flair for the dramatic on occasion," Evan sipped his bourbon. "You've obviously got something in mind, and I still don't know the whole story. Why don't you start with that?"

"If you read the document then you know what our friends the

Russians were up to during the Cold War and what nasty action they put in motion."

"Wait," Evan interrupted, "are you Russian? The accent isn't quite right although I haven't been able to place it."

"No, no, no. I am not Russian. I am German, to be specific for a long time I was what was known as an East German. During that period, I served with the *Ministerium für Staatssicherheit*-- you Americans called it The Ministry for State Security or the…"

"*Stasi*," Evan interrupted. "I remember hearing about you guys when I was stationed in Berlin. Quite vicious as I recall."

"I won't debate that description at this point except to say if you were to ask someone from the former Communist Bloc for a description of your CIA, they would probably use the same word. But going back to your original question, no I am not a Russian, my longtime friend is a Russian, and he is the one who came to me for help, but I am at a point now where I cannot complete the task assigned without some inside help. You, Mr. Davis, are my attempt to recruit some help from the inside. If I may go on?" Pausing for a moment, Dieter drank. "The Crimson Firebird Initiative began the early part of the seventies…" With that introduction, Dieter dove into the entire history of the initiative to include a description of the Academy, how the sleeper agents and weapons were deployed, and how the program should have been stood down after the fall of the old Soviet Union in 1991.

"During the entire time that the CFI existed, at most only four people simultaneously knew of its real mission and how it was to be deployed. Due to Andropov's transition from head of the KGB to General Secretary, the number dropped to three. Then, when Yury died, that number dropped to two. Because Gorbachev was not seen as being someone with the best interests of the USSR at heart, he was never informed of the program, leaving only the CFI Director and Deputy Director as the only ones knowledgeable of the plan's existence. When the government of the Soviet Union collapsed and then reformed, the CFI should've been stood down like many KGB intelligence programs during the Cold War. But because no one knew of its existence and since the CFI required no direct financial support, the program was left standing."

"Forgetting for a moment the fact that hundreds of sleeper agents are still running loose in my country, I'm more concerned about the --boxes –bottles –vials or whatever they are of *Chimera K629* that're currently unaccounted for. Or is it no longer viable?" Evan questioned.

"The *K629* was housed in a cylinder that was part of the complete Launch Preparation Assembly Kit or L-PAK. These were foam-lined, medium-sized plastic footlockers with the various components wedged in holes cut within the foam-like tool..."

"Shadowbox," Evan interjected.

"Yes, precisely. Additionally, there is a small kit of exfiltration materials – – an *escape kit* -- in the box for use by the agent that contains cash and gold Krugerrands. As for viability, some of the devices I've recovered may be viable and some may not. To be honest, my mission was to destroy weapons not determine if they could still be utilized."

"Okay, so you've been gathering up these relics that are scattered across the United States... since you have them why do you need me now?" Evan hoped he had found a legitimate reason to walk.

"The problem is, Evan, I have not found them all. I've been working off a partial list of the devices, and I have retrieved the ones of which I am aware. In doing this, I have also managed to stand down a majority of the sleeper agents who were in this country. All of the operatives I have contacted, have gone on to lead quite satisfying lives and wish to continue doing so. What remains, is a smattering of sleeper agents who are likely no problem to anyone, and one to three devices which are a problem to everyone should they be accidentally discovered and released into the environment or purposely detonated."

"What the hell do you mean *purposely detonated?*" Evan leaned toward Dieter, almost threateningly, "I thought the program was dead? Wasn't the only purpose of its existence in the case of the US first strike? Well, that isn't going to happen." Calming himself, Evan sat back in his chair, "Hell last, I read the missiles aren't even pre-targeted towards the Soviet Union anymore. So how could the weapons end up purposely detonated?"

"Fyodor Maldroski is my friend, and he was the Deputy Director of the program. After the rebirth of the Soviet Union in 1991, he left the KGB and managed to find a quiet life for himself as a retiree in Minsk. Like many who departed the espionage services during that period, he managed to erase his footprints on his way out the door, and that anonymity has contributed to his survival. It is he who asked me to ensure that all of the sleeper agents were stood down and the weapons destroyed." Dieter swirled his drink. "However, the person that he worked for – – the Director of the program, Sergei Kirill Mikhailov, did not go quietly into the night. He chose to first try to resurrect the old KGB from the heart of the new agency, the SVR. Of course, he was unsuccessful, and in the end, Sergei lost not only his power and position but all of the riches and property that he had ever managed to acquire during his career. At some point, in the midst of the chaos, he vanished." Suddenly restless, Dieter rose to gaze upon the planes as they taxied on the runway.
"Even though Fyodor had left the intelligence service, he still maintained a loose network of people who kept him informed. My friend heard rumblings that Sergei might be planning something – – which caused him to research what had become of the Crimson Firebird Initiative's resources." Dieter drained the contents of his glass and wasted no time in pouring another.

"Why'd your friend Fyodor suddenly have concerns for the United States and its well-being? A sudden post-Cold War concern for humanity?" Evan shifted in his chair, as he attempted to mask his frustration.

"Fyodor had a dozen concerns…" Dieter turned to face Evan. "but the well-being of the United States was not really one of them. You see, the CFI was designed as a response to a particular action from the United States. Without the initial cause for the intervention, things would be out of order, and the United States would have time to retaliate against the Soviet Union before succumbing to the effects of *Chimera K629*. In other words, by doing things out of order, mutually assured destruction would be a distinct possibility. But, Fyodor's top concern was for his own son who is one of the sleeper agents currently in your country. Whether the United States decided to retaliate or not, the use of *K629* would put his own son in the direct line of fire—probably as one of the first victims." Dieter returned to his chair.

"Why the hell would he put his son into the program, if the program was designed to destroy the Russians who launched the attack?"

"Even though Fyodor had no love for the United States, he realized his own country and its government was failing. He wanted to ensure his son would have a future. In his own mind, he could never see a point where the CFI would be launched, and he tried to figure out ways to prevent its launch should that ever prove necessary." Dieter tried to keep his voice calm. He sensed Evan was piecing together the various bits of insanity that comprised this monstrous plan.

"Forgive me but your friend is absolutely bat shit crazy." Evan was silent for a moment, shaking his head at the situation. "You mentioned that there were several of these weapons left unfound. I'm assuming that they are sitting somewhere in a footlocker just waiting to be detonated?"

"Yes, there are a few left. The L-PAK, as the name implies, is not the completed weapon itself, but the various parts required to assemble and launch the weapon. It requires the entry of an access code to be opened. That code is one of several measures the weapon has to ensure its detonation. If the agent fails to correctly enter the access code within three tries, the device will detonate several explosives immediately. Even though it is not ideal for optimum dispersal and therefore fatalities, it would allow for some measure of retaliation in the event of a compromise." Dieter studied Evan to gauge his comprehension. "Inside the L-PAK is a vial of *K629*, along with a cylinder containing a concentrated oxidizer – – which is necessary to ensure peak activation of the virus – – and the components to build a small rocket to launch the *K629* several thousand meters up to allow its most favorable initial dispersal. The rocket is tipped with a sharpened titanium nosecone that allows it to pierce through any roof during the missile's launch. This way, the weapon can be fired from inside a building instead of being exposed." Gulping his drink, Dieter continued, "Once the rocket is assembled, it is connected to a launch sequencer which was also inside of the L-PAK. When connected, the sequencer comes to life, and the agent enters a provided code. If correctly entered, a two-hour countdown begins on the sequencer's digital display; otherwise, it will activate immediately, another guarantee of detonation. Likewise, if the L-PAK is opened, but the sequencer is not connected within fourteen minutes – it will cause detonation."

Evan felt his chest grow tight as the full weight of catastrophic possibilities began to take hold. He closed his eyes while he concentrated on regulating his breathing – an anxiety control technique he had learned from a PTSD website. Upon reopening his eyes, he realized he was being stared at; to break the man's gaze, he leaned forward, unzipped a pocket in his backpack, and withdrew a bottle of Tylenol. Holding it up for his host to see, he gave the bottle a quick shake and explained, "Flying gives me sinus headaches." Deiter nodded in understanding as Evan popped two pills into his mouth and washed them down with a sip from his glass. Evan didn't need the pain killer, he needed the cover. It had worked, he was back in control of himself.

"Once all is connected correctly, the sleeper is supposed to take the escape pack and leave, but typical KGB…the countdown clock was a lie. Even though the digital display shows two hours, the device actually goes off in four minutes. The KGB had determined someone could disarm the device so it should detonate as quickly as possible. Fyodor was not even aware of this lie; I can only surmise that Sergei had made the four-minute decision."

Evan exhaled loudly. "Sergei didn't trust his own people, so he guaranteed a way to not only set the weapon off but also to ensure the agent's annihilation."

Dieter nodded. "If everything goes according to plan, once the rocket launches it proceeds straight up through the roof and continues for 10,000 or so meters up. Once the rocket fuel is almost expended, the vial containing the *Chimera K629* opens, along with the cylinder containing the oxidizer. This allows the concentrated oxidizer to fully activate the *K629*--a catalyst to make a more potent virus. The rocket's climb continues until all of the fuel is spent and a few seconds later it returns to Earth as an onboard altimeter triggers exploding bolts, causing it to split and allowing the *K629's* release and spread in a large plume. Since the spores of the virus are almost weightless, they'll carry wherever the wind may blow -- allowing them a broad dispersal of perhaps miles." Dieter again paused as Evan shook his head at the audacity of the sequence of events.

"Initially," Dieter continued, "we were under the assumption that each agent would be acting alone to activate and execute the device. In actuality, two operatives were assigned to each weapon to ensure coverage. If both agents reached the device at the same time, they would work together to ensure mission success. Or, if one lost his nerve, the other could complete the task on his own."

"I guess that's why you don't know how many L-PAKs are actually left?" Evan asked.

"True, it isn't all just simple math; not all of the 131 agents in the field were responsible for setting off weapons. Some of them were to assist as needed, to maintain the L-PAKs and perform other functions. This has made discovering and disposing of all the weapons extremely difficult. Thus far, I have a partial list of existing agents to locate the L-PAKs based on their geography and additional information gleaned from Fyodor's records. During discussions with those assigned to maintain the L-PAKs, I've been able to gain additional insight. As I said before, I'll need your help to find the remaining devices."

"Okay, but how do you plan on finding the final weapons if you've exhausted the information?" Evan needed to be informed to help with this next phase. At this point, he would be shooting in the dark.

"When the plan for the Crimson Phoenix Initiative was developed, the primary communication method for agents in the field was designed to be unidirectional. That means that..."

"You could talk to them, but they couldn't communicate back," Evan interrupted, he didn't need elementary explanation -- he needed indepth information.

"Correct you are. The plan was to use numbers of stations to send out regular communiqués as needed. Do you know what a numbers station is?" Dieter was unclear how much Evan grasped.

"More or less," Evan responded. "When I saw a reference in the documents, I researched. Most of what I saw made them sound like Bigfoot. There was some evidence of their existence, but nothing concrete and no one knew exactly why they had been in existence for since World War I. If in fact, they existed at all, to serve any kind of real purpose."

"They do indeed exist and for a purpose," Dieter assured Evan. "Perhaps you overlooked it in your research; as recently as 2010 ten Russian agents were arrested by your FBI after being caught decrypting numbers stations communiqués. In 2006, there was a more publicized case in Miami where spies were arrested and charged with espionage for receiving encrypted instructions broadcast by a Cuban a numbers station. So, they not only exist… they are still in use. When Sergei first began to stand up the CFI, he had several numbers stations reassigned to the project. The problem we have now is that due to the compartmentalization of Crimson Firebird, we have no way of knowing which stations may have been transitioned versus those that were quietly phased out over the years. However, I now have a lead on one of the stations, which we can utilize to find the final few L-PAKs."

"These numbers stations knew where all of the weapons were?" *Why didn't you just go there first?* Evan held his tongue.

"Not directly-- at least not as far as I can tell--what they do have is folders of information that are to be broadcast when the execution order for the CFI is given. Amongst that information is the actual geographic location of the L-PAKs themselves. I don't want to waste your time with going through all of that now, but if you do decide to assist me with this, I will give you information that explains how the numbers stations communicated the various types of Messages and the meaning of each type."

"So, you want me to go to this numbers station, knock on the door, and ask them for the information they have regarding the weapon locations?" Evan was finding it increasingly hard not to be snarky, and he still didn't have any idea why he was the only one who could go knock on that door.

"That would probably result in your being shot; you see the numbers stations are not manned by sleeper agents who have grown accustomed to living a comfortable life as Americans. The stations are manned by SVR military officers who have one duty--to ensure various Messages are transmitted when needed. They are dedicated to the point of being fanatical – that is how they were selected. Don't you think if it were that easy, I would knock on the door myself?" Dieter paused but not long enough for a response. "No, my friend, I want you to meet and befriend one of the sleeper agents. While you do that I will be transmitting instructions to the numbers station to release Execution Messages for the weapons release." This statement drew the expected agitated response as Evan rose up out of his chair. "Please, let me finish," Dieter requested. "It will be up to you to convince the sleeper agent that the Message is being transmitted on purpose to help locate the L-PAK so it can be disarmed-- and not as a response to the Crimson Firebird Initiative being put into action. We will repeat this process until all the weapons are found and destroyed."

Evan was openly agitated and suspicious of this plan and how it might actually work. He was possibly being used to help this Stasi agent launch an attack rather than prevent one. There was a certain simplicity to the details Heinrich had given him up to this point; he calmed himself to run through the details in his mind.

"What makes you think that the numbers station will keep sending out Execution Messages once they realize that no activation is taking place?"

"You are thinking like an American." Dieter said tapping his temple with his finger. "You have to remember in the Soviet Union no one trusted anyone else enough to provide full details. Bear in mind that at most there were only four people who truly knew the full scope and breadth of this program. None of those four people is working in a numbers station. The numbers station's staff will have no idea whether the desired result has happened or not. The assumption will be that whatever was supposed to happen has happened and they will go on with their day-to-day operation. Would it surprise you to learn that the sleeper agents don't even know the nature of the payload on the device that they're assigned to trigger? They are only carrying out their mission for the good of the Motherland." Dieter managed to keep his voice calm which helped reassure and calm Evan.

Evan was having a hard time wrapping his mind around people who could blindly operate without knowing the full picture. While in the Air Force, Evan didn't always know the full details, but he always felt he understood enough. Or did he? *No, no time to go down that rabbit hole right now.*

"What you want me to do is to get to know the sleeper agent, wait until he's given some sort of execution order sent via the numbers station, and then convince the operative to disarm the device he's been waiting a lifetime to trigger? Sounds easy enough."

"Please don't be flippant, Evan. I realize I've given you a lot of information to process, but it's necessary that you fully understand what's going to be expected of you, and to get you caught up so that when you walk out of here today, you can proceed with great haste."

"You still never answered my first question—Why me?"

"Because sometimes the best solution is not the obvious one. Sometimes the best person for a job is not an expert who can only think in an unemotional straight line but a person who comes with a new set of eyes while also bringing a sense of honor, empathy, and humanity. You, my friend, are *that* solution."

Evan stared at the brown liquid in his glass, contemplating its fluidity for a moment. He gave the glass a quick tilt to and fro which caused the contents to swirl before putting it to his lips and drinking the balance of its contents. Gazing out the window, he slowly shook his head pondering all he had just been told. "So, who and where is this sleeper agent I'm supposed to befriend?" He was resigned. Whether he liked it or not he was accepting possession of what amounted to a screaming baby wearing a shit-filled diaper.

"I will make travel arrangements for you under the guise you're writing a story for a magazine. This will give you a good cover to get to know the man. You will be traveling to a small town in Oklahoma, and the gentleman's name is Julian Shepherd. As you probably guessed by now, he is Fyodor's son."

"Abi my young friend! *As-Salaam-Alaikum*! How good it is to see you. Have you been staying busy with your new radio hobby?" Areef greeted the young man as he entered Oasis Mart.

Abi had done little except play with his shortwave radio since performing the demonstration of how numbers stations work for Qa'id. His research had led to few successes and much boredom as he encountered stations that were merely repetitive and not being actively used--at least as far as he could tell.

"Wa `alaykumu s-salāmu wa rahmatu l-lāhi wa barakātuh. Yes Areef, I have been enjoying the radio very much. Especially the numbers stations that were talked about and some of the magazines that you gave me. Fascinating stuff."

"Ah yes, I seem to recall you telling me about them. Has anything proved it all worthwhile?" Areef carefully guided the conversation as was his usual ploy.

"Yes and no. I have found several stations that are reliably transmitting, but none so far that are saying anything more than gibberish. It's quite fun to listen in, almost like I'm listening in to a secret conversation between two close friends. But, when I tried to translate the conversation I'm getting nothing." Abi did little to try to hide the disappointment in his voice; it always seemed Areef would offer some sort of solution.

"Hmm, I really don't know about such things. But I seem to

recall," Areef paused for dramatic effect. The reality was that Areef not only recalled but had purposely placed information along the path. "Something about coded stations in a box of papers that I picked up at an estate sale. Now, where did I put those…" Areef paused again, this time not only looking off into space, as if deep in thought, but placing his hand against his cheek as if he were exhausted. He looked up at the ceiling and pointed his index finger as if he were having an epiphany.

"Ah yes…" Areef headed towards the back of the store through the door marked *Private*. Sitting beside a small worktable in the office was a box he had placed there ten days earlier. At first, he was going to leave it in the store and let Abi discover it himself, but he realized someone else might find it first, and there was no telling where that could lead. Scooping up the box, he turned to exit the room only to find Abi standing in the doorway.

"…and here we are," Areef said, handing the box to Abi. Areef had taken great care in putting the box together. Inside were about two dozen highly classified KGB documents, interspersed among several hundred pages of meaningless treacle. He had taken the time to add a few handwritten notes here and there in English, translating just enough of the Russian to spark the young man's interest.

Patting the top of the box, Areef said, "Now you have a bit more to sort through, but some of it looked interesting. Not all of it is in English, but you are resourceful, and I think you can figure out how to translate it."

Abi was beaming, He bid his friend goodbye and went back to his apartment, anxious to explore the material. Abi flipped the box over spilling the contents onto his kitchen table. He shuffled the pages into a single large pile. Then, he picked up the first page. *So many possibilities to explore.*

The first few pages appeared to be some sort of strategy instructions for playing cricket. Those, he dropped directly into the empty box on the floor. He then encountered a dozen or so pages in German, and he stacked them in a pile at one corner of the table. The next few pages had Cyrillic lettering; which earned them a place at the opposite corner of the table. Abi whittled down the material until he reached the last few pages. There he found handwritten notes in English on a page of Cyrillic type – "Encryption/decryption algorithm," then more notes in the same handwriting on other pages-- "Transmittal Instructions," "Dates/Times for Routine Messages," and more. These pages were placed in a brand-new pile in the center of the table. *Gold!*

Up to this point, Abi had only ever considered listening to what the broadcasts said and learning what type of activities the intended audience may be up to or what information they may have regarding his side. Based on the words he had seen, including terms like 'encryption,' as well as 'transmittal,' he began to think beyond simply listening. Suppose he could direct the actions of the person listening to the numbers station in a way that benefited him? Could he count on them to perform whatever action he directed them to do? Maybe, he could have them taking actions against their own self-interest. Or even better – – what if he could have them attack the ones they were sent to protect?

His mind was spinning as he sat looking at the papers in front of him. He may finally find a definitive way to be able to strike back and gain the revenge long sought. With that thought, he closed his eyes and allowed his head to fall backward, enjoying this blissful satisfaction.

On the Tarmac of Atlanta IAP, Georgia

As Evan fastened the seatbelt across his lap, his mind was still reeling from the conversation with Dieter. He wasn't sure why he would've thought it unexpected for him to be using an alias in the beginning. Heinrich was really Dieter Sieg who was a former Stasi agent relying on the help of a part-time novelist who seemed to be continually getting himself into weird situations he didn't belong in but could not refuse.

He stuffed his backpack under the seat in front of him. Inside were several hundred more pages explaining the Crimson Firebird Initiative. Not all of the information was necessary, just the part about how communications were handled. But somehow, Dieter found it necessary to give him all the information so that he fully understood the scope of what this all meant. *Was there an East German/Stasi word for Glasnost?* Probably not, the Stasi were more concerned with torture and assassination than openness.

It was all he could do to resist the urge to pull out the backpack and start going through the documents. Even though the project was no longer classified, Evan could be arrested as a spy just for possession of the documents. The cell phone device Dieter had given him could also get him arrested. It was manufactured by some unknown Chinese company, and even though the design was clunky, it contained the latest in security technology that required both a pin code and his fingerprint. Aside from having the ability to transmit both voice and text to any other number in the world, it could encrypt both types of transmissions in such a manner that would prevent even the most skilled hacker from understanding. That included government hackers, which is why the phone was the preferred telephonic tool of those involved in the espionage arts. He would have to wait until he was home and behind closed doors before figuring out what he was going to do next and how it was all going to work.

Dieter said it would be several days before he could get travel arrangements set up for Evan to go to Oklahoma. Meeting Julian Shepherd was going to be its own thing. *What exactly do you say to a guy whose father is the designer of a population-ending program using bioweapons and who has been living as a sleeper agent for the past few decades?* He peered out the window and watched Atlanta slowly disappear below the aircraft, as the wing dipped and they headed north. *Nap – I need a nap*, was Evan's last conscious thought before going to sleep.

Chapter Six

After landing in Detroit, Evan drove back towards the west side of the state. His mind was alive with a storm of ideas, thoughts running back and forth like speeding cars on the freeway, trying not to collide. For Evan, this was a good situation-- if his mind was busy with thoughts of what to do next, anxiety would not be able to creep in. He was not familiar with Detroit, at least nothing near Romulus, but he needed time to think and a quiet place to put these pieces together and in some sort of order. There had to be some sort of logic to it all.

There was a sign up ahead for a nightclub, Aglow, a perfect island in the storm. Evan had seen several advertisements for the place, bragging about the club's lack of electrical lighting – – preferring to use hundreds of candles – – and its low-key music guaranteed to inspire casual conversation. "*The place where the candles and serenity set your soul aglow.*" A hokey slogan at best, but it sounded like a place where he could let his mind wander without disruption. There was another new club with no lights at all, and everyone wore blindfolds, but that was pushing privacy to the point of sensory deprivation.

Aglow was located in an active industrial district, in a building that had been TekNow, a computer firm that crunched numbers. When the power of mainframes was usurped by lesser machines, the company imploded and the warehouse, with unique features that included a liquid-cooled floor, was obsolete. The floor had kept the facility a chilly 50 degrees to keep the heat-producing mainframes happy and humming. The temperature was ideal for an entrepreneur who envisioned a club with thousands of heat-producing open flames. Area rugs prevented the patrons from being uncomfortably cold.

Evan was greeted by the sweet, familiar, and somehow

comforting scent of vanilla wax. He paused in the entryway as his eyes adjusted to the darkness before entering the main club. Playing in the background was the instrumental *Sleepwalk,* loud enough without being overbearing. Above the door, in gold script letters was the quote: *A man loves company - even if it is only that of a small burning candle--* Georg C. Lichtenberg.

"This might just work out okay," he said in a low voice.

Evan decided on an ideal place to perch. The interior was indeed lit by hundreds of candles. Most were grouped before large mirrors, which help reflect the flickering light throughout the club. The space was brighter than he had expected, but Evan had never experienced so many candles burning in one place other than some European cathedrals. Large brass and crystal chandeliers also hung from the ceiling and individual clusters of candles adorned each table. The décor was golden oak with a glossy finish, adding to the reflection and the warmth. People, mostly in couples, were scattered throughout the club but it was early enough that some tables remained empty.

Given his desire for solitude, a table may have been an ideal choice, but empty chairs were often inviting. Instead, he would resign himself to the historic lair of the single person wanting to remain along--the bar.

Centered on the back wall, extending into the sea of tables, was a large U-shaped bar surrounded by a smattering of tall chairs that reminded him of cows approaching a feeding trough. Evan preferred this to staring at himself in the traditional mirror behind the rows of liquor, or the bartender as he served the length of the bar. A conversation with a friendly bartender was at times a welcome but not this evening.

He took a middle chair in a row of three empty seats and glanced around finding nothing truly remarkable before ordering a Makers Mark with a single ice cube. Patrons drinking on one side of the bar ended up looking directly at the folks on the opposite side while the bartenders mixed drinks and a smattering of waitresses came and went.

Evan was lucky, his seat did not put him staring into the eyes of a stranger but instead a bank of twelve beer taps mounted on a horizontal bar at face height. He sipped his bourbon slowly while utilizing his fifty-yard stare mastered in Afghanistan--the appearance of intently focusing on something in the distance, while his mind was in another realm and his thoughts tried to organize. The day had been full of new information and that aligned with what he knew about the situation. But, could Dietrich, an ex-Stasi officer, be trusted and why would he approach Evan in the first place? Dietrich said it had something to do with the truths Evan had exposed as a reporter – so what? How did that connect with what he told him about Cold War KGB programs still awaiting wake up in the US?

A flash of red broke Evan's trance. Under the row of beer, taps were small and feminine hands, holding the stem of a tall red wine glass. There was an almost ballet-like grace in their movement as her fingertips rested on opposite sides of the glass, tapping one at a time, pinky to her index finger. The nails were coated in a deep red high gloss polish. The red polish, wine, and the candlelight had broken his concentration. He ordered another bourbon and observed the hands across the bar in earnest. The fingers seemed to be painting swirls on the glass with just one fingertip and other times the fingers moved in unison stroking the bowl of the glass and leaving patterns in the condensation. Evan could not tell if she was alone because of the beer taps but he imagined she was for the moment. This was a remarkably good distraction even if only evanescent.

The dark rich color of her nails was intriguing. Even though the candlelight added a certain luster to her skin, they seemed pale in comparison to the dark red hue. The light captured and reflected in the nail's gloss made for a remarkable show as well. He wondered what the name of the color was, probably something slightly decadent like *Sensuous Cerise* or maybe something more blatantly obvious like *Fuck Me Hard Ruby*. The thought caused him to release deep thought in favor of something more primal, and as he did, he raised his glass to his lips and slowly sipped his whiskey letting his mind wander further.

Take her home? Well, that would be as okay ending to this day… depending on what's hidden behind the beer taps.

As he set his glass down, she was again using both hands to caress the wine glass. He wasn't sure how you could move from watching a woman's hands to actually speaking to her, but if he figured it out, he might be able to find a way to set his soul aglow. When her fingers were still he could see the reflection of the single candle flames in each of her nails. Then both her hands disappeared and he felt let down. After several seconds, however, she drew a repetitive small curvy pattern on the glass. He focused and realized she was drawing a question mark. The realization caused him to sit up straight as his jaw went slack. She couldn't possibly be trying to...

The loud sound of breaking glass shattered the moment followed by applause--the usual sophomoric reaction to a restaurant mishap. The waitress gave a deep bow to her appreciative audience. Her good spirit caused Evan to chuckle. When he turned his attention back to the graceful hands of the stranger, he was disappointed to find they had vanished, leaving only an empty wine glass behind.

How depressing.

He spun in his seat, trying to catch a glimpse of her. No luck. The warmth of a hand on top of his caused him to spin back towards the bar.

He discovered a rather delicate hand with nails painted in a most decadent shade of dark red. The hand slowly slid from the back of his hand up his arm. His eyes glanced up a bare arm, to a bare shoulder with a cascade of glistening straight blondish-red hair. After giving the shimmering hair a brief appreciative stare, his view came to rest on an attractive face with large beautiful eyes and an inviting supple mouth.

"Uh...hello," Evan managed to say.

"Hello there," she responded in a smoky, warm voice. Even though what she said was brief, Evan was entranced-- watching as the words were formed by her lips and glimpsing her tongue between them.

Evan was spellbound by the sudden sensuality, when she slid her hand down his arm and upon reaching the back of his hand, interlaced their fingers. *So soft!*

She motioned towards the chair next to him. "Mind if I join

you?" Her head tilted, allowing the candlelight to dance across her shoulders and neck. She shifted her hips, starting to sit – having correctly assumed permission would be instantly granted.

Evan watched her body movements and after a moment of silence realized she already knew his answer. "Sure, feel free. I was here by myself anyway." As he spoke, Evan realized how pitiful his words sounded. He wasn't sure if he should say something to try and explain, or merely let her assume he was a pariah sentenced to another evening alone.

"Me too," she said settling into the chair while remaining turned towards him. "I'm here to enjoy a temporary respite from reality, to allow my mind to recharge while I have a quiet drink by myself." *Well, that's more or less the truth…*

Evan felt a bit of reassurance that her motive for being in the bar was similar to his, or maybe he should be concerned that she was friendless. *No, no not at all – – not her.* He had lived enough years to know just because a woman was beautiful didn't mean she was sociable or worthwhile. But there was something about the way this woman carried herself that told him there was something worth exploring. Allure? That was the word he was looking for – – she had an allure.

"I'm Nikki. Nikki Grey." She extended her hand.

As he took her hand and gave her a firm but not too strong handshake, he returned her smile. "Hello, Nikki, I'm Evan Davis." He was almost tempted to add "the author" but withheld that for later in the conversation. He looked her over while trying not to be too obvious. Her eyes were indeed beautiful; they were large and accented by exceptionally long dark lashes. He could not tell what color they were in the candlelight. Nikki's hair was straight and extended about halfway down her back. Her fair skin tone and the faint smattering of freckles across her nose were an indication of her natural hair color. He could not tell how old she was but figured she was at least a decade younger. Once you get past thirty, age seemed irrelevant except for music preferences. Seated, they were about the same height, so he knew she was not too short or overly tall. Her black spandex shirt was off the shoulder with a lattice pattern which allowed a glimpse of her bare upper chest. Nice.

Evan allowed her to break the handshake first and withdrawing his hand, he took another sip of his drink before offering to buy her – – "…another glass of red wine?" As soon as the words passed through his lips he realized his mistake. How would he know what Nikki had been drinking? Of course, why had she approached unless she was interested as well? This was a most eloquent standoff-- a delicate dance that even though both were enjoying, found them being cautious as to not let too many truths become visible too quickly.

"Sure," she answered, giving nothing else away.

Evan signaled to the bartender. He had no idea what he should say next, but before he spoke, she broke the silence.

"Mmm, Lana Del Ray -- I love her." Nikki closed her eyes as the music transitioned to a new song. He has rescued Evan again.

"Ah yes." Evan nodded his head. "She did *Jar of Hearts*."

"No, that was Christina Perri…similar voices and styles. Easy to confuse them."

Nikki had forgotten a base lesson in getting a man to like you-- don't contradict him. "Oh, you're right - the voices sound incredibly similar. Such sadness and pain in the lyrics." Evan nodded in time to the music.

Not a typical man. Nikki smiled. "Yeah, but Lana is a bit more aggressive. With songs like *Fucked My Way to the Top*, Lana she really lays it out there." *Her first strong words, how would he react?*

If only she had known Evan's past, there would be no concern over language. He was a firm believer that words held no ability to hurt, that was an honor held for the intent of the speaker. The word *fuck*, in particular, held no sway with him. Evan had worked with aircraft maintainers who used the word as often as any other in their vocabulary. When he was an embed, this nonchalance was taken to new levels. He had heard Army combat engineers use the word as an adjective, adverb, noun, object, conjunction, and even once or twice in its normal usage as a verb. Not only had he heard *fuck* used as various parts of speech, but he had also heard those different parts of speech used in a single statement with a few variations thrown in on top. "*Fuck*! Those *fuckers* really *fucked* us up this *fucking* time, there is no *fucking* way we'll get beyond this bucket of *fuck* treatment. Those mother fuckers are up to some serious fuckery. Fuckery? The word sounded both obscene and archaic. You would almost expect King Louis XIV to have uttered it describing rude behaviors at the Royal Court -- and just what was a bucket of *fuck* anyway? Evan had never figured that out, but it really didn't matter. The end result was that he had been desensitized to most language and listened to the intent of the speaker rather than the vocabulary. If Nikki was worried about putting him off, she should have been more concerned about her name. Evan never had much luck with any woman by the name of *Nikki*--a harbinger of doom.

"Haven't heard that one, but you've got my interest up. May have to check it out," Evan said earnestly.

Nikki gave Evan a sideways glance. He would too. He was the kind who wanted to know the facts. Curiosity made him demand answers. She was beginning to like this Evan, even though she guarded herself against it, at least for now.

The bartender delivered their order. Evan asked, "Is that Gray with an *A* or an *E*?"

"Grey, with an *E*."

"Ah, so British lineage?"

"Nope, one of those Ellis Island change-ups." Nikki smiled. "My family's claim to fame is Betsy Gray, a young Irish lass who fought beside her father and fiancé during the Irish Rebellion of 1798. Her father and boyfriend were members of the United Irishmen. Are you familiar with them?"

"Uh, no I find Ireland's history a bit difficult to follow." As he admitted this, he repositioned himself on his stool so he was at a better angle to give his attention exclusively to her.

"Most do. My kinsmen have a way of getting fired up in multiple directions but always end up fighting themselves," her voice changed to a more serious tone. "The United Irishmen was founded in 1791 to fight for Irish independence from England. They had been inspired by the American and the French Revolutions and sought to introduce parliamentary reform. None of this was based on religion, by the way, but pure Irish nationalism." Nikki paused, to allow him to take control of the conversation if he desired – instead, a careful examination of his face told her that Evan's attention was solely focused on what she was saying. No way she could know if he was intently interested in the story or in the way she looked telling it. Either way, he failed to take control of the conversation, so she continued. "By the summer of 1798, there was a short-lived armed rebellion that quickly floundered and eventually fell apart. Unlike the American Revolution, the forces from France came too late, nearly a full month after the British had crushed the revolution. Not much was actually known about Betsy other than her actions during the Battle of Ballynahinch on June 13th. Of course, this is all memorialized and turned into legend through folk songs and poems."

"Wasn't 1798 a little early for a woman to be fighting in a battle?" to Evan things had to make sense and if not, questions needed to be asked.

The question pleased Nikki, he was paying attention to the words, not just her looks. "Well, there is no real record of her battlefield accomplishments until the 13th. Betsy rode into battle that day carrying a green battle flag next to General Henry Monro, leader of the Irish forces. During the fight, the Irish mistook the British signal for retreat as their own and the Irish retreated, allowing the British to win the battle. At some point during the fight, Betsy was defending her finance from a British sword, and when she raised her arm in front of him the attacker cut off her hand just above the wrist..."

"Youch! Talk about giving your left arm for something." He grimaced comically at the thought, shaking his head.

"Yeah," adding a chuckle, "but in this case, it was her right arm…anyway, Betsy's father and fiance refused to desert her during the retreat; all three were captured and executed by the British. By July, most of the rebellion had been crushed with a couple skirmishes during the latter part of summer and on into the fall. General Monro was executed after the Rebellion, and there was a hunt to find others who had fought during the rebellion, and this was soon expanded to include families of those who had been involved and seizing their assets as reparation. At some point around Christmastime, the rest of Betsy's extended family decided it was a good time to head west to America." She took a sip of her wine before concluding the story, "When they got to Ellis Island they changed the surname from Gray to Grey - turning from Irish to British in the process, to throw off any pursuers." Nikki raised her eyebrows, tilted her head, and shrugged her shoulders to indicate the end of the story.

"But they couldn't hide that beautiful red hair or fair complexion so easily," Evan observed while allowing himself to admire both.

"True, but over the generations – and thanks to modern chemistry, red hair is no longer the exclusive claim of the Irish--- but mine is." Nikki sensuously turned her head back and forth, so her hair shimmered in the candlelight it captured. She stopped with one bare shoulder exposed and the other hidden by her hair then added, "And the carpet matches the drapes – – well, if there was carpet and not just bare floor."

She laughed at her own crude reference, carefully watching Evan's reaction. The carpet reference was a line to separate the players from the guys looking for something a little more serious.

Evan met her gaze, raising his eyebrows slightly, and offered a knowing nod. He knew exactly what she meant, and he welcomed a woman who was willing to expose a bit of herself as well as show a humorous side.

Well, not a player and not bashful either. So much more than what I could've expected. She gave him a sly knowing wink in response.

Their body language was changing and they now faced each other. Their knees were almost bumping as shared bits and pieces of personal history and geographical references. As they talked, Nikki occasionally reached out a hand and caressed Evan's arm draped across the bar. Eventually, her hand rested on his arm, rising to accentuate her conversation. There was a unique chemistry between them and it was growing more intimate.

"No way," Evan said shaking his head, "if you're from Georgia – – where is the beautiful Georgia Peach accent?"

"Total waaaay!" she suddenly brandished a full-on, deep Southern twang then switched back. "And besides, are you saying something is wrong with the way I've been talking?" She crossed her arms, turned her head, and lifted her face in faux outrage.

"First of all, nothing is wrong with the way you happen to be speaking – – I like it just fine. What I'm saying is, I'm usually able to pick up where a person is from based on his accent or language. With you, I hadn't been able to pin it down at all. I was thinking somewhere in the Midwest."

"Forgiven." Nikki uncrossed her arms and placed her hand back on top of his arm. "Anyway, back in high school, I worked for the school television station. Part of my training was to suppress my accent. I needed to sound more professional -- more televisiony. Of course, there are times when my Georgia Peach just comes bubbling right out," as she finished that statement, she let her full Georgia Peach loose.

"And here I was, thinking I was sitting here getting to know only one person when in fact she has multiple personalities," Evan chuckled.

"But see, you haven't even met all of my personalities yet. Some of them are much more fun. There's the businesswoman and the deeply concerned protector of abused dogs and cats. Plus the Naughty Catholic Schoolgirl and the Slutty Cheerleader." Nikki lowered her face and raised her eyes to make direct contact with his. Because this could also come off as slightly psychotic, she had practiced this expression in front of the mirror, so it came off as sensually hungry. Evan's reaction let her know she'd succeeded.

"My oh, my. Tell me, do you have the uniform for both the Naughty Schoolgirl and Slutty Cheerleader?" As soon as the words left his mouth, he knew he'd come off a little too serious and not quite as playful as he had hoped.

"What kind of Slutty Cheerleader would I be if I didn't have the uniform, and you can't be any sort of Naughty Catholic Schoolgirl

without the uniform all the way down to the patent leather shoes. Well -
- patent leather stilettos." Nikki was pressing every single exposed
button to make sure she had him lassoed before the evening ended. She
had been painting the picture of herself he wanted--intelligent, educated,
well-traveled, and full-on sensual. *But did Evan realize that?*

The small town of Melrose, Scotland sits just north of England's border.
Eildon Hills, which overlook the village, is rumored to be the burial place
of the legendary King Arthur. Even though the population is less than
2000 people, there are nearby attractions and adequate facilities to make
the lifestyle there comfortable. Adrian Ahlström was widely known
among the townsfolk, even though he was Swedish and not a full-time
resident.

Sergei knew when he adopted his persona in West Midlands that
he was not going to be able to live a full-time life as an Arab shopkeeper
without some means of occasional escape. He needed a way to live life
more as he had known it than under the social restrictions of Islam.
Melrose provided him with that escape, and his identity as a semi-retired
Swedish factory manager named Adrian Ahlström afforded him that
opportunity.

From time to time, he hung a sign on his shop door, letting
everyone know he would be gone for a few days. He carried a small
duffel bag with only one change of clothes and caught the bus to the
train station in nearby Wolverhampton. His train route varied greatly
depending on the time of day and his own feelings of paranoia. Once he
was a safe distance from Wolverhampton, Areef shifted out of the Arab
shopkeeper clothes and into his more Western clothing. Then he no
longer spoke with his carefully trained Arab accent but adopted a more
Eurocentric accent that was unlikely to be questioned. The next section
of his journey involved crisscrossing his way back to a small town just

north of London, using a circuitous route that probably could be followed, but would in all likelihood end with the pursuer being spotted by the experienced prey.

Once he reached his destination north of London, he walked from the train station to a storage building where he rented a garage. Sergei entered the garage as the nondescript Euro traveler and within an hour or so departed to continue his journey to Melrose as Adrian Ahlström. Aside from a variety of clothing, the garage was also home to a 1986 BMW which he used to complete his journey.

His Ahlström persona was much more cheerful and open. In the West Midlands, he found himself being severe and stern, but Melrose was a chance to resume his more social side.

After arriving at his cottage, he unlocked the door and opened all the windows to let it air out. He followed this ritual every time he returned to Melrose. Because he passed through town on his way to the cottage, all the local folks found it necessary to drop by and say hello to their part-time resident. He enjoyed that bit of friendliness as well. It had become a routine transition and a way for him to drop both Areef and Sergei on the floor and totally embrace Adrian for the time he was there.

With his social period over, and all of the windows closed, Adrian poured three fingers of Absolut and dropped into his easy chair which provided him with a beautiful view of the surrounding hills through the large front window. Even though he had assumed Adrian's personality, Sergei's plotting and mental wanderings continued through his mind. This calmed itself the longer he stayed in Melrose, but for now, Sergei had control and wanted to ponder recent events a bit.

Sergei knew he was one of two people fighting for Abi's soul. He found the thought of such a contest as humorous because he could not care less who ended up owning the young man's soul as long as he was able to manipulate Abi into doing what he needed. It was also impossible for Qa'id to know that Sergei had merely expanded from using one of them to using both after Qa'id and Abi became acquainted. Still, Qa'id did what he could to separate the young man from Areef so he would be the primary focus of his attentions and efforts. Sergei had no problem with this; Abi's new direction made his plan easier, giving him a better reason to explore and exploit the information Areef had passed on.

He had passed on documents which spelled out that Abi would need to use the shortwave radio to communicate with those who could trigger the execution of the Crimson Firebird Initiative. Sergei always found it interesting that Abi never seemed to question how or why tools and information showed up just when they were needed. The young man was smart but not intelligent enough to ask essential questions. There were variables at play here, of course. There was no way of knowing how long it would take Abi to actually translate the documents and then figure out what he would need to do to make it all work. Plus, Qa'id might play into timing, insisting that he wait for approval from some higher up before putting things in motion or worse-- diverting his attention elsewhere. *Did it matter as long as the end result was the same?*

No need to worry himself with that--a satisfactory conclusion to Sergei's plot was almost in sight. Over the years, he had the foresight to minimize the number of people who knew anything about the CFI, and with that limitation, he had lessened possible failures. Even though only one numbers station was still in existence, it could activate the sleeper agents, and that was enough. Nearly a decade ago he had hand-selected the two SVR officers. Both were orphans with no familial ties in the Soviet Union so they kept their heads down on the job in front of them and their life in Mexico. As long as they were being regularly paid, and getting the expected input from their headquarters, they would continue to stand at the ready until needed.

Sergei was not deluded enough to believe all the sleeper agents in the United States would perform as expected. Many had probably just gotten too fat and comfortable to want to bother themselves with such things. At the same time, he was sure that a sufficient percentage would perform as expected and that would be enough. He did not need a complete annihilation of the United States to claim success--just needed a devastating blow that could not be tracked back to his homeland. The bonus was that all the tools would misdirect blame and spur an all-out confrontation with an assumed enemy. The United States would be busy for decades chasing its tail and an invisible enemy in the Middle East. Meanwhile, the Soviet Union would emerge as the strongest nation on the face of the earth. What better legacy could he leave behind? What better revenge could there possibly be?

Adrian drained the vodka from his glass and returned to the kitchen for another. A knock at the door interrupted settling back in his chair with his freshly filled glass. Adrian answered the front door to find an attractive middle-aged raven-haired woman standing on the cottage's stoop smiling back at him.

"Is this a good time, Luv?" she asked, without attempting to enter just yet.

"Perfect timing, Freya. I just completed settling in and was wondering whether you might drop by to provide a sensuous diversion. Without it, I fear I might fill the rest of my afternoon with other chores."

"Well, then I am just in time." She stepped into the cottage and pushed past him. With no warning, she thrust her body against his in a tight embrace. Raising her face to his, she kissed him deeply. When the embrace mutually broke, she took a step back and began to unbutton her blouse.

"I can taste the Absolut on your tongue--why don't you go get me a glass. Maybe I will use it to finger paint your body and then lick it off." She used her index finger to trace her lips and then allowed the finger to slide into her mouth, sucking on it for a moment.

Adrian stood motionless with his mouth slightly open. "Come on, dear, I have to get on to my other job here in a little bit. I want to make the most of our time before then."

Freya turned towards the bedroom, dropping her blouse on the floor. Adrian moved to the kitchen and poured a second glass of vodka and then made haste following Freya's trail of clothing to the bedroom.

At this point, there was no knowledge to be gained by physically tormenting Fyodor. However, there was something to be gained for Maksim personally as he enjoyed inflicting pain on others. Even though he had been paid well for his first freelance mission in Kuwait, it was not a complete success. He was sure new jobs would come his way, but he had no way of knowing how long it would be before he could exercise his particular talents again. Therefore, he took his time with Fyodor.

Brute force had caused Fyodor to admit his position as a member of the KGB and supply detailed descriptions of some of his illegal operations in various *Rezidenturas* worldwide. Now that that first wall had broken down, it was up to Maksim to push a bit further to see if Fyodor would divulge anything regarding the Crimson Firebird Initiative. Even though had been involved to varying degrees with the CFI, Maksim only ever had contact with Sergei, so Fyodor was totally unaware of his participation.

"You and I both know more things occupied your days than what you've spoken of so far. Perhaps I need to be a little more persuasive so that you will feel free to talk about those things as well." There was the ominous sound of metal as Maksim searched through items on the table. With a grunt of approval, he picked up a pair of duck-billed pliers and returned to his seat in front of Fyodor.

Fyodor had no control over his reaction. His heart rate quickened, and he found himself trying to pull his hands back against the tape which bound them. Finally, a small bead of sweat started its journey from his temple down the side of his face. Maksim smiled at Fyodor. At this point, he had done nothing more than showing him a simple hand tool, but clearly, he was deep inside Fyodor's mind.

"Now, perhaps you have something more to say to me." Maksim bore into Fyodor's eyes as he grabbed Fyodor's hand and crushed it flat against the chair, leaving only his fingertips exposed. Fyodor broke from Maksim's stare to see the pliers brought towards his fingertips. Fyodor was panting, his mind filled with fear of the present and flashbacks from the past. Maksim never broke his gaze as he opened and closed the tool before pulling back. But that was when Maksim realized something was wrong, as the pliers found nothing to grip. Three fingernails were already gone. Maksim ran his thumb over the ends of Fyodor's fingertips and felt the rise of scar tissue-- whoever had ripped out his nails removed them from the root for a permanent and elegantly cruel reminder. This was a new situation. Maksim had always been sent to victims who had never been tortured. This time, he was dealing with a veteran, which made him wonder--*Am I being played?*

He felt the moisture growing underneath his hand which was gripping Fyodor's. The man was beginning to pant, and as Maksim searched his face for some sort of clue, Fyodor's eyes rolled back and his head went limp, falling forward. *No, not now!* Maksim started to panic. Pushing Fyodor's head back, Maksim could see that his face was drenched with sweat.

Fyodor knew the sharp pain in his chest, and the numbness of his left arm were indicators of a heart attack brought on by the stress. Fyodor had made peace with how he had lived and what he had done to save his son. He let his mind drift back to 1975 when he had ensured the boy's future.

The matron had returned from taking Dmitry to a waiting room where a guide was to take him to the Gamayun Education Centre for further processing. She returned to the counter and confronted Fyodor with a dour expression.

"What is your interest in this boy?"

"Part of my extended family..." Fyodor lied, not wanting a nosy bureaucrat to make too many connections, "They said the boy has high intelligence and is exactly the kind of candidate we are seeking for this opportunity."

The matron nodded, knowing full well another privileged bureaucrat was taking care of his own family rather than allowing the stringent selection process to take place. As Fyodor exited the building, she returned to her paperwork and forgot the incident entirely.

On his way home, after leaving the Kerzhenskiy Nature

Preserve, Fyodor made a short stop at a research facility located within the compound of the Nizhny Novgorod Higher Military Engineering Command School. The research facility tested the corpses of dead Russians for the effects of various explosives and military weapons. Many years after the Cold War it would be revealed that the Russians had tested human corpses instead of farm animals as was the practice in the West. There was public outcry for what had been done, and the practice was stopped. But this was 1975, decades before that would happen.

Even though he lacked proper paperwork, no one at Lubyanka questioned Fyodor's need to obtain the corpse of a male child. Based on his verbal request, an acceptable corpse was taken from a morgue freezer, the body removed from the bag and wrapped in a blanket. This was at the insistence of the staff since the body bag had identifications. The corpse was placed in the trunk of Fyodor's car. Usually, such a deal would require a payoff in vodka or some other contraband, but Fyodor declined to keep the exchange under the table. Questions could arise even into the distant future over something like this.

After departing from the base, Fyodor pulled his car to the side of the road and removed the body from the trunk and placed it in the backseat of the car. His flashlight illuminated the child's face, and Fyodor for a fleeting moment recognized the corpse as a human being. Sad. Whatever misfortune had befallen someone so young was just sad. He also realized that this child would never be mistaken for his son so he would have to go one step further with his plan.

Originally, Fyodor had intended on staging an accident, his car running off the road and into the fast-flowing waters of the *Oka River*. This way, there would be no reason to question his survival and his son drowning as the car was swept away. After a few days in the water, the body would be so swollen and unrecognizable, but the hair color would remain. Many people had known Dmitry and while bodies might begin to look alike after a week in the water if the hair didn't match it could draw unwanted attention and curiosity. Therefore, Fyodor came up with a different plan, running the car into a tree at high speed, and then setting fire to the wreckage—this would leave only skeletal remains. The new plan was trickier since he could get seriously injured. But alas, there was nothing else he could do to guarantee his son's acceptable *death*.

Fyodor's staged crash went fairly well--the impact concentrated on the passenger side, so he was not seriously injured. His car was equipped with seatbelts, though most Soviet cars were not, preventing his ejection through the windshield. As he climbed out of the wreck, still dazed, he smelled no gasoline. Luckily Fyodor, like most Soviets, kept several liters of gasoline in the trunk in case of shortages or a long journey.

Unsteadily, he walked to the rear of the vehicle and opened the trunk. He stabbed the floor of the trunk with a pocketknife to make an opening above the muffler. He unscrewed the top of the fuel can and tipped it over. Fyodor made it a few steps before the leaking gas made contact with the hot muffler and exploded. The explosion threw him to the ground, knocking the breath out of him. Fyodor remained still. He was both a Communist and an atheist, but still, he found himself silently praying for the decoy child.

Rolling onto his back, he sat up and watched the flames engulf the car. He assessed his pain and realized he was not seriously injured. As the inferno died down, the Duzhnny police arrived and took control of the situation.

The police determined Fyodor had taken the curve far too quickly and ended up crashing into a tree, then dazed, crawled from the car before it exploded. The cause of the fire was determined to be the gas can in the trunk. There was one fatality from the accident—Fyodor's son, Dmitry. Recovered from the wreckage were the boy's skeletal remains which were immediately released to Fyodor without questions.

Fyodor made arrangements for a small funeral within a week of the accident. The modest funeral was attended by the boy's aunt, his father, and his father's associate from work, Sergei Kirill Mikhailov. Sergei gave Fyodor a week off from work to mourn and recover. Fyodor spent the week playing chess in the local park. It was the end of the life of Dmitry Fyodorevich Maldroski just as the life of Julian Shepherd began.

Fyodor's son's death ensured his secrets were safe and he was far beyond anything that the KGB, Sergei, or even this man sitting in front of him could do to him or his child. They were free.

Maksim was doing his best to remain calm. He had not ever failed like this on any mission. Everything Fyodor said had been a carefully planted lie to manipulate Maksim.

Maksim put his face directly in front of Fyodor's and screamed before beating his head back and forth with his fists. After several minutes, Maksim slowed and then stopped – staring at Fyodor's bloody and pulverized face. He remained there for almost an hour staring as Fyodor's body grew cold. The only sound was the dripping blood from Fyodor's face onto the floor. Maksim took and exhaled several deep breaths, still trying to assimilate what had happened. He had never been played this way before. Or had he been played? The truth was that he had no idea. There was some comfort that this was the finale of Maksim's service to the KGB, SVR, *Siberian Rime*, and the Soviet Union. In fact, after he phoned in his report he was going to trigger incendiary explosives within this building, burning and destroying any organic content that might still remain. He would then disappear, after ensuring his trail held no clues.

"Complete," Maksim said into the phone.

"Did he break? Was there any clue he may have given information to someone else?" The concern in Sergei's voice was unusual but he managed to keep it controlled.

"Not at all, he spoke only of his job dealing with the Rezidenturas but nothing at all about any codename projects he may have known about." Maksim realized Sergei's voice had a strange tone as if he were not himself. He had no way of knowing this call had interrupted Adrian during a liaison in his Melrose cottage.

"Did he ever use the term *Firebird?*" Sergei was exposing part of what he was trying to keep secret, but there was no other way to ask the question and get confirmation.

"No, nothing like that. Just about the man's role in the handling

of S Directorate Illegals," Maksim said. *So, the man was hiding something —*
maybe this is why his voice is strange.

"Have you disposed of everything?" The authority in Sergei's
voice returned.

"It will all be gone in a moment." Maksim pushed the button on
a small remote which set off a series of explosions in the building across
the vacant lot. Within minutes the building imploded as flames caused
by white phosphorus explosives rose through the pile of rubble. By
morning, nothing would be left but smoking charred rock, and Maksim
would be on his way Germany to set up a new base of operations as a
self-employed assassin.

Sergei pressed the red button on the touchscreen of his phone
to terminate the call. His mind ran back over his lifelong
acquaintanceship with Fyodor. He had been a good man and a good
Russian, but he lacked vision -- oblivious to the ultimate goal the Soviet
Union still required of him. Fyodor had gone so far as to call Sergei *mad*
during their final conversation after the Soviet Union fell.

Sergei was doing his best to maintain and consolidate power
within Strategic Intelligence, during the State reorganization in late 1991,
but it was not working. In fact, he had become something of a pariah to
those coming to power--the Soviet's new intelligentsia. On his last night
in Moscow, Sergei reached out to his friend Fyodor who had already
begun erasing his own history to escape.

"Fyodor, you know the capability we still have in place – – the
weapon that only you and I control." Sergei spoke quickly as he was
consumed by paranoia that at any moment he would be locked in chains
and taken away.

"You cannot be serious, why would you do such a thing? What
good would it do to destroy the West at this point? Don't you realize
that through the failures of the bureaucracies of communism we have
brought about our own destruction?" Fyodor's voice rose.

"But don't you see? If we release the CFI now, I can regain
control…" Sergei pleaded.

"You're mad!" Fyodor concluded their final conversation.

Fyodor managed to erase his footprints sufficiently to remain in the Soviet Union, moving first to Stalingrad and later to Minsk.

"Adrian. What are you doing? – Come back to bed," Freya's interruption was welcomed.

After dropping his phone into a drawer, Adrian strolled back to his bedroom.

"Who was that on the phone?" Freya asked.

"Just some business from back home. Now the phone's off and I can give you my full attention." Adrian crawled across the bed towards Freya.

"Good idea, and the next time you go to the living room to answer a phone, you might want to put on a robe; you have yet to put any curtains on that front bay window."
She had a point, but right now he had other things on his mind.

Chapter Seven

Romulus, Michigan

Evan was surprised by the way the evening turned out, but he was not disappointed at all. As he exited the bar with Nikki, he realized he still had to consider all the things Dieter had discussed. But for this moment, Evan was going to remain in the present with this beautiful woman. As they stood on the sidewalk outside Aglow, Evan stared into her eyes—still unable to tell what color they were.

Perhaps a golden brown? Maybe a dark green? Greenish gold?

"They're hazel," she said, breaking the silence.

"I didn't mean to stare…they are just so – – lovely."

"Why thank you, kind sir," Nikki made a small curtsy. She handed Evan a napkin with her number.

"I was just about to ask you for that…"

In a sudden fluid motion, she pressed her body firmly against his, wrapped her arms around his neck, and leaned in, stopping just short of touching her lips to his. Instead, she used the tip of her soft, wet tongue to slowly lick his lips. The heat of her breath was like a furnace and added to the sensations her tongue, Evan was driven to push forward until their mouths pressed hard against each other. Their first kiss exploded. Their embrace tightened, and Evan's body began to react. He grew hard and knew she could tell.

"Mmm, I believe I know what's going on inside your head," she whispered into his ear as she allowed her hand to caress him before stepping back. "And here I am not even wearing anything slutty or naughty."

"Oh, yes you are, those eyes and that smile…you're devilishly naughty indeed."

They laughed, breaking the sexual tension as Evan walked Nikki to her car. He took her keys to unlock the door and then kissed her again. This time was more controlled but just as passionate and sensual. Evan opened the car door, leaned down, tightening her seatbelt across her body before fastening it.

"Worried about me?" she asked.

"Worried *for* you," he nodded. "There are a lot of crazy drivers out there, and I want to make sure that we get another evening together."

They kissed a final time. Nikki's hand moved between his legs, pausing at his inner thigh. As their kiss ended, he pulled his face back slowly, opening his eyes to find her looking back at him with an absolute hunger. Not saying another word, Evan closed the door. She started the engine and gave him a quick wave as she drove off into the darkness.

Damn! He glanced down at the napkin and noticed she had written her number and included her name with little hearts to dot the I's. He rolled his eyes. "Why did she have to be a Nikki?"

Nikki watched Evan in her rearview mirror until she made her first turn. His body language, the way he returned her kiss, and the way his body reacted while she kissed him—no doubt she had captured his attention. Her mission for the evening was complete. Beyond that, she was going to enjoy this unusual assignment more than most. This time it was not her job to extract information or to *remove* him. All she had to do was keep him out of trouble; keeping his attention on her would make that easier.

Once she was a safe distance from the club, Nikki parked at the back of a market's lot. After ensuring there was no one around, she pushed a sequence of buttons on her car stereo which opened a concealed compartment and withdrew what appeared to be an average cell phone. She pressed her fingerprint onto the screen and entered a six-digit pin before typing a one-word SMS to the only number listed.

```
>Contact
```

She typed and hit send.

The response was immediate,

She nodded and destroyed the communication using methods that met the United States National Security Agency standard before hiding the phone away. Nikki headed home happy with the successful beginning– and he was a good kisser too.

Melrose, Scotland

Dressed in his bathrobe, Adrian escorted Freya to the front door and enjoyed a wet and sensual kiss before handing her a €100 bill that she stuffed into her pocket.

"Again tomorrow?" she asked smiling.

"Mmm, perhaps. I have a few errands to run but maybe in the early evening. Available?" Adrian asked.

Freya cupped the side of his face, and ran her hand all the way down his chest, opening his robe to caress him below the waist. "Luv, you know I am always available when you're here. I cancel everything else on my calendar just for you." She gave him a firm squeeze and leaned in to kiss him again.

The relationship between them had started off as something strictly commercial, but over the years it had become more emotional and tender. The only semblance to their original encounters and was the exchange of currency at the end of each rendezvous. Adrian was sure he could probably stop giving her cash and still have sex but why bother. She needed the money and he could afford it. The arrangement worked for them, and that was good enough.

"One day, you're going to have to let me shave off that beard and find out who I've been shagging," she said, releasing one part of him and gently tugging on the end of his beard.

"Perhaps one day soon I will," he said as he caressed her cheek with his fingertips. The sentence he did not speak was: *If all goes well and I manage a clean getaway while the rest of the world implodes.*

With that, she gave him a final kiss on the cheek. As he closed the door, he inhaled deeply and enjoyed the lingering scent of her perfume. *It would not be such a bad life... in fact, being with her full-time might be precisely what I need in my latter years.* He smiled at the thought and then proceeded into the shower to wash the scent of their lovemaking away.

Adrian dressed in clothes suitable for wandering the country roads that beckoned him every time he visited Melrose. Taking his walking stick from the umbrella stand near the door, he set out on an eight-kilometer stroll that took him past the church and the Melrose Abbey and into the Market Square. He picked up some fruit and other odds and ends he needed, and found himself conversing with several of the merchants who were familiar to ask after his health and his life in Sweden—both he always assured were fine.

He made sure his sojourn back to the cottage took him past Gibson Park, to watch people playing tennis, or perhaps some schoolboys playing a pickup game of soccer in the open field. The town was large enough to have his own Rugby club but not a formal football league. These distractions were part of what Sergei looked forward to when he came to Melrose. He yearned for a quiet life like this -- without the cares of the city and without responsibilities beyond the vegetables and fruit he picked up each day.

After escaping tumultuous Moscow when the Soviet Union ceased to be, Sergei spent several years moving from place to place within western Europe. His moves were not caused by fear of being discovered, but because he was angry at his loss of stature and power and he could not find his new place.

Eventually, in 1999, he arrived in Melrose, Scotland and became Adrian Ahlström--a financial analyst from Gothenburg, Sweden. For the first time, he considered settling down. After all, he had managed to escape without a trace. Sergei had more than enough money left from KGB projects, sitting in a numbered account in Switzerland, and he had no emotional ties. His was a better transition than most, but his life's work had been obliterated and this weighed on him.

No matter how much money he possessed he would never be able to gain a position of power again. The more he spent, the more visible he would become, and visibility could eventually lead to his capture and being placed on trial. This had happened with many KGB during the chaos of transition. In the years since, the government seemed content to let sleeping dogs lie as long as they were outside their borders and did not make too much of a fuss.

Even now in Melrose he still received information regarding the new government and how his legacy was being destroyed. Every time he read a new dispatch, or looked at a Western newspaper, this destruction was obvious. Fortunately, there were operations only known to a limited number of people, like the Crimson Firebird Initiative.

CFI could be a decimating blow against the country he held responsible for his exile. However, as a realist, he knew the source of the attack would be linked to his homeland which he could not allow to happen. Otherwise, Crimson Firebird was the perfect tool for revenge… it relied on nothing that was not already in place, no one but Fyodor and he understood its mission or capabilities He needed two things, for Fyodor to be eliminated and to find a scapegoat. Then during a period of pondering, a possibility occurred to him.

During his years as a Rezident in the Middle East, he became aware of the rise of terrorist groups based on faith turned fanatical. The one thing the terrorists could be counted on for, aside from being ruthless and fearless, was that they could not see more than what was in front of them. Because he was willing to dive to the levels they sank to, all he had to do was look further down the road than them for a way to foil their various plots. Even if a battle was won, few within their ranks could look beyond the tactical. As a result, they took actions that made a sudden splash but led to their loss due to a lack of preparation. Many within their ranks saw massive attacks, such as 9/11, as a win but they underestimated the cost of making their Satan angry rather than annihilating him.

But suppose they were convinced they had a weapon that was so powerful it would entirely wipe out their enemy? Suppose they were convinced to hijack and use the Crimson Firebird Initiative not as a response, but as a first blow? With the right patsy, Sergei could win two ways, the United States would be destroyed, and his own country would not be blamed. If he gave partial information to his scapegoat, the weapon would be crippling and lead to a war between the West and the Middle East, while his own homeland reaped the benefits. He may even be able to return triumphant.

To that end, Sergei needed a way to recruit the right candidate to serve. He purchased a small storefront in West Midlands, England and established the persona of Areef Rahal. His past command of Arabic helped as well as his dark curly hair and olive complexion. Arabs had a tendency to be tribal while within their own borders but opened wider arms when away from home. After a year of preparation, he moved to West Midlands but kept his cottage in Melrose as an escape.

He waited until all was set before dealing with Fyodor. Sergei had a soft spot for the man and did not want to kill him needlessly. His contacts kept an eye out in case Fyodor resurfaced, but he did not. During the entire time, Fyodor was in Minsk, Sergei was aware of his location. With the selection of Abdul-Malik Kaseem as a decent candidate, dealing with Fyodor became an issue.

Fyodor was the type of problem that Siberian Rime was designed to rectify. This was one of several plans Sergei had developed that got fielded under the new Foreign Intelligence Service. The new management may not have liked Sergei, but they liked his ideas, and Siberian Rime was fully functional three years after his departure. Even though the program lasted only two years before it was transitioned into Zaslon, there were several star performers from the program who became approachable.

Maksim Fillyp Bondreovich was fourteen when he and Sergei first met. He was one of many youths identified as being of potential use to the KGB and was being monitored by the agency. It was obvious Maksim would grow to be physically intimidating, but what intrigued Sergei more was his highly cunning mind and his ruthlessness. Sergei coded his folder SI, particular interest--over the course of his training Sergei would receive regular updates on anything significant.

Once Sergei had departed, and the Siberian Rime program became a reality, he still received information about Maksim. When the program was folded into Zaslon, occasional information regarding Maksim, his whereabouts, and activities were sent on to Sergei. At great risk Sergei began direct contact with Maksim, convincing him that his position within the KGB had transitioned into an ultra-secret role. This gave Sergei something that most outside a government seeking revenge don't have, a private intelligence field asset. When coupled with his money and information, Sergei could exact whatever level of revenge desired--an astronomical level.

Sergei passed the disposal of the staff members assigned to the Vodyanoy Transmission Station in Mexico to Maksim, beginning in 2000. With every staff rotation, following the assumption of duties by the new team, Maksim disposed of the departing staff within hours, their bodies buried near the site. The goal was to prevent any knowledge of the site's existence beyond the current active staff and Sergei.

Maksim accomplished many such eliminations over the years, but the assignment he had just completed was the most difficult--the questioning and termination of Fyodor. Sergei had to know for sure that Fyodor had never spoken of the CFI to eliminate any risk. He now had that certainty.

When he arrived back at his cottage after his walk, he decided with the stage properly set -- the time to begin his plan in earnest was here.

Qa'id Al-Abidin's primary function in England was to recruit soldiers from the Arab expatriate population as well as Westerners seeking true faith. He was enormously successful as a teacher at a local mosque which allowed him access to young moldable minds. Qa'id had developed great skills of perception over his life that aided him in determining how best to approach new candidates and converts providing answers to questions they themselves did not know they were seeking. His cover also allowed him a certain amount of protection under the English law, because faith was seen as personal freedom rather than a means of violent revolutionary change. The disguise was indeed a deep one, as Qa'id possessed no religious beliefs one way or another.

When Qa'id was recruited into the Palestinian cause decades before, it was not out of a sense of religious fervor or feelings of religious indignation. Qa'id saw Islam as having connotations he could exploit. Growing up as a son in the sliver of the middle class in Saudi Arabia, he had been introduced to Wahhabism-- a version of Islam that stressed the strict interpretation of the Koran. But in adolescence, he veered into nihilism, and the concept interested him more -- the feeling that nothing in faith or society was worthwhile. He wanted to take that idea a step further and to have a significant role and power within the society. This path did not exist under Wahhabism since he was not born into the royal family. Not wishing to be limited by a failure of birth, he blended and morphed philosophies into something that more aligned with his personal goals.

Over the years, Qa'id's loyalty was fluid, moving from the PLO to various splinter groups when the PLO became political, Al Qaida, the Muslim Brotherhood, and finally the Islamic State. Each of those organizations benefited from his talents, but in the end, Qa'id always found himself seeking a new more aggressive group. He was careful to always be the power behind the figurehead and not the face of any cause.

This served several purposes, but mostly it allowed him the flexibility to move on.

Few people knew those who conducted the 9/11 attacks were not men of faith but rather men of violence. Many of them spent the days before their assault in bars, strip clubs and eating forbidden foods. One of the leaders was caught on camera drinking vodka in an airport bar before boarding the plane he would pilot into the World Trade Center. Qa'id admired these men as having the dedication to sacrifice themselves to bring about the seismic cultural shift. Of course, Qa'id would never make such a sacrifice himself-- how could he? If he died before he obtained the level of power he wanted, it would be a failure. Instead, he found and recruited the grist that would eventually be ground into dust by the mill of his revolution. The latest and most promising fodder was Abdul-Malik Kaseem. Aside from the payment he would receive for recruiting the boy, he saw new ways to strike out at the West using their own technology.

Even though his assigned function did not include recruiting resources to be employed in England, he saw a new way to wage war, from the time he met Abi on his seventeenth birthday. Shortly after meeting the boy, he gathered the details of how he and his mother ended up in West Midlands from Palestine. Using sketchy information from Abi and from his contacts in the Middle East, he blended a new narrative that helped direct the boy's hatred toward the West at a level the Islamic State could use.

Abi was intelligent and clever, but not smart enough to realize how effectively he was being used by Qa'id. Once a rapport was established, Qa'id used the details of the Abi's father's death to build a bond. Early on, he promised Abi he would find out more about the man who had murdered his father. In truth, there was no way Qa'id could discover much, so he merely used Abi's recollections.

With these details, Qa'id searched a database of Israeli Commandos to match--a man with three long scars on the left side of his face, from just below the eye to the neck. Major Moshe Levinsky fit the bill, and utilizing Photoshop, Qa'id extended some existing scars.

From that moment on, Abi had the identity of his father's killer. Hatred is much more effective when it has a face you can see rather than just imagine.

Qa'id recounted a story that fits. He painted Abi's father as a hero of the cause, trying to organize fellow Palestinians against the Israeli state. Qa'id connected everything negative back to this tragic night. Of course, it was Israeli assassins who killed his father--who else could it be? It was the PLO who came to the rescue – – too late to save Abi's father but in time to allow him to escape with his mother. The story blended Abi's memory with propaganda that allowed his father a hero's death, leading to a vow of revenge. Qa'id's craftiness paid off by drawing Abi closer to him and allowing him more control over the young man's perception of the world.

Abi was indebted to Qa'id and accepted this fabrication as the truth. Due to Qa'id's emotional support, Abi respected the man and desired to please him. This led to him to learn about a broad range of technical skills that Qa'id said might be of value to his people. Of course, Qa'id tempered this direction with adulterated quotes from the Koran that seemed to support the tasks he assigned to Abi.

Fakhriya was not without concern for the truths Qa'id used to indoctrinate her son. The night her husband was killed remained vivid in her mind, and she knew it was not the PLO that had rescued them but their friends who helped them leave the country. She worried her son would die on some battlefield in the Middle East as so many others were, trying to lay claim to a small piece of desert. Their life in England had been stable. She wished her son would realize that sometimes out of the most devastating situations a glimmer of good could be found.

As Abi spent more and more time at the mosque with Qa'id, he argued more with his mother. She wanted him to socialize with other students rather than this religious instructor. She wanted him to seek more understanding of their faith than by this one individual. Fakhriya wanted him to regain his humanity and stop talking like a zealot ready to die for some cause he didn't fully understand.

Qa'id realized there was a threat that he would lose Abi to his mother, so he took a bold step of establishing the young man in his own apartment nearer to his school. This cut Abi off from Fakhriya and at the same time allowed his protégé a stable base of operations.

Now Abi had come to him with a possible methodology for intercepting espionage transmissions. Qa'id wasn't quite sure what this could turn into, but he asked the young man to spend a little more time on it. Of course, Qa'id informed his superiors about the possible breakthrough and his plan to exploit the young man's talents in the West instead of sending him to Syria or some other battlefield.

Abi sat at his kitchen table with a spiral notebook to one side and two laptops on the other. He had dedicated one laptop to the duty of handling numbers stations broadcasts. He dutifully entered the words from the last transmission he intercepted into the search algorithm that was tied to the Project Gutenberg database. Even though he had continued to optimize his program, it would be at least a few hours before the program returned any sort of relevant text.

He considered the piles of papers on the table. *Areef may have come across something truly beneficial this time.* After his initial sorting of documents, into Russian and German piles, he subdivided into six stacks of varying heights. Directly in front of him was a bunch of numbered German pages that he arranged in sequence. The effort led him to discover that pages were missing.

Abi moved onto the next mysterious pile written in an unknown alphabet. One of the difficulties of learning Russian beyond the spoken word was the Cyrillic alphabet. Over time, many Russians adopted the Latin alphabet, but older, official documents were exclusively in Cyrillic. When he organized this pile, he set aside any material in Russian with English handwritten notes. This was the collection of papers that most interested him. He skimmed each of the pages until he came across the written words *encryption/decryption algorithm*--the commenter had drawn an arrow pointing to a particular section so this was where he would start.

He could not just type the Cyrillic words into his computer and run a translation program. There were two possible ways of dealing with this--change the keyboard to Cyrillic and enter each letter one at a time, or scan the document and convert the letters to text to be translated. Seeking a faster solution, he tried the second option. Since he did not have a conventional desktop scanning device, he used his phone to take a picture of a portion of the page that seemed of interest. He transferred the picture from his phone to his laptop. Once the file appeared on his desktop, he opened it and selected a conversion option for the image that would translate any lettering on the picture into text.

After taking several minutes to process the file, the program announced *No Text Was Found*, and Abi realized he needed to make a few configuration changes that would instruct the program to look for text in Cyrillic. He did this and then again started the program to process the document. This time it found the text.

> *Первые цифры сообщения содержат том в сборке который должен использоваться для текстовой части сообщения. В колкции всего 102 тома, и, что каждый агент три цифры, соответствующие каждому тому.*

Abi's eyes lit up; he quickly compared this bit of text with the picture he had taken of the actual sheet. This conversion did not have as many lines in it as his original document, but he pasted the text into the *Source* box and hit the translate button. The result appeared in seconds:

> *The first digits of the Message contain the volume in the assembly that should be used for the text portion of the Message. In the collation of only 102*

Abi's face reflected deep shock. It was not that he was no longer happy – – he had gone from being simply happy to euphoric. Not only did this work, but it also made some semblance of actual sentences. Comparing the text, the program had gleaned from the picture to the original document, he quickly figured out which words were missing, which were lacking some of the Cyrillic characters from the original document, and things that just looked wrong. He found a solution to photograph each of the pages and then use the conversion software to translate. Next, he would verify the captured text by comparing it to the original and manually correct any mistakes. Instead of changing his keyboard to Cyrillic, Abi would copy individual letters from other parts of the document and paste them where needed. He clasped his hands together as if in prayer, and lowered his forehead onto his fingertips while closing his eyes. Abi was delighted with himself. Again, Areef had led him to a door he was able to open and would be able to use for the good of the cause. Praise be upon him.

Abi set to work, photographing, transferring, converting, validating, and then translating each section of text from several pages of what appeared to be a self-contained section of the document. He created a new document with the combined result of the translations. When he finished the last section, he scrolled through the document from top to bottom and smiled to himself. *How could I have been so lucky to have come into possession of a document like this?*

Abi knew enough about cybersecurity not to risk transmitting the document to a printer using Wi-Fi so he connected his laptop directly to the printer using a cable. His current work was riskier than anything he had done up to this point.

Abi thought about how best to handle this information. He created two binders to organize the documents after first dumping out the class information they contained. The first binder would contain the original documents in case he ever needed to cross-check; the second was for translations. After he finished assembling and sorting the documents, he pulled the binder containing the translations towards him. Taking a deep breath, he opened it and began to read.

The first 3 digits of the Message contain the volume number within *Brandt's Compleat Collection* that is to be used to decode the text portion of the Message. There are only 102 volumes in the collection, and it is expected that each agent will memorize the 3 digits that match each volume.

Next, are 17 digits that gave precise decimal degree coordinates for the location of the Launch Preparation Assembly Kit (L-PAK). This information is only to be given during the execution phase and will only ever be used once. The entire United States is roughly located between East/West coordinates 20 and 50 and -65 to -123 North/South coordinates. This means that a shorthand will be used and the information can still be understood due to the limited scope.

For example, there is no need to use a full 3 digits for the numbers since it can be assumed that anything in the East/West that was numerically below 23 would need to have a one added as a prefix. Likewise, it is known that all North/South numbers will be negative so that bit of information will be omitted as well as any decimal points since the format of the data are known to the receiver.

So, the location of the *Luxor Hotel* in Las Vegas is usually seen as 36.095510, -115.176067 but when using the shorthand, it can be represented with the 17-digit number 36095510115176067. In an additional twist, even though the code is only going to be used once, the numbers will all be flipped in pairs with the odd last digit, flipped with the 16th digit (63905501111567670) and then the entire string reversed; the end result will be

7676511110550936. Finally, the result is divided by 3 which will lead to 02558837036850312. This is the number that would be transmitted to identify the L-PAK's location. Since the result was less than 17-digits, a leading zero was added.

Note: It is a mistake to treat these coordinates like longitude and latitude; all geographic references are displayed in decimal. Decimal degrees are much more accurate and allow for a greater degree of specificity.

The final 3 digits are the specific page number, within the volume identified above, where the Message will begin. Depending on the length of the Message several pages may be used beyond that initial starting point.

Within the numeric portion of the Message will be a scattering of miscellaneous words which are designed as decoys and distractions. When copying down the Message, the agents are directed to ignore the words and just write down the numbers, the result will always be a 22-digit numeric.

The text portion is actually a misnomer since it is still transmitted as numbers. Each number corresponds to a particular line and word within the text of the selected volume of *Brandt's Compleat Collection*. This portion of the Message will contain additional specific information that may be necessary, like codes or ciphers needed to get into the facility at the location provided or specific room number within the building where the L-PAK is located.

Sitting back in his chair, Abi pondered what he had just read. He found himself jiggling his left foot as he pondered what he had read. *Without the benefit of section titles, there was no way to tell what this 22-digit numeric related to or how it was used.* But, if he ever came across a 22-digit numeric he would know how to break it down. *Interesting. And the purpose of this 22-digit number?* It served to provide him with the location of the Launch

Preparation Assembly Kit. To this point, he had no idea what a Launch Preparation Assembly Kit or L-PAK was or even why it was. Lifting his eyes from the page, he looked at the stack of papers he had yet to process. *The answer is in there, somewhere. It is up to me to find it. Time to get to work.*

Chapter Eight

Kalamazoo, Michigan

As soon as Evan turned his car onto the highway, his cloudy mind began to clear; despite his new acquaintance, he was a man with responsibilities. *Zax!*

If he had kept to his schedule, Evan would've been home within ten or eleven hours of leaving the dog. Looking at his watch, he realized, thanks to a stop at Aglow, he had been gone almost thirteen hours and was at least another two hours from home. Zax did okay on his own, but this was a bit much -- and almost to the point of being cruel. He withdrew his phone from his pocket and looked at the screen long enough to pick a familiar name from his list of contacts.

"Hello?" the female voice answered after four rings.

"Hey, Artiste, I need a favor. Are you busy?"

"Mmm, baby, always free for you," Houstynne mewed.

"That's why you stay on my Favorite Human list. I need you to go to my house and let Zax out. I went to Detroit today, and it took longer than I thought, so he could really use some relief."

"Sure, no problem by me but he's only ever met me once. Will he be okay with me just walking in without you?"

"Absolutely, Zax has a great memory plus he is the worst watchdog in the world – always friendly to everyone."

"Gotcha. Any problem if I bring Ellie along, she loves dogs?"

"Not at all, in fact, Zax will love making a new friend-- especially after being alone all day. The back door's unlocked-- just be sure to stand back as Zax comes plowing out the door as soon as it's open."

"No worries, Hun… I'll take care of it for you."

"I really appreciate it, give my best to Ellie and let Zax know I'll be home in a couple of hours."

"Will do!"

Evan's mind wandered to his conversation earlier in the day with Dieter, but soon he found himself pondering Nikki's beautiful eyes. Not just beautiful, they were amazing and hypnotic. The light of the candles reflecting off her hair, the feel of her fingertips, her scent, and most of all that kiss. As often happened, he found himself going over every little bit of their encounter, vacillating between how she was another *Nikki* and how the next step would feel beyond.

He would give her a call because he couldn't be stupid enough to write off a beautiful woman just because of her name. *Maybe I can start referring to her by another name instead of Nikki and that will end the Nikki curse. Yeah, right -- sometimes, I am a special kind of stupid.* There must be something incredibly special about her, as she had made him forget about the threat of the Crimson Firebird Initiative to instead consider the sensuality of her lips on his.

Pushing those thoughts to the back of his mind, he floored the accelerator to the almost legal seven miles above the speed limit. He had a few folders to read before he went to bed--folders that would probably lead to another sleepless night.

Ann Arbor, Michigan

As Nikki walked into the apartment, she knew instinctively what to expect and where everything would be. The apartment was located in what used to be an abandoned office building in the center of downtown. As part of a gentrification project, the rooms were converted into luxury apartments, costing three or four times more than any other residence. Of course, there were complaints from longtime residents of being pushed out of their homes by inflated pricing, but an old and deteriorating building had been saved. The property values improved and a new generation of taxpayers arrived. Sometimes to save something you had to help it evolve.

She dropped her keys into the glass mosaic bowl by the door and wheeled her small suitcase into the bedroom. Nikki's bag contained only a few personal items plus her daily toiletries since the vast majority of what she needed for the mission was already in the apartment. The agency's logisticians saw to it that her housing was completely furnished. In addition, her closet was fully stocked-- a separate team at headquarters kept a file on Nikki that included her sizes, style, and color preferences.

The widely accepted paradigm that secret agents conduct espionage operations after being equipped with the latest technology and released alone into the field was the stuff of *James Bond*. The reality was any spy in the field was backed up by several teams in the background who prepared things in advance. For Nikki, this meant her entire lifestyle was in place so she could begin operations as soon as she arrived.

After taking a few minutes to unpack her small bag and stripping off all of her clothes, Nikki pulled an oversized T-shirt over her head. The refrigerator was stocked with the foods she enjoyed and her favorite German wines. She selected a bottle of 2004 Hoch Heimer Victoriaburg. She deftly uncorked the bottle and poured herself a generous glass before replacing the cork and returning the bottle to the refrigerator. Nikki opened the drapes in the living room, revealing a panoramic view of the buildings, before lounging on the couch. The sun was setting in the distance, and the golden light was reflected in the windows of the buildings.

As she sipped her wine, many thoughts ran through Nikki's mind. She thought about her journey. Way back she had been an emancipated teenager, named Ashley, working as a dancer at the *Neon Cactus* in New Orleans - the first of many roles she would assume. Even though she had never thought of herself as a runaway, many would've described her as one. In 1999, she had completed high school in Atlanta a year ahead of her peers, and even though she was only seventeen, Ashley was more than ready to take on a life based on her own terms.

Her first move was to attend Louisiana State University in Baton Rouge-- not her first choice, but it offered her enough tuition assistance so she would only be left with living expenses. Such expenditures she felt she could cover with a part-time job. Quickly, she found out that she had woefully underestimated what it actually cost to live on your own. With no help from her parents, she discovered waitressing was not going to cover what she needed, even with the best of tips. She overheard two students talking in a campus bathroom who was unaware she was in a stall.

"Are you serious? You actually let those drunk, gross guys at the *Neon Cactus* touch you while you dance around naked for them?"

"I'm not always dancing naked. For the first song, I am wearing a bikini. Then for the second song, I take off my top and show off my boobs, then for the last song I remove my bottom, and then I'm dancing naked for them – – and that gets them really fired up for a lap dance which is where the real money is. Also, I don't really let them touch me – – I make them *pay* to touch me. Last night, I made $300 in just four hours. That was totally worth it, a quick shower and a few shots of tequila afterward and I can forget the whole thing while I shop for a new pair of shoes."

"That just seems so wrong--you don't have sex with any of those guys -- do you?"

"Well, the only one I've had sex with so far was the owner and I had to do him to get the job. And I had to blow the bouncer just to meet with the owner. But that wasn't so bad, and it was over quick enough. Some of the guys have offered me money to have sex with them… haven't done it so far but if I do, I get to choose which ones."

"I just can't believe you're doing this-- we spent so much time guarding our virginity in high school, and now you're just giving your body away."

"I ain't giving nothing away. I'm renting short bits of time with it, and in exchange, I'm able to shop for whatever I want and I don't have to worry about the little allowance from my parents."

As Ashley sat and listened, she wondered if she should consider doing the same. She was receiving no allowance whatsoever and $300 for a day's work was more than she was earning now in a week. At no point did she ever consider having sex with anyone she didn't want to; she was smart, and was always found attractive by men. This taught her at an early age that she needed to control the situation or she would be victimized by it. Ashley was in control of every situation. But before she ever walked through the front door of the *Neon Cactus,* she needed to prepare.

The first step in her process was to take a hard look at her body in the mirror. She had not seen the girl talking in the bathroom that day, but she imagined her looks were probably above average but less than model perfect. Standing in front of a full-length mirror completely naked, she evaluated her own attributes.

Her hair was long and straight, and its reddish blonde color had always garnered compliments, so, she would love it alone. Likewise, her most outstanding feature, her large hazel eyes, were an attention-getting feature. There was nothing she would want to do but get lash extensions. Looking down at the rest of her body, being brutally honest, all she saw was average. Her breasts were average sized, nicely shaped and uniform in appearance. The first boy she ever allowed to get to second base had made the memorable comment that her breasts were "inviting." She watched herself in the mirror as she ran her hands over her breasts and by doing so caused her nipples to harden. *Yes, these are a sensually-carnal invitation.*

Ashley's stomach was not completely flat, but the skin was flawless which helped. She did have a cute naval which at one point she considered piercing but decided not to. Turning around she could see that her ass looked okay but was not a bubble butt that some men seem to prefer. Her legs were average length but did have a nice shape. Luckily, the tattoos she had picked up over the years were small enough to be considered cute and not over-the-top.

Walking over to her closet she picked out her white strappy heels that were three inches tall. After putting them on, she returned to the mirror. The shoes not only made her legs look longer and shapelier, but they also added a pronounced lift to her ass. An investment in taller heels before her audition would be worth the cost. She needed to invest in a Brazilian wax too even though it would take away any proof that her hair color was natural.

For the next week, she rehearsed dancing several hours a day in her apartment to bump and grind music. She hoped her neighbors would forgive her for playing the same songs over and over again. In addition to practicing her own moves, she tried to learn others from watching YouTube and checking out dance scenes from the sexiest striptease scenes in movies. Ashley was a quick study and soon had a variety of moves she could perform with the utmost skill.

Ashley figured the best time to audition would be on a Sunday afternoon. She would get there right as the *Neon Cactus* opened so the club was not too busy for the manager to give her a shot. Maybe there'd be a few regulars on hand as an audience. Ashley wore a pair of loose-fitting jeans, sweatshirt, and tennis shoes rather than showing off her physical attributes upfront. She styled her hair perfectly and she applied the right amount of sultry makeup to captivate the manager.

As she pulled into the gravel lot of the *Neon Cactus*, she was totally unimpressed by the outside of the building--a long, flat structure severely in need of paint. Aside from a small porch, which served as the entrance, the building was totally nondescript. Perched on the roof was a muted neon sign with a large picture of a cactus adorning the club's name.

She grabbed a small gym bag that contained her change of clothes and her shoes, took hold of the door handle and paused. Closing her eyes, she exhaled and then took a deep breath before opening the door. She stepped into the small vestibule. The place was an assault on her senses. The first thing to hit her was the sheer stink. Even though no one had smoked inside in years, cigarette smoke had left every surface stained and stinking of nicotine, including the curtains and shabby furniture. Years ago, the law had changed to ban tobacco smoking in all indoor facilities, but even without lighting up there was enough ambient nicotine in the air to keep even the heaviest smoker sated while he was inside. When the smell of smoke abated, Ashley's nose was attacked by the smell of stale, spilled beer and a mixture of cheap competing perfumes and colognes.

Once her eyes adjusted, she noticed red and blue neon, cactus-shaped displays, beer signs and three large platforms that served as individual stages. Between the stages, there was a bar surrounded by stools. To the side was a DJ's booth surrounded by a grouping of several worn and cracked faux leather armchairs that had seen better days. Two were occupied by gray-haired men, who looked like fixtures, holding mugs of beer. Several doorways covered with curtains served as VIP booths for private lap dances. No music was playing, and all of the stages were empty since the club had just opened.

A deep voice startled her, "You coming in for the afternoon's performance, sweetheart?" She hadn't noticed a large black man who served as the maître d' and bouncer.

"Um, no. I wanted to see the manager about getting a job."

"Well, aren't you in luck. Mr. Wharton is in today and just may have time to see an audition." He made no effort to conceal it as he looked her over from head to toe. "Do you want to get changed?"

"Yeah, do you have a changing room?"

He motioned for her to follow him into the main room and stopped in the section of the club with tables and chairs. With the added neon light, his name tag could be read--*Marquis*--affixed to a form-fitting tuxedo vest and topped off with a silk bowtie. Marquis was intimidating-- so large he'd block all daylight walking through a door. "Go ahead and change here."

It takes a lot of nerve to get undressed in front of strangers, let alone in an open room. The two men were staring, sensing something worth watching might be about to occur. Until that moment, Ashley was unaware she had a deeply buried talent. Her survival now counted on being able to assume a role immediately and with full commitment and this talent emerged. She transitioned into the persona of Toccara -- erotic dancer.

Without pause, she pulled her sweatshirt off and revealed her metallic green bikini. Marquis watched Toccara remove her tennis shoes and take out her newly acquired dancing shoes with four-inch clear Lucite heels specifically chosen to accent her attributes. Toccara unbuttoned her jeans. Without raising her head, she gazed at Marquis.

She winked and turned around, bending over at the waist, and exposing her bikini-clad ass. In response to this move, one of the men from across the bar whistled. She stepped out of her jeans, slowly folded them, and then sat back down. While she was seated, she put on her heels, looking up at Marquis. "Ready."

"Not quite, pretty lady; we need to discuss your *admission fee* to see the boss-man." Marquis was excited, his voice slightly higher from its usual baritone.

She was prepared for this. Toccara took his face in her hands and pulled it towards her, and then moved to one side of his head so that she could whisper into his ear. "I know exactly what you want… the problem is that my makeup is all ready to go for the audition – – including just the right amount of hot red lipstick on my soft and supple mouth. I really don't want to mess that up right now, could we maybe make some sort of arrangement to take care of the fee later? I promise." She pulled her face back and stared into his eyes while she let her hands slide from his face to shoulders, then down his chest and stomach before sliding them behind to grab his ass and pull him towards her. She felt the effect she had on him.

"Well, that's highly unusual," his voice rose. "But I guess as long as the fee is paid at some point it'll be okay." With that, he reluctantly pulled back from her grip. "I'll go get Mr. Wharton, he's probably in the back talking to the dancers." He disappeared through a door marked *Private* near the restrooms.

After watching this exchange, the two old men were laughing. She tilted her head, smiled, and took a quick bow before sitting down. She inhaled deeply and slowly exhaled to help her nervousness fade. Her new persona had controlled the situation and prevented her from doing anything she absolutely did not want to do. Now all she had to pass the audition and somehow get out of having sex with the boss.

Wharton leaned around from behind her chair and placed his face directly in front of hers. His sudden appearance caused her to jump slightly. He was older than she imagined, but in the subdued light, age was hard to determine. Wharton wore tinted glasses that hid his eyes, a beard, and even though she thought his hair should be gray, it was jet black and slicked down. The gravelliness of his voice was evidence that he was a major contributor to the stains and smell that now saturated the club.

"Okay, honey, the center stage is yours. Show me what you got." Wharton pulled out a chair in front of the middle stage. Then, he tilted his head back and yelled, "Tony, let's see what she can do with some *Cherry Pie…*"

"You got it, boss," the answer came from inside the DJ's station.

Before Toccara even got past the bar, the first few notes of the Warrant song were playing. Rather than being unnerved, Toccara turned it into an opportunity by beginning her routine as she sojourned to the stage. This included a quick side trip to run her fingers through both men's hair and caress their shoulders as she danced by. When she reached the stage, she took the three steps that led from the floor up to the platform without pausing. She had not warmed up and that might affect her more intricate moves, but luckily this was a song she had practiced to so she was able to adapt.

Toccara's moves caused enough interest for the two regulars to move from their comfortable spots into what they referred to as the drooler chairs-- the closest vantage point short of a lap dance. She gazed directly at each man as she danced in front of him rather than staring at the wall behind. She had read somewhere online that most dancers look away so as not to embarrass their clients. Toccara made sure her glance was one of invitation versus judgment, and that changed the entire dynamic between them.

Toccara was going to attempt to be fully nude by the end of the first song to show off everything she had in three minutes. One move involved removing her top while she performed a 360° spin, using a single hand to release the strap and having it fall off before she returned to her starting point. This worked perfectly, leaving her topless just as she returned in front of Mr. Wharton. She dropped to her knees and leaned back, performing a shoulder shimmy while raising herself up. When his eyes greeted her, she knew she had him inside her dance. To her surprise, he reached forward without warning and slid his hand up from her stomach and then felt of both her breasts. As he did this, she took his hand in hers and after allowing it to grope her for a moment, moved it back down her body to the spot between her legs before releasing it. While she did this, she first made direct eye contact, then bit her lip as she lifted her face up towards the ceiling. This seduction was not lost on Wharton.

He was testing her, even though it was against every law in the state, the club was known as being "full contact" and "high mileage" which meant that customers were allowed to touch the dancers within reason. One of the bigger challenges for new dancers was to keep from cringing or withdrawing. Toccara more than passed this test, because she not only allowed his caress, she had him convinced that the fantasy of the always horny dancer was alive and well within her.

From where she was positioned, Toccara rolled to one side and then back, placing her legs over Wharton's shoulders. Using him as a platform to steady herself, she lifted her ass while sliding her bikini bottoms down to her knees. Then lifting her legs straight up in the air, she slipped them all the way off -- ending the move with her feet on either side of him. Her knees were up, and her legs spread far enough apart so he could see her Brazilian wax. Toccara was only in this position for a moment before she spun to one side to dance off and reward the other two men for making the effort time to move closer. Wharton sat back and observed the individual treatment. He grinned. *She was good, she was damn good.*

Toccara did not notice as Wharton left. When the song was over, she crawled around the stage and picked up several bills from the two regulars. Wharton, of course, left nothing -- his reward would be a job at the *Neon Cactus*. She picked up her bikini and put it back on before taking the stairs down from the stage. At the bottom of the stairs, she was met by one of the club's dancers who smiled and nodded as they traded places. One of the men called her over and requested a lap dance. She was more than willing but wasn't quite sure of the protocol or pricing. So, she offered to give him a free lap dance if she was hired, producing a howl from the man who had not requested one.

The bartender slid her a glass of ice water. She took a few sips of water and waited for her breathing to return to normal. Even though she wasn't out of shape, dancing was not a sedentary activity and with her anxiety level peaked she was a little winded. She took off her shoes and had just pulled her jeans on when Marquis approached.

"Boss wants to see you back in his office." He motioned over his shoulder towards the door marked private.

"Give me a sec, I want to finish getting dressed."

Leaning forward and lowering his voice, Marquis said, "If you're serious about the job, you might want to take all that off and put the heels back on before you walk in there."

Without giving it much thought, she nodded and slid out of her jeans. While continuing to stand, she then stripped out of the bikini and slipped her feet back into her heels before bending over and tightening the straps. Then without pausing, she raised back up and sashayed through the door wearing nothing but her heels. She was not sure what to expect but she did have a plan in mind.

The small office was lit by a single gooseneck lamp on the desk, and Wharton sat in the only chair in the room behind the desk. She stood in front of him as he leaned back and looked her over from top to bottom. As her eyes adjusted, she could see that off to one side was a sloppily made bed.

"What's your name, honey?"

"Toccara. Toccara Rose," she replied.

"Nice name. Well, Toccara, where were you dancing before?"

"Never have, anywhere. I'm a student at LSU, and I need money to get me through school."

"Hard to believe" he shook his head in disbelief," ... you must be a natural. We've got a few students from LSU dancing here, no problem with that. The terms of the job are very simple: You show up and on time when you're on the schedule - if you fail to do that twice -- you're out of here. Usually, you get four nights a week, with at least one of them being on the weekend. If you want an extra shift or two, let

Marquis know and he'll call you if someone else fails to show. It's up to you to compensate Marquis for taking the time to call you." Wharton paused to ensure she understood the terms. When she nodded, he went on, "You get to keep all the tips you make on the stage and all the tips you make for lap dances. You charge $30 for a lap dance in the main club area that lasts one song, or you might be able to upsell it to a hundred bucks for five dances there or three in the VIP area – – the club gets half." At the end of every shift, you pay Marquis $100 in addition to the lap dances. That's the fee for the privilege of working at the *Neon Cactus*."

"I pay you to work, rather than the other way around?"

"You got a problem with that?" Wharton's voice purposely had a hard edge to it, but then he softened his tone as he continued, "Just don't think of it that way, honey, think of it as being an independent contractor. I supply the facility, the stage, and the customers – – you sell what you can, how you can – then, in turn, you give me a share of what you make to cover my expenses. Looking at you, and the way you dance, you should easily clear $200-$400 a night, and that's after all your expenses. On weekends, you could easily double that."

Doing the math in her head, Ashley realized that this could easily net her $40-$60,000 a year for only working four nights a week. All of that money would also be tax-free. This was ideal. "Okay, I'm in."

"Fine, keep in mind that the stage dance is not the entrée, it's just the teaser." Wharton winked at her, and Ashley nodded. "And there are some rules about using the VIP booths to have sex with customers that you need to understand. You do it in the club, the *Neon Cactus* gets a flat $200 for full, $100 for oral. That means if you sell it cheap, we may get more than half. The more mark-up, the more you get. Girls usually try to get $200 or $300 for a feel up with oral and maybe $500 for full. You have to give the cash to Marquis *before* you take the guy into the booth. Got it?"

This part of the business held no interest for her; she did not plan on giving any more than she wanted to on any given night. So, she just nodded in agreement.

"You can do what you want outside the club, but never, ever take it from in here to out there – or you're gone. Got it?" As he said this, he hit the desktop with his fist for emphasis.

She nodded again,

"Also, there is a finder's fee you need to pay -- today. I found you, I get to try you out. You're already dressed for it, so just get over there on the bed and I'll be along after I make a quick call."

Ashley had done some research on Wharton. He had a sixteen-year-old daughter. Even though the age of consent in Louisiana was fourteen, wasn't he decent enough to think about his own daughter? "One thing I think you ought to know--I'm only seventeen."

Wharton was silent for a moment and then nodded. Toccara was too good a talent to let walk out the door and perhaps into the door of his competition – – but now he knew she was young. Not so much underage in a legal sense, but too close to the age of his own kid to simply screw her and not be haunted. The one thing he learned being in this business was that some rules were hard and fast, and others were rewritten every single day.

"I guess you get to pay a different finder's fee. For your first ten lap dances, I get 100%. Deal?"

"Deal." She turned to leave.

"One bit of advice, kid, never do anything you don't want to do -- with anyone you don't want to do it with. Understood?"

She didn't want to insult him by telling him that's what she had just done, so she nodded and thanked him.

Ashley would have to deal with Marquis before she left the club; she was not exactly sure how to get out of that obligation. After dressing she approached the entrance where he was on his phone. He motioned for her to wait then put his phone down.

"Boss tells me you are now part of the *Neon Cactus* line up and that all your fees are paid in full and up-to-date." Looking her over from head to toe again his face betrayed his disappointment, "We're good." He motioned her to the front door. Ashley walked back into the sunlight, climbed into her car and headed back to her place, having secured a job that would help her get through the next three and half years of college.

Overall things did work out until her senior year at LSU, only stretching her boundaries if the financial need arose. Her relationship with Wharton and Marquis became less guarded and friendlier. Then in the summer of 2002, things suddenly changed and her career path took off a new direction. Toccara had taken a Sunday afternoon shift to take care of some unexpected book costs. As she walked from the dressing room to the stage, she looked around the club for prospects who might want a lap dance after her stage performance. There was a smattering of regulars, but she also noticed two unfamiliar men in the section of the club usually occupied by couples. The men were deep in private conversation.

She took the stage and delighted the five guys in the *drooler* chairs, giving them the individual attention that had made her one of *Neon Cactus'* most successful dancers. By the end of the third song she was naked, and each man was aroused by the sight of her fit body and their individual fantasies.

She departed the stage still naked and provided single song lap dances for two clients; a third opted for three songs in a VIP booth. The booths were tight with built-in unpadded benches for the customer to sit and an overhead bar which for the dancer's performance. Toccara had become an expert using the small space and providing the most erotic experience. Once she closed the curtain, her body moved into overdrive. Most of her clients were too overwhelmed to take advantage. Aside from allowing them to touch her anywhere, she felt she could do the same, taking many of them over the edge… or at least to the precipice.

As she stood at the bar, tucking her bills into her purse, she glanced over at the two men still in the deep conversation. She felt she should make an effort just in case there were a few extra dollars to be had. She placed a hand on each man's shoulder and leaned forward.

"Gentlemen, isn't it time you take a break from your serious conversation for something much more entertaining?" She massaged their shoulders and then ran her hand across the sides of their faces before striking a pose. "Something more entertaining, like this?"

The younger of the two did not appear happy with her interruption, as if they had been about to solve the world's problems and create international peace. The older man, who was on the heavy side and easily in his early fifties, smiled at Toccara as he enjoyed the view of her naked body.

The younger man shifted his glance from Toccara to the older gentleman and shook his head in disgust. "You're a silver-haired lecher. We have important things to discuss. I am not sure why you even dragged me into this place."

"Easy, my young friend. We are here because the scenery is just so remarkable." The older man glanced at Toccara again looking directly into her eyes. He reached out and cradled her hand between the two of his while he rose out of his chair.

"My dear, you must forgive my rude friend – – he's far too young to understand the value of beauty and the need to surround one with it to balance one's life. While neither of us cares for a dance right now, perhaps we can be persuaded later." He turned her hand palm up, kissed it and then place a hundred-dollar bill into it. Toccara had never encountered anything like this before; as soon as the bill hit her palm, she closed her hand around it and winked at the older man. She ran her fingers through his thick hair and leaned forward, kissing him on the cheek before departing. Without realizing the significance at the time, that exchange changed the trajectory of her life.

The two men continued their intense discussion which ended when the younger man slammed his hands on the table, spilling both men's drinks. He then stood up, knocking over his chair. Marquis was a mountainous man, but he was also agile, and within a second he stood at the table, surveying the situation. The seated man, who had been splashed by the drinks, held his hands out towards Marquis, advising him that all was all right, and the younger of the two stormed out of the *Neon Cactus* without saying another word.

"Tell me, Marquis, the dancer with the entrancing eyes and beautiful hair who was just on stage – – what is her name?" the man asked, acting as if nothing had occurred.

"Her name is Toccara Rose, she's been here a few years," Marquis said. "She's a co-ed at LSU." He shifted from bouncer role to concierge.

"Ah, excellent. Could you give me a moment to clean up a bit and then ask Toccara Rose to come and join me for a drink?" The man reached out to shake Marquis' hand.

Marquis accepted the handshake and when he withdrew, discovered it was graced by a twenty-dollar bill. "Sure, glad to be of service. Just give me a wave when you're ready for Toccara." Marquis slipped the cash into his pocket and returned to his station.

The man went to the restroom. Using a combination of paper towels and a hand dryer he was able to clean up the drink. He glanced in the mirror and combed his thick silver hair. Even though he was only fifty-two his hair had gone prematurely gray; he felt this gave him an aura of distinction. He returned to the table and noticed Marquis had it cleaned up and a fresh drink delivered. Leaning back in his chair, he waved to the bouncer who made a call on his cell phone. Shortly, Toccara entered from the dressing room, in a floral bikini with a short black mesh wraparound. She came up behind the man and wrapped her arms around his shoulders, leaning forward so she could kiss him on the cheek before sitting down.

"So, I am told that you are a senior at LSU. What are you studying?"

"That's not fair," she said leaning back, "you know something about me, but I know nothing about you – – not even your name."

"Forgive me, my name is Mordechai, most people just call me Morty. I am here doing a bit of recruiting in the local area for my company. Now, tell me about your major." Morty leaned closer to create an air of intimacy.

Toccara also leaned forward. "Earth science with a minor in information technology. Are you looking to hire scientists with computer talent, Morty?"

"Perhaps, why don't you tell me a bit more about your history and how you ended up working here at the *Neon Cactus*."

Toccara told a version of her personal history that left out some parts and emphasized others. She was not used to telling the truth about herself within the walls of the club and was not sure why she felt at ease with Morty. She ended with, "And then I showed up today for work and met a guy named Morty who offered me a job paying a bazillion dollars a year."

Morty laughed at her joke, but it was the words and way that she spoke about her personal history that convinced him she could be the candidate he'd been searching for his entire career.

"I take it that the guy who was here earlier didn't get the job, right Morty?" She was pushing to learn more about this man.

"Well, he wasn't exactly an applicant – – more of a failed intern. But that is neither here nor there. I would like to meet with you again to discuss more concerning a possible opportunity and what kind of salary might come with it. I will tell you that it is considerably less than a bazillion dollars, but it is quite good compensation with some attractive fringe benefits. Would you be willing to meet with me maybe on Tuesday evening – – for dinner?" Morty kept thinking that everything about her seemed to be just as he had imagined.

"Well, I usually don't meet people outside the club."

"I understand. Perhaps, it would be best if you thought it over a bit and then gave a call if you feel like pursuing this further." Morty reached into his jacket and took out a business card from an interior pocket and slid it across the table.

Picking up the card without looking at it, she tucked it into the side of her bikini top and nodded. "Since we're here today, can I interest you in a VIP dance?"

"I'm afraid not… I thoroughly enjoy admiring you but I fear that lap dance might lead to my premature demise." He accentuated this statement by patting his chest with his hand as he spoke. "However, since you were kind enough to take the time to talk to me today, I feel I do owe you some compensation." He handed her what she assumed was a single folded bill. She took it from him and leaned forward kissing him

on the cheek. "Please give this some serious thought, and give me a call
– – anytime," he said before walking out of the club.

Toccara sat back down and looked at the bills in her hand -- five
neatly folded hundred-dollar bills. She withdrew his card from her bikini
top. The only information was his name, Mordechai Shalach, and a
phone number. No title, logo, no address – – in other words damn little
information. Typically, such lean details would've led her to throw the
card away, but something about this intrigued her, so she placed the card
back into her top.

The first few notes of Alannah Myles' *Black Velvet* came over the
speakers as the voice of the Master of Ceremonies announced, "Now –
coming on to center stage for your viewing enjoyment and tantalizing
pleasure – Toccara Rose!"

She tucked the bills into her purse. She would let Ashley deal
with Morty later, right now Toccara had a performance to give.

The next day Ashley called Morty. She wasn't sure what inspired
her to make the call so quickly, but she had a feeling about the man and
what he might have to offer. Somehow, your gut knows an offer that's
going to change your entire life, and you don't want to let it slip through
your fingers.

Since meeting her twenty-four hours ago, Morty was able to read
a full dossier on Ashley's life. He knew everything about her, including
the five dollars she charged last week for a Pumpkin Spice Latte at
Starbucks. So, when she called, he was hard-pressed to suppress his
excitement. He arranged dinner the following evening at Juban's, an
upscale Creole restaurant. As soon as he hung up, he phoned Juban's
and booked a private dining room. Since he was well-known to the staff,
he had no problem getting one of their nine dining rooms at a moment's
notice.

As he watched her walk into the restaurant, Morty realized he
was meeting with someone other than Toccara Rose, the exotic dancer
from the *Neon Cactus*. Although dressed more conservatively, she was
quite lovely while exuding an air of sensuality just under the surface.
Perfect. He began by asking for her actual name. Morty spent their time

over dinner asking for more details about her personal history to see how much of the truth she was willing to divulge. He was pleased she was upfront and honest about most things, only being evasive about family matters.

Her research on Morty had revealed nothing, except for his name being Hebrew in origin. So, she walked into this meeting virtually blind, but somehow, she sensed something positive. Since this was the first time, she had seen him in decent lighting Ashley spent time examining his face for exterior indicators of the man she was meeting. His face was placid and lacked worry or stress lines many men of his age had started to show. *A lot of sincerity and humor there too.* Between Morty's queries, Ashley also glanced around at what seemed like a formal dining room in an upscale house. The décor was clearly meant to create a homey illusion. After dessert and coffee were served, Morty said something softly to the waiter, before he closed the doors, leaving them alone. Ashley was about to speak when Morty held his finger to his lips. He selected a rather morose classical violin piece from his cell phone and nodded his approval as the music began.

"What you cannot hear in between the notes is the white noise that blocks eavesdropping equipment. This will ensure we are the only ones who can hear our conversation." Ashley's demeanor changed and Mordechai knew he would have to get straight to the point. "I assume you were unsuccessful in finding information about me, so I will fill you in. I am the United States recruiter for the Israeli Institute for Intelligence and Special Operations—the Mossad. The Mossad is not unlike your Central Intelligence Agency… it is our job to perform espionage operations that will keep our country and our people safe. Unlike what Hollywood and the newspapers would have you believe, we are not a bunch of rogue assassins running around trying to change the world without governance." Morty noticed this prompted a knowing grin from Ashley. "We are there to prevent bad things from happening by providing information and analysis-- as our motto states: *Where no counsel is, the people fall, but in the multitude of counselors there is safety.* To supply that counsel, many resources are required. Great care is taken with our selection process, and we recruit people to be agents who are only of the finest moral character and with the highest level of intelligence."

"Considering I'm a stripper working in a seedy nightclub, I'm not sure you have the right person. I'm not an Israeli and…"

Morty shook his head. "You are from the United States which has values analogous to Israel's. The nationality is less important than the values you possess and your skills. Likewise, I understand your line of work. You made a decision based on your needs and you never compromised your morals."

"Okay, I guess that's true enough. But I'm not Jewish– – how many Methodists does the Mossad have?"

Morty chuckled at her question. "You will be the first I know of, but that is not a bad thing. You see, what is happening here is something that I have dreamt of for years. I have often felt that placing a female agent into the field could at times be more useful in some situations than the best male agent. Many nations use female agents in roles where their sensuality might be of benefit for gathering information." Sitting back in his chair, he took a sip of water before continuing. "However, Israel has always had issues with doing this because of a cultural chauvinistic protectionist attitude about women. In many ways, the nation has better equality between the sexes than most of the West, but there are still those who see women as flowers that must be protected." The comment caused Ashley to smirk, Morty nodded knowingly and then continued "Also, the few times the Mossad tried to field female agents they found they were placed in morally compromising positions beyond their comfort and beyond what was needed to succeed. In other words, they gave up too much, too quickly…if they had been smarter they could have gotten the same results without the compromise. I have been on a bit of a crusade to change attitudes and bring in women who are strong enough and smart enough to be able to handle these types of situations."

Morty paused, as if listening to the music but in reality allowing Ashley to process the information. "Aside from cultural issues, I received enormous pushback from my superiors that most women are not capable of the mental compartmentalization required to be placed under deep cover. What I have seen convinces me that you have such talents and capabilities. Additionally, your studies in Earth sciences may prove handy for certain undercover assignments, and your cyber assurance training will also be put to the test as we are increasingly a data-driven world. In many ways, you are an answer to my dreams... so, if we wind up with a Methodist in the Mossad, so be it."

Ashley nodded at the thought as it sank in; after a few years of being nothing more than a man's fantasy she was now being appreciated for more than the superficial. "I'm assuming there would be some sort of training program? I still have another year of college before I graduate – – what about that? I know you said the paycheck wouldn't be a bazillion dollars, but how about half a bazillion? Would there be..."

Morty reached out his hand and took hers in his to establish a close rapport. "Let's start with the basics. There will be a training program, in fact, there will be several. We will make adjustments so that you can do them as time allows... by the way, most of them will be in Israel or outside of the United States -- that part is done for your protection since giving you this type of training within the borders of United States would be illegal." Releasing her hand, Morty studied Ashely's face to detect any adverse reaction seeing none he continued. "You can finish your school, in fact, we will immediately become your employer, and you will not have to worry about rent or any other expenses as they will all be covered in addition to what you are paid as an agent." Morty intertwined his fingers while placing his elbows on the table, then leaned forward in his chair towards her. "As for your pay, to start it will be similar to what you are making as a dancer, but the amount will go up when you graduate from all your training and become an active field agent. In fact, you will make more as an agent than if you went into corporate life." Morty ticked off each of her concerns and when he finished, he allowed for a moment of silence before asking, "Have you ever fired a gun?"

"Um no. Never had a need to." Somehow Ashley sensed this might come up, but she was surprised this requirement came up so quickly.

"That is entirely all right-- for some missions a weapon will be optional, but for others, it'll be absolutely required. There are many firing ranges around here where you could go to practice."

"Okay," she said nodding.

"You and I seem to have a certain rapport, which is a good thing because I will be your training mentor through this process until you are an actual field agent. This is something that I want to be successful; you can count on a good deal of support from me. I hope that is acceptable to you."

Ashley considered this for a moment. She liked his almost fatherly manner and the way he seemed to sense when she was anxious-- explaining details that would calm her without asking. "I like that fine, Morty… I think we can work well together."

"Good! So – – a lot of information, in precious little time. Now you have one crucial decision to formalize. If you decide not to do this, I'll walk out then you'll go on about your life doing whatever it is you want to do and working at whatever job you get. I am offering you something different, something where you can make a difference in the security of our nation and Western civilization. I am offering you a career unlike any other -- and all you have to do is say yes."

Ashley cleared her throat. She did have many questions that kept popping up one right after the other. This offer was unique. She finally came up with one question she needed answered. "What about love?"

"The job you will be doing has unique demands and at times unique job requirements. It can be dangerous, it can be exciting, and it can be deadly. But, it is not in empty life, and it is one where you can still experience the joys of love and family. The Mossad will do what it can to help you balance the two; it is ultimately your choices that will determine how well that balance works out. Policemen get married, soldiers, commandos, politicians, etcetera -- all of them have families and more. You will be no different -- I was married at one time, now alas I am a widow, but I do have children and grandchildren I love and enjoy immeasurably."

Morty could see Ashley was not ready to make this serious

commitment. Luckily for her, he was not willing to let go of his ideal candidate and therefore was prepared to make a slight capitulation.

"I will tell you what, I will give you until six PM tomorrow to decide. I realize that is less than twenty-four hours, but it is more time than if I forced you to give me a decision right this moment. If you call me tomorrow, we will proceed. If not -- comme ci comme ça."

"Oh, and I don't speak Israeli... Hebrew?"

"Actually, that was French. It means like this, like that – – what I meant was that things will happen as they will happen. In Israel, Hebrew and Arabic are the official national languages, but most people speak fluent English and before you ask, we have many agents who don't speak Hebrew at all." Morty smiled as he revealed this fact, wanting to end their meeting on a positive note.

Morty dropped several bills on the table to take care of the check and then walked Ashley outside to her car. He decided to walk back to his hotel rather than catching a cab. As Morty strolled, he smiled at the thought that he was actually going to see something he had always wanted. The Mossad would have their own honeypot capability. He never fully understood why it was acceptable to have male agents act as sexual lures to male targets, but it was wrong for women to be employed the same way.

Rather than calling Morty the next day, Ashley texted a single word to him: "Yes." At nine o'clock that evening, Ashley found Morty standing at her front door with a briefcase. He was wearing the same crumpled suit but had on a freshly pressed light blue shirt underneath. After entering, he fanned out the satchel's contents on her coffee table.

"This is your Israeli Diplomatic passport and, passports for Germany, Spain, United Kingdom, and Italy. Plus, we have also obtained an American passport for you. You know, I was quite surprised that you did not have the tourist passport of your own already-- you seem to be the kind of woman who has seen more of the world that her own hometown."

Ashley shrugged but was secretly happy to be seen as worldly. Picking up one of the passports she opened it and was surprised to be greeted by her own face looking back at her. *How did they get that picture of me?*

"These airline tickets are for your first three courses, one of which you will leave for on Monday. The rest are between now and the end of the year. These files contain information on three primary cover personas which you should come to know and thoroughly memorize. You won't need these immediately, but they will be used in the future, so you need to be entirely familiar with them. Finally," he spun the open briefcase around so she could see the contents in the bottom, "this is a new cell phone and a 9mm semiautomatic pistol. I will need you to give me your old cell phone tonight before I leave here… you will not need it or the numbers in it any longer. As far as the pistol goes, you need to immediately begin going to the range several days a week and become an expert with this weapon. It will be your primary tool for defense while you are in the field. As I said before, it is optional for some missions, required for others. Most agents choose to carry one all the time."

With that, Morty turned the briefcase back towards himself and began picking up all the items that he had dropped onto the table. Then he reached into his suit pocket and pulled out an envelope and handed it to her. Ashley opened the envelope and found a cashier's check for $35,000.

"This is money to settle any affairs and accounts that need resolving before you enter this life. You will not be returning to the *Neon Cactus* ever again. You will not seek to speak to anyone from there, and if someone recognizes you, you will deny it. This is a major turning point." Morty took the envelope from Ashley, dropped it into the briefcase and closed the lid. He flipped the locks on the briefcase with a loud click and spun the combination dials. Placing his hands on the top of the briefcase, he smiled. "By the way, until you have a real security safe installed, this briefcase will serve as a vault of sorts as it is rigged with explosives should someone try to open it without the proper combination."

"Morty, you plan on leaving a bomb in my home?"

"Tsh, not a weapon per se but protection for the contents of the briefcase. The combination is the month and day we first met, and as long as you have the combination, there is no problem. The quicker you install a proper safe, the faster you will no longer need this briefcase."

With that, her life changed in so many ways and became a blessing and a curse. She enjoyed her undercover work immensely – – the freedom, responsibility, and the deep cunning it took to do what needed to be done. At the same time, there were things she regretted and times when she questioned orders. Over the past fifteen years, she had gone from being a gatherer of information for the Mossad to being someone who could work the most challenging missions where world peace was in jeopardy.

The sunset had faded, replaced by the artificial lights in the buildings surrounding her. Her wine glass was empty, and it was time to either get another one or turn in for the night. She opted for another glass.

Chapter Nine

West Midlands, England

Abi's vision was blurry, and if the task at hand involved much more than repetitive actions, it would have been negatively affected. He had been at this for almost thirty-six hours without a break, and even though he was near completion, Abi was too numb to feel any great sense of accomplishment. He thought the job would be relatively straightforward, however, the conversion software was not as accurate as he had hoped and he spent lots of time comparing, correcting, and adding to the text. Abi also realized there was a great deal missing from the documents. Eventually, his hard work would pay off.

He learned that four different types of Messages were transmitted by the numbers stations. A Routine Message was the most free-form. The alert sound was anything other than what was reserved for the other three; the communication itself followed no particular pattern or logic. It was meant to be a complete distraction, causing complacency or confusion. Based on this information, he began to question the transmissions. *Was it possible they were simply meant to confuse?*

The next three types of Messages were much more interesting, each having a specific alert tone and function. Warning, Preparation, and Execution Messages were the direction and action parts of the messaging system. Abi decided the Warning and Preparation Message codes could be used to test the validity of the scheme and to ensure it was still in operation. Both of these types of Messages required some sort of action from the person on the receiving end.

A Warning Message identified by the prefix of a bridge of classical piano music was meant to alert an agent that action would be required within seven days. However, a Preparation Message might lead to obvious signs that the Message was received.

Prefixed by the sound of a ringing church bell, the Preparation Message had a greater sense of urgency. This Message was sent 24 hours before expected action, including necessary travel, which could mean the agent would need to react within one to 12 hours. This urgency resulted in greater visibility of reaction, but if the person was skillful, this could be disguised as being commonplace, especially if used in concert with a response to the Warning Message.

For example, after getting a Warning Message, the receiver might tell his friends about a sick and distant relative. When the Preparation Message arrived, he would announce his departure to tend to his relative or attend a funeral. In this way, day-to-day life could serve as a masquerade.

The fourth kind of transmittal was the Execution Message which Abi had just finished translating.

> The Execution Message will set things in motion, and it is signaled by the laughter of a child. The agent will depart from their home station and travel to the individually assigned location. Up until this point, the agent will have no idea of specifics regarding the designated area other than it is within 1 to 12 hours of the home station. The Message will provide the final destination to which the agent is traveling; using the 22-digit code previously discussed.

> Once on site, the agent will enter the identified facility where the L-PAK is located, retrieve and gain access to the device using the code provided in the transmission, perform any required assembly, and then immediately initiate the countdown on the instrument. Once countdown has begun, the agent will have two hours to depart the location before weapon ignition. An exfiltration kit is included in the L-PAK to facilitate the agent's escape.

There has been no effort made to synchronize the launch of all weapons, as it is not required for mission success. Instead, due to the sequencing of events, all weapons will be launched within a 5-10 hour window which is adequate to provide the maximum combined impact of multiple devices.

Details of the weapon are as follows…

Abi faced another dead end as *nothing* followed. He was finding this increasingly frustrating. Still, he was steadily gaining an understanding of how the entire sequence worked and enough knowledge to postulate triggering a launch himself. *Wouldn't that be something to use the weapons of one Western Satan against another? Would anyone even realize I am the puppet master who made such a play? Somehow, I'll need to make sure they are aware, and why they're being held to task for what they've done to the world and to me.*

Working on the last page of the document, Abi realized his plan may not be as quickly put in motion as he had hoped. This section discussed validation codes which must exist within the Execution Message.

The methodology for the Execution Message transmission is to provide various numerical data that may be necessary, including the exact volume of *Brandt's Compleat Collection* for decoding, followed by encoded text along with any supplemental data, and finally, a Validation Code which would be preceded by a series of nonsense words. Each transmission must be accurately recorded verbatim as it will only be played once and making a recording is unsafe and would leave behind evidence. It is also possible, after receiving and decoding a lengthy transmission that an incorrect validation code will result from an invalid Message.

The Validation Code is a four-digit number at the end of the Execution Message which is preceded by a random sound effect. It is decoded using the Perpetual Table (based on a month and year) with a cross-check using the same volume within *Brandt's Compleat Collection of Great World Literature* identified in the prefix of the Execution Message. Decoy Validation codes are easily identifiable – if the Validation code provided is only three digits, or greater than four digits, the Message can be ignored.

The Validation code has two indicators, the first being the month the Message is sent. For example, if the agent were given the code 8639 in April 2004, the Perpetual Table would provide him with the numbers 147, 27, and two. Next, the agent would retrieve the book identified in the Message prefix, Milton's *Paradise Lost*, and turn to page 147, find line 27, and then search across to word number two. All of this effort would yield the word "downy," which begins with the letter d, the fourth letter of the alphabet – the same number as the month of April. Therefore, one of two indicators is proven to be valid. If the letter's number had been higher than 12, you would have divided by three until it was less than 12; for example, T is the 20th letter, divided by three is 6.66 which you round to seven or the correct validation code for July.

The second indicator of the validity of the Execution Message is based on the geographical reference given at the beginning of the Message. If the coordinates provided within the 22-digit code are 0307232885894012, this decodes to identify 2804

Opryland Drive in Nashville, Tennessee; the Grand Old Opry. The agent would take the numbers for the address and add them together to get a total of 14. They then divide that by three to achieve the rounded number five, or the same number of letters in the word that was found during the first indicator check. Since both signs were correct, the Execution Message is valid.

Brandt's Compleat Collection would be easy enough to find and even if it were out of print, Abi would somehow be able to locate a copy of the collection. The Perpetual Table was another animal entirely. He had yet to come across anything called a Perpetual Table or any document in German or Russian that resembled any sort of table. Without this, Abi was not going to be able to send an Execution Message, at least one that wouldn't be invalid. This presented a rather large conundrum – one his tired mind was not prepared to deal with at this point.

Abi stood and stretched his body before finishing up the project that had occupied him for nearly two full days. He gathered up the last of the original documents and slipped them into the appropriate binder. He locked both binders in his radio room, checking the padlock twice before returning to his kitchen table. There he gathered up the remaining documents, segregating the landscape and portrait sections. Once sorted, he stored this organized pile on a shelf in his kitchen cabinet. Next, he was careful to delete all documents from the computer. Finally, he retrieved the computer he had set on the floor two days before. The screen displayed a result window that said *Algorithm Complete* with an *OK* button. The text below it read:

That it never stands between you if I don't possibly see those things which are shown. 569. Hibbert down don't, display now unusual for things which are not and even though hopeful understanding.

Yes. Never can be wound sure to never possible. Why not be told if not truly way shift one for. Complete.

Gibberish. All that effort and nothing but gibberish but now Abi was on a different path, one that actually led to something. Sure, he didn't have all the parts yet but he was getting closer and soon he would be able to do something satisfying that mattered in the bigger scheme of things.

Abi deleted the processed text and then the original sound file that the program had attempted to decrypt. After he shut down the computer and stretched again, he arose and wearily walked off to his bedroom to sleep for the next fourteen hours, uninterrupted by man, beast, or nocturnal visions.

Atlanta, Georgia

Dieter made contact with those who had assisted him in conducting the meeting with Evan, thanking them and providing them with their recompense. He then left the Hartsfield–Jackson Airport and proceeded directly to downtown Atlanta, returning to his suite at the Hilton. After the complete failure of communism and socialism in Europe, he found that he enjoyed the comforts that even the average person enjoyed under capitalism. Dieter opened the curtains upon entering his room that revealed an excellent view of the Olympic Park. *Interesting coincidence … all of this started near an Olympic Park, and now I am near another, thousands of miles away.*

Dieter sat at the desk and immediately began making phone calls to arrange Evan and Dmitry's meeting – or Julian as he was now known. At the beginning of his career, Dieter had been an independent and skilled field agent with the Stasi, but after rising through the ranks, he'd gained resources that took care of most simple contacts for him. Now that he was without Stasi resources, he found himself calling upon his field skills again. A well-placed call to the corporate offices of the Ranchers & Farmers Bank convinced them that *Der Spiegel* magazine was interested in publishing an article regarding American banks and how they serviced the needs of agriculture.

His call was transferred to Brian Eddy, one of the firm's vice presidents, and within a few minutes, Dieter convinced him that an interview was a positive thing for the bank. Pressing his powers of persuasion further, Dieter guided Brian to select a branch located in northern Oklahoma as a prime example of bankers and farmers working together. The state line dividing the regions serviced by the bank provided an added line of interest. This choice, of course, would lead to the necessity of interviewing the regional manager.

"An American will conduct the interview – we often try to use in-country personnel to make things as smooth as possible," Dieter said matter-of-factly.

"Good, good. I'm sure that'll also help with any language issues. I'm fairly sure few people speak fluent German in Alva, Oklahoma," said the bank vice president, faking a chuckle.

"Indeed. So, I will need to send my reporter to – what was the name of the town again?" In truth, there was probably any number of veterans who spoke fluent German in that area.

"Alva. I'll email you all the details shortly, after we get off the phone, including the person who will act as a liaison for the bank, if that's okay with you."

"That would be wonderful; I will send you the information about our reporter as well, once the details are completely worked out." *No need to give them too much information to play with upfront.*

"Excellent, thank you very much for your interest in our institution. *Auf wiedersehen.*"

It was Dieter's turn to fake a chuckle at the banker's attempt to speak at least some German. "Ah yes, indeed – goodbye and *grüss gott*," Dieter said, adding the blessing used by many Bavarians for positive karma.

True to his word, Brian forwarded information on the bank in Alva within the hour. As expected, the bank selected Julian Shepherd to serve as the reporter's liaison. Before Dieter received this information via email, he had already placed a call to his private office staffing service.

His instructions were simple, contact the bank and set up an interview between Evan and the regional manager. Then, once the meeting was set, the staff arranged for Evan's flight from Detroit to Oklahoma City along with the necessary rental car.

Dieter was napping on the couch when a call came a few hours later, confirming the arrangements had been made. Dieter forwarded the email confirmation to Evan and the initial meeting was set up for the following week – not as quick as he had hoped, but better than it could have been.

It had been a fruitful day. His meeting had gone smoother than expected with Evan, and now things were set for the next stage of the operation. Soon, it would be over, and the world again would be safe, at least for a little while. In the back of his mind, he still worried about Fyodor and not being able to get a hold of him. He wished he could share the good news with his friend

He straightened his clothes and grabbed his phone; he owed himself a bit of a respite, and the Georgia Aquarium was an easy walk from the hotel. Dieter's fascination with fish had begun while he was serving with the Stasi, as a relaxation technique when nothing else would calm his nerves. He could stare into the abyss of the fish tank in his office for hours, watching how each of the fish moved and interacted. This allowed him to leave behind his concerns for the world on land. He'd never had an aquarium at home but now that he found himself back in the game, he found himself longing for the solace it offered.

Alva, Oklahoma

"Brian, are you sure I'm the right choice for this?" Julian was trying desperately to get out of being assigned host for the *Der Spiegel* reporter. "You know I only speak Sooner."

"Language doesn't matter – the reporter is American, and even though he's from Michigan, I'm sure the two of you will find enough

188

commonalities in language to be able to converse." Brian's attempted joke fell flat, so he tried to stress the importance of the task. "The publicity is going to be good for the bank. Even though I can't think of a single one of our farmers who might read *Der Spiegel,* our Board of Directors and investors might find favorable international attention a good thing." Brian allowed Julian to make his objections, even though it was fruitless.

Julian remained silent, he realized there were two options at this point; he could accept the assignment or have it foisted on him by his boss. Rather than being seen as contrary he swallowed hard and said, "Fine, I'll do my best to make us look good."

"I appreciate it."

"But if there is an international incident because I don't understand Michigander correctly, I'll lay the blame squarely on you." Julian wanted to change the tenor of the conversation before it ended to maintain his relationship with Brian.

"Understood, maybe you should listen to some Motown records before he gets there. I'll provide their contact with your information so they can set up the appointment directly with you and your folks." Brian's mind had already left the conversation, and he was pondering whether or not he could fit a quick nine holes in for the end of the day.

"Got it, I'll update you as this moves along."

Both men hung up almost simultaneously, without the necessity of formal farewells. Julian swiveled his chair until he was facing the window that looked out onto the park. He realized increased exposure like this was bound to happen as he moved up the corporate ladder, even though Julian had done what he could to avoid publicity. This was a bit more of a concern because it was international as opposed to local, but he thought he might be able to control this a bit better by having the writer refer to him as a bank spokesperson in the article rather than using his name. Also, the article was about the bank and how it functioned and not him personally, so that seem to be a bit less risky. *Doesn't matter at this point.* He spun his chair back to the desk and turned his attention to his paperwork.

A little bit later in the day, when he talked to Camille, he mentioned the appointment, and she made a big deal of it. "We should invite him to the house, Jules, and show him some local hospitality while he's here."

"Fine, fine. Don't you think you're making a big deal out of nothing? I don't even know how long he's going to be here at this point."

"You know as well as I do that if he's coming all the way out here, he will at least be spending one night in town before he leaves. This could be good for you; this could be a step up to the next level." Camille was always looking for ways to support her husband.

Julian realized the argument was lost, and rather than risking her being upset with him for several days, he gave in now rather than allowing it to linger. "Okay, baby, you win. Once I get the information on the visit, I'll add dinner at our house to the itinerary. Deal?"

"Deal. Any possibility you can break loose for an hour or so?"

"I suppose so, what's up?"

"I had to reposition your recliner, and I want to make sure it works in its new place. I figured you could come home and sit in it while I relive a few memories from the summers I spent on my grandparents' ranch … want to help me out by playing Bronco?"

"Mmm, on my way – cowgirl up." He made quick excuses to his staff and drove home slightly over the town speed limit. Julian returned to the bank an hour or so later with the knowledge that the chair's new position in no way affected the riding skills of his beautiful lady.

Western Michigan

The morning after the meeting with Dieter in Atlanta, Evan reviewed his travel arrangements and confirmed with Dieter that all was fine. He preferred his Android over the encrypted phone Dieter had provided, but he was trained to object only to those things he could change and otherwise make the most of it.

Zax lay on the couch watching Evan play with the new phone. Every time Evan moved for a coffee refill or to retrieve something from another room, Zax jumped off the sofa and followed. After being deserted the day before, the dog wanted to make sure wherever Evan was going, he got to go too.

The report from Houstynne the night before had been positive, other than repeated requests from Ellie to take Zax home and some begging for her own puppy. By the time Evan arrived, Ellie and Zax had calmed down, and they were snuggled up on the floor snoozing together.

"You didn't have to stay until I got back," Evan said to Houstynne.

"No worries, Ellie was having fun playing, and we decided he could use company until you got back." Houstynne stretched and yawned.

"Well, I appreciate it. I'm so glad you were around."

"No worries, Wordsmith, just remember…" Houstynne continued with Marlon Brando's *Godfather* voice, "someday, and that day may never come, I will call upon you to do a service for me."

Evan was tired, but not too tired to laugh. "I understand, Don Houstynne, I stand by to serve—with all respect."

Houstynne leaned over and scooped Ellie into her arms. "Be glad you didn't have to carry me out to the car," she said.

Evan opened the door to Houstynne's car so she could put Ellie into her car seat. Houstynne waved from behind the steering wheel.

"Thanks again, Artiste." He watched until her car pulled out of sight, and then went back inside.

Zax lifted his head and looked at him for a moment before lowering it again and going back to sleep.

"Some watchdog," Evan said and turned off the lights and headed to bed.

The next morning, Evan thought over everything. Not only his lengthy conversation with Dieter but meeting Nikki and how pleasurable that had been. Hopefully next week in Oklahoma he could convince Julian Shepherd to help disarm the weapons that had entered the US nearly 30 years ago. He would much rather contemplate Nikki and where their relationship might go, but the Crimson Firebird Initiative had to be derailed as quickly as possible to prevent any devastating accidents. Evan's sense of calm had returned. There were many things yet to be answered, but he could now focus on the end result rather than infinite possibilities. Also, Nikki provided a pleasurable mental diversion that kept him from considering things he could not control. In the chaos, Evan found peace.

Unlike Superman, he did not have to be on duty 24/7 and since the next thing requiring his attention was not until next week, there were a few days to spend some time with Nikki. Maybe. With that decision made, he got up from the table and went back to his bedroom to comb through the mess that covered his dresser. Evan was by nature immaculate but he had gotten out of the habit of sorting through the things from his pockets like change, business cards, receipts, and anything else he happened to collect. He grabbed his phone after locating her number scrawled on the napkin and entered her contact information into his cell—a sign of hope.

Zax settled next to Evan's chair for the occasional scratch behind his ears. Evan was not usually indecisive and knew being indecisive could lead to disaster, but there were times when he had to consider more than just what was in front of him, like now. In times like these, the best he could do was to allow himself to relax and contemplate. Petting Zax contributed to that by providing a distraction he could fiddle with as he allowed his mind to freely wander. Here he sat with the phone in one hand and Zax's soft fur in the other. Nikki was not a simple black and white issue, and when feelings were involved, he would overthink a situation. At this point, he had no desire to be emotionally involved. But he couldn't find anything negative about his encounter with Nikki to cause him to avoid her. Even his own Satori remained silent.

Evan had learned about Satori from one of the soldiers he was embedded within Afghanistan. The strict definition of Satori in Buddhism refers to a sudden feeling of enlightenment about one's own true self. Private First-Class Darnell had learned about this philosophy while being homeschooled and spent an evening on patrol explaining a bastardized version to the other soldiers in the platoon.

"A state of Satori should be seen as a way of becoming truly aware of everything around you and how it could possibly affect you both positively and negatively. With some training, you could even use your own Satori like an early warning system."

They were in a war zone and any constructive mindset was readily accepted. Since returning home, Evan could still get in touch with the Satori deep within, but mostly he just paid closer attention to gut feelings and instincts.

"Hello?"

The sound of a female voice interrupted his train of thought. He had unconsciously pushed the connect button and called Nikki. He took a quick gulp of air and put the phone next to his ear. "Hi, this is Evan. We met yesterday at the candle bar in Ann Arbor?"

Nikki knew who was calling as only one person had this number. She felt pleased not only because the contact she had made seemed to be bearing fruit, but also because she liked him. "Of course, I remember you. Do you think I just run around kissing every guy I meet in a bar?"

"Now, now. I didn't say that at all. But it is nice to know my kiss was that memorable. I thought we might be able to get together later this evening, possibly for dinner?"

"Um, tonight?" She allowed the pause to linger as she rolled from her side to her back and then lifted the sheet covering her and allowing it to drift down on her naked body. "Actually, tonight doesn't look real good."

"Uh," Evan was not sure what to do with that information. It wasn't exactly a refusal.

"Wait ... let me see if I can rearrange a few things to free up my evening."

"Okay, while you're rearranging things be sure to leave yourself enough time to pick up your Naughty Catholic Schoolgirl outfit from the cleaners."

Nikki grinned. *Not too blatant, with just the right amount of horny.*

"Not sure that will work out for tonight though as my stilettos are with the shoe cobbler getting some new heels put on them." She allowed her bedroom voice to seep into the conversation; after all, it only seemed appropriate. She was lying nude on her bed covered only by a sheet, caressing her tummy with her free hand.

"Well, then I will let that slide this time. Give me a call back if you're able to arrange something."

"Mmm. Definitely." Nikki disconnected, dropped the phone on the bed and stretched. She would call him back in an hour or so and confirm dinner; he was the only thing on her schedule until this mission was complete. For now, Nikki could be lazy and take her time getting up and into the shower. Her mind was flowing and she felt the need to linger in bed just a little bit longer. With that decision, she closed her eyes and allowed her mind and hands to wander.

After ensuring that the call had been disconnected, Evan found himself mouthing the word "damn" and even though he was silent, Zax lifted his head before yawning and going back to sleep.

Melrose, Scotland

After Sergei's walk, he fixed himself a small meal, washed the dishes and set about gathering various tools. He flipped the corner of the worn green carpet in the hallway to reveal a bare wood floor. He ran a blade along the crevice between two pieces of wood until he removed a combination of caulk-like dirt and dust. Sergei pried up four boards and shone his flashlight underneath, illuminating the earth a half-meter or so beneath his cottage. He dug down into the rocky soil with a small garden trowel until he hit a flat aluminum plate.

Sergei set the light beside the hole and took a prone position to reach into the hole at a better angle. Using his fingers, he worked around the edges of the plate until he was able to pry it up. Shining the flashlight into the hole, he could see a combination dial and then entered the correct sequence of numbers for the lock to release with a soft click. He turned the metal handle and pulled up, opening the door to the buried safe.

The safe was large enough to hold many items, but due to his position, it was hard to see them all. Among the things readily visible was a cell phone, a block of various international currency sealed in plastic wrap, a variety of passports, a pistol, several loaded magazines, and the object of tonight's search—an encrypted cellular phone. He grabbed the phone, powered it on, and waited until he acquired a signal.

Well, now we are ready to begin. He scrolled through the phone's contacts, selected a group entry and texted the group the same four digits that had opened the safe—6592. Since there was no need to wait for a response, Sergei turned the phone off and returned it to the safe. After smoothing the soil over the safe, he replaced the boards, returned the crud back into place between the crevices and flipped the carpet back.

Sergei turned on his stereo which was already cued to the music he loved – classical Spanish guitar. As the music filled the cottage, he stared out of the window with the satisfaction that after so many years the final act of his orchestrated revenge had begun. Except for a few details he needed to provide to Abi when he returned to West Midlands, everything else was ready and waiting to destroy the villain in his life. Sergei was soon asleep and snoring as the events began to unfold. This was the most relaxed he had felt in years.

Chapter Ten

Matehuala, Mexico

Nastia loved her current assignment at the Vodyanoy Transmission Station. Unlike other KGB assignments, this one supplied her with time to enjoy a rich, full life out of uniform in a great setting. This was different; she was a flyspeck in the overall population which allowed her to move around almost unnoticed.

Nastia made a few friends and enjoyed a few intimate liaisons during her years in Mexico, but mostly she appreciated her privacy and space. She had grown up in a crowded orphanage. It was only due to her cleverness and intelligence that she was able to find a better path. She never took for granted the independence she had gained.

With Yury on duty this morning, she ran her errands and spent the heat of the afternoon to relax at the *Cinemas las Américas 1 y 2*. When she first heard about the movie theater, she assumed only American movies were played, forgetting but that North America included Canada and Mexico. Over time, her Spanish improved so it no longer mattered if the film was in English. She appreciated Latin cinema and its powerfully moving plot lines. Today she was primarily interested in the well air-conditioned theater.

She sipped her ice-cold bottle of Pacifico which tasted great with her popcorn while totally immersed in the movie. Her focus was broken by the electronic tones of a cell phone. Nastia glanced around to shoot someone an evil glare until she realized the sound was her own beeper, which caused a sense of panic. She managed to fumble in the darkness until she found the device and saw the numbers 6592 quickly fade, eradicating any record. The numbers were only to transmit a Message at some point in the future. The actions she was required to make following the transmission were immediate and uncompromising.

Nastia rushed to the Vodyanoy Transmission Station and parked next to Yury's motorcycle. She entered the proper sequence of buttons and switches to open the biometric panel. The machine completed the retina and fingerprint scan before the concrete floor opened, revealing the stairway down into the numbers station. She descended the staircase, pausing to ensure the door automatically closed. Yury sat behind a console in his camouflage uniform. He was trying to tune their transmitters to a particular frequency.

"Have you accessed the one-time pads from the safe?" she asked.

"Not yet, Commander Zamurovich, I am trying to find the proper channel in case the broadcast occurs. I don't want us to miss it." Yury didn't bother to turn around.

Being formerly addressed as commander was a surprise though she was acutely aware that she outranked him. Perhaps, with the change in alert status, Yury returned to his formal self. Shaking her head to focus her thoughts, Nastia proceeded to the locked door which safeguarded their high-level communication equipment, as well as two large four-drawer safes. After submitting to the retina scan, she opened the door. She was quite sure neither of them had ever opened the safes. Pulling the chair along with her, Nastia approached the safe marked number one. Even though the Cyrillic was still used in Russia, it was written in Arabic numerals. If the date was an even number, Nastia would've gone to the safe marked with the number two. She spun the dial and opened the top drawer to find two rows of one-time sheets used for the decryption of transmittals. Nastia withdrew the one-time sheet numbered 6592 and closed the safe's drawer.

Back in the control room, she handed the sheet to Yury and told him she was going to change into her uniform. They were required to wear their military uniforms once the readiness status of the station had been upgraded. Once alerted, the pair were no longer involved in espionage but returned to being military assets. At some point in history, an unnamed KGB colonel had decided that in order to prevent his soldiers from being shot as spies they would wear uniforms. That way, if captured they would be identified as combatants, required to be treated in accordance with the Geneva Convention.

Aside from the uniforms, several other procedural changes were enacted as soon as they received the numeric SMS. The station was put on full alert and utilized four separate radio frequencies available for any incoming broadcasts 24/7. They were expected to decrypt the incoming transmittal using the one-time pad and act upon the directions immediately. All station personnel carried a loaded sidearm at all times for a protection of their mission from anyone that attempted to thwart their efforts — this included both external and internal threats. The one constant was the sending of the Routine Message. Unless they received some countering order, the Routine Message was to continue being sent on a schedule.

Nastia changed in the secure communications room, opened the second drawer of safe one and withdrew two Stechkin APS pistols along with six magazines, each containing nine rounds. She loaded one of the pistols, slid it into her holster and placed two of the magazines into the pouches of her belt. Picking up the remaining Stechkin and magazines, she laid them on the table in front of Yury. He diverted his attention from tuning the radios just long enough to slide a magazine into his pistol and put it into his holster. For the moment, he left the ammo on the table.

"Have you been following the news, Major Trechnikov?" Nastia asked while assuming the same military formality that Yury had adopted. "To be honest, I have not, but I am unaware of anything going on that would've caused us to go into a state of full alert."

"It is probably nothing, Comrade Commander, just a test of some sort." Yury was still concentrating on tuning the proper frequencies on the old radio.

Since Yury was not facing her, he could not see Nastia roll her eyes. One of the first things explained by the duo they had replaced, was that the station never rehearsed or tested anything. Everything done by the station was real-world, real-time. A *test* was just not an acceptable answer. The numbers station could go on full alert and then stand down later, but even that was not a real possibility. Apparently, Nastia was the only one concerned about what was coming next and why.

Yury sat back in his chair, finally satisfied. He spun around and raising his hands said, "Well, we are ready."

After an hour of listening to static on the radio, they were both ready for something different.

"When we first got here, Comrade Major, you said it might be possible to use the existing antennas to access TV signals; did you ever do anything about that?" Nastia asked.

"Actually, I did one better; I installed a line from the antenna that would allow our regular cell phones to work. That means we could use a cellular phone as a hotspot and then set up the laptop so we could watch Netflix or stream video from one of the movie channels."

"Since it appears that we may be here a while, I think you ought to do just that." She handed her cell phone to Yury. "Here, mine has a full battery at the moment. We can rotate back and forth."

Within the hour, he adapted the wire to the external antenna and they binge-watched *Black Mirror* while four channels of static roared in the background.

Lansing, Michigan

As Evan pulled into the parking lot near Capital Prime Steak and Seafood, he breathed deeply to calm himself. Nikki had suggested meeting there since it was midway between them. He looked forward to seeing her again to verify everything he remembered about her. *Could a woman really have a smile that dazzling and eyes that alluring? Great, now I sound like a frigging Hallmark card.*

As he walked toward the restaurant, he saw her approaching from down the street. The setting sun illuminated the silhouette of her body through her light-colored dress and set her hair on fire. Evan's throat tightened. "I gave myself a little extra time to get here … I don't like to run late," he began speaking when they were six feet apart.

"Me too. In the end, it all worked out perfectly." She gave him a hug and then a kiss on the cheek.

Evan breathed in her spicy fragrance which he did not recognize and let it permeate his senses. When the hug regrettably ended, her eyes opened and their beauty left him speechless. She looped her arm through his and entered the restaurant where they were guided to a private table for two. Evan felt a sense of ease even though the place was more upscale than he would have chosen. Nikki was in her element and exuded confidence. Evan accepted the sommelier's recommendation to complement their filet mignon.

The conversation during dinner was light and more thoughtful than their prior discussion in the bar. They chatted about their personal histories, accented by a few entertaining stories. Occasionally, whenever Nikki said something humorous or laughed, she reached out and placed her hand on Evan's arm. Her touch was light, warm and thoroughly enjoyable.

As he watched her talking, he found himself noticing the sensuality of her lips, the way they moved as she formed words, and how they gave him an occasional glimpse of her tongue as well. More than once as he was watching her mouth, he looked up and found that her eyes were upon him. *Did she notice I was staring?* He found himself captivated and wondered, beyond the physical, what might lie in her heart.

Nikki's choice of a restaurant was neither close to his place or hers and allowed things to cool between them while keeping his interest hot. She had a way of heating up his sexual imagination which made him painfully aware their geographic situation prevented any of it from being immediately possible. Because neither had a private space close by, they were forced to limit themselves to the environment they were in, which allowed her to say *no* without even speaking the word.

The discovery dance was something Nikki enjoyed. Having thoroughly studied Evan's bio as well as his psychological profile, she had come to learn a great deal and could craft the conversation accordingly. She mentioned her love for dogs, motorcycles, creativity, and the loss of a parent so Evan would open up about his experiences. All evening, Nikki caressed Evan's soul. By the time the night was over, he would be enamored. What she hadn't counted on was a mutual attraction.

Nikki knew the way a man perceived his breakup—particularly divorce—as a failure, which created life-long negative feelings for his ex-spouse or partner. She listened as Evan opened up from his heart about his ex-wife and his sons. Rather than laying blame, he admitted their relationship had just failed as they each wanted different things. Refreshing. The meal came to an end with cups of dark roasted coffee and a pair of shortbread cookies.

"Have you ever tried these?" Evan recognized the imprint on the baked goods.

She shook her head and pulled his hand with the cookie toward her mouth. Evan's attention was on her lips as she parted them and took the cookie into her mouth. He went slack-jawed.

She sucked his index finger, twirling her tongue a few times before allowing it to slide out. "Had to get all the crumbs."

If she were to place her hands in the right spot, Nikki would feel his body physically responding. "I … yeah," was all that Evan could respond at first. "Well, you obviously like the cookies if you're going after the crumbs. Would you care for another?"

"That sounds like fun, are you going to feed me that one too?" She was no longer worried about being too forward. He liked her attitude and she was reeling him in.

"I would say that depends; if I feed you my cookies, will you be the plate?"

"Mmm, as long as you lick it completely clean," she said raising the stakes.

The waiter delivered the check and broke the tension. To Evan's surprise, Nikki reached out and took the bill.

"I suggested the restaurant, so it's my treat. Next time you choose and pick up the tab."

"Deal, or maybe I'll cook." Evan wanted to make sure the next time they'd have the privacy to explore their shared attraction.

"Ooh, that would be nice. I would even get to meet Zax and see what a world-famous author's house looks like."

"Well, I don't know about that. What you'd see is a minor-league author's house and get to pet his dog."

"Petting your dog is in line with what I'd like to do, so maybe," she smiled and nodded to the waiter.

"That's a definite possibility." Evan reclined in his chair.

Nikki leaned forward and placed her hand on the inside of his knee, sliding up to his inner thigh where her fingertips caressed him before withdrawing. "Could be a fun evening." *Yes, hun, exploring you could be a lot of fun.*

The sun had set but the city lights prevented any stars from being visible. Evan pressed his body to Nikki's when they reached her car before kissing her deeply. Her hands held him close and caressed his face. Nikki could feel his hardness. It was probably a good thing he could not feel how wet she was or their first time would have ended up in the backseat of her car. After several long kisses, she broke away as he reached around to open the car door.

"I cook pretty good Italian by the way."

"Sounds good. Maybe I'll plan on spending the night."

This left him speechless as Nikki drove off.

Morty withdrew the cell phone from his pocket and allowed his retina to be scanned. He had a single SMS from his active agent in the United States.

>2nd Encounter. Very Pos. Rapport est. Ready

Morty smiled. Ashley was always ready for anything but this one was different. She would only need to insert herself if things went sideways. Tonight, things may have begun to move sideways. A Full Alert order had gone out to a single numbers station located in North America. Whether this related to the Crimson Firebird was still unknown. However, since only one station was contacted, it was likely Sergei had surfaced to execute the operation. For now, there was no need to upset Morty's asset, at least not until he had more precise information. He typed in a three-letter response:

<ACK

Morty's cheeks collapsed as he sucked on the cigar between his teeth, then he blew out a huge puff of smoke, staring out across the horizon. German intelligence had been a valuable asset to the Mossad since Israel's founding, due to collective national guilt over the Holocaust. The Stasi had supplied the bit of information he possessed. Technically a former Stasi agent, Dieter had been the one to inform him about the chilling Crimson Phoenix Initiative. Dieter's request was an easy one: to send a single asset into action for a limited scope of duties.

Ashley Grey was Evan's guardian angel. She was going to protect him from any difficulties. Morty smiled. *The man has no concept of the superior capabilities of this lovely woman he randomly met in a bar. She is one of the best operators I ever recruited and has a captivating smile too.*

Morty dropped his cigar on the ground, grinding it into unrecognizable bits with his heel for the wind to carry away.

West Midlands, England

Qa'id stood in his small apartment with his cell phone pressed against his ear, trying to hear the voice through the static of thousands of miles. His superiors had understood the importance of the numbers stations;

now the additional information was too vague to fully understand what the broadcasts were designed to do. It was merely background instruction not useful intelligence. Qa'id pressed hard to convince them of the value of what had been uncovered so they would be aware when things would be triggered and the progress through the levels of the Messages.

After some back-and-forth discussion, it was decided that Abi would be allowed to proceed with the course of the investigation. Qa'id was pleased with that permission, and also at not having to reveal that an L-PAK was tied to some sort of weapon system. He was told to come up with a codename for the project.

Qa'id thought before speaking. "Since this information came to us seemingly through divine intervention, and because it so heavily involves the use of numbers in mathematics, we should call this operation *Allah's Numbers.*"

Qa'id listened to the silence on the other end of the phone. He had spent years connecting random bits of information into something that matched the religious dogma of the organization. This talent had served him well and he expected nothing less this time. By invoking the name of *Allah* in the title of the operation, which could be considered blasphemous by some, there would be an automatic emotional connection to the deity.

"Agreed," said the voice. "See if Abdul can gather more information from his source regarding these transmissions. Perhaps he can find a way to speak to the numbers station and get them to act on our behalf." The voice wished him well and terminated the call.

This was the second time within a week Qa'id had called those above him. The first time was to explain Abi's discovery of numbers stations and how he was monitoring unnamed espionage assets. This time was a bit more ominous, as the documents revealed an actual program that was using numbers stations as a method of communicating with field agents who appeared to be tied to something sinister, involving L-PAKs. At this point, no one had any idea what an L-PAK was or why it may be substantial.

Qa'id connected many random ideas concerning the type of weapon and what control he could gain. The implications were wide-ranging with endless possibilities. He left a voicemail asking Abi to call him as soon as possible.

Staring off into the distance, he imagined himself elevated in position within the Arab world after dealing a huge blow to the West. But unlike the others before him, he would not sacrifice his own life in the process. Yes, he would live to enjoy the adulation and rewards of being a hero rather than being a quickly forgotten martyr.

Adrian's departure from Melrose was more hectic than in the past, but a quick explanation that he was needed back in Gothenburg to handle a few urgent issues placated anyone who may have been interested in tracking his movements. Freya, of course, made a fuss about him leaving. He could not tell how much of that was emotion versus concern over the loss of income, but he welcomed her sentiment. After their last rendezvous, he handed her a sealed envelope containing bills of various denominations that totaled €800. It was not unusual for him to give her a larger payment on his departure, but he had never given her this much. Perhaps it was out of sentiment because he knew this time he might not return.

His route to West Midlands was a reversal of his journey to Melrose. However, this time he was turning back into Areef. Sergei disliked this identity since he had to adapt to cultural norms that differed from his typical behavior. *Soon, this will no longer be necessary, and I can get rid of this damned itchy beard.* He secured the door of his storage garage before leaving for the train station.

Part of the identity of Areef was that he neither owned nor used a cellular phone to allow for better mobility and control over situations. Abi would certainly be trying to get hold of him but Areef controlled when he'd get the papers and Abi would become so anxious that he'd forget to question the source of the material.

Once back at his apartment, Areef ate a late meal while organizing a box of documents and a stack of random material written in Cyrillic. These documents explained how to contact the numbers stations after being put on Full Alert; he also included documentation regarding *Chimera K629*'s purpose and fatality estimates. He omitted any direct reference to the Crimson Firebird Initiative to prevent investigators from discovering the origins of the program. Once he had the documents and extraneous pages in order, he placed them in an old leather satchel and removed the top drawer from his bedroom dresser. Turning the drawer over, he dumped the contents onto his bed and withdrew his penknife to cut into the rear wooden panel of the drawer, revealing a small compartment. Using the penknife, he pried a tightly rolled sheet of paper from it that he had hidden decades ago. He began to unroll the item he'd retrieved as he walked back to the kitchen table. Once spread out he could read the random letters and numbers on it. In the upper right-hand corner was 6592. He placed it between two random sheets of paper inside his satchel, locking its keyless latch. *The fact that the bag is locked will make this seem more authentic to Abi, and it will challenge him as he will need to pick the lock to gain access.*

The following morning, he walked to his shop early so that he had sufficient time to place the satchel among a pile of books on his consignment shelf in the back of the store. Oasis Mart usually opened every day of the week at nine o'clock in the morning except Fridays when it was closed. Areef flipped the switch on the neon light that said *Open*, even though it was a little earlier than normal.

As expected, Abi was the first customer who hurried through the door. *"As-Salaam-Alaikum!"*

"Wa-Alaikum-Salaam," Areef responded with equal gusto, forgoing the longer version of the greeting so they could get right down to business.

"The box you gave me before you left … did you get any more from the same source perhaps?" Abi paused for a moment and then remembered his manners. "I hope you had an enjoyable time away."

"Yes, yes my young friend, quite pleasant. As for the box, it came as part of a lot that I bought at a storage locker auction. I seem to recall that there was only one box I gave you but if I do remember, there was a briefcase made of leather like a schoolboy's book bag. It may be among the things on the back shelf."

Without responding, Abi headed to the back of the shop to rifle through the items on the shelf. At last, underneath a pile of books and loose magazines, Abi found the locked satchel.

"Do you remember getting a key for the satchel or any keys at all from the auction?" Abi called to the shopkeeper.

"Hmm, not that I recall. In fact, I think I remember being concerned that I could not sell the satchel if it were locked as it would not be worth paying for it to be professionally opened. If you are interested in it, you can take it with you as I have no use for it."

"Thank you, old friend."

"I take it you found something interesting in the box I gave you, perhaps some new stations to listen to on the radio?" Areef was playing up the part of the interested uncle.

"Yes. I truly appreciate you thinking of me." Abi cut himself short as he could not wait to get home and break into the bag.

"Well then, perhaps there will be even more in the satchel."

After the young man departed, Areef walked to the back of the shop and brewed himself a cup of tea, feeling very satisfied with himself; he only needed to sit back and watch what happened. He was a skilled puppet master.

Chapter Eleven

West Midlands, England

Abi barely took the time to close and bolt the front door once he got back to his apartment. He sat the satchel on his kitchen table and then went to retrieve a butter knife from one of the drawers before sitting down directly in front of the latest mystery gift from Areef. At first, he considered a direct brute force attack to pry the lock open but thought better of it. Perhaps he had seen one too many spy movies but what if tampering with the lock caused some sort of mechanism within the satchel to destroy its contents?

He looked very carefully at the lock and then retreated to a different drawer in the kitchen that contained miscellaneous items in the hope of finding something useful. After several minutes of searching, his efforts were rewarded as he withdrew a plastic-coated paper clip from the drawer. He removed the plastic coating from the paperclip and bent the piece of wire until it was straight. He sat with the straightened paper clip in one hand and realized as he looked at the lock that he had no idea how to use one to open the other. Hoping for a miracle, he slid the paperclip into the lock mechanism and twisted it one way and then the other. Upon completing this maneuver, he attempted to open the latch again and found that he was still locked out.

He tried to calm himself and take a closer look at the lock to see if he could find some way in without harming the mechanism or the satchel. After spending a bit of time looking at the mechanism from all angles, he realized that he simply had no skills as a locksmith. There were only two options available to them at this point; he could either attempt to pry the lock open, or he could take it to someone with more expertise. He considered both options carefully and decided that it was too much of a risk to bring someone else into this secret, so prying the lock open was probably the better choice. With that conclusion reached, he picked up the butter knife, placed it under the lip of the lock and attempted to twist the knife to pry open the lock. After several tries, the lock remained in place, and he had bent the tip of his butter knife.

Picking the satchel up he looked at it from several different angles and tried to determine another way to gain access to its contents. He then recalled a lesson he learned earlier in the semester that the easiest solution was often the best. He determined that he could cut the leather at the bottom of the satchel and most of the contents would simply fall out – those that didn't would still be accessible by reaching his hand into the bag. Abi smiled to himself at the cleverness of his idea and then made a second trip to his kitchen junk drawer to retrieve an X-Acto knife.

At first, he was going to make the incision with the bag laying on his side but then decided that he would lessen the risk of damaging the contents if he held the satchel upside down, allowing gravity to draw all of the contents away from the bottom of the bag before cutting through the leather. He stabbed at the leather on the left-hand side bottom of the satchel until the knife blade pierced the leather, and then pulled it across to the right making a relatively straight cut from one end all the way to the other. Laying the knife on the table, he pulled the two sides of the satchel open and began to withdraw the contents a handful at a time.

Once he had removed all the pages he could feel, he flipped the satchel over and shook it in case anything else remained. A single piece of paper floated out of the satchel, and Abi picked it up and examined it. The page was covered with letters and numbers arranged in some sort of table and in the upper right-hand corner he could clearly see the numbers 6592. The young man smiled as he realized that what he held in his hands was an actual page from a one-time pad. He was not sure where this path was going, but he was sure that fate was smiling upon him.

Abi followed the same methodology as before, separating the documents into similar stacks. This time there were documents completely in Cyrillic with no English markings, some documents in

German, and other pages in English. Since English was the easiest to deal with, he examined those pages first and found nothing of interest. Next, he examined the German pages and determined the subject matter was sporting events. Even though it seemed unlikely, something might have been encrypted there, so he would have to wait until he could fully translate all the words. He set this section off to the side.

He already knew the process the Cyrillic documents were going to require, so he decided to take a few minutes and eat breakfast before starting. Leaving the documents scattered about his table, he locked his apartment and set out for his favorite food vendor. One of the few things that he actually enjoyed about British culture was the variety of street food that existed, even though he tended to be a repeat visitor to the same few stands. After enjoying a muffin, egg, and two slices of beef bacon, he returned to his apartment and began working. As before, he added these pages to the binders with the originals going into one and the translated documents into the other.

This time, rather than allowing himself to be hypnotized by the process, he took the time to read each printed document. The results were thrilling and terrifying. He discovered a fully-fielded plot to launch bioweapons against the United States internally. Along with that discovery, he held the instructions to alert and execute the launch of those weapons. When his mind finally grasped the full impact of what he'd discovered, he understood he had all that was needed to avenge his father's death. *Qa'id, I must contact Qa'id and tell him what I have found.*

Abi completed the translations and reread all the documents. While the information regarding *Chimera K629* was fantastic, what thrilled Abi were the details of alerting the numbers station to begin its actions. Abi was starting to accept that he may truly hold the key.

Transmittal process for sending directives to the numbers stations will be possible only after Full Alert. Once the Full Alert status is reached, the numbers stations will begin to monitor the frequencies provided on Table R below. These frequencies will be monitored

24/7 by the numbers stations until they receive the execute order or are told to stand down. Multiple frequencies are monitored by each numbers station, and therefore directives should be provided for all frequencies listed, if possible, rather than just one.

All transmittals will be encrypted using the referenced OTP sheet identified by the four-digit numeric when the Full Alert transmission is sent via beeper/text SMS.

Abi glanced at the sheet with the number 6592. Even though almost 10,000 possible one-time pad sheets existed, the kismet of his finding only a single sheet indicated this must be the correct one. What concerned him most was how to know if the numbers stations were on Full Alert without having any visual verification, and if they were not, how he would get them there.

Instruction transmittals sent to the numbers stations will be in the following 15-character format:

1. A single letter designating the type of Message the numbers station should transmit (Warning, Preparation, Execution). The letter used will correspond to the Message type.

2. The three-digit number of field assets that should be notified by the particular Message; 999 indicating all assets.

3. A one-letter designation of the time zone for the specific geographic regions where the desired L-PAKs are located. Z indicates that the choice of region is up to the numbers station itself based on current situation.

4. A three-digit number for the date of execution (day of the year) along with a four-digit number for a particular time. Four 0s followed by three Xs are to be used if the Message is to be sent immediately. In the case of a Warning Order, the Messages are to be sent on the next regularly scheduled transmission time.

5. A three-digit number indicating the number of minutes until the next transmission to the numbers station, except 555 which would indicate that the numbers station should continuously monitor the frequency for the next Message.

6. Once the 15-character string is created, all numbers must be converted to letters. Match the letters to the numbers, starting with A being 0, B equals 1, etc.

It all seemed quite straightforward. There was enough leeway to be able to create and send the instruction transmittal even without knowing all of the information regarding locations and actual numbers of available assets. Even with the little information provided regarding *K629*, it would not take an enormous number of detonated weapons to have a massively detrimental effect. As Qa'id had taught him from the Quran 22:19: *"Punish the unbelievers with garments of fire, hooked iron rods, and boiling water to melt their skin and bellies."* Wasn't this *K629* exactly that?

As he read back through the pages, it suddenly occurred to him how he could monitor what was going on with the numbers stations. If he were to send a directive to the numbers stations instructing them to transmit a Warning Message, he only needed to monitor for changes in the broadcasts from the station to determine if they were reacting to his instructions. Flipping back to the front of the binder solidified his hypothesis. He knew what each of the outbound Messages would sound like and what they would contain, or at least enough to determine their meaning. He would have no way of telling the actual actions that were taking place as a result of the Messages until the weapons were actually detonated, but he could monitor the steps beforehand. Without giving it another thought, he asked Qa'id to come by to discuss his new discovery.

Qa'id arrived at Abi's apartment within the hour. Abi explained his plan to test both the status of the numbers station and the ability to trigger events. Qa'id considered his young asset's intriguing words.

"You can send an Instruction Transmittal that will tell them to send out a Warning Message to their various field personnel and then you can monitor whether or not the numbers stations actually sent the Message?" Qa'id asked. Not only did they have more to work with, but they also had real possibilities, not just conjecture.

"Yes, and not only that but I can tell them to choose which field agents to notify and where. Then I would have them remain vigilant for the next step in the process." Abi pulled out a piece of paper and demonstrated the construction of the basic 15-character code required. He stepped through each item in the process and in the end produced a 15-character string: W999Z0000XXX555.

"Now, I will take that string and convert all the numbers to letters, and then run it against the one-time pad sheet that I have right here." He picked up the paper with the designation 6592. "That will create a new string which I will transmit to all of the frequencies listed here on the bottom of the page."

The older man heard Abi's words and saw the documents, but just like watching a cake being made, he only cared how it would taste when it came out of the oven. "How long before you would be ready to do this?" Qa'id said, hoping to bring about the end of the conversation and get to the point.

"Well, I have a microphone for my radio already. I would have to make sure the radio itself can access each of these frequencies and then I would have to transmit the script. Realistically, I could do this in the next few hours." Abi shrugged.

"Perhaps, it would be a better idea if you recorded the instructions and simply played it repeatedly rather than going to the effort of actually speaking on each of the frequencies. That way, you can ensure that each of the communiqués was identical. Aside from that, how long before you know if you have had any effect?"

"The numbers stations send scheduled Messages a few times a week with the field assets instructed to monitor at specific times and days. I suppose we would have to wait until we are on a specific day and at the particular time to see if the Messages actually sent. According to the documentation I have here, the Routine Messages are sent on Mondays between 0230 and 0400 Greenwich time, then on Thursdays between 1820 and 2030, also GMT."

Qa'id realized it was already Monday evening and too late for that scheduled time, but Thursday was a few days away and an excellent possibility. "Here is the plan: first, make sure that your radio is capable of broadcasting to at least most of the frequencies listed. Second, produce the required string to instruct them to send a Warning Message to all assets. Encrypt that string using this sheet you have and then make a recording of the result. Third, send the Instruction Transmittal immediately to all frequencies possible. Once this is done, verify its accomplishment with me. Then we will meet on Thursday and monitor the actions taken by the numbers stations." Qa'id nodded his own approval as he finished providing instructions.

Qa'id was stepping beyond permissions, but he saw little risk in doing so. *It will be irrelevant that I placed a bunch of Russian spies on alert in America. The fact that I could is what will matter in the long run.* Qa'id provided Abi with a blessing for his efforts before he left. *After all, if you're going to use a religious dogma as a motivator it needs to be consistently reinforced.*

As soon as Qa'id departed, Abi set about verifying the capabilities of his radio. He was disappointed his radio could only access seven of the channels listed, but Qa'id said to verify that *most* could be reached, and seven was the most, by one. Next, he put together the 15-character string using the guidance provided in the documents. Abi had created the series once already, as an example for Qa'id, but he went through each step to verify everything was correct. Finally, he retrieved OTP sheet 6592 and encrypted his 15-character string. In that step, W999Z0000XXX555 converted to WJJJZAAAAXXXFFF which became YRSCGUUHMICOZVS. Once Abi completed the encryption, he used the one-time sheet to decrypt the 15-character text that resulted and was able to retrieve the exact text he had entered. It worked.

He was unsure of the need for the next step and saw no reason why he couldn't just manually broadcast the same information seven times, but he followed Qa'id's instructions. He made the recording inside of his radio room to avoid outside noise that could allow a geographical track. He utilized his phone's half-speed playback to distort his voice. Once Abi completed the process, he listened to it several times to ensure that each letter was easily identifiable. There was the danger of background noise, so he wired his telephone to the radio.

Abi decided to wait until after Isha prayers that evening. They were scheduled to start at 10:05 PM and conclude about 40 minutes later which would allow him to get home by 11:00 PM to broadcast the communiqué. The instructions were to broadcast on each frequency twice to ensure receipt by various numbers stations. Due to his older radio, it would be far easier to play it twice in succession. *Sometimes you just have to take a leap of faith.*

Since Qa'id had left all of these decisions to him, he saw no need to call him before the transmissions were complete. That evening, Abi went to Isha prayers in his neighborhood mosque and returned home in time to begin broadcasting. He played the recording once, then waited 30 seconds before playing it a second time. Abi then tuned the radio to the next frequency on the list and repeated the process until he had covered all seven frequencies. When all was complete, he spun the dials on his radio to ensure any frequency was wiped off the unit.

This time Abi actually had information that needed to be destroyed, so he gathered all the notes he had made and lit a fire in his kitchen sink. When the burning was complete, he ran the water to wash away the ash. He opened the windows to let the smoke escape, using a fan to assist in the effort.

Very satisfied with his efforts, he also felt fulfilled that he had at last launched his strike back at the West. Before going to bed, he shut down all of his computer equipment and locked the two binders and one-time pad page in his radio room. His final action that evening was to send a one-word text to Qa'id, knowing he would understand precisely what he meant – *Complete*.

Morty rolled to the side of the bed and reached for his ringing phone on the nightstand. He had no idea what time it was, but due to the lack of light streaming in from his windows, it was still night. *"Ma kore itkha?"* he asked, speaking Hebrew. Rather than repeating the phrase, "What's going on with you?" in another language, he paused.

"Mordechai? Is that you?" Dieter asked. More and more over the past few months, English was his go-to language outside of Germany.

"Yes, yes, this is Morty. Dieter?" It had taken a moment through the fog of sleep to recognize the voice.

"Yes, I'm sorry to call you so late, but there has been a rather significant development." Dieter was unaware what time it was in Israel. He was reacting to his first instinct upon receiving a call from his contacts.

Many former Stasi officers migrated to South America after the fall of the DDR; those who still needed an income and could speak passable Spanish managed to market their skills to the Bolivarian National Intelligence Service. As a result, when Dieter needed intelligence service in the Western Hemisphere, he reached out to his old friends in Venezuela with resources, including those who monitored specific shortwave radio frequencies just in case Sergei attempted to trigger Crimson Firebird before he was able to disarm any weapons.

"Just a moment." Morty made his way into his office to retrieve a notepad and pen. "Go ahead, what is going on?"

"It appears that Sergei has surfaced, placed all of the numbers stations involved on Full Alert and sent an Instruction Transmittal for them to send information to the sleeper agents. Based on the documented process, the numbers stations will transmit a Warning Message during their next scheduled broadcast. From there, the entire timeline gains speed and things will begin to happen rather quickly." Dieter scanned the email on his laptop from his contact in South America.

"When is the numbers station's next scheduled broadcast time?"

"Thursday evening, your time." Dieter had not discovered anything new in the document.

"At this point, I don't see anything actionable for me … at least not until the Warning Message when we can establish some sort of definitive timeline. Am I missing anything?"

"No, I saw no actionable intelligence yet; it is just something that we both need to be aware of. You might want to let your asset know so that they're prepared to take immediate action when necessary." Dieter was taking steps that were unlike the way he'd operated with the Stasi. He found sharing information strange but oddly liberating as it meant more than his own judgment was needed to make decisions and accountability became shared.

"Agreed, I will contact them in the next few hours to ensure their vigilance. No need to call this evening when we have a day or so before things may go into motion." Morty stifled a yawn. "Anything more for me this evening?"

"Nothing more … I wanted you to be aware of the situation as it develops," Dieter said almost apologetically.

"No worries, when you work to bring things together it is always beneficial to share all the information you possess. I will let you know if I hear anything from the field you need to be aware of."

"I appreciate your candor. I will keep you in the loop as things proceed. Goodnight." Dieter decided to interject the one Hebrew word he knew into the conversation. "Shalom."

"Peace to you as well." Morty hung up, entered the messaging software for his telephone and selected Ashley's number. Having worked with her for some years, they had developed an efficient shorthand.

After Morty had entered these words, he hit the transmit button and received an SMS moments later.

Morty returned to his bed and fell asleep. Over the years, he had developed the ability to work with very dire information and still will himself to sleep. Otherwise, he would have gone days without sleeping. This information was nothing more than a preliminary salvo for what was coming next. This incident had been handled before the call was ever made; what happened next would require new actions based on the information itself.

Romulus, Michigan

There was a certain excitement that affected her entire body when Ashley received preparatory orders like the one that had just arrived from Morty. Since she had first tracked Evan Davis in the candle-filled bar, she had been preparing. Now that things were underway, Ashley felt the strange, familiar calm that came at the beginning of every mission. She retrieved a Phillips screwdriver and went into her bedroom closet, kneeling down to see the small air intake vent. She unscrewed the vent and reached inside. A foot or so inside the faux duct, she could feel a football-sized item wrapped in thick cloth. Inside was an Italian-made Beretta PX4 Storm compact with three spare magazines and two boxes of 9mm ammunition. Over the years, she had gone through a myriad of weapons before finally settling on this one. It was small enough to be easily concealable but at the same time large enough to utilize a full-size magazine and operate as a semiautomatic. Until this point in the mission, she felt no need to be armed, especially since a weapon's accidental discovery may cause problems while initiating an intimate relationship. Now that she may be called into action at any moment, keeping the weapon with her at all times was a requirement.

She opened one of the boxes of ammunition and loaded all three magazines before inserting one of them into the weapon. She then wadded the cloth into a ball and stuffed it back into the duct before replacing the vent. Ashley returned to the living room and inserted the two magazines into the hidden pockets within her bag. The gun was placed on the coffee table and then covered with a magazine. The boxes of ammunition were stuffed in the back of a drawer near the main entrance of the apartment. With a weapon and extra ammunition within easy reach, she felt ready for whatever came next. Taking a deep breath, she exhaled and allowed herself to reoccupy her identity as Nikki and wondered why Evan had not called after what she considered to be a successful date on their last evening together. Being physically intimate with a subject was frowned upon by the Mossad, but it had never been forbidden.

Over the years, Nikki had found herself attracted to a few subjects whom she felt were worthy of being intimate with. Evan was indeed different. He was not in the espionage business nor was he a holder of a great wealth of information. Evan was a regular person who was honest with an outgoing demeanor and a sense of humor that meshed with hers. He seemed to know who he was and his place in the world. Nikki found his confidence appealing and so did Ashley. Breaking conventional American dating protocols, she reached for her cell phone and sent a text to Evan thanking him for a lovely evening. *After all, who says a man always has to make the first move?* They made a plan for dinner at his place. Perfect.

The evening was going well so far. Zax had endeared himself to Nikki from the minute she walked through the door, rubbing himself against her like a giant cat and looking at her with his soulful, brown, puppy eyes. Even though he had not spent lots of time cleaning up his place, she did not run in horror when he gave her the guided tour. She was impressed with the open-floor design that flowed from the living room to the dining area, to the kitchen. Evan's own sense of order led him to place the couch as a divider between the living and dining areas; the kitchen separation was an island counter. Nikki questioned why there were only three chairs surrounding a table for eight.

"I saw the table in the store and liked the warm wood tones but they had it marked down because only three matching chairs were on hand. As a result, I ended up with a table that has lots of space for three people to have dinner. I also like the other end as a standing desk of sorts."

At present, the table was completely cleared except for two adjacent place settings. Nikki took note of his thoughtful arrangement. *Planned for intimacy.*

Dinner consisted of homemade baked ziti, following a field greens salad. Evan had also made his first tiramisu. By any outside account, the evening was a thorough success but Evan felt it had been a bit more than just successful since they were making a deeper connection. Their conversation was again of life stories and histories but he allowed himself to look deep into her eyes and admire the gleam of light off of her hair whenever she moved her head a certain way. Since they were seated close, she often touched his hand or arm as she spoke. He was not sure if he was imagining it but her hand seemed to feel warmer with each touch. His body's reaction was internal but it would not take much for it to become quite physical.

As he busied himself in the kitchen, he stole glances at Nikki over the island. She had not indulged in blatant sluttiness to elicit a sexual reaction from him. She'd chosen a wardrobe to show off her best assets; a pair of strappy heels that gave her ass a significant lift – she'd caught him noticing before she kicked them off, jeans tight enough to draw his attention to her curves, a blouse pulled down across her neckline to leave her shoulders bare, her hair was down, and she only had on some subtle makeup so he could see her natural beauty.

Nikki felt the entire evening had been wonderful. She had learned so much about this attractive man. He'd created a truly romantic environment for them from the music to the candlelight and she found herself drawn into its spell. His house was lovely but not overly opulent and she couldn't have imagined a more appropriate dog for him. Sometimes on a mission, she had to think about each action to create a rapport with her subject. None of this was true with Evan; every time she caressed his arm or smiled with a sexually arousing look in her eyes, she genuinely hoped for a response.

"Now, I will apologize for this ahead of time, in case it isn't up to par. It's the first time I've ever made tiramisu," he called over the clatter of plates and silverware as he assembled the decadent dessert.

"I am sure it'll be perfect. I've always been a big fan."

"Well, try it and let me know what you think," he said glancing at her hopefully over their steaming coffee.

Rather than using a fork, she reached out with her finger and drew it through the smooth creaminess on top of the tiramisu. Nikki placed her finger in her mouth and closed her eyes, reveling in its sweetness and the whisper of almond flavor that permeated the entire dessert. "Mmm. Total mouthgasm." Nikki removed her finger from her mouth and opened her eyes to find Evan staring at her.

He was speechless and the seductress in Nikki was unleashed and came to the forefront. Running her finger through the top of the tiramisu again, she leaned forward and painted his lips with the creaminess. Evan closed his eyes and parted his lips, allowing her to slide her finger into his mouth. He swirled his tongue around her finger. He heard her movements but before realizing what they were his mouth was being hungrily devoured by Nikki's. This kiss was different than any they had shared before. It was not just an intimate moment but filled with desire and want, a need to explore further. Craving.

He pushed all the dishes out of the way. Nikki climbed up on the table and sat with her legs on either side of his chair. She leaned forward and they kissed again. This time Nikki used her hands to caress his face as they explored each other's mouths. When the kiss broke, Evan lowered his mouth to her bare neck and shoulders as she tilted her face away to give him better access.

Nikki allowed slight moans and other sounds to escape her lips as Evan kissed her bare shoulders and ran his hands over her back. She lowered her face, and when Evan pulled back, he found himself looking deep into her flashing eyes. Slowly she smiled as if she suddenly had a brilliant idea to share. She removed her shirt in a single motion, leaving her breasts exposed to his gaze before tenderly exploring his neck with her mouth. Evan ran his hands down her back, starting from her shoulders down to her waist at the top of her jeans. The feel of her flesh was smooth and warm, bringing his sensual side to life as she began to nibble more urgently on his neck.

Nikki raised herself up as she gazed at Evan before unbuttoning her jeans. She lay back and lifted her hips to slide her jeans and panties off, but after getting them down to her thighs, she hesitated and spread her arms out. Evan watched from between her legs. He could not remember anything like this before in his life and he wasn't quite sure how to react. The view of her body stretched out before him was beautiful. He watched as her stomach raised and fell with her breathing. Above that, he could see the hardness of her nipples and the outline of her chin as she stared up at the ceiling.

Evan extended his arms until his fingertips reached the waistband of her jeans bunched around her thighs. He curled his fingers under the waistband and sat back. Sliding her pants down her legs and over her feet was a sensual reveal, leaving her completely nude in front of him. He paused to simply enjoy the gentle eroticism of the view. The way the candlelight reflected luminously on her naked flesh reminded him of that first night in the bar. How far they'd come in such a short period of time.

He dropped her clothes on the floor and rose from his chair while unbuttoning his shirt. He was beguiled by the sensual, delightful woman. His mind couldn't decide between passively enjoying her beauty or taking action. Without warning, Nikki sat up and took him into her arms. She kissed his chest while she ran her hands down his bare back, occasionally allowing her nails to lightly scratch him. She raised her face and explored his mouth with her tongue, while her hand slid from his back to his front to unbuckle and open the front of his pants. Evan allowed them to drop to the floor around his ankles while she clawed at the waistband of his underwear so that they fell as well. Both were physically aroused and barely in control as they allowed their hunger to be unleashed.

Nikki pushed his shoulders back to signal him to return to his chair, following him forward. Moments later she used the table for balance, lowering herself onto him as he entered her. The two of them were now on his chair, face-to-face with bodies pressed tight against one another. As the entire evening had been an exchange of control, this was no different. At times, she would sit forward against him holding him tight and guiding their pace. Other times, he had her arch back and rest her upper body on the table so he could caress her breasts and run his hands over her body.

It was a time of discovery, and at the same time, things just seem to flow together as if they had known each other all their lives. It was utterly what lovemaking was supposed to be between two people who not only connected on a mental and physical level but who also allowed their spirits to entwine.

The morning after, as Nikki slowly opened her eyes, she was greeted by an energetic Zax. He bumped Nikki with his muzzle. She really wasn't quite sure what he wanted, so after giving him a quick pat, she rolled over and found Evan naked and lying on his back. She smiled at the memory of the night before, and as she did so, she extended her arm across his chest and then her leg across his legs, pulling her body into his. Without opening his eyes, or giving any indication, he was awake.

"You realize, now that Zax knows you're awake he won't leave you alone until you play with him or at least feed him and let him outside."

"I wasn't quite sure what the morning routine was here ... you see this is my first time..."

"Sure, it is, but we'll have to make sure you know the routine because I see more mornings like this in our future."

She mumbled something and nuzzled into his neck, noticing she had left a few small bite marks and bruises.

Evan was imminently satisfied just lying here for the moment with her warm body pressed against his. He could still feel the events of the night before on different parts of his body as he allowed each to become awake on his own. He allowed his free hand to caress the side of her naked body from her breasts to the curve of her hip and had just begun to feel aroused when a hundred pounds of demanding Goldendoodle landed on top of them both, having jumped from the side of the bed.

"Zax, dammit. This is not how we greet guests in the morning," Evan said, pretending to be mad at the dog but realizing all he wanted was attention from the humans in the room.

"Maybe you should let him out first." Nikki untangled her body from his and rolled over so Evan could get out of bed.

"I have other ideas..." Evan threw back the covers and let Zax out without his robe. When he returned, he found Nikki was face up, under the sheet, her eyes closed.

"Breakfast is served," she said, throwing back the sheet to reveal her naked body. "Devour me."

An hour later, they remembered to let Zax back in who was waiting patiently on the front porch.

Nikki brought a cup of coffee into the master bathroom. "Hey babe, I made coffee for you. I will leave it here on the counter," she said as Evan pulled back the shower curtain.

"Thanks, beautiful; you didn't have to do that. Sure, you don't want to join me?" He shot her his best seductive gaze.

"I'll have to pass. I need to get ready to hit the road. Got a few things I need to get done today." She had nothing else to do today but she needed to be in control.

"I brought your bag in from your car last night when you were sleeping; it's in the bedroom."

"Aw, thanks, lover," she said over her shoulder. She unzipped her bag and found nothing appeared to be disturbed. Her handbag was also just as she had left it.

Last night, Evan had told her about his time in Afghanistan and how he sometimes went to the range with his own pistol. Between those two bits of information, she knew that she could easily explain away having a gun in her purse but would prefer not to have the conversation. As she was standing by the couch examining her purse, Evan appeared drying his hair.

"Shower's free," he said kissing her neck.

Nikki threw her arms around Evan, pressing her body to his. His body smelled fresh and clean while she still smelled of their sex. Nikki felt his arousal and released him, heading for the shower.

An hour later they stood beside Nikki's car. Evan's arms were wrapped around her waist.

"I have to go out of town on Tuesday for an interview, but can we get together when I get back?" he asked.

"Of course, going anywhere interesting?" Nikki was a little surprised. She would need to ask Morty how to proceed.

"Not really, some small town in Oklahoma. I have a flight out of Grand Rapids in the morning." He kissed her and leaned down to open her door.

"I really had a great time last night, dinner, dessert, you for dessert, us as another dessert," she said, trying to suppress a smile.

"And then you for breakfast—delicious," he added laughing.

"Mmm, my knees are still weak. Have a safe trip, babe, can't wait to see you when you get back."

After another kiss, Nikki gave Zax a quick scratch behind his ears before she drove off. Evan reached down and stroked the side of the dog's face as he watched Nikki's car vanish around the corner at the end of the street.

Once she was a few miles down the road, Nikki pulled into a gas station and sent Morty a quick text on her encrypted phone while she fueled up.

```
>Subj going on trip. Follow?
```

Usually, she would've waited until later to send the information, but Morty's last text to her about *wheels turning* and *next level* meant that even minor things needed to be reported. Since it was early in the evening in Israel, she waited for a reply.

```
<Remain in place. Call.
```

Morty seldom asked for her to call in the middle of an operation. Usually, what she needed to know was given upfront and after the launch and she was allowed to be as creative as needed to accomplish the mission. Now was not the right time for her to call; she had no secure place to communicate. It would have to wait until she was back in Romulus.

```
>ACK - 2 hours
```

With the text sent, she put down the phone and pulled back on to the highway. A notification tone sounded seconds later and she picked up her smartphone from the center console and flipped it over.

```
<ACK
```

That meant it was important, but not earth-shattering. She could crank up her radio and enjoy the drive while bathed in the afterglow of the last

18 hours.

Chapter Twelve

Evan spent most of Monday afternoon reviewing the documents Dieter provided to be prepared. He still couldn't believe the madness of the Crimson Firebird Initiative and hoped he was putting the project to rest forever. After watching a very dull movie on TV, Evan packed and dropped Zax off to be boarded so he wouldn't have to impose on Houstynne.

Evan had never flown through the Oklahoma City airport before; overall it was a functional facility, and it was relatively easy to find his way from baggage to rent an Impala for his drive to the Ranchers and Farmers Bank in Alva. Dieter's staff had made all his travel arrangements, including a stay at the local Holiday Inn Express. Realistically, with the amount of money he was being paid, a classier hotel would seem fitting, but then again this was Alva Oklahoma.

His interview with Julian Shepherd was not until the next morning, and the bank had allowed three days for it. Even if this were a legit job, Evan wasn't sure how he'd fill the time as financial news was not his thing. The three-hour drive was incredibly mind-numbing with miles and miles of fields, cows, oil well pumpjacks, and lots of flat tan and brown. Luckily, the sedan had a fantastic sound system complete with satellite radio so he tuned into the Eighties Music station, cranked the volume, and watched the miles roll past.

During the drive, Evan's mind kept wandering back to the last time he was with Nikki. She had made a deep impression on his psyche and his heart. This morning when he was getting dressed, he could see the scratches she'd left down his back. Driving through the barren landscape he felt a deep sensual satisfaction as he allowed his imagination to conjure up remembrances of their night together. In his heart, he hoped Nikki would turn into more than just a momentary dalliance.

Driving into Alva was a brief experience at best. The road seemed to turn from rural to small town without warning, and then after a short drive through a business district, the buildings immediately faded back and disappeared. He located the bank and then found the Holiday Inn Express to check in and get organized.

Having spent a lot of time on the road, Evan found comfort in unpacking his clothes into the dresser, hanging his dress clothes, and laying out his toiletries around the sink. When this was accomplished, he fell back on another ritual of trying the local cuisine. He had spotted El Maya Mexican Cuisine on his drive through town and decided this was his choice for dinner.

The restaurant was a typical small town, the Chile Relleno was excellent and the Dos Equis was ice cold – a perfect pairing. When Evan returned to the hotel, he texted Nikki but then deleted it before sending. Evan didn't want her to think he was too … too … something. So instead, he spent the evening idly watching TV and checking his phone to see if she had texted him. Just before turning out the light, he recalled she had asked to read some of his fiction, so he emailed her a section of a work that was in progress. This way, he could reach out and touch her without it seeming too … *I am a writer and can't come up with a word for what I'm "too" about?*

Any anxiety he experienced was quietening as he began to mentally take control of his situation. He had heard some other PTSD sufferers talk about an almost unnatural calm they felt upon reentering the combat zone. The requirement to focus on self-preservation appeared to keep the horrors at bay. He left the television on while he dozed off to sleep comforted by the soft slur of fading conversation and the dim blue light from the screen.

One of the things Evan hated most in motels was the continental breakfast, so he visited the local McDonald's and wolfed down an Egg McMuffin with a large coffee in his car before returning to the motel to change into his suit. Looking at himself in the mirror he was satisfied that he appeared to be a respectable financial journalist. The bank was crowded as he made his way to the customer service desk where a rather young-looking Asian gentleman greeted him.

"Hi Brad, I am Evan Davis, and I have an appointment with—"

"Mr. Shepherd," the young man finished for him. He rose and extended his hand. "I was told you would be coming. Mr. Shepherd is waiting for you. Can I bring you a cup of coffee or something?"

"Um, coffee would be great. Just cream please." Evan shook the young man's hand and then followed him up a set of stairs and then down a short hallway towards an open office door.

Brad knocked on the door and announced Evan's arrival before excusing himself. The man behind the desk rose and extended a hand towards Evan, which he shook firmly.

"Mr. Davis, so glad you could come out to the wilds to visit us," Julian said.

Evan took a mental inventory of the man. After all, he needed to convince himself to give up his intensive espionage training and to accept his story of not committing treason but of saving the world.

Julian was six feet tall, which surprised Evan because during the Cold War he had always heard all Russians stood eight feet tall. Overall, he was more or less athletic with a slight middle-age spread. His hair was solid black and neatly combed with a smattering of gray around the temples. His broad smile appeared to be earnest and his blue eyes seemed to add to his trustworthiness. All in all, the perfect appearance for a banker – *or a sleeper agent pretending to be a banker.*

The two men spoke about where Evan was staying, how his travel to Alva had been, and if he had ever been to Oklahoma. They decided to go by their first names. Brad appeared with a cup of coffee and closed the door behind him.

"Brad is one of our two interns…" Julian launched into a polished explanation of how the intern program worked for the bank.

Evan made notes about the intern program and continued writing as Julian gave a detailed history of the bank, including local folktales about Bonnie and Clyde attempting to rob one of the branches during the Great Depression.

"From what I understand, Bonnie was quite a looker and probably could've had a career as a writer if she had not met Clyde."

"Probably wouldn't have helped the reputation of the journalist," Evan stated with a straight face.

"Well, you're probably right, friend." Julian smiled broadly. *Well, he at least appears to be paying attention.* "Now, I do have a couple of meetings this morning – and you're welcome to attend them with me – but this afternoon I thought we would head out across the county and meet some of the customers. The local folks should be able to talk about how the bank has worked with the ranchers and farmers in the area. Then, this evening, if you feel up to it, my wife, Camille, thought it would be great to have you over to our new place and do some steaks on the grill so we could show you a little Sooner Hospitality. If that would be okay with you."

When invitations like this came up, Evan always tried to figure out how he could decline but this invite would allow them to speak privately and provide the opportunity to sway him over. Dieter had given him a sealed envelope with the name *Dmitry* written on the front and said it contained a letter from Julian's father – a *Hail Mary* to be used if all else failed. Evan would bring the letter that evening.

"My calendar is clear, and a steak along with local hospitality sounds like the perfect way to spend a Wednesday evening in Alva. I truly appreciate it."

"Super, I will call Cam and let her know. Camille enjoys meeting new people." Julian handed Evan a family photo from his desk.

Evan wasn't sure what a sleeper agent's family was supposed to look like but somehow this wasn't it. They had the appearance of the typical American family. Perhaps Julian's family would keep him from doing anything destructive.

"I'll leave it to Camille to tell you all about the kids tonight but I will let you know upfront that I'm very proud of all three of them."

"As well you should be. You've got a fine-looking family."

By the end of the first few days of Full Alert, Nastia realized there was simply no way they could both remain at the station 24 hours a day seven days a week. The Vodyanoy Transmission Station didn't have a large enough stockpile of food, space was too cramped for privacy, and there were no shower or bath facilities. It did not take long before personal quirks and lack of hygiene and food caused agitation.

Nastia decided the station could be vigilantly manned for short periods by just one. Yury agreed; he'd had no notice when they were called to duty with no time to make personal arrangements or to grab his belongings before being buried in this hole. It was decided they would exit the station on alternate days for an hour or so to return home for a shower and secure the next day's provisions. On one of Yury's breaks, with Nastia manning the station by herself, the next transmittal came in.

The static disappeared from one of the monitored channels – a solid indicator of an impending broadcast. Nastia grabbed a pen and pad of paper with a shaky hand. She held the pen tightly and pressed it hard against the paper in an effort to stop her hand from quivering. A strange voice came over the radio, slowed down mechanically for clarity. She began writing Y-R-S-C-G-U-U; there was a slight pause before he continued H-M-I-C-O-Z-V-S, and then silence. Fifteen letters. As the voice started again, she flipped to a clean sheet of paper. Once the second transmission was complete, she compared the sheets and found them to be the same. She had recorded the transmission correctly. Now she needed to decrypt it.

"I was able to get the oranges but I could not find any mangoes," Yury's voice came from behind her.

"Come here … the next transmission has been broadcast."

No sooner had Yury placed his bags down on the counter, the static on another of the four frequencies went silent. Nastia tore a few pieces of paper from the notebook and handed them to Yury, who prepared to write.

Nastia realized the transmission was the same; regardless, she recorded each letter again. After completing the first broadcast, they turned to a new page to record the second transmission. Their recordings matched. For a moment, they stared at one another with the full realization they had received their order. Nastia broke her trance and decrypted each letter—the result was the 15-character string WJJJZAAAAXXXFFF. She performed the decryption again, and the result was the same; satisfied she handed the OTP sheet to Yury. Nastia watched Yury intently as he decrypted the string one character at a time; after completing it once, he did it again, and the result was the same. The final step was to perform the reconversion on the string so they could get their order. Nastia performed the conversion in her head, and Yury created a small table that showed A was equal to zero, B to one, etc. They were at last ready for the final validation of the 15-character string. In unison, they began reading the final result one letter at a time.

"W—nine—nine—," they read aloud. Suddenly another frequency went silent. There was no requirement to record the transmission again. The multiple frequencies were used to ensure that the transmittal was received. Neither spoke, as the voice recited the same 15-character string; when the transmission was complete, without saying a word, they resumed reading the Instruction Transmittal.

"Nine—z—zero—zero—zero—zero,   —X—X—X—five— five—five." When they completed the last letter, they raised their eyes and nodded to each other.

"Comrade Commander I verify the decrypted and converted Instruction Transmittal," Yury said in a stilted and formal voice.

"Agreed, we have identical results, Comrade Major."

The process up to this point was relatively easy and routine. Yury was instructed to retrieve the process book from the safe. They worked together and after several minutes of breaking each part of the string down, they found they were to send out a Warning Message to all field assets. The choice of the geographic location subset was up to the station. Both the date and time indicated that the Warning Message needed to be sent during the next regular transmission time. The numbers station was also instructed to monitor the standard frequencies 24 hours a day for the next transmittal.

"Well, so much for this being nothing," said Yury in resignation.

"I guess, but I wonder what is going on in the world that is causing this." Nastia realized she should've kept her thoughts to herself.

"Commander Zamurovich, we are loyal soldiers of the Russian Federation. It is not our duty to wonder what has caused something but merely to act and follow the orders we are given. We are to trust our leadership always to be correct." Yury said repeating the party line.

"Agreed." Nastia shut down their discussion, not wanting her career or safety to be jeopardized.

Both sat quietly for a few minutes before Yury rose and returned to the counter. He put away their provisions in the small refrigerator. *I am not sure of the Comrade Commander's dedication to this mission.* For the first time, he doubted the loyalty of his partner of almost a decade.

Nastia studied the code again—this was her mission but she also assumed her mission was to prevent accidental disasters. *Was this perhaps an intended catastrophe?* Unlike Ballistic Missile Launch Officers who knew their weapons precise capability, she had no idea of the capability of this program's weapons. There were definite holes in her knowledge and she was not in a position to find any answers. During her last scheduled session outside the station, she had spent much of her time watching TV news headlines. There was no conflict between the Soviet Union and the West. *So why are we preparing to trigger execution?*

In 1983, Lieutenant Colonel Stanislav Yevgrafovich Petrov of the Soviet Air Defense Forces had prevented the launch of Soviet missiles against the United States when he decided the system had malfunctioned when it reported inbound US missiles. He was met with neither applause nor condemnation for the action, and the Soviets did not speak of this publicly for almost 22 years. Nastia took this event to heart—sometimes you needed to apply a little common sense to your orders to prevent disasters from happening. There were only 72 hours for her to figure out how to avoid a possible catastrophe.

Abi awoke from his night's sleep, not haunted by the past but excited by what lay ahead. After the communiqué was sent on Monday night, he spent the next day smiling as he went about his business, extremely confident about his actions. Nothing would happen until Thursday evening, and he imagined what would take place shortly after. He would be crushed if he didn't hear any transmission from the numbers station, but he remained optimistic.

On Tuesday, he spent time between the mosque and reviewing the binders for accuracy. Of course, he found no errors, but he did find additional useful information. He decided it might be best to begin preparing the next set of transmissions rather than waiting for confirmation. *After all, as soon as it is confirmed that my transmission to the numbers station is successful, shouldn't I be ready to send the Preparation Message to get things moving along?*

Wednesday was a bit more unsettled, as Abi had breakfast with his mother and the meal ended with an argument.

"Abi, you need to be spending more time on your studies and less at the mosque," Fakhriya said. "Allah will understand that time must be budgeted and priorities made."

"No. You don't get it, Allah would not be forgiving if opportunities are missed. My mentor, Qa'id, stresses the need to make the most of those times when fortune smiles upon you," Abi argued.

It was not missed by Fakhriya that Qa'id was no longer referred to merely as his teacher but was given the elevated title of *mentor.*

"That is another thing; this man is taking up entirely too much of your time. My son, you are young, you should be spending your time playing soccer with your friends or perhaps finding a good girl with whom to plan a future. You will have time in the future for listening to mentors once your life has a steady path."

"Mother, there is no time like the present to seize opportunities when Allah presents them. In days or hours, things can shift so greatly, and those things that matter most will seem trivial and silly." Abi realized he had gone too far.

"Abi, what do you mean days or hours? What have you done? What are you a part of?"

Abi wrapped his arms around his mother's shoulders, moving his face close, and paused before speaking. "Mama, do not worry. I am just excited at the possibilities in the future and my increasing opportunities. I have no classes this afternoon, perhaps I can find a few friends, and we can kick a footie around for a bit. It seems like it is going to be a beautiful day for that."

Fakhriya closed her eyes and placed her hand on his forearm. She rested her head as a sign of approval. She then opened her eyes and stared straight ahead. At this point, she was not sure what she should do next, but Fakhriya was sure the boy she had raised was now lying to her. "Will you come by after, for dinner?" *Perhaps by then I will have an idea of what to do.*

"I will try," Abi lied; he was not sure of what he might need to do but did not want to commit to anything that would cause any issues.

"That is all a proud mother can ask." Fakhriya rose and turned to hug her son properly, while her mind raced for a solution to rescue him from Qa'id and those who would use Abi's intelligence and dedication for nefarious purposes.

As the hours of Wednesday afternoon slowly dragged on, and having heard nothing more from Qa'id, Abi decided to construct the text of a Preparation Message. This time, the same as last, he would leave enough leeway in the communication for the numbers stations to provide any lacking information.

Abi wrote a quick outline of what he wanted the communiqué to include. He was going to have the numbers stations send out a Preparation Message to all the assets, again leaving the decision regarding the geographic subset up to the station. He would use four zeros followed by three Xs for the transmission time, but unlike the last instruction, this would result in the immediate transmission of the Message. The numbers stations would monitor his transmission frequencies 24/7.

After constructing the 15-character code, with those instructions, Abi reviewed his handiwork. Once this communication was sent, the only action remaining would be to transmit the final communiqué in the series to launch the bioweapons. A chill ran through him as he realized how close he was to avenge his father's death and his own misery, but the cold turned to a burning anger. He pounded the table top with his fist and then returned to the reality of his mission.

Abi converted the code into numbers and used the OTP to encrypt the result. For a moment, it seemed strange that he would use a one-time pad more than once, but he proceeded. The KGB had weighed the risk of multiple transmissions to relay OTP number information versus using the same sheet for all three transmittals. It was decided if Crimson Firebird were put into action, confusion in the aftermath of a nuclear attack would prevent quick decryption. The time lag would be sufficient enough to allow the use of the same sheet more than once since decryption would take far longer than it would take to go from Warning to Execution.

Once Abi had encrypted the string, he created the file that he would play when it was time to broadcast these instructions to the numbers stations. This time recording the communiqué was much smoother but he heard the anxiety and excitement in his voice so he did it multiple times before he was happy. He again burned all paper used to create the transmittal in his sink, opening his windows to allow the smoke to escape. Later that night, when he was headed out of his apartment to attend *Salat al-`Isha,* he overheard two neighbors discussing the smell of smoke in the building and how residents should not be barbecuing food inside the apartments as it created a fire hazard.

Upon returning home from prayers, Abi lay in his bed, staring at the ceiling. His mind was racing from one thing to the next, and he was energized by the prospect of actually hearing some result from his actions by this time tomorrow. Upon having a sudden epiphany, he picked up his telephone and played his recording. As he heard his voice, distorted by the slow speed of the playback, he could clearly hear each letter of the code that would bring things to the brink. He played the recording three times, each time counting off the letters from one to 15. Abi had memorized the code and could say it without reference. He did so once, just before exhaustion took him from consciousness.

The afternoon was spent going from one farm to another in a full-size pickup truck that sported the bank's logo on the doors. The article might have just been a cover story but Evan was learning a lot about farming and the business of agriculture. Julian was a terrific host and ensured that Evan understood everything. Julian knew the people of this county and they knew and liked him as well. In the back of his mind, Evan wondered if Julian were really prepared to give all this up just to execute a mission given to them so many years ago.

"Did you grow up here?" Evan asked as they were driving for the next farm.

"Naw, I'm a transplant. I met a semi-local girl when I was in college, and we got married. She convinced me this would be a great place to live and raise kids. As usual, she was right."

"Semi-local?" Evan inquired.

"Yeah, Camille spent her summers here on her grandparents' spread. Her father and mother were trying to keep her from the evils of Kansas City. I really can't blame them. As a result of that upbringing and her university education, I've got a wife who can operate in the world of international finance, break a horse, rope a calf, and make homemade jelly. She does it all while looking fantastic, too." Julian smiled. He loved to brag about Camille. She was something extraordinary, and he knew it.

"Sounds like."

"Since the kids have become more independent, she has taken

on several leadership roles with local charities and spends her time doing work instead of a job. I am lucky enough to have a position that's both." It suddenly occurred to Julian that he may be revealing too much about himself that really wasn't needed for the magazine article. But at the same time, Evan seemed like an earnest guy who wasn't out to dig up dirt but was interested in what was actually going on here. He did get a feeling that Evan had questions he wasn't asking. Maybe eventually they would get to those.

Turning from paved state road to a dirt road that led up to a farm in the distance, they were on the last stop of the day. Most of the farm operations the bank dealt with had been handed down through generations. This one was no different, and the current patriarch of the family could trace his family's ownership back to the original dash for property in 1889. In fact, Yancey Van Dijk was very proud of the legend that his family could be counted among those who gave Oklahoma its Sooner State nickname.

The tour lasted a little over an hour, with Yancey showing off some new equipment purchased with a line of credit from the bank. Julian possessed an encyclopedic knowledge of the farm's history and his bank's part in its success. Evan knew little about agribusiness and it was completely evident that Julian was an expert. Both men were invited to stay for dinner but Julian politely turned down Yancey's offer, explaining that dinner was already planned at his homestead. After shaking hands, Evan and Julian got back into the pickup and headed for the bank. Evan would arrive at the Shepherd household in an hour and a half; first he wanted to shower the dust off and make himself presentable in tactical pants and an Elvin Bishop T-shirt, since the evening was casual.

Camille greeted him with a hug and unlike the portraits in Julian's office, she had her hair pulled back in a simple ponytail and was dressed in a pullover shirt and jeans that she somehow made seem elegant. Unlike many people who looked nothing at all like their portraits, Camille was every bit as lovely. She scolded him for bringing a bottle of wine which she then happily noted was her favorite. While Julian was busy with the grill, Cam took Evan on a tour of the house.

"We're still getting settled in but we really like having a bit more living space available than our last place," Cam said, taking him room to room.

"I truly like the layout of your home; mine has this huge center room that comprises the living room, dining room, and kitchen that everybody makes such a big deal of but I like yours better."

"Now this is Julian's home office. He doesn't actually use it much; it is more a storage place for all his books and office stuff." Camille allowed Evan to take a look inside.

Her body language expressed that she did not intend him to actually enter the room. One of the first things he noticed was the gold lettering of *Brandt's Compleat Collection of Great World Literature* displayed on the bookshelves. Dieter had mentioned a collection that was used as part of the decrypting scheme but did not give him any details.

"Very nice," Evan said as he withdrew his head from the room.

Camille guided the way further down the hall and showed him their kids' bedrooms. None of their children would be joining him that evening, as the high schoolers were at a football game and the college student was away. Camille demonstrated a great pride of her new home, so he played along with the appropriate sounds of approval. With the tour done, she guided him back through the house and after a quick stop at the refrigerator to obtain two Corona Lights, she guided him out to an expansive deck where Julian was grilling.

"What you think of *Casa de Shepherd?*" Julian asked as he accepted a beer and continued to flip steaks.

"Quite a beautiful place; looks like the whole banking thing is working out well for you." Evan was testing his new friendship. He didn't have much time to make a whole lot happen and really wasn't sure how to proceed.

"Yeah, well you know how it is, it was either do the banking thing or dig ditches and I didn't have a good enough reputation to be allowed to dig a ditch."

Camille left after giving him a quick kiss on the cheek but before passing through the sliding doors, she turned. "You okay with a salad, some large russet potatoes, and collard greens?”

“Sure, I’ve been a fan of soul food ever since my tour in Afghanistan,” Evan responded with a smile.

“They cook collards in Afghanistan?” Camille was honestly surprised.

“Well, not the locals. There was an Army Master Sergeant named Emeric Cormier who was the chief cook at the chow hall. He took it upon himself to prepare authentic Louisiana collard greens and other Southern delights at least once a week. The whole time I was there I never had the guts to ask him how he managed to get pork fatback into a Muslim country but somehow, he did.”

“Learn something new every day. Well, mine is prepared based on an old family recipe, so you know they’re better,” Camille said, adding a bit of over-the-top pride.

“I have no doubt, looking forward to them.”

“Camille is usually friendly to new folks but you seem to have established a pretty good rapport right off the bat,” Julian said as he used a spice grinder to add a bit of flavor to the meat.

“You might be responsible for some of those positive vibes. Thanks for the wine tip. Camille seems like a great lady. You’re very fortunate. You said you met during college?”

“Yep, been married since 1992. At first, Camille wasn’t sure if she was ever going to let me out of the friend-zone but I was persistent. She had never dated a white guy and really wasn’t sure what to expect or how her parents would handle it. That kinda went away the first time I met her folks. They had come to the school to see her over a weekend, and I hit it off right away with her dad. By Sunday night, he was asking her why she wasn’t dating me.”

Her father did indeed like him but upon finding out they were actually dating a few weeks later, he made a special trip to the school just to speak privately with Julian. Their conversation lasted several hours and he gained her father’s blessing to date Camille with the promise to do his best to make her happy. The two were married three months later.

“I take it your family handled it okay?” Evan asked.

"I am sure they would've, and they would've loved her too, but they never had the chance. They were gone before the two of us even met. I don't have any other extended family." Julian examined the steaks to see if they were properly done.

Evan wondered if he'd known other sleeper agents, seeing how easy it was to vary your past with the right story.

"Honey!" Julian shouted over his shoulder. "I'm taking them off the grill. They still need to rest about five minutes but then they're ready."

Their dinner was among the most enjoyable Evan could remember in a long time, except for his meals with Nikki which were in an entirely different class. The conversation never lagged; Camille, asking Evan questions about his history or offering family stories of their own. Julian remained quiet as Cam controlled the conversation. His love and appreciation for his bride were clear. The evening ended all too quickly without Evan finding an appropriate time to bring up his real purpose.

For a few moments after dinner, enjoying cigars on the back deck, Evan approached the topic. "You seem to have a wonderful life here." *It would be a pity if your mission as a spy ever destroyed everything that you and your wife have built so why don't you help me prevent that from happening.*

"Agreed. Some people just can't adjust to rural living, but there's a way of life here that doesn't exist anywhere else. Don't get me wrong, I like the occasional trip to the big city, but I enjoy living my life day-to-day right here; just me, Camille and the kids enjoying each other."

Julian had never really thought about the nuts and bolts of his life but when someone from the outside commented on what he saw, it caused him to reflect. He was lucky, and even though he had been sent here for one purpose, he found a whole new reason for his existence every day. *Perhaps it is time to separate me entirely from that other part of my life and let it fade to black while I continue on down this path.*

Evan pounced, "You know there are things that—"

"Well, gentlemen, now I've found where you escaped to." Camille took the cigar from Julian's mouth and puffed. "Have you managed to solve all the world's problems?"

"Well, I was just about to explain to Evan my idea for bringing about world peace, but that was before I was interrupted by your beauty. Now I've lost my train of thought." Julian wrapped his arm around his wife's waist.

Evan gave a nervous laugh and realized his opportunity was lost. *Well, at least I have two more days.* Feeling a bit like a third wheel, Evan excused himself and made his move for the door. After a lengthy farewell process, and a promise to return, he departed for his hotel.

"He seems like a really nice guy, Jules," Camille said, hugging her husband.

"He is. He's unlike any reporter I've ever met. It's a shame he doesn't live closer," Julian replied, guiding her back into the house and closing the door for the evening.

As he was pulling out of their driveway, Evan saw the silhouette of Julian and Camille, her arms wrapped around him as he waved. Evan was unsure why this man would consider doing anything to destroy his happiness. Interrupting his train of thought, he heard the sound of his phone alerting him to a text.

```
>Call me ASAP
```

Rather than responding, Evan sped back to the hotel to call Dieter.

"Hello Evan, how are you getting on with Julian Shepherd?" Dieter inquired.

It was not exactly the conversation Evan was expecting after being told to call ASAP. "Very well, I think, but I haven't been able to approach the real reason for my visit yet. I may need an extra day or two."

"You don't have it, in fact, you may only have 24 hours more," Dieter said. "It would seem that things have already been put in motion, probably by one of Sergei's minions or perhaps Sergei himself. Either way, at approximately 1:30 PM tomorrow, Julian will receive a Message telling him to prepare to perform his primary mission."

Evan was silent. His mind was reeling as he tried to grasp the impact of Dieter's words and losing the little time he thought he had.

"Are you still there, my friend?" Dieter asked.

Friend? "Uh, yes. Yes, I am still here, just a little stunned. I just went from thinking I had a few days to make things happen to now having, what, 16 hours?"

"Yes. About 16 hours. Do you think it is possible?"

"Do I have any choice?" Evan shot back.

"No. None of us do. If this fails, the results will probably be catastrophic." Dieter realized if Evan lost all measure of hope, he may just give up and the entire situation would be in peril. "You said yourself you thought everything was going very well and you have some measure of rapport with the man. That'll have to be the basis for getting him to do what we need him to do. Don't forget you also have that envelope. If all else fails, that might help to convince him."

"Then why not just hand them the envelope, have him read it, and hope for the best?" Evan demanded.

"The letter is from a father who he may feel abandoned him years ago. It is just as likely a letter from him will turn Julian off, and he will no longer listen to anything you have to say. I don't think we want to start out that way."

"I suppose. You know you're causing me many sleepless nights."

"Now you know what I've been dealing with since I first heard about the Crimson Firebird Initiative. Do you think you have all the resources you need to address this tomorrow?" Dieter asked.

"Either I do, or I don't, either way, it's too late to do much about it. Any more good news?"

"Yes, I'll be sending you a package via FedEx that has a modulator in it. If you recall, I told you that once an L-PAK is opened you have 14 minutes to connect it to the sequencer or it will self-detonate. You attach this device in between the sequencer and the rocket, and then when you enter the code to launch the weapon, this device will use that unlock information to shut the entire system down, including all self-destructs. We developed it earlier in the process, and it works very well," explained Dieter.

"I guess that makes sense, we would need some way to shut the whole thing down once we actually get to it. Is that all?"

"Nothing more for now, please let me know what happens. I'll keep you informed of anything more I find out on this end." Dieter had not known Evan long enough to feel one way or another about him but he realized he had placed the man in a damn near impossible position and up to this point he had never given up. He admired that.

"Goodnight," Evan said, hanging up. *If I live through this one, I'm never going to open any mystery envelope left on my porch again.* Evan prepared for another sleepless night.

Chapter Thirteen

Evan arrived at the bank just as it opened on Thursday morning at 9 AM. He was hoping Julian would also be in on time, but as that did not occur, Evan was left talking to Brad. Brad actually seemed like a very nice kid, but Evan's mind was on anything other than idle chit-chat. No topic seemed off limits from how much a journalist makes per year to whether or not Evan expected his salary to increase. Evan's usual response to questions about journalism was to claim that he wasn't one, except by accident. So, he made up answers as he went along. Just as Brad was going to start another series of queries, his phone rang. He looked over at Evan and nodded several times. Because Evan's mind was spinning in different directions, he didn't pay attention.

"Well, it appears Mr. Shepherd will not be in until 11," Brad explained. Apparently, he had to make a side trip to a construction site. He asked that I let you know, and to give you access to his office if you need to do any work, or to assist you in any other way possible."

"Disappointing, but I really could use the time if you would let me into his office so I could use the conference table I would appreciate it." He hated losing two hours but perhaps rifling through Julian's desk would offer additional ways to approach this.

"Right this way," Brad said. After letting Evan in, he announced that he would bring him some coffee and offered to get anything else he might require.

"Coffee would be great and then just some quiet so I can write." Evan hoped to put an end to any further interruptions.

Evan sat at a small conference table and took out his notebook, pretending to make editorial changes to his notes. He kept this up until Brad appeared with his coffee. Evan stood, went over and closed the door, taking inventory first of the bookcases that contained plaques, trophies, and knickknacks from local charities, a smattering of business textbooks, and more pictures of the family. Everything backed up the story of the man Julian appeared to be.

On one side of the office was an old Blaupunkt hi-fi system. Evan carefully examined the console. He lifted the split lid and found a bottle of whiskey and some glasses sitting atop a record player. Opening the lid on the other side was an old-style radio. Sandwiched between the various scales of frequency numbers were rows of city names that he guessed at one point were linked to the spectrum displayed on either side. *Good luck getting Paris or Luxembourg from Alva Oklahoma.*

He pushed one of the buttons underneath the tuning display. Nothing happened, so he pushed another. Evan didn't realize the unit used tubes, so it was going to take a moment to warm up before it was operational. After several tries, he gave up and closed the lid, figuring the unit didn't work. As he turned to walk away, a sound started emanating from the console at first low and then getting louder.

"…other local news, a break-in was foiled by an alert neighbor when…"

Evan quickly reopened the lid of the Blaupunkt and pushed another button he hoped would turn off the radio. He got lucky at his first attempt to shut off the sound. The listing for frequencies included a line for MHz. *Was it that easy?* After all, he had learned about numbers stations, and how they were being used for the CFI; he expected the receivers that the sleeper agents used would be highly technical and spy-like. Evan did not expect something this easy or openly visible. Closing the lid, he walked back to the conference table. Based on what Dieter had told him and what he had read, Evan knew exactly where Julian would be at 12:30 PM this afternoon.

Evan shifted his position in the chair so that he could look out the window onto The Square and allow his mind to wander a bit. Minutes were ticking by and he still had no idea how he was going to approach Julian for assistance. It was in that position that Julian found him when he walked in precisely at 11 o'clock.

"Sorry to keep you waiting; a banker's hours never seem to be banker's hours," Julian said. "I thought we would head into southern Kansas today and hit the Farm Co-Op in Kiowa. It will give you a chance to meet a group of farmers all in one place and get a different viewpoint of agribusiness as well. Most of the folks up there are farmers and not ranchers. But we need to get going if we hope to catch them while they're all still together." Julian gathered up a notebook.

"Uh, sure. Sounds great." Evan hoped this would provide them the opportunity to talk.

"Super, I've asked Brad to come along. He doesn't get much of an opportunity to get out of the building and see what we really do."

"Okay, but I wanted to talk to you," Evan tried to interject.

"We will have plenty of time this afternoon but now we have to hit the road," Julian overruled.

The ride to Kiowa was mostly silent and Evan was deep in thought. When they arrived at the Co-Op, Julian introduced Evan to all of the farmers having their morning coffee. Many had left and begun working but the few who remained were more than willing to talk about anything and everything. It seemed as if they had just arrived when Julian announced they needed to leave for other appointments. As they were getting in the car, there was a test of the tornado siren which, according to Brad, indicated it was exactly noon.

The drive back from Kansas into Oklahoma was quiet except for a few comments here and there. Upon arriving at the bank, Julian explained, "I need you to excuse me for a few minutes, I have a private phone call I need to make." He attempted to park Evan in the chair outside his office.

"Really, I think we need to speak if you would just—"

"In a few minutes … have a seat I'll be with you as quick as I can." Julian closed his office door.

Evan collapsed into the chair while listening intently. At first, he heard the radio playing. Next, a single tone played six times, followed by silence, and then it repeated. Finally, he heard a church bell and the faint sound of an unintelligible voice. Finally, the repetitive tones played again. *It is now, or never.* Evan walked into Julian's office without knocking and closed the door behind him. Julian was sitting on the floor in front of the stereo with a legal pad and pen. The lid to the stereo was open and static flowed from the speakers. Julian turned to him with an ashen face. Whatever was written on the legal pad was not decrypted, but the gravity of the Message had not escaped Julian, and he was frightened.

"Julian, I need to tell you that I know who you are and why you were sent here," Evan said, trying to feel his way through the situation.

"I don't know what–"

"Just give me a minute to explain … then you can decide if you want to try to deny everything or if we can try to work together to prevent a serious catastrophe."

Julian shook his head for a moment and then nodded very slowly, indicating he was ready to listen.

"You were sent here as part of a bigger plan called the Crimson Firebird Initiative. You probably have never heard of that name before but that was the way the KGB operated when this whole thing started. The program was designed to be a strike back option should the United States ever exercise a nuclear first strike option. The Warning Message you just received was sent not by the Soviet government or anyone of any authority. It was sent by a man named Sergei Kirill Mikhailov who initially thought up the entire Crimson Firebird plan. He was thrown out of the KGB when the Soviet Union fell in the Nineties. Since then, he has been biding his time waiting for an opportunity to get revenge on the West."

Julian remained seated on the floor. His head was lowered so Evan could not see his facial expressions. It was unbelievable how much this man knew. He and his peers had been warned about this at the Academy, in fact, there had been rumors that inspectors would appear from time to time in the field to test them. *Was this a test? After so many years?*

"I know you were trained to use something called an L-PAK. Do you know what kind of weapon that is?" Evan waited a moment for Julian to respond, but when he said nothing he continued. "The L-PAK is a launch system for a bioweapon called *Chimera K629*. It will destroy this entire nation in just a couple of weeks, and once it starts there is nothing that can stop it."

The students at the Academy were never told about the payload of the L-PAK. It was simply described as a weapon of retaliation that would strike down their enemy. They were instructed how to remain hidden to survive once the weapon was launched. Based on what Evan was saying, no one would survive.

This has to be some sort of loyalty test; there is no way the Soviet Union would ever allow such a weapon to exist. "You don't know what you're talking about; I'm a banker in a small town in Oklahoma. I was born in this country and have always been loyal to it. So what that I sometimes listen to random radio broadcasts as a hobby. Do you really think an espionage service would use an unencrypted, over-the-air radio transmission as a method of communication? What silliness." Julian rose from the floor in an attempt to take control of the situation. He was following his Academy instructions in the case of being outed but his mind was elsewhere—worried about his family and how they would recover from this.

"Fine. Fine," Evan said waving his hands above his head "All of this is just imaginary but how would you explain the fact that I know any of this? After all, I am just a writer from Michigan."

"Exactly. How and why would you know any of this? It's not what you do for a living. Or maybe you are with the Soviet KGB or whatever they call it these days and you are looking for a patsy, or perhaps you're CIA," Julian argued back, still trying to regain control.

Their exchange went on for several minutes with Evan trying to point out the logic and Julian fighting back as if it were all some sort of set up designed to frame him. The entire situation was at an impasse. Finally, Evan withdrew the envelope he had been given by Dieter from his pocket and walked over to where Julian was standing.

"I was told if nothing else convinced you, to give you this envelope."

He attempted to hand it to him but Julian refused to take it, instead staring silently at Evan.

Finally, Evan set it on top of the Blaupunkt and turned to leave. "Take whatever time you need to read it; I'm going back to the hotel. You can reach me if you change your mind and decide you want to help prevent this evil from happening. So, read it, and think about it. But also think about your wife and your children and your life and everything else that will cease to exist if you don't help me end this now." Evan realized his words would not bring about success, but maybe Julian's emotional attachments would.

Abi was able to find a website to monitor shortwave frequencies from a variety of geographic locations worldwide. He was able to find the frequency that was employed by the Vodyanoy Transmission Station. Abi could not believe his ears when he heard the transmission made over the numbers stations frequency. His mind was crackling with excitement, and Qa'id was also grinning from ear to ear. They actually had control of the numbers stations the transmissions. They were in control of weapons that were poised and ready to strike out at the Great Satan.

"Amazing," Qa'id said in awe of their power.

"I have already prepared the next broadcast to send to the numbers stations. It has them notify the field people to begin preparing to launch the weapons they have," Abi said with a good deal of pride.

"Good, good." Qa'id's mind raced. "Based on what you've read, does anything else happen at this step other than preparation?"

"No, it just brings everything to the highest state of readiness but does not actually start any action." Abi could at last show off his superior knowledge.

"Fine, I trust you have composed sound files so you can play them over the radio as you did last time?" Qa'id waited for his nod. "Good. Go ahead, send the communiqué out and then monitor what response the numbers stations take. But take no further action."

"Yes, Qa'id."

Qa'id hugged his young protégé before leaving. He had a phone call to make and approvals to acquire before moving on to the next stage. As soon as Qa'id departed, Abi prepared the radio for transmission. After hooking his phone into the radio, he played the MP3 file on each of the frequencies. There was no way to know that only one of the numbers stations was still in existence, but the Vodyanoy Transmission Station was intently listening for his transmissions.

Nastia said nothing more to Yury about her concerns. After the Instruction Transmittal was received, they immediately prepared the Warning Message, using the appropriate alerting tones and various voice recordings. A simple Message to tell the receiver to standby on alert since the Preparatory Message could be coming shortly. They were not instructed to send along any further instructions.

Yury's focus shifted to watching TV but not before he returned all of their radios to monitor the preassigned frequencies, turning down the static to a dull roar.

Nastia stared off into space, wondering what was going on and how she could verify what they were told to do when suddenly she heard the drop of static on one of the frequencies. She turned up the volume. Yury did not notice the change as quickly as Nastia but when she reacted, he knew immediately what it was. He grabbed a notebook and pen. They recorded the string as it repeated. Nastia was sweating profusely. *My God, could this actually be happening?*

"Validated," said Yury.

The conversion and decryption were a much faster process this time. Within a few minutes, they knew the following:

The station is to send out a Preparatory Message to all

field assets. The choice of the geographic location subset was up to the station. Both the date and time indicated the Message was to be sent immediately. The numbers station was instructed to continue monitoring the standard frequencies 24 hours a day for the next transmittal.

Once their mission was known, Yury stood up and walked into the secure communication room to withdraw the necessary materials from the safe to compose the Preparatory Message.

Nastia remained at her station, slowly drumming her fingers on the countertop while her mind worked furiously hoping to find a solution to her dilemma. Then she had an idea of how to at least slow things down.

"Comrade Major. Since the decision as to which geographic subsets are to be alerted is left to the station, I have decided that we will only alert the stations located in California at this time. When additional information is received, we can bring the other subsets online as needed."

Yury was not surprised; he felt she would find ways to back off from their mission but was not sure exactly how. "Affirmative, Comrade Commander." This was a minor change, and well within the Commander's purview to direct, but he was not going to allow her to prevent the mission of the station.

Yury opened the box with the individual Message instructions for the resources located in California where there were five separate weapon sites. For each location, there was a different breakable aluminum capsule containing precise decimal geographic coordinates. Yury had no way of knowing that four out of the five sites had already been disarmed by Dieter Sieg's efforts. The final site was located near Los Angeles.

He broke open the first capsule and unrolled a small paper scroll. All of the digital information needed to construct the Preparation Message was contained on the scroll. Additionally, at the top of the scroll was the information for the specific transmission frequency for the corresponding Message.

It had taken two hours to complete construction of the first four Messages, and Yury was glad to finally be breaking open the last capsule to discover the frequency, digits for the volume within *Brandt's Collection*, the 17 digit location code, the starting page number within the reference book, and several coordinates for the line and word numbers.

Yury constructed the script needed for the Preparation Message. Unbeknownst to him, the first three digits of the Message 039 indicated that the volume to be used from *Brandt's* was Mark Twain's *The Adventures of Huckleberry Finn* which he had read in school.

The major transferred the information obtained from the sheet taken out of the capsule onto his notepad. The location code, 31843583713876745, was for a site near Los Angeles. The number 155 indicated the page number within the book where the agent was supposed to read the portion of the Message. There was a sequence of numbers that provided a particular line and word sequence, beginning with the page number previously provided. Yury transcribed the seven sets of numbers one at a time, verifying their accuracy: 2502, 3209, 0109, 2405, 2406, 2407, 2408. Once he reached the bottom of one sheet, he proceeded to the next page to obtain the words required.

The major had the required digits for the Message and inserted random words to pad it with distractors. The random words came from a sheet with the numbers interspersed within the document at specific intervals. All of the words provided were available in all the voices on the tapes stored at the station. Occasionally, Yury would add a verb here or there just to make an uninteresting group of words more notable but that was more to alleviate boredom than the standard procedure. Each line contained just the words that were supposed to be said as a phrase. Longer groups of digits were meant to be spoken as a single numeric, rather than individual numbers. When he completed the task, he handed a single sheet of paper to Commander Nastia Zamurovich, so she could double check what he constructed against the numbers provided in the aluminum capsule. The script for the last location he provided was as follows:

PICKLE
03
WINTER WOOD
9
JUICY SOCK IS TOWERING
3184
CHILDREN DEVELOP
358
THE HESITANT ELF NODS WHILE DRINKING FAR-FLUNG YAK MILK
371387
DEPENDENT HARBOR
674
REPLACE
5
STEP BACK
155
A WELL-OFF WOMAN OBSERVES SCRAWNY SNAILS
25023
ALIENS WEAR HATS
209
THE INNOCENT SUSPECT IS BLUE
0
1
0
KITTENS ARGUE WITH MOUNTAIN GOATS
9240
RAGGED RED WRIGGLE
524
A CLAMMY LONG-TERM APPARATUS
06
GRAB SUPER

After she had completed her comparison, she wrote the required frequency in the lower right-hand corner of the sheet, as she had done with the others, and then nodded to Yury while handing back the sheet and scroll. Yury gathered the five scrolls and placed them in the small cardboard box along with remnants from the capsules. He folded the flaps closed and then taped it shut before returning it to the safe. He pulled the voice files to construct the sound file for the first of the five Messages based on the script.

Unlike Routine Messages, which directed a particular set of voices to be used for its construction, Preparation and Execution Messages were to be built from the voices that had been used within the last seven days to be less conspicuous—just another layer used to disguise the broadcasts as routine.

Yury constructed the first three Messages before handing the work over to Nastia to complete the last two. He watched the TV and ignored her efforts. This gave Nastia an opportunity to write down both 17-digit location codes. Even though the station did not calculate the code, they were trained as to how the calculation was done, so she could figure out the identified location. *Maybe if I know where things are supposed to happen, I can discover what is going on.*

When she completed construction of the last two sound files, she carefully slid the two location codes into her breast pocket, before spinning her chair around. "All five transmission files are ready. Do you want to send them out?"

"No, you go ahead and do it. I'm into this show," Yury responded without looking away from the screen. In fact, this was a test. The first time she refused to do something, he would know she was no longer willing to perform the mission.

Nastia prepared the first file. After adjusting the transmitter to the frequency, she hit the play button on the laptop. Instantly, the Preparation Message was sent from their transmitter. The sheets were not in any specific order, but the sequence of transmission was irrelevant. Neither Nastia nor Yury had any way of knowing that only the third transmission was heard.

After the broadcast was complete, Nastia decided it was time for a break and a shower at home. She changed from her uniform into civilian clothes in the other room and transferred the sheet from the breast pocket of her uniform into the pocket of her civilian pants. After obtaining a list of foods from Yury, she drove directly home to take a little time to figure out where things were about to occur. Google Maps showed the first location was somewhere near San Francisco, and the other was near Los Angeles. She wished she had been able to get all five coordinates, but Nastia accepted her situation. She wiped her laptop browsing history. Even though a computer technician could retrieve it, that would take time and what mattered now was happening in a matter of hours. The last thing Nastia did before leaving home was burn the sheet she had removed from the numbers station in her kitchen sink.

Simon Dennis sat motionless in front of his portable shortwave radio on the workbench in his garage. He was surprised at how quickly it had all occurred, just over three hours ago he had received the initial Warning Message, and now he had just finished listening to the Preparation Message. *They never told us it could possibly happen this quickly.* He studied the most recent transmission unaware it had been prepared by Yury and transmitted by Nastia from the Vodyanoy Transmission Station. Simon smiled, not only inwardly but outwardly. The 51 numbers signaled an end to his torturous prison sentence.

He hated his wife with whom he had never had children. He hated his manual labor job, especially his boss who saw him as a malingering lout. He hated his home—he had expected so much more from the promise of life in America. Most of all, he had hated the routines forced into his life by his mission – reading the books, monitoring the radio, being careful not to be too visible or too vocal. *Now, I can finish this and go home a hero.*

After taking a few minutes to decrypt the location code, he took out a grid map of California he'd obtained a few years ago and quickly found where his L-PAK was located. He had been told it could be up to 12 hours away, but he was pleased to discover it was within a few miles. Aside from the opportunity to fire some sort of weapon against a country he had a seething hatred for, he knew that the L-PAK contained an exfiltration kit.

The Academy had never discussed the specific dollar amount, but there was both cash and gold in the package. With the passage of time, the price of gold alone had increased over 300 percent; enough to escape and to place a stake somewhere else, to abandon Simon Dennis and return to being Alexi Vladislavovich Kozlov. Simon had always known that his given family name meant goat; perhaps by re-embracing his name, he would be released from the curse that had made him a goat in life.

Later this afternoon, he would figure out which book from the useless set of anchors would help him finally gain the freedom he sought. Tearing the top sheet off his notepad, he folded it and placed it in his pocket before turning the radio off and leaving the garage.

Ashdod, Israel

Morty held the phone back and looked at the screen for a moment to contemplate his answer to Dieter. Dieter would not be calling the shots on the triggering of the weapons which were now in the preparation phase.

"Go on," Morty said.

"I have no way of being sure who directed the Message be sent. Fortunately, it appears the Message was sent to only one or two geographic subsets," Dieter said in a calm voice. It was not normal for him to share information until he had all the details, but the only way any of this could work was based on trust and transparency.

"Where precisely, do you know?"

"So far, we can only confirm California, but we are continuing to monitor the situation. I have informed my asset of what has happened, and he is accelerating the process of turning one of the sleeper agents to deactivate at least one device if not more. Where is your asset located; can they be put on the road at a moment's notice?" Dieter asked, getting to the point of the call.

"Yes, the agent can be prepared to travel within one hour of being notified. Do you know where my asset needs to go?" Morty asked.

"Not yet, probably will not know until the Preparation Message is sent to that location. It will be within a 12-hour drive or so from Oklahoma City. I can let you know as soon as the Message is transmitted and decrypted," Dieter explained.

"That will be fine. You only need my person to provide situational overwatch, correct? Nothing direct?" Morty asked.

"Yes, no direct involvement unless mine encounters resistance or something unknown."

"It would seem this entire situation is turning into something unknown," Morty said trying to lighten the mood.

"Undeniably; as it is with most operations of this sort, there is always that element that comes up and bites you in the ass."

"Agreed. I will notify my resource. Please let me know if you need the operator to come into play."

"Thank you, I will," Dieter said.

Morty then terminated the phone call and sent a single word text to Ashley.

>Pack

Even though the hour was late in the United States, the response was almost immediate.

<ACK

Morty rolled over and fell back to sleep almost immediately. He knew whatever was going on now would be there when he woke up.

As Simon Dennis pulled up to the abandoned warehouse, he noted the building was exactly three stories. The decision to make the trip to the L-PAK's location was made in haste, following yet another argument with his wife about money. Of course, the argument was staged so he'd get time to look up the information for the Message from *Brandt's Collection* and make the trip to the site. Even though he had not intended on the argument becoming physical, she said some things she knew would drive him to hit her, again. This time rather than cowering or running into the bedroom and locking the door, she left without saying a word. *Good riddance, this is almost all over with anyway.*

Simon got out of his late-model truck while clutching a small tool bag. He was not sure what he might need and he did not want to have to cancel his plan due to the lack of a screwdriver or pliers. The entrance was locked with a hasp and padlock. The hammer in his toolkit made short work of the hasp and gained him quick admittance to the building.

Simon had taken the time to scope out the lot and could not find any sign of security guards or other anti-theft measures. The building looked as if it'd been abandoned for years. He planned to gain access to the L-PAK and most importantly the exfiltration kit and the money therein. Without the Execution Message, he would be unable to launch the weapon, but at this point, Simon wanted to gain access to the cash to set up his escape. He would come back later and launch the damn thing.

Following the instructions from the Preparation Message, he went to the third floor of the building and found door number 64. Gripping the doorknob, he turned it, hoping to gain easy access, but of course, that was not to be. Withdrawing his trusty hammer from his tool bag along with a sturdy screwdriver, he put the blade of the screwdriver in the key slot and hit it several times. When he withdrew the blade of the screwdriver from the doorknob, the workings of the lock came with it. This time when he attempted to turn the doorknob, it gave way.

He used his flashlight to examine the large room from the doorway and discovered floor-to-ceiling steel shelving on three walls. There did not appear to be any windows or other visible ways in or out of the room. Closing the door behind him, he stepped into the center of the room, and thinking of the Preparation Message, he shone his light into the three corners. But nothing was placed directly in any of the corners. He recalled that the final part of the text was the number 465. Shining his flashlight into the corner on the left side of the room, each of the shelves was labeled with numbers. The labels in the corner on the bottommost shelf were 123, the second shelf was 223, and the third 323. The top shelf was numbered 423. Turning to his right, he walked to the next corner and saw the number on the second shelf was 265.

"Bingo!" Simon pointed his flashlight upward to a wooden crate on the top shelf above the label 465.

He located a small stepladder and tipped the oversized wooden box to the edge of the shelf. He eased it down one shelf at a time until it was on the floor. Simon never realized how lucky he was that his jostling of the box did not upset the mercury tilt triggers that would have set off the explosives prematurely. Examining the box, he concluded, *This is not what this is supposed to look like.* Three separate metallic bands were wrapped around the middle of the container to prevent it from being opened and signal any tampering.

He cut through the bands and used his claw hammer to pry open the top. After pulling handfuls of wood shavings out and dumping them on the floor, he exposed a box the size of a small footlocker. Simon lifted the L-PAK out of the wooden crate and set it on the floor. He examined all four sides as well as the top and could not gain admittance into the box. Simon stared at it for a minute thinking about what to try next. He scrambled to his knees and ran his hands over the surface of the box, feeling for a secret panel with no success. Turning the box over, Simon again ran his fingers over the surface and discovered a spot that was not completely level. There was a rectangular pattern pressed into the surface. Pushing down on it yielded no result. There did not appear to be any separation between the surface and the panel.

Reaching into his tool bag again, he pulled out a craft knife and traced the rectangle. He did not press very hard because he did not want to damage the contents. On his third trip around the rectangle, the knife suddenly plunged deeper into the box, indicating that he had cut all the way through. Once again, he dragged the knife around the rectangle, pushing it harder; he attempted to lift the corner of the panel but met some resistance. Removing the knife, he sat back again. While seated directly in front of the box, hoping for some sort of clue, the panel suddenly popped out of place, revealing a digital panel. Beneath the panel was an old style LED display that currently showed six zeros, and underneath the display was a standard numeric keypad with numbers zero to nine. Simon laughed. He was almost there and he knew it.

When each student arrived at the Academy, they were given a new birthday. In most cases, it was the same year and month as their original birthday but a different day. In his case, he was told that his new birthday was December 17, 1968. Before they left the Gamayun Education Centre, the students were informed that their birthday was much more than a sign they were getting older, it would be used in the field as the entry code for the L-PAK.

Now that he was faced with the need to gain entry, he entered 12 – 17 – 68. As he typed each digit, it appeared on the LED, replacing the zeros. Upon entering the last digit, the display flashed the number 121768 twice before returning to showing all zeros again. *What the hell? I know my own damn birthday.* Perhaps, he had entered something wrong along the way, so Simon keyed in the number once again, this time making sure the proper number was displayed on the screen before going onto the next one. Again, when he entered the last eight, the display flashed the number 121768 twice and then returned to zeros.

Simon sat back down in front of the box and stared at it disheartened. This was yet another failure of what had been a horrible life experience. He knew he was in the right place and was positive he was entering the number accurately. Why was it not working? If he could find where the lid connected, he could possibly pry it open. The only thing he could figure, after several fruitless minutes of searching, was that the box must be some kind of interlocking lid.

Simon lay back on the floor. Looking towards the ceiling, he closed his eyes and recalled the day at the Academy when they told him the date of his new birthday.

"Simon," Professor Zheleznova had said, "from this point forward your new birthday will be December 17, 1968."

"But Professor, my birthday is the twelfth of November, it is not even in December," argued Simon.

"It is now, don't you recall we said that you would get a new birthday as part of your training here?"

"But all my friends got birthdays that were in the same month as their old one, why can't I have a birthday in November like my real one?" Simon pushed.

"Tell you what, we will make a deal. You let your new birthday be December, and we will leave the day on the twelfth. Deal?" the professor proposed.

"Deal," said Simon.

The deal caused Simon much confusion from that point on. The paperwork created for him showed a birth date of 17 December, and every time the issue came up he was sent to the central office where they made corrections manually one document at a time.

Maybe that is it…

Sitting up again he moved to the footlocker and knelt in front of it. This time he entered the numbers 12 – 12 – 68. Upon entering the number eight, the LEDs began to flash very quickly, rather than just flashing twice as they had before.

"Ha! I got it," Simon said without realizing they were the last words he would ever speak.

The logic circuits within the L-PAK had determined that the wrong code had been entered three times, and to protect itself the L-PAK triggered its own self-destruction mechanism. Because the circuits were older, and the mechanism was likewise old, it took a few seconds for the explosive reaction to occur, but when it did the result was massive. The sequence of the events was driven by physics rather than by what the developers hoped would happen.

The initial explosion accomplished its function of killing the person without the proper codes and created a large clear blast zone. Due to Simon's proximity, the concussive wave from that explosion vaporized his entire body while it blew out the windows and a good portion of the structure of the third floor. Because the blast wave traveled faster than the bits of Simon Dennis that had been turned into a fine mist, the sticky red mist covered what was left of the structure rather than blasting through it.

Next, a secondary explosion was supposed to blast the concentrated oxidizer along with the *Chimera K629* into a large plume meant to travel far and wide since the initial explosion had destroyed the structure. However, two things occurred that prevented this from happening. During the initial explosion, the container holding the oxidizer had begun to fail and then the solid fuel that was supposed to launch its deathly payload high into the air unexpectedly exploded. The explosion completed the structural failure of the container, releasing the oxidizer which acted as a catalyst feeding the fireball the fuel's explosion.

Within seconds, the entire contents of the third floor were blasted by an ultra-high-temperature heatwave from one end to the other, and a massive fire burned the remnants. The tolerable storage temperature for *K629* was between -21 and 52°C (-5 and 125°F). As a result of the secondary explosion, the temperature within the blast zone exceeded 200°C (400°F). Those temperatures were maintained long enough to cook the *Chimera K629* inside the vial that held it, before the secondary explosion to release the bioweapon.

The device that was to trigger the secondary explosion proved to be very resilient, and within a minute of the fireball sweeping the floor, it exploded and threw the burned spores of *Chimera K629* across a wide area of the part of the structure that remained. The spores instantly bonded with the sticky red remnants of Simon Dennis when they landed.

Chapter Fourteen

Matehuala, Mexico

Over time, Nastia found it necessary to enforce TV rules. This was the only entertainment available, but after discovering Yury watching porn she realized some sort of limitations needed to be in place.

The first rule was no porn, and at least every four hours or so, a news broadcast was viewed to learn what was going on outside of the station. Yury didn't object but believed their leadership would provide any relevant news. They took turns deciding on programming as well as the volume during hours of rest.

The excitement of transmitting the Messages had been two hours ago, and the station returned to its dull television viewing routine. They watched the news at 1800 hours and Yury was free to turn on something else. Nastia was not surprised that nothing out of the ordinary had occurred yet. The Messages would've been received about mid-afternoon in California if everything went as planned. Nastia had no idea what action would be triggered but thought it would occur within the first six to 12 hours. Perhaps there would be some indication when they watched the news at 2200 hours. So far there had been nothing noteworthy in world news.

West Midlands, England

Areef paced his apartment while wringing his hands. He had given Abi everything needed to place things in motion, but nothing was said after the latest set of documents. In fact, Areef had not seen his young friend at all. That concerned him, but not greatly. Still, his blood was racing. He was in a place he had not been for many years, in the thick of the game waiting for the next move. All of his cunning planning was culminating; he could almost taste the victory. *At last, after all this time, a victory.*

Hidden in the corner of his shop office was an escape bag. Within moments, he could take the bag and disappear into the population. The problem with escape plans was knowing when to execute them. Too soon, and something minor could go irreparably wrong which would cause the entire thing to collapse. Too late, and the criminal authorities might be waiting for him. His timing was crucial. Once he had decided to escape, he would make his way back north to Melrose and assume the identity of Adrian Ahlström full-time while allowing Areef Rahal to evaporate. Melrose would be a comfortable place to live out his remaining years, and Freya would be a pleasant diversion.

Alva, Oklahoma

Julian's watch confirmed what he already knew—though it felt like several hours, only three minutes had passed. After his confrontation with Evan, Julian moved to his desk and spun around to face his beloved window looking over the park. His training included lessons on how to remove obstacles in your mission, but that was so distant now. He was in a different place. *Is this worth taking a man's life?*

A popping sound caught his attention, and he spun the chair around to face the Blaupunkt. He didn't need to monitor the frequency for at least another hour, so he'd switched it off. As he did, he saw the envelope Evan had left on top of the stereo. Looking at it, he noticed the name Dmitry was handwritten on it. Picking the envelope up, he returned to his desk. The envelope was sealed with the only markings being the handwritten name. He slashed the length of the envelope with his letter opener and pulled out a single piece of paper and unfolded it. He noticed it was handwritten in English:

My Son,

I know if you are reading this, you are probably terribly confused, and in all likelihood, I am no longer in this world. It was never my intent to leave you abandoned and in this sort of situation, but alas things have occurred that have brought us here. I will not go into deep details about what has happened; I am choosing to rely on the person who gave you this envelope to provide you with that information. Instead, I want to try to explain why you should listen to the presenter of this letter and do what he may ask.

You may think it cruel that I sent you away to a program at such a young age. But it was my love for you that caused me to take such action. I knew that our country, and the government I was part of, was going to fail and I needed a way to protect you from that and from the consequences of being my child. I can only hope that you've had a happy life as a result of my action — a happy life that could not have been possible otherwise.

Now your life is threatened by my connections. The man who directed the Crimson Firebird Initiative has chosen to use its capabilities to exact personal vengeance. To allow him to do so would be catastrophic for the United States, but more importantly, it would be destructive to you and all you have built over the course of your life. I beg you to preserve that life by assisting the person who has given you this letter. Help him to do what is necessary to prevent a cataclysmic disaster.

As I told you that night, many years ago: never forget your mother, I love you and know we want only the best for you. Even though I told you back then never to forget that you are Dmitry Fyodorevich Maldroski, perhaps it is time to let that go and fully assume the person you are now. You are the one great and pure thing I ever accomplished in my life. To preserve that, you must do what's needed to destroy the remnants of the horrible part of my legacy.

Love,
Papa

In the span of one afternoon, everything Julian knew or had become was being threatened. The secret mission he had begun at the tender age of six was now exposed. His anxiety rose as he checked the time again—only four minutes had passed. He felt as if someone was removing his skin bit by bit. Every minute that passed felt like torturous hours.

Romulus, Michigan

Before she even read the SMS, Nikki knew she was being called into action. It was time; too many things were moving in various directions for her involvement not to be required. As soon as she read Morty's single word, she fetched her small nylon duffel bag on the closet's top shelf. Everything she required for three days was packed in it.

She packed the ammunition that was stashed in a living room drawer. Finally, she took the pistol from under a pile of magazines on her coffee table and slipped it into the waistband of her jeans. Nikki checked her reflection from behind to check her shirt covered the sleek weapon.

Nikki poured her wine down the kitchen drain. Until this mission was complete, she would need a clear head. Any level of alcohol in the blood was a detriment to reaction and thinking speed.

Before returning to her couch, she withdrew a Diet Coke from the refrigerator and popped it open. Sitting back down, she took her TV remote in hand and changed the channel to a 24-hour news station. *So, what the hell happened in the world now?* She allowed herself to breathe deeply and regain her calm. There was no way to control her thoughts from drifting to Evan and longing to know how deeply he was involved.

West Midlands, England

Qa'id had just gotten off the phone after convincing his leadership that the time for action had arrived. His mind was crackling with thoughts of what might happen once the West was tamed and had blown itself up without any direct confrontation. He was surprised he'd heard from them this early. It was just before Fajr in the Middle East, which meant they were either up extremely early or had never gone to sleep the night before. Either way, he had the endorsement to send the Preparation Message to the numbers stations to direct all operatives to prepare the launching of their weapons upon receipt of the next Message.

Regardless of the time in the Middle East, it was 1:00 AM in West Midlands, and while he had no problem calling Abi at this hour, he thought it best to let him rest because the next day or so would be quite busy. Then, if all went as expected, life could turn into one continuous stream of motion as events exceeded their wildest expectations. *For now, I will let them sleep, but when I awaken him, we will use Allah's Numbers to change the face of the world.* Qa'id settled into his easy chair and turned on his television, tuning to a movie from the West that he would undoubtedly condemn as haram to his minions.

Alva, Oklahoma

It was after 9 o'clock at night when Evan suddenly felt hungry. *I haven't eaten a damn thing since breakfast.* It wasn't that he was hungry but he learned from his time in Afghanistan and Kuwait that running on empty wasn't wise and at times like this it was best to eat when you were able. So, he drove through Alva four times trying to decide what he wanted to eat. He finally gave up and pulled into a small convenience store. When all else failed in the field, if he could find a frozen burrito he could survive until the next regular meal.

He bought a beef and bean as well as an El Diablo burrito. Rather than heating them in the store, he went back to his hotel room where he was surprised to learn there was no microwave. Fortunately, the clerk at the front desk agreed to let him use the microwave for employees. She had handed him Dieter's FedEx package earlier in the day. Apparently, she was working an extended shift.

The clerk presented the burritos to Evan on a paper plate. "Enjoy, be careful of the El Diablo – my boyfriend ate one once and ended up on the toilet for two days."

"Wish I knew that before I bought it. Thanks." Evan smiled. Once back in his room, he unwrapped the hot burritos, prepared for the molten lava cheese in the middle. He sucked in air to cool it off. Evan finished off the beef and bean first, and then the El Diablo in four bites. *I've eaten MREs; in a contest of me versus food, I win.*

It was a force of habit to turn on the news and hit mute whenever he entered a hotel room. If he had been looking at the TV, he would have seen an aerial shot from a helicopter of a city block of warehouses on fire. The assemblage of buildings was surrounded by flashing blue and red lights from the fire trucks and other emergency vehicles. Had the sound been on, Evan would also have heard the fire was of an unknown but suspicious origin.

Matehuala, Mexico

With the advent of satellite broadcasting and the 24-hour news cycle, people around the world could share the same news in real time. As soon as Nastia flipped from Yury's sophomoric comedy to the news channel, the screen was filled with pictures of a massive fire. She blinked several times. With Yury present, she could not react though she wanted to.

"I have a friend who is a fireman; he says that one of the scariest things in life is running into a fire without knowing how much worse it is going to get while you are in there," Yury said.

"Yes. I can imagine it is quite intense." Nastia tried to keep her voice from shaking as she realized this location could very well match the coordinates she had decrypted. *But what purpose would a fire serve and why would you go through all this effort just to have one started?*

They watched the broadcast loop for several minutes. The cause of the fire was under investigation as there was suspicion of arson given an unauthorized vehicle had been found on the premises. No one had been apprehended yet.

"This is boring," Yury said, hoping to pressure Nastia to change the channel.

"Fine, change it."

As soon as he was again absorbed in his movie, she pulled out her personal laptop to research the fire.

Near Los Angeles, California

Once the fire was under control, investigators set about their work. District Fire Investigator Steve Davison and his trainee Maritza Ramirez prowled around the building determined to be the origin of the fire. The building was supposed to be three floors tall, but it looked more like one. The firemen illuminated the rubble and smoking cinders, looking for a precise starting point. Neither could smell an obvious accelerant, but they could smell something familiar and metallic. There was no smell of burnt human flesh which would have indicated the arsonist had been condemned by his own creation.

As the fire had progressed and the floors had collapsed, material from the third floor had landed below. As a result, when the senior investigator noticed a faint sheen on a bit of wallboard, he was unaware that it had originally begun on the third floor. Even though the wallboard had been scorched, the red of Simon Dennis' blood could be faintly seen, as well as what appeared to be grains of embedded salt. The investigator made a mental note, but this did not register as a cause for concern.

"Steve, come take a look at this," Maritza said, shining her flashlight on something she found.

Even in the worst explosions, parts of the bomb usually remain—an inconvenient rule of physics. As the mind of the senior investigator spun into action, he quickly realized he was looking at the timing device of some sort of explosive. His mind connected the wallboard and he broke into a cold sweat. "Leave, now!" Steve grabbed Maritza by the shoulders and pushed her towards the perimeter's entry.

"What the fuck?" she argued before being shoved forward by her supervisor.

"Dammit, Marty, GO! Move your ass, this thing might be biological," the older man said trying to get her to react.

Alva, Oklahoma

When Julian arrived home from the bank, he requested to be alone in his office to work on something important. He had a small portable radio with similar shortwave capabilities as the Blaupunkt in his work office. No additional broadcasts had been made. Julian sat in his large executive-style chair and stared at the oak shelves that lined the walls. There was, of course, the most visible reflection of who he truly was—*Brandt's Collection*, and dozens of framed pictures from his life with Camille. Photos in front of their first house, Camille pregnant with their first child, and their children's athletic teams coached by Julian. All were images of a good life. *All pictures of a life that was a lie. Or was it?* There was just more to the story than what met the eye. Now what? The small silver clock on his desk, a thank you from a local charity, showed the time was after 8 o'clock; he had been in the office for several hours.

"Babe, are you hungry? You never came out for dinner. Not sure what you're working on but you do need to take time to eat." Camille stuck her head in the door.

"Yeah, you're right." He followed Camille into the kitchen and picked at his food.

"Jules, what is going on? I have never seen you like this before." Camille reached her hand out only to have him pull away.

Julian pushed away his plate and clasped his hands as if in prayer. He continued to look down before staring at Cam for several minutes, just appreciating the woman she was. The pained look on her face conveyed her deep concern. *Oh, how I love you.* Julian realized that regardless of what he was going to do he would first have to explain why. He would have to confess that he had lied to her their entire lives.

Before he could speak, she laid her hands upon his. "Babe, it doesn't matter what it is — we'll handle this together, just like we have everything else."

Julian could not handle the intensity of her stare, and he broke it off, lowering his head. "No human being on this planet deserves the kind of love you have for me. After I'm done talking, you may not feel this way about me anymore," Julian said in a small voice. When he raised his head, he expected to see fear on her face, but there was still soft love reflected in her eyes.

"Go ahead, Jules, whatever it is it will be okay." She squeezed his hands in hers. "Besides, whatever you have to say isn't a matter of life or death."

No, at least not yet. Julian began to explain how he had arrived where he was today.

Camille asked questions, but until now, everything had happened decades before. His father leaving him at the Academy, his training, and move to the United States—all were past history and none involved Camille. He had lied to cover up his true identity when he talked about his family being killed, but aside from listening to a radio a couple of times a week, Julian really hadn't done anything, at least not until now.

"What about your parents, are they still in Russia?"

"My mother died before I was born, but that's a whole other

story. I think my father's death, at least based on what he's written." Julian removed the letter from his pocket and slid it across the table.

Camille placed her hand over the top of the letter. "So basically, you're a spy who really didn't do any spying. Is that about it?"

"Well, more or less, until today. Today I received a Message that I need to prepare to execute a mission. But as soon as I got the Message, Evan confronted me with the truth behind this mission."

"Evan? You mean the reporter? He's some kind of spy too?"

"To be honest I don't know, we never got into that. Evan was sent here, somehow connected to my father, to try and stop me from doing anything and to help defuse the weapon I was expected to launch."

"So, where does this leave us?"

"Cam, I love you. I love our life. I don't want to do anything to hurt that and if I do what I am supposed to do, I will destroy not only our life but possibly thousands of other lives. That is just not who I am, it never was. I was told when I was a kid that all this had to do with some greater goal of saving the Motherland. Now, it's just politics. According to Evan, it isn't even the Soviet government that launched this. It was some crazy guy who thought up the whole program. Someone named Sergei." Julian couldn't stop the tears from welling up in his eyes—a combination of extreme emotion and frustration.

"Baby, the good thing is you don't have to do any of it. Just tell Evan where this thing is and let him defuse it." Cam stroked Julian's arm to calm him.

"It's not that easy, I don't even know where it is. I have to wait for the next Message to give me a location, and then another Message after that to tell me what the codes are to open it. Then, Evan and I would have to figure out how to diffuse the damn thing. The scariest part is, this isn't even a nuke, it's a kind of biological weapon that could kill everybody."

Until now, Camille had not understood the severity of the situation. A biological weapon? Those things contained germs and viruses that killed people by the millions. Now her husband, the man she loved, was supposed to somehow stop this? What if he got killed? What if he failed?

"Baby, I'm sure Evan has some way of turning this thing off before it blows up. They wouldn't have sent him here otherwise." Camille paused for a moment and let logic take control of her thoughts. "How long before you get the rest of the information you need so you can defuse this thing?"

"I don't know. I'm supposed to monitor the radio and listen to the next Message. The problem is, I wasn't alone coming to the US, and there are hundreds of others watching for the same Message," Julian explained.

Camille let it all sink in. "Well, hopefully, Evan has friends too." She picked up the letter.

"You know, the only person on Earth who ever made me feel like I was the most important guy alive, aside from you, was my father. I never really understood what he was trying to do for me and what pain it caused him," Julian said when Camille lowered the letter after reading it.

"Why don't you finish eating, baby, you're going to need your strength to save the world," she said. Camille slid his plate back towards him and turned on the kitchen TV.

Julian happened to glance up just as the picture shifted to the scene of a warehouse district fire near LA. The reporter was speaking to a witness when someone in a hazmat suit ushered them away. Everything in his mind connected it at once; his knowledge of his mission and what Evan had told him about *Chimera K-629*. Julian dropped his fork and scrambled from his chair into the other room to locate his phone. He ran past an open-mouthed Camille as he headed to the door.

"It's started," he said.

Camille turned and looked in horror at the TV just in time to see an aerial shot of the inferno burning out of control as the firemen were pulled away due to possible hazardous waste.

As Nastia searched for information regarding the fire in Los Angeles, she was not disappointed. Speculation as to the cause of the blaze began almost immediately. Based on prior recent incidents and general patterns of behavior, Muslim extremists were blamed almost instantly. As soon as those accusations were spoken, counterclaims of racial profiling and generalized racism began. *It isn't profiling when there is proof that a particular group has historically been so violent.* As time passed, additional information was posted. There were photos of the abandoned pickup truck that was registered to Simon Dennis. It all seemed routine until information regarding the possible cause of the fire was leaked. Parts of a bomb were discovered and then suspicions that it was a dirty bomb. *Was this some sort of chemical attack on the United States?* Before her thought was fully formed, her stream of consciousness shifted from chemical to biological attack.

Nastia leaned back in her chair and let the ramifications sink in. There was no reason for the Russian government to launch a bioweapons attack against the United States – at least not at the moment. *At the moment? How about any time ever?* She ran through what she knew at this point: The station had released a Preparatory Message, a few hours later a weapon was set off which caused a massive fire, and the nature of the weapon appeared to be biological. Those were the facts, but there were many things she wasn't sure of. For instance, if the station had sent the Message to five different operatives, why didn't the others also set off their weapons? The world political situation was quiet so why was this happening? Who could she contact to verify that what they were doing was sanctioned and legitimate?

Nastia did not realize that Yury could see what she was doing on her computer. Yury appeared to be engrossed in his movie, laughing or making crude comments from time to time. He could not see her screen well enough to read all of the text but he was able to get the gist of her research. *Why would she need to find out what has happened? That is not our function.*

Nastia was exhausted, and looking up at the clock on the wall realized that due to the hour, nothing more substantial would materialize until tomorrow.

"Yury, could you please turn down the TV a bit? I am going to try and get some sleep. Tomorrow will likely be a hectic day." She stood and stretched after closing her laptop.

"Of course." Yury lowered the volume. "I will take first watch tonight … I'm not very sleepy anyway."

"Thank you, Comrade Major. Goodnight." Nastia entered the secure communications room that housed the collapsible cot they traded off using while sleeping in the station.

"Goodnight."

It was a little after 0100 hours when Commander Zamurovich went to bed. At 0230 hours, Yury was fairly sure she was asleep since he could hear her deep and steady breathing. Her laptop was secured with a password. This was more an irritant than a stumbling block. Yury withdrew a small flash drive from his pocket and plugged it into the USB port on the side of the laptop. He then flipped the laptop over and removed the battery as well as the charging cable. After waiting five minutes, he reinstalled the battery and reattached the charging cable, then turned the machine back right side up, opened the lid of the laptop, and hit the power switch.

As expected, the computer booted from the USB device rather than the hard drive, easily bypassing the simple security Nastia thought would protect her. After the machine booted from the USB drive, it automatically installed software to allow the laptop to be monitored remotely. Yury removed the USB device and rebooted to the locked screen. He returned the computer to the exact position she had left it.

Yury yawned as he starting another episode of *Hill Street Blues,* dozing in his chair, prepared to awaken if Nastia stirred.

Even with the stress of all that was going on, Evan forced himself to sleep with a heavy dose of melatonin. He was jarred awake by the sound of someone pounding on his hotel room door. Evan had fallen asleep, still dressed, lying on his back in the bed, balancing a half-full Diet Coke on his chest. Startled, he spilled the soda as he awakened. Cursing, Evan grabbed a towel and opened the door. He was a little surprised to find Julian.

"I'm in, but first I want some answers." Julian pushed into the room.

"Okay, I'll try to let you know what I know," Evan said as he closed the door.

The two men stood a few feet apart, and even though neither was confrontational, it almost appeared to be an old-fashioned gunfight.

"First, I want to know who sent you,"

"I was contacted by a guy named Dieter Sieg who was friends with your father. I guess they met each other many years ago on the job. Dieter used to be with the Stasi. He was the one who gave me all the background and told me about the Crimson Firebird Initiative and what was going to be necessary to try and stop it."

"Why did he contact you specifically?"

Evan could not help but smile at the question and shrug. "I don't have the foggiest damn idea; I've been asking him the same thing since the very start. The only answer I ever got was that he knew about some stories I wrote when I was in Afghanistan and Kuwait. Based on my journalism and experience, he thought I might be good in this instance. I am by no means a spy."

"Great, so you're a reporter, but you're acting like a spy. If you know what I am, you must know that there were over 100 of us that came to the United States. What about the rest of them? Do they all get their own reporter?"

"First of all, I'm not a reporter; I'm just a writer who needed money so I wrote news stories. I can only tell you that you are the only one who gets a personal visit from me, and I guess it's because your father wanted this handled with some degree of finesse. Most of the others have already been contacted by Dieter and his associates. There may still be more out there. Dieter was going to trigger the different phases so we could observe what was going on and deal with each one individually, if possible."

Julian took a seat but never took his eyes off Evan. "Dieter is responsible for what just happened in Los Angeles?"

Evan took a seat at the foot of the bed facing Julian before shaking his head. "No. That was our old friend Sergei, or one of Sergei's minions. That's why I confronted you the way I did; we're out of time, and we need to do this now."

Julian let that sink in for a moment. "Okay, so I get the Preparation and Execution Messages. We go to wherever this thing is located and we get access to it. The part I know only sets it off, so how do you plan on defusing it?"

Evan nodded. "I was wondering about that too." Opening his dresser drawer, Evan removed the still unopened FedEx package that had arrived earlier. Handing the box to Julian, he continued, "Dieter sent me this. Apparently, it's some sort of device that we plug into the sequencer of the L-PAK. We have to do it within 14 minutes of opening the box … if we get that done this device will defuse the weapon."

"Fourteen minutes?" Julian examined the unopened box.

"Yeah, apparently there are a whole lot of booby-traps built into the L-PAK that nobody ever told you guys about. Dieter's team discovered them as they diffused the other weapons they were able to locate," Evan explained.

"The bastards didn't even trust us? Unbelievable. What about after all of this? Suppose we actually succeed, what happens then?"

"Nothing, I suppose. All of this is being done under the radar. I don't think anybody in the United States, like the CIA, DHS, or FBI, is even aware of it. If they are, I have to believe they would've intervened by now. I guess if we defuse this damn thing, you go back to being a banker and I go back to being a writer," Evan said.

Julian set the FedEx box on the desk and looked directly at Evan. "Fine, fine. As you may know, I'm unaware of where this device is even located until I get the next Message. I was instructed in the Warning Message to monitor specific frequencies for the next Message in the series. Once I have that, we can travel to where the L-PAK is stored. Then, we have to wait for the Execution Message before we have the codes needed to complete my end of the operation."

"Why don't you grab your stuff and come with me back to my house; that way we're both in the same place when we start getting this information and can take off more quickly," Julian added.

"Agreed, I'll pack up," Evan said, rising, as he extended his hand.

"This is not the way I'd expected any of this to turn out you know. I had no idea what the end result of my mission was, or I would've abandoned it years ago." Julian shook Evan's hand.

"Sometimes, we place too much trust in others and they abuse us," Evan said. He gathered his belongings and stuffed them into his suitcase.

Julian changed the TV to a news channel, this time with the sound up. Once Evan had packed his belongings from the bathroom, he completed packing his suitcase and put his laptop into the backpack. Evan picked up the FedEx box from the desk and tore it open. Reaching inside and digging through Styrofoam peanuts, he removed a small, cigarette-pack sized, black device that had what appeared to be coax connectors at either end. He offered it to Julian who waved it off.

"No thanks, I'll enter the codes, you get to defuse it."
With that said, Evan slipped the device into his pocket and they picked up Evan's bags and left the motel room to head back to Julian's house. Evan followed in his rental car and during the few minutes alone, Evan realized he felt more optimistic than at any time since picking up that first manila envelope. With Julian on board, things were moving in a direction that might lead to permanently extinguishing the Crimson Firebird.

Chapter Fifteen

West Midlands, England

Abi tried to focus on the illuminated screen of his phone which had woken him. The screen remained a blur to his tired eyes as he finally gave up and answered.

"As-Salaam-Alaikum," Qa'id said in a jovial voice.

"Waʿalaykumu as-salām," Abi responded, less with joy than as a reflex.

"My young friend, it is indeed a great day to be alive for today that which you have provided will be put to use."

Abi sat up in bed, now fully awake. "You mean that we can—"

"Hush now. Not over the telephone. I will be there in a few minutes." Qa'id hung up without speaking another word.

Abi showered and dressed. He had just finished putting his clothes on when he heard a knock at the door.

Qa'id strode into the kitchen. "The Preparatory Message you sent yesterday, that went to all of the numbers stations and you told them to notify all of the locations of the need to prepare?"

"Um, yes, err, no. I mean, yes, I sent it to all of the numbers stations, and no, I did not tell them to send it to all of their locations. Like so many things, I don't have enough information, so I left that choice to them."

"No matter. This morning I want you to resend the same communiqué, only this time direct the stations to notify all geographic locations; we want to have all the weapons ready. Have you perchance seen the news this morning?" Qa'id asked.

"Uh, no. Your call woke me up. I was up late last night and skipped morning prayers so I could be better rested for whatever today might bring. I hoped that Allah would understand that—"

"Yes, yes, Allah understands when more important priorities

sometimes need to be done in his name and prayer must take a backseat. It is a good thing because I need you to prepare this new communication immediately. Can you create the new script for broadcast right now?"

"I suppose so, it may take a little time to do the recording, but I can get it out within the hour," Abi offered.

"Yes, yes, that would be fine. Do it and do it quickly. Before sunset today we will set this entire operation in motion and as the Quran 5:33 tells us: *'Maim and crucify infidels if they criticize Islam and in doing so place me in power.'* After you have the next transmittal ready, take time to look at the news as there are interesting goings-on in Los Angeles in the United States. I believe the first strike has been made and now we need to ensure that all of the weapons have been brought into readiness. Prepare and record the communiqué but do not broadcast it until after you return from Dhuhr, your noon prayers. That way you may pray for our success and it will truly be blessed by Allah." Qa'id did not explain that doing it this way would also allow the numbers station to send the Message at the start of the day in the United States, increasing his chances of success.

Before he exited, Qa'id hugged Abi, and kissed him on both cheeks, promising his return later in the day. Then as quickly as he had blown in, Qa'id departed, leaving Abi a bit unnerved. Gaining his grip on reality, Abi quickly pulled out the materials needed to alter the previous transmittal and perform the necessary encryptions before recording the sound file. As promised, within an hour he was set to rebroadcast the communiqué to all numbers stations, instructing them to send out the Preparatory Message to all geographic locations.

With several hours before Dhuhr, Abi searched the internet for the incident in Los Angeles. Abi sat reading, his mouth hanging open at the thought of what all of this meant. *Was this truly what Allah wanted?* For the first time, he was trying to reconcile the revenge he desired with what he believed might be Allah's intentions.

Nastia was not quite sure what woke her up. It could've been the overhead fluorescent lights being suddenly turned on or Yury opening and closing the drawers of the safe.

"Major Trechnikov, what in the hell is going on?" Nastia asked.

"I'm sorry, Comrade Commander, we have received another communication. This one is directing us to notify all geographic locations. I am beginning to construct the new Messages." Yury slammed the safe drawer and departed.

Nastia felt sick to her stomach, realizing what this new transmittal could mean. Unless she did something, she would be partly responsible for the world's first biological war. *And I have yet to figure out who is actually directing we start this damn war.* She sat up, throwing her legs over the edge of the cot and putting on her boots before buckling her gun belt in place. Nastia found Yury hard at work creating the scripts for 29 separate Preparatory Messages as she walked unsteadily into the control room.

"I will assist you in a moment, Comrade, but first I need coffee," Nastia said.

"No problem, Comrade Commander, it will take me a little while to get the scripts completed." Yury did not look up from his work.

As Nastia sipped her coffee, Yury broke open the aluminum capsule for one site, and then a few minutes later for the next. It would not take him very long to create the scripts, as with most repetitive work the more you did it, the faster you became. While sipping her coffee, she switched on her laptop to search for new information concerning Los Angeles. What she read bordered on terrifying.

Even legitimate news agencies were reporting that some sort of chemical hazard was found in the burnt rubble of the warehouses but they still had not called it a weapon. Because of the possible danger, several blocks around the warehouses had been evacuated, even though the fire was now out. The fringe news agencies spoke of rocket parts being found as well as traces of an unknown pathogen.

More far-out sources were reporting some sort of imminent invasion was possible. Rumors were also flying that the United States was preparing for a military retaliation as soon as the origin of the weapons could be firmly identified. *Even if they are blaming the Arabs now, it would be hard to believe that all traces of Russian origin could have been wiped from the weapons. It is only a matter of time until World War III begins.* Nastia bit her nails.

Yury unquestioningly continued to create each of the scripts for the new Preparatory Messages while monitoring Nastia. So far, her actions were suspicious but not traitorous; her opportunity to prove her loyalty would come very shortly when it was time to begin transmitting all of these Messages.

As expected, it did not take Yury very long to construct the scripts. As was the procedure, he handed them off to Nastia to verify the information transferred from the scrolls in the aluminum capsules matched what would compose the sound file for each location. Once that part of the operation was completed, Yury built the necessary audio files for each of the 29 geographic areas. He offered to do this on his own, which was a surprising relief to Nastia. With the five Messages previously sent, the total was 33 locations—all the sites for which the Vodyanoy Transmission Station was responsible. Because Yury was using his computer to construct the sound files, he could no longer monitor Nastia.

She was trying to construct a list of contact numbers to let someone know what was going on. The more things she read about Los Angeles, the more she realized she had to do something. Nastia wished she had spent more time getting to know Yury. If she had, she might know what to say to convince him to help. But that opportunity was lost, and she could only hope that logic would rule.

It was almost 1100 hours when Yury announced that he had completed all of the sound files and they were ready for transmission. He had already begun to attach the necessary cables from the laptop to the transmission radios when Nastia spun her chair around from her workstation to face him and interrupted.

"Comrade Major, are you aware that we have received no outside validation of the requirement to send any of these Messages out?" Nastia asked.

"Yes, Comrade Commander I am well aware. But if you recall our training, that is not an unusual occurrence. In fact, we are relied upon to carry out our duties based only on the transmittals we have received so far. What is your concern?"

"I am concerned that we may be obeying orders from someone or something other than our headquarters. I'm worried that the system may have been compromised and if we take this action, we may inadvertently start a hostility that has global ramifications."

"So, what do you propose we do? We can't just sit here and do nothing. If the Messages are legitimate, their broadcast may be part of a much bigger plan and without their being sent the plan could fail. Do you want to be responsible for that? Besides, we have no way of reaching out to anyone from here," Yury responded.

"But we do. We could contact the Russian Embassy in Mexico City. One of us could go to the embassy and use their classified communications equipment to speak to someone at the SVR. Maybe we should just pause until we hear something further and more definitive."

"Perhaps, maybe you are right. Perhaps we should validate this before we do something further." Yury nodded.

"Yes. Did you see the news reports of the fire in California? I believe that is a direct result of the Message that we sent out. The fire is in the same location that was in the communication we broadcast yesterday."

As he heard this, it was hard for Yury to control his reactions but he did. For her to know the exact location, she must've compromised the transmittal. *What else has she compromised?* "I saw what was on the news; did you find some more information about it?" Yury finally managed to say.

"Yes, yes I did. " Nastia turned her chair back toward her laptop.

"Let me show you, this may help you understand my concern." Then she froze.

Yury's reflection had appeared on the screen of her laptop and he was now standing directly behind her. Nastia had no clue that he had already drawn his weapon with a round in the chamber, and the only thing left to do was to squeeze the trigger.

The sound of the shot rang out and echoed in the concrete room. It would be some time before Yury's hearing returned to normal. He fired the shot into the back of Nastia's skull, with the barrel pointing downward to try and avoid a ricochet should the bullet exit through her face. As a result, the laptop and counter were covered by the explosion of blood, mixed with bone fragments, hair, and brain. Looking down at her body which was slumped forward, Yury slowly slid his pistol back into its holster, and after fastening it, he leaned forward and spat on Nastia's body.

"*Chornyy predatel,* a fucking traitor," Yury said, and after standing straight again, he went to the secure communications room where he removed the blanket from the cot and brought it back into the main room using it to cover Nastia's body. He would figure out how to dispose of the corpse later. Right now, he needed to complete his mission and transmit 29 Messages as he had been ordered to do. By 1300 hours, he had completed the transmissions and had returned to watching TV, this time he could watch what he wanted and when.

Alva, Oklahoma

Julian called Camille while he was driving back from the hotel to let her know that Evan would be staying with them until the situation was resolved. During the call, she let him now that she had arranged for their teenagers to spend the night with friends to keep them away from any danger that might arise. By the time they arrived, Camille had made up the guest room for Evan; she only spoke to Julian who shrugged as she left the room.

Evan felt the chill from Camille. He couldn't blame her; after all, Evan had lied and exposed her husband's past. There was nothing he could do about it.

"Give her a little time, she'll get over it." Julian led Evan down the hall to his room.

Once alone, Evan lay down intending to sleep but had no way to turn off his mind. Now that Julian was on board, things would only get more complicated. He welcomed the way his mind focused as it prevented uneasiness from creeping up on him. He was almost to the point of dozing off when he realized Dieter needed an update. He sent a simple text:

```
>J Onboard. Standing By.
```

The response came back almost instantly:

```
<ACK
```

Acknowledge? Was his last thought before allowing himself to give in to exhaustion.

After a restless night, Evan was awoken by the smell of the most wondrous of breakfast foods —bacon. Voices came from the other room but he remained in bed to give them privacy. The tranquility did not last long, as a small knock was followed by Camille saying not to rush but breakfast was ready.

After taking a shower and getting dressed, Evan found Cam in the kitchen. She handed him a cup of coffee.

"The cream and sugar are on the table. I hope you slept well."

"Uh, thanks," Evan said taking the cup, gingerly sipping as he moved to the table. "I thought I heard Julian."

"Oh, he's up and gone. Fridays at the bank are very busy, so he wanted to go in and put a few things right before you two go about saving the world." Camille offered a worried smile.

Evan was not sure what to say. It was hard enough to explain things to Julian, now he needed to do the same with someone indirectly involved. Someone confused and possibly hurt over what she had discovered about Julian's hidden past.

"Yep, that's me. Put on a mask and cape then go save the world," Evan said trying to lighten the mood. Evan had always used humor to deal with extreme stress. At the moment, however, he felt more in control than he had since returning home from Afghanistan.

Camille sat down to drink her coffee as he ate breakfast. The news channel televised the scene from the Los Angeles fire, which now included the arrival of the men in their hazmat suits. Evan greedily dug into his eggs and bacon. "I had a light supper last night, so forgive me." He took seconds of eggs and another biscuit.

"No problem, I like it when my meals are enjoyed." Camille refilled his coffee cup and sat down again as if she was waiting on something specific to occur.

Evan decided to put a stop to their polite dance. "I know you probably have a lot of questions but I only have answers for some of them at best. Is there anything specific?"

"There is one thing: how did you like your breakfast?"

Evan was confused, "Um, it was incredible. Delicious. Exactly what I needed. It's been a long time since I've had any kind of bacon other than that precooked microwave stuff so it was excellent."

"Good, from what Jules tells me you guys may be taking a road trip." She could see her words had perplexed Evan, so she explained further, "I've accepted it. Julian is the man I love, despite his past. It's what he does from now on that matters. As for you, you lied but for a purpose. You need to be the person who makes sure my man comes back alive. I don't know if you're CIA, FBI, ATF—"

"None of those," Evan interrupted, "I'm just a writer who got pulled into this."

"Uh huh, being a writer is really risky." The sarcasm dripped off her words. "But if you were some kind of secret, double, naughty spy you couldn't tell me anyway. Like I said, I don't care who or what you are –you take care of him and you bring him back to me. Whatever it is you two have to do to stop all this badness from happening, you better do it.”

“Camille, I will do everything possible.” Evan met her intense gaze.

There was a heavy pause as Cam looked into his eyes for reassurance. “Since we’re stuck here waiting for Julian, you want to move into the living room where we can be a bit more comfortable?”

“Uh, sure, as long as I can take my coffee with me,” Evan said smiling.

“Always, until noon, it is expected that coffee will be carried any and everywhere in the house.” Camille laughed.

The more time Evan spent with her, the more he realized what a lucky man Julian was; he wondered if he may have found similar luck with Nikki. As morning became afternoon, Evan prepared after raiding the refrigerator and finding the makings for a pair of Montecristo sandwiches on rye, using some of the leftover bacon. During their lunch conversation, Evan described his time as an embed in Afghanistan while she filled him in on her three children’s academics and sports.

“They are so different than either of us was growing up.” Camille paused, realizing everything Julian had ever told her about growing up was probably contrived. *No, I am beyond that, I need to worry about now.*

Both of them turned toward the front door, as Julian suddenly burst in. “I got the Preparatory Message. I need to decrypt it to find out where we’re going!” he yelled on his way to his office. He knelt on the floor, flipping through the pages of Jules Verne’s *20,000 Leagues Under the Sea*. “I was able to break apart most of the code in the office but I need the books to figure out the rest.”

“Any idea where we’re going?” Evan asked.

“It looks like somewhere in Kentucky to the middle of nowhere between two cities. We’ll have to figure it out on the way.” Julian let out a frustrated groan, grabbing the book to sit at his desk.

“I have your bag packed,” Camille said.

“Excellent, I also realized we’re going to need your help here at home to do this." Julian located the page and counted the lines.

"Huh?" Camille said.

Julian paused from his work. "If Evan and I take off for the wilds of Kentucky, someone is going to have to monitor the radio for the Execution Message, write down all the numbers, then text them to us so I can break the code to get the launch codes. Evan, grab a box from the garage—we need to take *Brandt's Collection* with us." He returned to counting lines.

"Okay, baby, whatever you need me to do," Camille agreed.

Camille and Evan packed all 102 volumes of *Brandt's Compleat Collection of Great World Literature.*

"This isn't making sense to me," Julian said, shaking his head.

"Problem?" Evan asked.

"I really have no way of knowing for sure until we get there. I have some wacky numbers that may or may not be an address; maybe part of it is a combination or cypher. We were always taught that once we had the information, and arrived on site, everything would be evident. All the numbers would somehow be used in locating the L-PAK. I guess I was just looking for something more definitive."

"Okay, we'll figure it out when we get there. Speaking of that, which car do you want to take? I have a rental that will be anonymous," Evan suggested.

Julian nodded. "Good idea. Can you handle a gun?"

"Yeah—you think we'll need them?"

"Maybe. I have a pair of 9mm, semi-autos, that work?"

"Yep, do you know if the penalties for armed espionage are heavier than just plain old espionage?" Evan asked trying to use humor to break the growing tension.

"In for a penny, in for a pound." Julian folded the paper with the decrypted information. He moved a few boxes in his closet and revealed a small safe from which he withdrew two Ruger SR9 pistols along with a box of ammunition. He loaded the magazines and set both weapons on the desk blotter in front of him.

"Are those really necessary?" Camille asked.

"It takes a good man with a gun to stop an evil man who has one," Julian replied. "It's just a precaution."

"Uh-huh." Camille shook her head. "Nothing heroic, okay?"

"Okay, babe – I promise. How long do you need to get ready?" he asked Evan.

"I just need to throw a few things in my bag and I'll be ready to pop smoke."

"Let's hit the road in the next five," Julian suggested. Julian grabbed his small black duffel bag and slipped two pistols inside. He considered packing additional ammunition, but with 34 rounds between them, *if the need arises, more bullets aren't going to help.*

Camille was in the kitchen, preparing sandwiches. He wrapped his arm around her waist, pulling her close. As she had done since they first started dating, she pressed her ass back against him and slowly ground back and forth. Julian felt reassurance that they were still connected. She spun around within his arms but rather than raising her face to kiss him, as she often did, she lay her head on his chest and held him tight.

"I love you," she said.

Julian felt his body relax for the first time in the last 24 hours upon hearing those words. The bond between them was still there, and it would stay. When this was over, they could continue the way it had been. But he had to get through this first. He tightened his grip on her, and as he did, she raised her face to his, and they kissed.

"Everything is packed up if you're ready to…" Evan went silent when he saw their embrace.

"Ready," Julian said as he released Camille. Then leaning forward and placing his lips against her ear he whispered, "I love you too."

"I packed you guys a couple sandwiches to get you started, along with some chips and carrot sticks."

"Gee, Mom, thanks!" Evan commented in a faux childlike voice.

Camille nodded in resignation. "You know, if we live through all of this, you're going to have to come visit us from time to time."

"Certainly," Evan agreed.

The two men waved to Cam as they backed out of the driveway and headed off towards Kentucky. Cam watched until the car was out of sight and then she let the tension relax. Her shoulders slumped, and she allowed the tears to come.

The anger Qa'id felt was born from somewhere deep within him. The response from his bosses in the Middle East was not one he expected nor was it welcome. He knew they would acquiesce but he thought he would be allowed to go forward to the next step and use the weapons. That was not to be, with the news coming out of California, along with the panicked reaction from different factions and the older religious men wanted no part of it. All of them had been around long enough to realize this was more blame than they could afford; it would scare off donors and new recruits for their organization.

Qa'id spent nearly two hours arguing with them. His logic was actually quite sound. Eventually, the West would figure out the origin of the bombs and blame Russia even though there may be Radical Islamic fingerprints on parts of the cataclysm. The West could be counted on to have a knee-jerk reaction, which would cause a devastating counterattack. The way this weapon would destroy the West would allow them to move in and take an abundance of resources. In the end, Islam could own the world. *And, as the mastermind behind all of this, I will be in charge of some part of that world.*

He found himself soundly rejected. They abolished the entire program ordering *Allah's Numbers* shut down with all evidence destroyed. Additionally, he was ordered to fly back to the Middle East so discussions could take place immediately; several members of the leadership doubted that his motivations were purely religious. Some of them had been around long enough to have watched Qa'id's actions over the years—not only was this a question of ethics but they also seemed to see it as his grab for power.

By the end of the conversation, Qa'id was so unnerved he could barely speak. He stood in his flat without moving for several minutes, letting everything settle. This was a devastating blow on many levels, not only was the program dead but in all likelihood, he would be too as soon as he stepped off the plane in the Middle East. Right now, he had a chance, an opportunity to continue on as planned. After all, there was no one here to stop them. Abi had never spoken to anyone in the leadership and they had no direct contact with him. The only one that Abi trusted and accepted direction from was Qa'id. Therefore, *Allah's Numbers* would proceed and now was the time for the Message to go out to launch all weapons in the United States.

When Qa'id finalized this decision, he broke his phone in half, cutting off all direct contact with those cowardly leaders. Now he could not be easily tracked. Looking down at his hands, and the pieces of the phone, he realized he had crossed a bridge. Succeed or fail, this was it.

On the walk from his apartment to Abi's, Qa'id dropped his phone parts in various open storm drains. Of course, who would scrutinize a religious teacher in England when it was Russia who launched an attack against the United States? When he arrived at Abi's apartment, he could see from the young man's body language that something was wrong.

"Have you seen the news, Qa'id? What we have done, it was not just explosives but some sort of biological weapon. What are we unleashing into the world?"

Qa'id rested his hands on Abi's shoulders and smiled. "Calm yourself, my son, it is natural to recoil from those things that are horrible. But at the same time, we must do those things that are necessary to change the world in dramatic ways that will prepare it for Allah's chosen people."

"But Qa'id, how can this be what Allah wants? It just doesn't make sense."

"Hush now, it is not up to us foolish mortals to determine what Allah wants. We're handed tools by divine destiny and by using them we will act upon his unspoken will to bring about the changes that he desires." Qa'id had used similar speeches to convince bombers that suicide and murder were moral. *What bullshit. I am really good at this.*

Abi tried to speak again but Qa'id silenced him with a look. He realized the boy had hundreds of questions but there was no way he could take the time to answer. Time was very limited; if he failed to act quickly, Qa'id would lose his window.

"Now, you and I both know there is one more Message for which those agents are waiting to trigger all of the devices. You need to put the instruction communication together directing the numbers stations to broadcast the Execution Message." Qa'id could feel Abi's body stiffen. He could not afford for him to lose faith and fail to act. "Abi, while you are creating these communiqués, I will stay here with you to keep you company and in case you have any more ominous concerns that need to be addressed immediately. Then after you are done, and the transmittal has been sent, we will talk about all the other questions. We can spend as much time as you want to discuss those things while we wait for our glorious victory."

Qa'id realized he was going to have to kill Abi once it was done. *I can't afford anyone with doubts to have knowledge of my part in this scheme.* Looking over the young man's shoulders, towards his kitchen, he could see a knife block. *That will make it smooth and quiet.* "Now, my young friend, it is time to go to work. Keep in mind while you're doing this that the Koran 47:4 says, '*Do not hanker for peace with infidels; behead them when you catch them.*'"

Abi hated it when Qa'id did this. Basically, the old man had told him to shut up and color. For now, he would do just that, but he wanted answers. Yes, his part was to honor his father and avenge his slaughter, but should he be lashing out in such a devastating way? These thoughts plagued him as he put the final transmittal together for the numbers stations. *Back when this began, it was so easy and almost joyful, now it is so, so dark.* He wrote the script on a new notepad.

It was not unusual for Nikki to enter a trance-like state when she knew her mission was about to go fully operational. This time was different, however, as somewhere in that trance were thoughts of the man she was getting to know. Evan had somehow pierced that hard exterior and had found his way to Ashley, the woman Nikki really was. As she sat in her apartment, staring at the TV, she found herself absentmindedly flipping the channels one at a time.

When her phone alerted that she had a new SMS, she did not immediately pick it up. Instead, she closed her eyes and slowly exhaled, letting the nothingness fade to enter a sweet calmness; she needed to become the weapon she was trained to be. When she picked up the phone, all she saw was a set of coordinates she copied into her GPS. Her destination was somewhere in Kentucky, about six hours or so away. She sent Morty a response letting him know that she had the information and her ETA.

<MT

On her very first mission, Morty had sent her the same text. She had asked him what it meant afterward, and he told her it stood for Mozel Tov.

"The usage is more Yiddish than Hebrew. The literal translation of Mozel Tov is 'good constellation,' but it has come to mean both congratulations and good luck. When I am sending you off to do your job, I will always wish you the best of luck but when you are successful, I could also use the same words to say congratulations," Morty had explained with a fatherly smile.

"Sort of like Aloha."

"I don't know, you don't speak Hebrew and I don't speak Hawaiian," Morty had replied.

Mozel Tov indeed, Morty, and I will need it. She took another cleansing breath and prepared to leave. As she climbed into the driver's seat of her car, she knew that in the trunk, hidden underneath the rear deck where a spare tire normally would be, was what the Mossad called a Tactical Kit. Inside the kit was a standard grouping of items that might be needed while in the field. It included a Kevlar bulletproof vest, flash bang grenades, long distance listening equipment, binoculars, and one piece of lethal equipment—the M2010 Enhanced Sniper Rifle (ESR).

The ESR was the same weapon used by the U.S. Army's sniper corps and had excellent reliability up to about a thousand meters. Nikki was taking the sniper course when the Israeli army managed to get a hold of a few of the weapons, and she was one of the first to be able to fire it outside the US. She immediately adapted to it since it was the first sniper rifle she had ever fired. Her natural calm under pressure allowed her to take longer and longer shots until Nikki was 95 percent reliable at 1200 meters, 200 meters beyond the weapons accepted distance limit. The weapon kept her out of harm's way while carrying out her mission with deadly efficiency.

She turned on the vehicle's radio and found a Detroit radio station that was playing Led Zeppelin's *D'yer Maker*. Turning the song up as loud as she could stand, Nikki dropped the car into gear. *Time to keep bad things from happening.*

Chapter Sixteen

As Fakhriya climbed the unfamiliar stairs, she had one goal in mind-- to finally level with her son about his history. She had long known a lot of his anger and angst were based on the past, particularly what had happened to his father. However, those feelings were mistaken and misdirected. She had never found the appropriate time to provide him with the information he lacked, but now she was determined.

She heard a noise in the stairwell and looked for a place to hide. She exited onto one of the floors and cracked the door open. Soon, she saw the feet of a man coming down the stairs and as his face became visible, she recognized Qa'id. She leaned against the door and closed her eyes, dreading at having to confront her son after his visit by this horror of a man. As she leaned against the door, she carefully listened to Qa'id's fading footsteps. When she heard the door at the bottom of the stairway close, she knew it was safe to journey up to her son's apartment.

Standing in front of Abi's door, Fakhriya paused for a moment. She had severe doubts about her timing and ability to communicate to her distant son but she was doing the right thing. With that, she knocked on the door. It took several minutes for his door to open, and when it did, she was confronted with an unfamiliar vision of her son. Even though it had been just a few weeks since they had last seen each other, he had lost weight. His face was drawn and pale. His exhausted eyes appeared stressed. Without saying a word, she opened her arms, and the young man walked directly into them. After a long hug at the door, Abi stepped back and motioned for her to enter. Fakhriya again offered her open arms to him but this time he sidestepped her.

"You have a wonderful place here, Abi." Even though he had lived there for weeks, he had never invited her over, preferring to see her occasionally in her own place.

"Yes, it is quite adequate." Abi had lost control of his emotions briefly when he saw her on the threshold of his home but now, he fought to maintain control and distance.

"How is school? Are you doing well at school?"

"School is school," he said flatly.

"And your friends? How are you doing with…"

"Mother, my friends are all right, I'm all right, school is all right. Please, I am busy right now, why are you here?" Qa'id would be back any minute with food, and he did not want the two of them to be in the apartment at the same time.

Fakhriya was nonplussed by his reaction; she was going to say what she came to say regardless of his reaction. It was time Abi knew the truth and it was time she stopped carrying this burden. She sat on the couch and indicated she wanted him to sit too. Abi sighed and sat down next to his mother.

His mother's voice was calm and quiet. "Abi, what do you remember about our last night before leaving Palestine? What do you remember about what happened to your father?"

Abi inhaled deeply, even though he was anxious and upset by his current situation, the memory of that night was so vivid that the mention of it caused him to drop his attitude. "I remember being awakened by the loud noises of people arguing. I came into the living room, and you held me and tried to calm me down. Then, I heard Papa's voice from outside, and there was more arguing and yelling. One of the ruffians then grabbed me away from you and dragged me outside where I saw Papa on his knees before an Israeli commando named Major Moshe Levinsky…"

"Wait. How do you know the man's name? How do you know they were Israelis?"

Abi thought for a minute. He couldn't tell his mother outright that Qa'id had added those details about that night. So, his mind raced for an alternate explanation. "I searched online for Israeli soldiers with the long scar I remembered. I found a picture of Levinsky, and his scarred face is one I will never forget."

Fakhriya nodded, not out of agreement but out of understanding. For now, she let her son continue his remembrance of that night.

"There was much more shouting, and then Levinsky took out his pistol and shot my father." Abi paused for a moment to quell the deep emotion that was rising within him. He then swallowed hard before continuing. "At the time, I did not realize he was dead, but after some more shouting, one of the men dragged me back into the house. After that, the commandos gathered together and left. You picked me up and we started our journey out of Palestine." Abi felt completely drained. Even though this version did not include all the details that he regularly dreamed, he still felt the weight of every single emotion.

His mother sat in the silence. She knew remembering this event would take an emotional toll on her son. She was not there to make it worse but to provide the truth. "Abi, you were too young to know everything, so much happened and your mind has tried to fill in the blanks, and maybe other people have told you things to fill in the blanks." As she said this, Fakhriya felt Abi's eyes burning through her at the veiled reference to Qa'id.

"The people who came to our house that night were not Israelis, they were with an offshoot of the PLO. Nowadays, they would be called radical fundamentalists. They're the same people who formed ISIL or the Taliban. Perhaps some of the exact same people." Fakhriya watched Abi to see if he rejected what she was saying.

"Why would the PLO attack our home? My father was loyal to the cause, and a good Muslim."

"Yes. Your father was faithful to the cause of getting a Palestinian state, and he was also a very devout man taking the teachings of the Quran very seriously. It was because of that that he had been working behind the scenes with the Israelis to bring about peace, to bring about what is now called the two-state solution. But there were those who believed that doing such things was haram, a blasphemy, not only against our people but also Allah. Your father thought as I do, that all people can live together in harmony." She reached out her hand and placed it on Abi's shoulder. He did not attempt to shrug off the contact, and she saw that as a good sign.

"They wanted your father to confess to what they viewed as his sedition against our people, but he would not. He knew that regardless of what he said that night, in the end, they were going to kill him. He was not going to give them the satisfaction of admitting that what he did was wrong because he never saw it as wrong but only the correct path leading us to peace. When those thugs realized they were not going to get what they wanted from him, they murdered him in our front yard. We were able to escape because of friends who were willing to help us regardless of what these radicals wanted. The battle that took place after we left the house was indeed between the Israeli Commandos and the PLO but the sides of the fight were very different than what you've been led to believe. It was the Israelis who came to rescue your father and then avenged his murder by eliminating those who had killed him. In doing this, they also made it possible for us to escape because those men would've tracked us down." Fakhriya was satisfied. At last Abi knew the truth about that night and how his father had sought to bring about peace.

"If what you're saying is true, then how come I remember the face of Major Moshe Levinsky as his killer?"

"I don't know, show me the picture."

Abi took out his laptop and searched for an image using Moshe Levinsky as a keyword. However, the images that loaded were different from the face Abi remembered and the picture he'd been given and studied for so long. The picture was also clearer than the one he had and the scars on the man's face were not the same. This was not the man who had killed his father.

Fakhriya could tell by her son's expression that whatever he'd discovered somehow didn't match the narrative he had been provided. "Can you look up anyone's picture using that? I seem to recall your father mentioning the name of one of the leaders of that sect, a Dawood Zaman. See if you can find him."

The man in the photo was older than the face he remembered from that night but he still recognized the man. The scars in this picture were correct, and the image was clear enough for him to see the man's eyes as well. Dawood Zaman, a radical fundamentalist with the PLO, was the man who had killed his father. Not an Israeli, not anyone backed by the West or funded by the United States. Someone of his own race, someone of his own religion, someone of his own origin. Abi felt completely drained.

Fakhriya watched her son's shoulders slump as he realized his emotional responses had been so wrong. Abi's eyes looked up from the computer screen into hers and for the first time in a long while, she saw her son. The moment might've ended with a hug, it might've ended with an enormous sigh of relief that the truth was now known but both of them looked towards the front door as they heard the doorknob being turned and Qa'id entered the apartment.

Evan enjoyed long drives. He liked nothing better than dropping into the driver's seat, flipping the radio on to some appropriate traveling music, something from the Seventies and Eighties, and then going. It really didn't matter where he was going, he just liked being in motion. But this trip had a mission to be accomplished at the end that could mean life or death for millions.

They split the driving. Julian was not a bad traveling companion and they took the time to review details that would have to be handled in Kentucky. Julian explained in deep detail how the codes worked as well as the various Messages types. Having been privy to classified information during his time in the Air Force, Evan was surprised at the simplicity of the Crimson Thunderbird Initiative.

"It was actually quite genius. No codebooks were necessary because of *Brandt's Collection*. The other parts of the decryption schema were simple arithmetic or flipping schemes and not very hard to memorize," Julian explained.

"I get that but I was expecting something based on a Fibonacci sequence or something designed by crypto scientists in a lab. Not based on divide three here, add four there, reverse the numbers, leave numbers out, put some more numbers in. It's just so simplistic," Evan said, not taking his eyes off the road.

"Well, consider this. The codes are only used once and are only used in preparation for the actual execution of the mission. Even if the CIA could figure it all out, by the time they knew what was going on it would be over."

"I guess you're right." Evan changed the subject for the sake of distraction. "How'd you know Camille was the right one? I mean how long were you dating before you felt you were in love or that you wanted to be with her and no one else?"

"Ah, I think there's something more behind what you're asking. You can tell me about her when you're ready. As for how I knew, I just knew from the first moment I saw her. The sun caught her hair and was gleaming just for me, then she turned her head, and I caught a glimpse of her eyes which were so beautiful. Then, her face lit up while she was looking at me and I was smitten."

"Smitten? She smote you?" Evan asked.

"Smote, smoted, smitten. Yeah, that's it, I was instantly and always smitten," Julian said laughing.

"Interesting. Let me tell you about the time I got smitten," Evan said.

The drive itself may have been uninteresting but the two men were becoming close friends even though an unexpected destiny had thrown them together. As Evan described his first glimpse of Nikki, they proceeded east towards a certain mission with an uncertain outcome.

"So nice of your mother to visit. What great timing too." Qa'id set the groceries on the table. He was not quite sure what was going on and he did not like the fact that Fakhriya was present. *That bitch is a problem.*

Abi tried to suppress his anger but finally gave up on that idea and stood to confront Qa'id. "How could you lie to me about what had happened? You altered the photo of Major Moshe Levinsky to match my memory of that night so I would blame the Israelis and the West for what happened to my father. My father was a man of peace and you have turned me into a tool of war." He took a step towards Qa'id, who quickly lunged around him.

"Now Abi, you know that everything I do is for our people and for Allah. Yes, I played on your sentiments to help motivate you into doing the right thing and so that we would be successful in this effort. Now we are! That is thanks to you, and thanks to your immeasurable talents. Regardless of why you were motivated, you have been successful." Qa'id's mind was turning over options. In addition to killing Abi, he would also have to dispose of Fakhriya. *But in what order?* Also, at play was the timing as the preparation of Execution Message had been completed but had yet to be sent. Qa'id did not have the technical knowledge to do that himself. *So, disposing of Abi would have to wait, for now.*

"Don't try to placate me with compliments. I have you figured out now, I just don't know why you couldn't be honest with me," Abi raised his voice.

"Because I needed you. I could not afford for you not to do what you have done. Our people needed it; Allah needed it. I have told you over and over again we are taught by the Quran in 3:85. We are now making that a reality."

"You lie! I have looked up things that you've said. You are twisting the words and parsing down the passages to mean only what you want them to say." Abi took a step towards Qa'id still unsure of what his next step would be.

Qa'id was done with this dance. As Abi was getting louder, it was just a matter of time until one of the neighbors gathered to find the nature of the disturbance and then the entire thing would fall apart. He was not sure where he was going with this course of action, but something needed to be done. Grabbing Fakhriya from the couch, Qa'id spun her body around and secured his arm across her chest. Abi backed up. Qa'id spun around towards the kitchen to withdraw a knife from the butcher block. He held the back of the knife against her throat.

"Now, just calm down my young friend," Qa'id said. "There is only one way for this to end with everybody okay. You need to finish your mission for our people. You have the communiqué prepared so all you have to do is transmit it on the correct frequencies. It will only take a few minutes, and then I will leave, and this will all be over. Whether you like it or not, you will be a hero of Islam."

"What's he talking about, Abi? What is it that he wants you to do?"

"Don't worry about it, Momma, I will take care of it and then he will leave us alone." Abi picked up the laptop and took it to the radio room as his mother gasped. The truth was going to come out and for this, he felt much guilt. Without giving it much thought, he broadcast the transmittal to the first numbers station frequency. He changed the tuning to the next frequency when the idea hit him that Qa'id knew how many frequencies there were but not what they were. With that, he tuned the frequency to where it was supposed to be and then continued to turn the dial until it was set for a few megahertz higher. Abi played the sound file. For the next one after tuning in the correct frequency, he turned the dial a few megahertz lower. He continued like this until all seven were done. He faced Qa'id. "It is finished, now let my mother go."

"Not yet, I want you to destroy the evidence," Qa'id demanded.

Abi gathered up the script for the communication he had just sent. He then deleted the files and performed a wipe of the disc. Abi picked up a large can of charcoal lighter fluid and soaked the papers in the kitchen sink. As he was squirting the lighter fluid, he had an idea. He struck a match and dropped it into the sink which ignited with a whoosh. He squirted the lighter fluid into the flames and trailed it across the counter and onto Qa'id's arm which caught fire.

Qa'id reacted without thinking, he released Abi's mother who ran into the other room screaming. Qa'id dropped the knife to slap at the flames on his arm. Abi set the can of lighter fluid on the counter and grabbed two knives. Turning towards Qa'id, he stabbed him repeatedly in the chest until at last Qa'id finally fell on the floor motionless.

Abi's mother's screams were not registering. He needed to extinguish the burning clothes of the man who was bleeding to death on his kitchen floor. Taking a pitcher of water, he flung it at Qa'id, extinguishing the flames. The older man lay motionless on the floor, the pool of blood around him slowly expanding. He could hear the rattle of the man's breathing as air exited his lungs through his wounds. Shortly, Qa'id would be dead.

Abi went into the living room and took his mother into his arms to calm her as she had calmed him so many years ago. His father, the peacemaker. His father, whose death had been avenged the very night he was killed. His father's death that resulted in an enormous amount of harm to them both but in the end they had survived. The question running through Abi's mind was how they would get out of the mess created by Qa'id's lies.

The keen logic that enabled Abi to be a good cryptologist and understand computers came to his aid now. As his mother calmed down, he began to think. At some point, the body in the kitchen would have to be dealt with, and Qa'id's was the only name on the rental agreement. Abi had not been around long enough to meet any of the neighbors. He only had minimal property that could be carried out in a single trip. Perhaps the solution was clearer than he thought.

"Mother, I want you to leave now and let me take care of things. I will meet you back at your place in an hour or so. Also, would it be all right if I stayed with you for a while?"

"Of course, but what do you plan on doing? You killed a man, Abi, an evil man, but a man just the same. The police will need to be called."

"Say nothing about any of this to anyone. I think I have a way for all of it to go away and cover up my involvement." Abi guided her to the door. He grabbed his backpack and slipped his laptop and several items inside before handing it to her. "Take this with you so that I am not overburdened when I leave. Also, wash the clothes you are wearing as soon as you get home."

Fakhriya took the bag and hugged him. Now, Abi needed to get to work. He first gathered anything that could be traced back to him and placed it in a duffel bag by the door. He stripped naked right in front of the door, putting his clothing near Qa'id's body, before showering, being sure to wash twice. Once he was done, he dressed in fresh clothing.

The radio and other evidence could stay. In fact, it would allow investigators to trace the items to Qa'id. Qa'id had repeatedly called Abi his secret weapon and he was counting on this being true.

He took a final look around the small apartment for any other evidence. What he was about to do could possibly harm other people but he would do his best to minimize that possibility. Asr was the most popular prayer of the day, in the early evening everyone was home from work and available to attend without encumbrances. As a result, his building would be mostly empty as everyone had gone to the mosque. Those who remained would have to fend for themselves, but sometimes things like that were necessary.

Abi cracked his front door open to ensure the hallway was empty. Going back into the kitchen he was careful not to step in the growing pool of blood as he retrieved the lighter fluid. He shook it to verify it was half full before spraying it liberally on the kitchen counters and floor. Abi then scattered scrap paper from his trashcan around the kitchen.

In addition to scraps, he tore the pages out of the binders he had carefully constructed since the beginning of this nightmare. He finished all of this off by squirting a trail of lighter fluid from the kitchen into the living room and to the couch. He then dumped the remaining fluid on Qa'id's corpse. Striking a single match, he lit the trail of lighter fluid. It seemed that within moments the fire in the kitchen was roaring.

Abi gathered his duffel bag along with the empty can of lighter and quickly closed the door behind him. Before he left the floor, he went to the center of the corridor and pulled the fire alarm. There was a good chance the fire brigade would arrive before all of the evidence was destroyed but that was a chance Abi would have to take since he did not want to harm anyone else in the building. Once outside, it was as if no one had been alerted by the alarm so he hustled towards Areef's store.

He was done. Whatever had happened was not his fault. Qa'id had tricked him and lied to him to manipulate his actions. *If I had known the truth, I never would've done any of it.* Now he would walk away and hopefully not have to pay for the results of Qa'id's untruths. At least the broadcasts he made this morning, at least most of them, would likely never be heard by anyone. There was the one correct frequency but he had no way of knowing if his script was even valid. At this point, he could only hope it wasn't. As he walked down the street, he wiped off the can of lighter fluid with his sleeve and then threw it into a storm drain.

He needed to let Areef know he was no longer playing with the radio. Hopefully, the police would never be able to connect Areef to the radio in the apartment. Abi wanted to ensure his friendship with the shopkeeper was still intact.

After walking several blocks, he found himself in front of Oasis Mart but discovered the doors to the *dekkan* were locked. There was no small sign hanging on the glass door. Shielding his eyes from the sunlight, Abi peered through the door into the shop but could see nothing because all the lights were off. Abi had no way of knowing that Areef was now gone for good. He had slipped away the night after retrieving his escape bag from the shop and abandoned the identity of Areef Rahal for good. Very late tonight, Melrose Scotland's newest full-time resident, Adrian Ahlström, would arrive.

⚜

As Yury sat watching the TV, he could not help but occasionally look towards the blanket-covered body of Nastia. He had not really gotten to know her personally. They collaborated professionally but aside from that, they were nothing more than passing acquaintances. He had convinced himself that he should feel no guilt after all he was just doing his duty but it was unpleasant that this had occurred inside the station. He would have to somehow drag her body up the stairs to dispose of it and then he would have to clean up her puddle of blood. *How long does it take for a body to start stinking?* He was just about to type that question into his computer when the static on the radio went quiet. *This is the order to send the Execution Message!*

Yury glanced up at the clock and recorded the time as 1217 hours. He sat forward ready to listen, seconds later he dutifully recorded all 15 letters and transcribed them again when the broadcast repeated. He validated that they were identical, and set about translating them into necessary actions.

The numbers station was to send out the Execution Message to all field assets as soon as possible. All geographic location subsets were to be included. Even though this was the final task, the numbers station was also to monitor the standard frequencies 24 hours a day for the next transmittal.

Curious, but I guess not inconceivable that they would make such a request. After all, they must have many assets in the field and don't want to lose control of them just because their primary mission has been accomplished.

The data to compose the Execution Messages were stored in similar aluminum capsules to those used to secure the information for the Preparation Messages. Most of the text required for the Message was contained in the scroll retrieved from the capsules. The one part that had to be calculated for each Execution Message was the Validation Code. That information was listed in perpetual tables that were also located in the station's safes. Because each of the Execution Messages was custom-made for each recipient and longer in length than any of the prior Messages sent, it was very time-consuming to put them all together. Yury found himself wishing he hadn't killed Nastia until after this task was complete. *Too late now.* He glanced at the blanketed lump across from him.

Tricia Le Clair sat at her kitchen table, where she had been for the past week, glued to her shortwave radio. Unlike some others from her graduating class at the Academy, she had been eagerly waiting specifically for this day to come; the day she would prove to her father she was every bit as good as her brother.

Tricia had come from the family of a mid-level bureaucrat in one of the major Soviet labor unions. She was the firstborn and her father had always made it abundantly clear that he wanted a son. Even her name, Afanasi Pyotrovich Mishka, was masculine and had she kept it she would've spent her life explaining. When her brother was born, some of the pressure was relieved, but at the same time, she lost the attention of her father, an event she had never completely gotten over. The choice to send her to the Academy was her father's way of disposing of her while placating her mother. Even though she was very young when she entered the Academy, that deep-rooted desire to please her father remained throughout her entire life.

Now, she was, at last, going to be given a chance to perform. It was an opportunity to make her father proud, even though she was a woman. She'd remained single, though opportunities had presented themselves. Tricia found it easier to be on her own and dedicate her life to the mission. Due to her genetics, she was almost six feet tall, and because she spent her extra time in the gym, she was solidly muscular. Her profession was construction welding, which also contributed to her muscular physique.

Since receiving the Warning Message, and then the Preparatory Message on Thursday, she'd taken time off from work to dedicate all of her attention to the next phase. She was within only a few hours' drive of the L-PAK. As soon as the Execution Message was received, she would be on the road within minutes.

She had already packed an overnight bag, which was sitting beside her front door, and she had readied a firearm as well. A Sig Sauer P-938 lay on her kitchen table next to the radio. Tricia had excelled at firearms training while at the Academy, failing to become class champion by a single point. She went to the firing range at least twice a week to maintain her deadly accuracy with the weapon. In addition to the 17-round magazine already loaded, she had packed two extras. Once she was directed to proceed, she would carry the gun on her person along with at least one of the extra magazines. But all that was for later. For now, she listened to the dull static of the radio, waiting for her call to duty.

Then, the radio went silent. Tricia's entire body was on edge, and she leaned forward towards the radio. The pencil she had been fidgeting with was now at the ready to write. When she heard the sound of the tones on the radio followed by the child's laughter, she knew at last her opportunity had come. As she wrote down each number, her mission became clear. She would be on the road within an hour and soon she would make her father proud.

Matehuala, Mexico

Yury listened as the final Execution Message was played. Once he had gotten through the first 10 or so, the rest was easier. Then, it was a simple matter of playing the right sound file on the appropriate frequency. It'd taken him just over six hours to construct those files, and now it was 1823 hours.

He hadn't the time to research how long it took for a body to begin to stink but Yury was acutely aware the air was becoming dense. With sunset in Matehuala in two hours, it would be at least four hours before he could safely drag a body from the station and put it into the trunk of his car. Then, since the mission was complete, for the moment at least, he could allow himself to take a few hours and go to town for a proper meal, some proper drinks, and perhaps a-not-so-proper brown-eyed girl with long dark hair. He smiled as this plan came to fruition. Surprised by the sudden silence, it took a moment for him to realize that his task was complete. He annotated the completion time on the script as 1834 hours.

Evan noticed the girl's name when she presented the menus, and as was his habit, he addressed her as Andi throughout the meal. Some of the most beautiful women in the world were from Kentucky. Andi was no exception with beautiful long blonde hair and pale blue eyes. Her friendly smile definitely lit up the room but Evan did not feel his normal interest.

"I'll have the barbecue brisket sandwich but can I get a salad instead of fries?" Julian asked.

"Sure honey, absolutely no problem," Andi replied in a voice that was sweetly coated with a southern accent. "And for you?"

"Uh, the same but I will be sinful and have the fries. Oh, and can I get a side of mayo with that, Andi?" Evan asked.

"No problem at all, honey, you must've been to Germany. I dated a guy once who was in Germany when he was in the Army. He said everybody over there eats their fries with mayonnaise. Be back in a bit with your drinks."

"You know, I think she likes you," Julian said as he slapped the table in front of them.

"Yeah, that's me, world-famous author with a girl in every

town." Evan reached over and grabbed the sugar in anticipation of his iced tea.

"You ain't gonna need that unless you're trying to get diabetes. You're in the South now and tea always comes sweetened unless you ask for it otherwise."

Evan returned the sugar decanter. "Are we almost there?" Up to this point he had avoided asking.

Julian tapped on his cell phone screen several times. "As near as I can tell, we are within about 50 or 60 miles of where we need to be. I think we should probably get a hotel room somewhere around here so that we are close-by when Camille calls with the info for the final Execution Message."

"Sounds like a plan," Evan said as he sat back in his seat so Andi could place an oversized glass of iced tea in front of him. Evan took a sip of his tea and winced. "Yeah, between this and the sweetness of our waitress, Andi, there is definitely a chance for diabetes here."

Nikki raised the binoculars to her eyes and at the same time pointed the parabolic dish towards the diner on the other side of the highway. She was parked between two 18-wheel trucks that provided a level of cover. Nikki noted that while Evan was being polite, and maybe the light side of flirtatious, the waitress' flirting back was not having an effect on him at all. The thought made her smile and feel a little more secure.

A brief discussion with Morty let her know there was still more information needed before these men could act. The mission was to act as a guardian angel. Her situational awareness was in high gear and she could not detect anyone else watching the men. But, as she had learned over the years, that could change in an instant simply by a car turning off the highway.

So, here she sat in her car watching Julian and Evan drink iced tea and eat barbecue while she was drinking a lukewarm Diet Coke, feasting on Cheetos. As she licked the orange powder from her fingers, she listened to their conversation through her headphones and continued to watch.

Chapter Seventeen

"So, anyway, after I graduated from the University of Kentucky with my Associates Degree in Radiological Technology, I got a job working for an assisted living facility with their own medical clinic on site. The problem was, I was dealing with the same people day after day, and because they were older, they kept dying on me." Andi was using her hands to emphasize her story while shifting her gaze between Evan and Julian. Chuckling at her own story, she added, "Well, not actually dying on me but dying after I'd gotten to know them. It was heartbreaking, really."

Both Julian and Evan nodded. Evan regretted asking her a personal question even though he enjoyed her syrupy accent. Julian wondered why she hadn't realized the natural progression of the profession before she took the job. Nikki was thankful no one could hear the comments he was making or how loudly she was rolling her eyes at the entire conversation. She had met many people who didn't understand the consequences of their decisions. This philosophical musing was interrupted when Nikki heard Julian's cell. He looked at the screen and without saying a word, he let Evan read the text.

"We have everything we need," Evan said solemnly.

"Absolutely," replied Julian, who then raised his hand as a signal for Andi to bring their check.

Before she could place the two checks down, Evan glanced at both, did a bit of quick math, and dropped two twenties on the table. He knew it was unusual to leave an 18-dollar tip, but they didn't have the time to wait for change. Upon leaving the diner, they sat in the car as Julian decrypted Cam's text.

"Which book?" Evan asked.

"I need Austen's *Pride and Prejudice* and also *Walden* by Henry David Thoreau," Julian responded as he continued to replicate the numbers from his phone onto a notebook page.

"You need two books to decrypt this one? I thought only one book was ever used." Evan handed the copy of *Walden* to Julian from the backseat.

"Only one is actually being used, *Pride and Prejudice*. *Walden* would never be used for encryption," Julian explained as he flipped to the back cover of the book and began to peel back the endpaper. He cut a square around the edges of the hardcover of the book and used the tip of the blade to peel the surface, exposing a plastic card. "Ta-da," Julian said with a bit of a musical lilt in his voice, "this card contains a Perpetual Table which will help us validate the Message once we have it completely decrypted. You kept saying things had to be more complicated … this card is that wrinkle in the fabric. Without it, you would never know if what you had was right or not."

Evan continued to dig through the boxes looking for the copy of Jane Austen's *Pride and Prejudice*. As Julian decrypted the Message, it verified they were in the right location, though there were details he didn't understand. Before he could be confident, he needed Austen's book for the final decryption.

Evan dumped the books onto the floor. "Got it!"

Julian flipped through the book searching for the right page and the start of the code needed for the final launch codes. Evan noticed Andi smoking a cigarette outside the diner as she talked on her cell phone. A truck was visible in their rear-view mirror. It was parked behind them but something seemed out of place. A car suddenly backed up in the gravel lot, causing a storm of dust as it disappeared.

"Okay, you about ready?" Julian said.

"You broke the code that fast?"

"Yeah, I've read this book many times." Julian glanced over his shoulder and dropped the car into reverse. Shortly the highway was taking them to the final destination.

Evan asked, "The validation and everything else checked out?"

The details didn't really concern him but he did care about what they were getting into next. A bit of anxiety had started to build but a few deep relaxing breaths calmed it and let him again focus on the task at hand.

The men didn't pay any attention to the car that followed them onto the highway as it had found a berth behind an 18-wheel truck and remained hidden. Nikki was in a perfect sweet spot, far enough back as not to be seen or noticed. She decided against attempting to use the parabolic dish while moving, hoping she'd catch up on the details once at the destination.

Julian's drive was uneventful. Evan flipped from one news channel to the next to hear any updates on the fire in California. They didn't speak. Julian was worried about his relationship with Camille as well as what he and Evan were going to encounter. Evan was lost in his thoughts about Nikki and the whole needing to save the world thing as well.

"Take the next exit and then turn right," the voice of the GPS startled both men from their trances.

They turned off at the exit and proceeded down a small two-lane state road through hills. Over the next 40 miles, the GPS continued to guide them. Evan noticed the miles remaining tick down. They were very close.

Nikki backed off more down the state road since there was no traffic or sufficient curves for cover. A Geo tracker on their car would have made it less stressful to protect them along the way.

As they crested the top of a hill, they saw a valley before them with a cluster of a dozen or so nine-story block buildings dotting the landscape. The buildings had one or two blackened windows per floor. Julian slowed the car and looked towards Evan quizzically.

"Those my friend, are where bourbon gets smooth," Evan said matter-of-factly.

"Huh?"

"I took a tour a few years back. They store those huge wooden barrels of bourbon in those huge warehouses. Sometimes they age five years, sometimes 10. I heard about one bourbon that is only sold after it has aged for 25 years. The longer it ages, the more intense the flavor and the higher the alcohol level. Is that what we're looking for, a rickhouse?"

"Dunno. I wasn't expecting something nine stories high."

"You have reached your destination," the GPS announced as they stopped at a chain-link fence surrounding the rickhouses.

"Any idea which one?" Evan asked.

"Yep, number 4723." Julian tore the decrypted Message from the notebook and stuck it in his shirt pocket. Taking the two pistols out, he handed one to Evan and then cocked his before slipping into his belt. There was a combination lock on the gate. Consulting the paper in his pocket, Julian spun the dial until it clicked open. After the two men stepped inside, Evan closed the gate and pushed the loose chain back through the fence to hold it shut.

Nikki found a superb vantage point of the buildings, about 300 meters away from the top of a hill. Nikki's Enhanced Sniper Rifle was prepared for use. She lay on top of her car and watched through the trees. The distance was too far for her parabolic dish to work so she needed to rely on herself.

As Tricia drove down the state highway, she slowly passed by the gate to the rickhouses where Evan's rental car was parked. Without knowing whose car it was, she parked her car a half-mile from the entry gate and walked back to conceal her presence. When she arrived back at the gate, she could see two men walking among the buildings inside the fenced compound. Tricia prepared for something hostile, drawing her weapon and slowly entering the gate. She attempted to outflank the men and catch them off guard when they rounded one of the buildings.

"I can't find any building markings," Evan said.

"Wait, what is that there?" Julian pointed to a cornerstone of a building with a crudely painted number.

"Okay, this one's 4728," Evan said, gesturing to a building off on the right. "It might be that one."

Rather than trying to walk through the scrub, they proceeded along the manicured side of building 4728. They cleared the end of the building only to be confronted by a large and muscular woman with her weapon drawn.

"Sorry, we were just out looking around; we didn't mean to be trespassing." Evan raised his hands.

Tricia followed her training, determined to maintain control through fear, so she pointed her weapon slightly to the right of Julian and fired.

Nikki was repositioning herself since she had lost sight of the men. Tricia had moved so stealthily into the area that Nikki was caught by surprise. She dropped her binoculars and knelt, watching through the scope of her rifle with her finger on the trigger.

Julian spent time studying the woman's face and then it suddenly occurred to him perhaps why she seemed familiar. *"Zdravstvujte tovarishch,"* Julian said, "hello friend," holding his hands out so he would not appear to be a threat.

A clear look of puzzlement crossed Tricia's face. It had been decades since she had heard Russian and it took a minute for her to translate her thoughts.

"Akademiya? Gamayunskiy obrazovatel'nyy tsentr?" Tricia finally responded, lowering her weapon.

"Yes. The Gamayun Education Centre. We both were trained there. We are both here now for the same reason," Julian surmised.

Evan was perplexed, not knowing who this person was, or what would happen next. *Was my trust in Julian misplaced?* Rather than panic, Evan felt a deeper level of Satori take hold. He slowly lowered his hands since her focus was on Julian. He wrapped his fingers around the 9mm tucked into his belt. As they continued talking, he pulled the weapon free but kept it concealed.

"Son of a bitch, son of a bitch, son of a bitch," Nikki kept whispering to herself as she watched the events through her scope. No one had ever gotten the drop on her before and the situation was too unclear to fire. She did not need to leave a body trail, but she could not afford for her protectees to be harmed.

"The Message shouldn't have been sent; it was sent by an evil man acting on his own not the Soviet government," Julian explained keeping his voice calm and steady.

Tricia was puzzled. *How can this man know all of this? Is this some sort of trick?* She had been trained and existed here solely for this mission.

Evan looked for an opportunity, not believing that Julian's words were effective. Tricia lowered her weapon a bit, releasing her two-handed hold, and dropping it to her side. Evan saw his chance.

"Drop it!" He pulled his pistol and pointed it directly at Tricia's head. The gun was locked, loaded, and ready. A flash crossed Tricia's eyes as she made a decision; she raised her gun but before she fired Evan watched the side of her head explode as blood, bone, and brain flew out. A muscle reflex caused her grip to tighten and her weapon to fire wildly as her body spun and crumpled to the ground in a limp pile.

Julian was frozen for a moment trying to process what had happened. He had not heard a shot but Evan must have fired. "Why the hell did you shoot her? I might've been able to talk her down."

"I didn't shoot!" Suddenly, Evan grabbed Julian and threw him against the building. "Someone is shooting at us," he said between gritted teeth. With his weapon in the ready position, he searched for a shooter. There was a departing shadow on the hill with the silhouette of a rifle. "Shit!"

"Who the hell is that?" Julian managed.

"I have no fucking idea but he's stopped shooting and he could have taken us all out. I think he's on our side."

The two men leaned against the building for several minutes, catching their breath and trying to regain a sense of calm. Evan had flashes of memory from his time in Afghanistan but rather than instances of things out of control, they were of times when he overcame panic to control events. When no other shots were fired, Evan re-holstered his weapon. They approached Tricia's body.

"Were you friends growing up or something?" Evan asked.

"No, not really. We once competed in a shooting contest. I won, she lost. Just like today. Maybe I was just luckier," Julian philosophized. "She was obviously more dedicated … Can we get this done now?"

"Fine by me."

When they reached the door at the end of building 4723, they found it was secured with a cipher lock. Julian again entered the four digits he had decrypted but nothing happened. Upon trying again, as his hands became steadier, the mechanism of the lock released. The two men stepped into the darkness.

"Those two bastards have disappeared from my sight again," Nikki whispered. There was little she could do if there were a threat in the building but she could ensure no one came up from outside. From where she was, she could see the door they entered through and the only other portal, an emergency exit on the end of the building closest to her. While watching through the scope, she texted Morty:

```
>1 Hostile Down - Cleanup Req
```

Once she hit the send button, she gave her full attention to panning the area to ensure no harm would befall Evan and Julian. The cleanup request was to remove any trace of the agent she had killed as well as her vehicle.

"What is that smell?" Julian asked.

"That wonderful aroma is the angel's share." Noticing the questioning look on Julian's face, Evan continued, "Once bourbon is stored in one of these rickhouses, the magic happens as the molecules work their way out through the barrel. The good stuff stays on the inside. What you're smelling is what has worked its way out, mixed with the scent of wood and caramelized sugar. It's the two percent that's lost or the share that's given to the angels."

Providing this explanation allowed Evan the opportunity to journey form reactionary fear to total calm and readiness. However, if it wasn't so dark, Evan would have seen Julian's hands were still shaking. Evan led the way down a path between racks of whiskey barrels stacked three high, towards the center of the building where you could look up and see all the way to the roof from the floor. Rising over 30 meters, row upon row of barrels were visible thanks to the dim light from one of the few windows.

Evan led them towards a steel door at the end of the walkway and pushed the call button, but nothing happened. "This elevator doesn't appear to be working. Please tell me you have some magic code to get it to work?"

"Nope, and we need to get to the ninth level, and find row 97."

"Every time I think we're getting close…" Evan said, examining the shaft for some way for them to get to the top of the building

Yury arrived back in the station just before sunset. Had Nastia still been alive, she would have chastised him for coming in drunk, unshaven, and covered in the smell of a Mexican slut. Yury enjoyed the smell that covered him of cheap perfume, tequila, and sex. Memories of an afternoon well spent.

As he pulled his motorcycle under the car cover at the back of the station, he noticed a complication. The station was designed to look like all the other maintenance buildings of Comisión Federal de Electricidad along Highway 57D, including several outside lights and a few lights along the road. The entire locale was under satellite surveillance by law enforcement. This was the reason for their synchronized departures and arrivals, to avoid being captured by the satellite's camera.

Now, he needed to get a dead body from the station into the car and out of the area. This would be best done in the dark of night but that was also the time when the satellite was overhead. *Before it gets so dark that the lights come on, I will shoot them out.* If he had known the satellite had infrared photography, he would have known he need not bother.

With Nastia permanently out of commission, and the mission complete, he chose to return to his usual work outfit of shorts and a T-shirt. After entering the station, he retrieved his weapon and went up and out of the building. He quickly shot out the two lights near the building and the three along the access road before retreating back inside.

He had always heard when someone was executed the last thing they did was shit themselves. As he was forced to rummage through Nastia's pockets for her car keys, he realized this was true. He located the keys and dropped her body onto a blanket to drag near the stairs. Next, he wiped down the blood from the counter and mopped the floor. With those chores finished, he threw the rags and mop head and rolled it in the blanket with the body. Using some parachute cord, he tied the bundle together.

This was the first dead body he'd ever had to deal with, usually having left such details to enlisted men. He had no idea how hard it was to move dead weight up stairs. So, he dragged the body up a few steps and then took a break before dragging it up a few more until he reached the maintenance house.

After turning off the interior lights, Yury cracked the door to the outside to make sure it was dark enough for his plan. Once reassured, he dragged the body to the back of the maintenance building and then opened the trunk of Nastia's car. He quickly discovered the body would not fit, forcing him to dump the body in the backseat. He slumped down panting in the driver's seat with the door open.

He planned to take the car and the body out into the desert. By the time it would be discovered, evidence of the crime would have been taken care of by the wildlife. He would have to walk back on foot but realistically he should make it back by dawn. He drove off with no headlights onto the access road leading to the highway.

Highway 57D was a major artery for Mexico, transporting a myriad of cargo both legal and illegal. One of the illegal commodities was refined gasoline. The police had found they could easily track down drug operations by monitoring the usage of electricity so the drug lords now relied upon generators to avoid being tracked. Then, law enforcement moved to track purchases of fuel. It did not take long for the Cartels to start handling their own fuel distribution.

Rafael enjoyed driving for Benito since he no longer had to get up early in the morning to go to a backbreaking job that paid little money. Now, all he had to do was drive this tanker truck starting at one end of Highway 57D and deliver its payload at the other. Another plus was that it was done at night when the roads were least busy. If the road was deserted, he was to drive without his lights to minimize his visibility. Night vision goggles illuminated any danger as he cruised along at speeds of 170 kilometers or more. But tonight, he did not see the car entering from a side access road. As he pumped the brakes and attempted to change lanes, his trailer slid sideways and collided with the car.

"Holy shit! Look at that!" Asher had been working for the DEA for a little over a month, as one of hundreds monitoring the live satellite feeds delivered to the agency's headquarters in Washington.

His supervisor looked over his shoulder. "Play it back."

"Right here," Asher said pointing to the screen as the heat signatures of two vehicles suddenly merged then vanished as the screen was filled with a huge yellow and red blob which was evidence of a collision and massive explosion. "Way more than just two cars colliding, huh?"

"That's fine, Asher, you're right it's out of the ordinary but traffic safety is not our concern. Make a note of it in your log and get back at it," she said before she walked away.

Asher smiled to himself, as he brought up his electronic logbook and annotated the date, time, and location along with the comment, "Awesome car wreck."

They managed to climb using the exposed crossbeams, like a jungle gym and were almost 20 meters above the concrete floor. Both men were breathing heavily, the air was dense with the smell of the angel's share, and as they rose through the building, the temperature was also rising along with the humidity. They did not speak, choosing to conserve their oxygen.

Evan wiped the sweat off his hands and pulled himself up as he found a place for his feet to keep him steady. Julian used a more disciplined approach, with the muscles in his legs propelling him upwards while his hands grabbed for stability.

When at last the two men had reached the top floor, they were faced with the task of finding the L-PAK location. Getting to the right row was relatively straightforward as the nine indicated the ninth level; the rows were counted from the north end of the building going south, so all they had to do was take the wooden plank path to the seventh row. The walkway ran the length of the building down the center, with each row extending on both sides. The men quickly found row seven, but then came the hardest part of identifying the specific barrel. Julian had provided the number, 839001, but each row had three layers on the left and on the right.

"How many barrels you figure are in here?" Julian asked.

"If I remember right, there are 20,000 barrels in a nine-story rickhouse. Believe it or not, that's a million gallons of bourbon," Evan explained. "That means about 2200 barrels on this floor, with about 150 on each row, or 50 on each of the three levels, with 25 on each side of this center walkway."

Julian shook his head, "You did that math fast, maybe you should be the banker."

"You didn't bring a flashlight, did you?"

"Nope, but I do have an app for that." Julian smiled as he pulled his phone out of his pocket.

"Me too; you take left, I'll take the right."

A few minutes into the search, Julian called out that he had found the right barrel. The barrel was on the second level of the rack, so they'd have to pull the barrel off the rack and set it on the floor.

"How heavy is this thing supposed to be?" Evan asked, placing his palms on the top of the barrel and nudging it to get an idea. To his surprise, he was barely able to lift the barrel. As the barrel fell back into place, there was the full sound of sloshing.

"Assuming that the L-PAK is not something to drink, are we sure that we have the right number?" Evan asked, verifying the number.

Julian examined the size of the barrel. It was a standard, charred, 53-gallon aging oak barrel that had been used for centuries. They could have placed the L-PAK inside the barrel before camouflaging it with bourbon. Julian attempted to lift the barrel, then tried the next barrel which was much heavier. Evan did the same with the barrels on the opposite side of the row and found they were much heavier than barrel 839001.

"This is it but I have no idea how we're going to get it off of this rack and onto the floor," Julian said.

Evan retrieved a fire ax at the end of the of the walkway and held it out for Julian. "Maybe, we need to open it in place and then drag the box out on the ground. The L-PAK's been soaking in bourbon for 40 years so don't think there's much we can do to harm it by draining the barrel and pulling it out."

Julian backed against the wall as Evan swung at the barrel head. The swing was met with considerable resistance, and the ax bounced off the wood. Evan shook his head. "I guess the pressure of the liquid against the barrel head is preventing us from being able to brute force our way into it."

"Let me have the ax." Julian struck the rack holding the barrel.

The board was less resistant and cracked, giving way after several blows. Both men watched as the barrels fell a level. Without saying a word, they worked the barrel back and forth until it slid off the rack and onto the walkway. Evan gestured to roll the barrel towards the center where they'd have more space to work. This time they swung at the side staves and a flood of whiskey spilled onto the walkway and down through the building. They loosened the staves and exposed the L-PAK.

"Oh yeah," said Julian in victory.

Once the L-PAK was free, they found themselves perplexed as Simon Dennis had been as to how to find a way in. Fortunately, Julian was more observant than Simon, and he noticed the depressed rectangular pattern that existed in the upper left corner of the box. Taking the knife from his pocket, Julian traced the rectangular pattern on the box, cutting through the material.

The panel popped out of place and exposed the hidden digital panel. Julian stroked his chin. Evan noticed a simple LED display showing six zeros. Underneath the screen was a standard numeric keypad with numbers zero to nine.

"Do you know the six digits? Is that part of what was in the Execution Message?" Evan asked.

"Yeah, I mean, no. This code is simple; it's my birthday. The code in the Message is for the sequencer, once we get it all put together. Here goes part one." Julian leaned forward and depressed the numeric keys one at a time: zero-nine-two-three-six-nine. As he typed each digit, it appeared on the LED and replaced the zeros. Upon entering the last digit, the display flashed the number 092369 twice before returning to all zeros again. He paused for a moment, expecting something to happen but after a few seconds, nothing did. "Mmm. Well, I thought it was my birthday I can't think of another logical six-digit number."

"So, your birthday is September 23rd?" Evan started to ask.

"Yeah, I must have hit a wrong key—I'll try it again," Julian reached out and slowly entered the same number again, hoping for a different result. Again, when he entered the last nine the display flashed the number 092369 twice and then returned to all zeros.

"You know at some point there are self-defense mechanisms that will do things we might not like," Evan said, remembering Dieter's words.

Julian reviewed everything he could remember from the Academy. Then it struck him like a lightning bolt. He reached out again, and this time entered the numbers two-three-zero-nine-six-nine. Upon entering the last number, rather than flashing twice, he heard a click, and the lid of the box lifted slightly. "With all the idiosyncrasies they had us learn to be entirely Americanized, this they screwed up. The Russian date format is different than the United States. Here we use month, day, year. In the Soviet Union they use day, month, year."

Evan nodded and then shook his head, anxious to move to the next step. He looked at his watch and made a note of the time. "That 14-minute clock is ticking, we need to get moving." Evan tapped his watch.

When he lifted the lid of the box, Julian was greeted with a foam shadowbox construct he remembered from decades before. He withdrew each piece and built the weapon almost from muscle memory. The pieces that screwed together had small aluminum caps on the ends that resembled small cups to protect the threads. Julian set them to the side, screwed the pieces of the rocket together, and connected the wiring. When it was complete, he had a rather short rocket with a thick wire coming out of the bottom, waiting to be plugged into the sequencer.

"Got your little modulator piece handy?" Julian asked.

Evan dug through his pockets and handed the small device to Julian who attached the wire from the rocket to one of the modulator's ports and then connected a second wire that originated from the sequencer. Once the connection was made, the sequencer came to life, and another LED screen display lit up, this one with the capability of handling eight numbers. Again, below the screen was a standard numeric keypad.

"This is the one that you got from the Execution Message?" Evan asked.

"Yep, this is it. Providing I do this right when I enter the eighth number, the screen is supposed to show a two-hour time clock which gives us time to get the hell out. However, from what you said, the minute I enter that last digit, your little box will begin to do its stuff, and the entire rig will be deactivated and made inert," Julian said, unfolding the piece of paper yet again. "Here," Julian handed the paper to Evan, "I can't hold it up to the light, read the paper, and enter the numbers. You read the numbers and I'll punch them in."

"No problem, but do note that my guy told me we only get one chance for this part. If the number is wrong, the thing goes off and takes us with it. Not the way I wanted to end my afternoon in a Kentucky rickhouse." Looking at the piece of paper Evan found it covered with smudged fingerprints and smears caused by sweat. Evan tried to discern which eight numbers Julian would need from the jumble he was looking at. "You do mean the numbers here at the very bottom, right?"

"Yep, just read them off one at a time."

"Seven," Evan called out, and Julian repeated the number just before he punched it in. "Two-nine-zero-four-three." Evan paused for a moment as he looked over Julian's shoulder to see the numbers 729043 on the display.

Julian, noticing the pause, nodded and turned his attention back to the keypad.

"Six," Evan said, then Julian echoed and pushed the number six key.

"Zer... no, wait ... I can't read what you wrote here. Is this an eight, a three, or a zero?"

Julian illuminated the page but the number was badly smeared. "Damn, I don't know."

"We don't have enough time to climb back down to make sure we have the right number. What you think we should do?"

Julian gave a heavy sigh and leaned back against one of the barrels as his head fell forward into his hands. He wouldn't have to worry about his relationship with Camille if he got this wrong; he wouldn't have to worry about anything anymore. He made fists and hit himself in syncopation as he went over the options in his head. Zero-eight-three, zero-eight-three, zero-eight-three, and then, without giving it any further thought, he opened his eyes, leaned forward, and pushed the number eight key.

Evan watched in shock. He wasn't sure why Julian had made his decision but it was done. He held his breath waiting for whatever was coming next. Looking at the screen, he could see the numbers all in a row 72904368 - then the screen went blank.

Both men sat motionless, waiting for something to happen, waiting for anything to happen. Thirty seconds passed and then a full minute. Neither man was breathing. The silence was broken by the ring of Evan's phone.

"Congratulations, you deactivated it. The modulator has left the weapon inert and the team will be there shortly to pick up the device for disposal. You've done well," Dieter said.

Evan thanked him before disconnecting the call. "That was Dieter. Apparently, we did something right; the weapon has been deactivated."

"My God, it's over."

Evan lowered himself to the floor next to Julian. Looking at the now inert device, Evan realized the aluminum caps might just serve another purpose. He picked up two caps and dipped them into the nearly 40-year-old bourbon that remained at the bottom of the barrel. He sat beside Julian and handed him a drink. "Here's to us, and a mission accomplished successfully." Evan extended the makeshift cup.

"To us," Julian echoed as he tilted his cup and tapped Evan's before taking a strong pull on the wondrous amber liquid.

"Damn," said Evan after taking a drink, "That's so smooth, it has to be over 150 proof."

"Good, let's get drunk." Julian emptied the cup and rose for two refills.

"Sure, why not. Save the world, get drunk. Works for me." Evan let his head fall back against the barrel as he closed his eyes. "I really need to call Nikki once we get out of here, maybe she would be up for a weekend escape."

"Hello?" Nikki called. She had given up waiting on the hill and figured they had been successful when there was no explosion. Nikki found the elevator and when nothing happened, she located the power box and flipped it on. This time the door opened and she pressed the ninth-floor button to find her lost protectees.

"Nikki?" Evan asked as he and Julian stood behind whiskey barrels with their weapons drawn.

"This is Nikki?" Julian slipped his gun back into his waistband and picked up his bourbon.

"That's her." Evan lowered his weapon but did not pick up his cup just yet. He was stunned and confused.

"Evan, I'm on your side, and from what I understand, the world is safe because of you guys," Nikki said as she approached.

Evan tucked his weapon under his belt and found another of the discarded aluminum caps to fill with bourbon for Nikki. "So, you were the one on the hill?"

"Uh huh. Once I heard the world was safe again, I thought we might have a few things we need to discuss. Since everything seems to be done here, how about a ride back to Michigan?"

Julian understood what Evan was about to ask. "Sure, I'll take care of returning the car to the airport. We just need to get your stuff, and we can all take off."

After finishing their bourbon, they departed the building. As they walked towards the gate, they noticed a black SUV, and two men dressed in jumpsuits. Both men carried large duffel bags and aside from a brief nod gave no acknowledgment to the people making their way out of the area.

Nikki turned to Evan, "Why don't you take a minute to say goodbye your friend. I'll go get my car and pick you up in a moment."

Evan nodded and watched as she disappeared from sight.

"She seems nice and she's a pretty good shot too," Julian said, not quite sure what he was supposed to say.

"Yeah. Apparently, Nikki has a great many hidden talents," Evan agreed.

"Hey," Julian put his hand on Evan's shoulder, "the last 48 hours have been kind of a big unmasking of hidden things but none of that means that what you were feeling before isn't still valid. Why don't you listen to whatever she has to tell you and then figure out what you're willing to accept? Just look at what Camille and I have to deal with. For some reason, however, I have great faith that it will all work out. I have that kind of faith in you and Nikki too. I saw the look in her eyes." Julian patted Evan's shoulder and pulled him close.

"You know, you are a lot different than I expected you to be. I'm glad this all worked out, and I'm glad I met you and Camille," Evan said as he hugged him back.

"Maybe you and Nikki can come out and see us later when we've all figured out who we all really are." He opened the trunk of the car and released the magazine from his gun and then Evan's.

Evan grabbed his backpack and suitcase as Nikki's car approached. They shook hands and hugged again.

"By the way, what made you finally decide the last number was eight?"

"I didn't. I was going for the zero and missed."

Evan could tell from his expression he was being earnest. Julian shrugged his shoulders, got into the car, and with a final wave he disappeared in a cloud of dust.

Evan turned towards Nikki, and she immediately grabbed the sides of his face and pulled him forward to kiss him passionately. When the energy of the kiss had lessened, from desperate hunger to one of white-hot passion ready to ignite, Nikki looked directly into his eyes.

"Nikki, I…" Evan started to say.

Placing her index finger to his lips, Nikki said, "Shhh. We have six hours before we get back to Michigan, and I plan on telling you everything about me. Then you can decide if we are something that's going to happen … First things first, my real first name is Ashley, not Nikki." She scanned his face for some sort of clue.

Not a Nikki? My life just got a whole lot better. "You're right; we have six hours before we get back to Michigan. Why don't you just tell me the parts of the story that matter from this point forward, rather than everything that doesn't matter that happened from this point backward? Then, once everything it is all out the open, we can find somewhere to pull off and maybe do something more interesting than talking to break the tension."

Ashley's eyes flashed; this was not the reply she'd expected, or maybe it was? After all, she had never met a man quite like Evan before. She leaned forward and gave him a quick peck on the lips before turning up the volume on the radio and flooring the car. They left nothing behind but a wall of dust.

Evan relaxed and let the words of the Modern English song *I*

Melt with You bounce around in his brain as he waited to discover more about this beautiful woman he'd fallen in love with.

Chapter Eighteen

Sergei was aware of the complete failure of the Crimson Firebird Initiative by the time he arrived in Melrose, but there was nothing he could do. He was sure he had covered his tracks and lying in bed with Freya, he tried to make peace with this failure. He lay on his back, staring at the ceiling, feeling her naked body as she changed positions.

"You know, I think the time has come," Adrian said as he caressed her back with his fingertips.

"For what, luv?" Freya shifted her body and glided her hand down between his legs. "Time for a bit more of this?"

Adrian's body reacted to her touch and his priorities shifted. "Yes, time, first for this and then I believe you need to get some scissors and a razor and find out what I look like beneath his beard. Since I'm going to be living here full-time now, I ought to adopt a new look, don't you think?"

She raised herself up on her elbows and considered Adrian's face for a moment, using her hand to stroke one side and then the other. Then Freya straddled him to look down upon his face. "Hmm, you know I've always wondered what was under there. You know what else? I've always wondered how those bare cheeks would feel against my inner thighs. But maybe I should feel it this way one last time."

With that, she moved further up on his body, imagining the look and feel of her man without facial hair.

As Ashley slept, Evan snuck into the dining room to use the phone Dieter had given him one last time.

"Hello, Evan, I am so glad everything turned out well in the end. Isn't it lovely when things go as planned?" Dieter said.

"Yes, well, it all worked out in the end. I just wanted to take a moment to say goodbye since it appears our business together is over."

"Yes, yes, our business is indeed at an end. Just to let you know, we did finally obtain a master list of all of the devices, and they have all been neutralized. So, the world is safe from the Crimson Firebird once and for all. Also, I have sent a final cashier's check to compensate you in some small way for your efforts. I hope you will find it adequate for what I have put you through." Dieter had the phone on speaker so he could stand before his newly purchased saltwater aquarium, a reward for the success of their mission. He was dropping bits of frozen brine shrimp into the water and watching his new aquatic roommates swim towards the surface to devour the supplied bounty.

"Thank you, that is unexpected but greatly appreciated."

"Perhaps, you should consider taking a long vacation with your lady friend. You have been through a lot together and an escape would be a nice way to celebrate the success." Dieter could see a shadow approaching through the frosted glass of his front door, so he closed the lid on the fish tank, wiped his hands on a towel and picked up his phone. "For now, my friend, I need to go but please feel free to keep this phone and reach out to me should you ever feel the need."

"I'm not sure that would ever be necessary but I will hold onto the phone as you suggest. Thanks again." As he sat at the dining room table, fidgeting with the phone in his hands, Ashley's arms wrapped around his shoulders and her bare breasts pressed against his back.

"Come back to bed, sweetie. I need to make love with you again," Ashley whispered into his ear.

"I can help you out with that need." Evan took her by the hand and led her back to his bedroom.

Zax raised his head for a moment as they passed before falling back to sleep.

Bavaria, Germany

Dieter opened his front door.

"*Herr Sieg?*" asked a young man dressed in a suit, holding a document box.

"*Ja,*" Dieter replied.

"*Mein namen ist Vincent Singly, von der Anwaltskanzlei Ferguson, Brice und Rushing in Boston. Ich bin hier, um mit Ihnen über eine Angelegenheit zu sprechen, die wir für einen unserer Klienten behandeln. Vielleicht könnte ich hereinkommen und mit dir darüber sprechen?*"

Dieter considered the young man for a moment, realizing he must be some sort of junior associate with the firm, who'd drawn the short straw and had to play delivery boy. "Let's try that again in English, as your German, while well-intentioned, is a bit more formal than what we speak here in Bavaria. Please, do come in, Vincent." As Dieter said this, he motioned the young man into his home and led him to the dining room where the young man set the box on the table. After offering Vincent something to drink, he sat down across from him and motioned for him to proceed.

"Thank you, I understand that the German I learned in college is not what is spoken on the streets here. But when this assignment came up, I was the closest thing to a German speaker that the firm had, so I'm the one that was selected to come over here for this. Starting from the top again, I am from the law firm Ferguson, Brice, and Rushing in Boston. One of our clients, hired us to handle the hand delivery of this box of documents should a particular set of circumstances occur."

"What type of circumstances?"

336

"According to his specifications, he was supposed to contact us every two weeks. If he ever failed to get in touch with us, we were to deliver this box to you." Vincent reached into his coat pocket and withdrew an envelope which he opened, removed a document from inside of it, and then unfolded. "If you would be so good as to sign the bottom of this receipt attesting to the fact that I have given you the box, I will be on my way." Vincent was obviously in a hurry to depart.

Dieter looked over the simple document which stated they had presented him with the box. It was sealed with monofilament tape to prevent it from being opened without leaving evidence. Dieter took Vincent's pen, signed his name to the document, and returned the pen and paper.

"Thank you very much, Herr Sieg. With that, I will be on my way."

"Why are you in such a rush?" Dieter was suddenly suspicious of the contents of the box which Vincent seemed to be in a hurry to abandon.

"Uh, my flight back to America is first thing in the morning, and I wanted to spend a few hours this afternoon seeing some of the sights in Munich."

Dieter nodded. "And who could blame you? Munich is a beautiful city with lots to see as well as good food and drink." Dieter held his door open as the young man walked through it. *"Tschüss!"*

Dieter returned to consider the box. After examining the exterior thoroughly and finding no clues other than a client number, he cut through the monofilament tape. On top of the stack of folders was a sealed envelope, with his handwritten name. He removed the folders and set them on the table. There were at least 100 of them. Then, sitting down he opened the letter and read.

Dieter,

> *My old friend, it is with a heavy heart that I have to do this to you, but it is the only way that I could guarantee that this matter would be taken care of properly. What you are in possession*

of now is all of the projects that I worked on while I was with the KGB. I have always assumed that they were all closed, but due to recent events, I realize that this assumption is incorrect. I cannot allow such projects to be turned loose on the world without a conscience weighing the consequences of doing so.

I have been working to try and ensure that each of these projects has been closed out, but if you have received this box, it means that I am no longer able to do this, probably for some reason beyond my control. So, I pass them on to you knowing that as a man of conscience you will attempt to take care of them.

The account listed at the bottom of this letter is with the Bank of Zürich and has a balance of $1.9 million Euros. I hope this should be more than sufficient to compensate you for your time and efforts in this task.

I will never forget what you did for me that night in Berlin. I can only hope that you will be able to help me with this as well.

Fyodor

Dieter stroked the side of his face with his hands as he considered the letter, and then he took the first folder on the pile, opened it, and began to read.

As Freya walked away from Adrian's house and up the path, she encountered an unfamiliar man approaching. Later, she would only recall he was fairly nondescript in his appearance and did not look directly at her as they passed. She was in a bit of a hurry, heading to the local bistro to pick up sandwiches for lunch. Freya turned to see if the stranger was going to Adrian's house, but he continued to walk past without stopping.

Walking past the house until Freya was out of sight, he turned back around for Adrian's door. Inside Sergei had just started to play *An Andres Segovia Recital*, a vinyl recording he had picked up when he was in Czechoslovakia in the early sixties. The first track had started to play when Sergei was interrupted by the sound of knocking at the door. Without turning down the music, he walked towards the door, becoming Adrian on the way.

Maksim had been waiting several moments when the door opened and he was greeted by Adrian. A sudden realization dawned on Adrian's face as he became Sergei for the final time. Maksim seized the opportunity and thrust his hands out taking Sergei by the throat, immediately cutting off his air supply, and then walked him back into the house, kicking the front door closed as he crossed the threshold.

As the notes of Segovia's acoustic Spanish guitar rose in the background, Maksim stared into Sergei's eyes noting the man's surprise and fear as he held his throat tight in his hands, preventing the man from obtaining a much-needed breath. Even though Sergei fought valiantly, pounding Maksim's arms, and kicking with his bare feet, he was no match for the much younger and stronger man. As Maksim watched the life depart Sergei's eyes, he could feel the man's body grow limp as he lay him back on the floor. Even after he knew Sergei was dead, he continued to hold his throat for a full minute longer.

The soundtrack provided by the stereo continued as Maksim dragged the corpse into the bedroom and placed him onto his bed. He found the floor safe exactly where he was told it would be, under the green rug and below the floorboards of the hallway. The safe had been there for years and was an older model he was adept at breaking into. Using a stethoscope, he listened to the tumblers, spinning the dial back and forth. Lying down next to the hole in the floor, he removed the contents from the safe until it was emptied. He spun the dial and returned the boards and rug to their place. Maksim then took a plastic garbage bag from his pocket and filled it with the safe's contents.

Returning to the bedchamber, where Sergei's body lay motionless, Maksim withdrew a cigar from his pocket and lit it. After the ember at the end of the cigar was glowing, he placed it between two of

Sergei's fingers and angled the tip of the cigar so that it was in contact with the bedding. Then, Maksim moved to the doorway and waited. It did not take long for the old cotton bedding to first smolder and then burst into flames. As soon as the bed was completely aflame, Maksim turned to leave but before departing Adrian's home, he went into the living room where the music had just gone silent. He turned the album over to the B side and started it, the soundtrack again filling the house as an accompaniment to the crackle of quickly spreading fire. Maksim walked out the door and then towards the Melrose city limits, away from the direction that he had seen Freya headed.

In 15 minutes or so, Freya returned to find the house engulfed in fire. She called the fire brigade, instinctively knowing there was no way Adrian would be saved.

Once Maksim arrived back at his car, he dialed the number for his most recent client and informed him that the mission was complete.

"Very good. Payment will be transferred shortly. There will be more things I will need you to do for me from time to time. Please keep me updated as to your contact information," the voice on the phone said.

"No problem, this number will be good for a while," Maksim said. "I will ship this safe's contents to you as soon as I get to the next DHL office. Nice doing business with you."

"And also with you." Morty disconnected and then considered his new asset. *Imagine that, an ex KGB agent and Siberian Rime asset working for the Mossad. Has to be another first.* Morty sat back and lit his cigar.

"Hello?" Evan did not bother to look at the screen before answering the phone. *Unidentified caller.*

"Evan, it is Dieter. I am sorry to call you on your private number and disturb you this way but I needed to talk to you immediately." The anxiety in Dieter's voice was palpable.

"Okay, what's wrong? I thought we had fixed everything." Evan closed the master bathroom where Ashley was showering.

"I did as well. But then I had a visit today from a lawyer who gave me a box of papers. A box of papers from Fyodor."

"Dieter, I keep telling you I am not a spy or some kind of mercenary. I am just a writer. Why would you be contacting me now because you got a box of papers? Do you need them edited?"

"I understand your trepidation, this is not what you were trained for but it is what you are good at. Now, tell me, have you ever heard of CRISPR?"

About the Author

Sheldon Charles is a decorated Air Force veteran, whose career has taken him around the globe, and given his writing a unique international flair. He is the author of *Three Paperclips & a Grey Scarf, Blood Upon the Sands* and *From Within the Firebird's Nest*. His last two books (*From Within the Firebird's Nest* & *Blood Upon the Sands*) earned Amazon bestseller badges after being ranked Number One for War Fiction and Middle East fiction, respectively. Sheldon

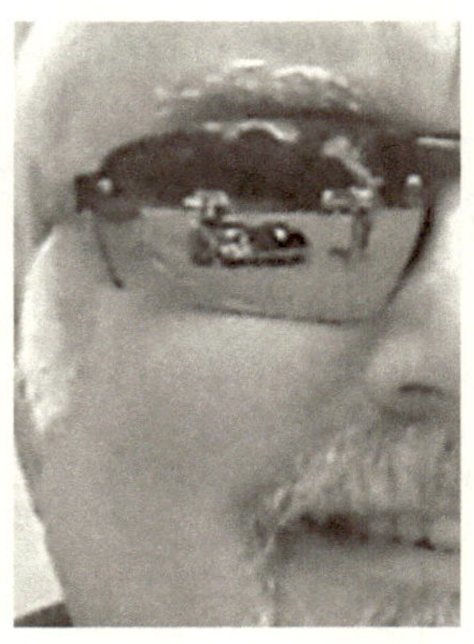

currently resides in Michigan, where he is a member of Michigan Writers.

From the Author

At about age eight, I went to my first sleep away camp at Lake Arrowhead, California. I could say many things about the camp; just like anyone else who has ever gone to camp, it is impossible to escape without more than a few *One time at camp* stories.

Every night of the week, there was a huge bonfire down by the lake right at sunset. It seemed like there were thousands of us gathered there, but in reality, it was probably only 2-300 boys gathered around in a semi-circle being led in cheers, songs and watching skits. All of this was new to me, and camp was a big bag full of new stuff of which to be a part. At the end of the evening came an act that changed my life.

The character's name escapes me now, but he walked out slowly from the darkness, using a cane, and wearing a jungle explorer jacket with a pith helmet. A long beard and wire-rimmed glasses finished his look. Everyone fell silent as he walked to the center of the fire ring and slowly sat down on a small stool a few feet in front of the fire. The intensity of the moment increased as he took off his glasses and cleaned them using a handkerchief he had taken out of one of his many pockets. The only sound to be heard was the crackling of the fire that roared behind him.

Even among us first timers, there was a sense of expectation as he cleared his throat and began to speak. He told us a story. The story was a combination of local legend, tall tale, and humor; all told using various voices and sound effects he provided. As he spoke, he used facial expressions and hand gestures to emphasize points. The assembled crowd was no longer silent as we laughed, cheered, and shouted comments while he kept us enthralled. The teller of tales would eventually stand and walk from side to side as the story came to the climax; his gestures becoming more wild and inspiring excitement.

When he finished the story, he would slowly drop his hands to his side and lower his head – as the absolute silence returned. As if on cue, we all exploded in loud cheering and applause. Over the course of my life, I have come to realize that what I witnessed was a master storyteller sharing his craft. I went back to my cabin every night of camp inspired and knowing the career path I wanted for my life. I wanted to be a storyteller too.

As an avid reader, I found myself drawn into writing. My first public display of my talents was in 2009 when I climbed back on a motorcycle after a thirty-year hiatus. While riding, I found myself flooded with thoughts, words, and visions of tales I should tell. So, I did. I started a blog to record those events. I found myself writing about people, adventures, and observations. It was not long before I expanded into fictional tales written. The blog evolved into a weekly, when I was assigned to Kuwait, then writing about my experiences living in the Middle East… Humorous and poignant.

It was there, during a meeting, I expressed a small bit of regret that I had yet to become the storyteller I envisioned only to have LtCol

Dan Ellis, point out that I had become the storyteller – using the written word. Sometimes it takes someone outside of you to point out a truth you are too close to see. I am grateful Dan did, as it caused me to write and publish my first novella and to begin writing tales in earnest.

Someday, I may get a chance to be a purest, experiencing that feeling of walking out before a crowd in front of a roaring fire, wearing an appropriate costume with the right props ready to tell tall tales. However, for now, I find great joy in telling stories through the written word and sharing them with readers. I hope you enjoy them.

You can always find an up-to-date list of my Evan Davis tales and all of my other books, at my website: **www.valkyriespirit.com** Also…

Sign up -- Be the first to know when there is a new release by signing up for the Email Newsletter. I will only send emails when there is book news and will never release your email to others, ever. To sign up drop a line to newsletter@valkyriespirit.com

Review it --- Consider posting a short review with the vendor where you found this book. Reader reviews help others decide whether they'll enjoy a book.

Connect with me -- I'd love to hear from you, please stop by my Facebook page for updates on new titles, cover previews, and general discussion: www.facebook.com/TheRealSheldonCharles/

Shel

shel@valkyriespirit.com

Hired by *Al Hakim*, a Kuwaiti horse breeder, to improve the world's bleak perception of his beloved country, Evan Davis enters Kuwait with six months to produce articles about its people and culture.

A journalist by necessity, Evan soon forms a close bond with his employer and his interpreter and cultural guide. But when some shocking information is anonymously put into his hands, his eyes are opened to the plight of an entire people group. He must choose between a newly formed friendship and exposing a tragic truth to the world.

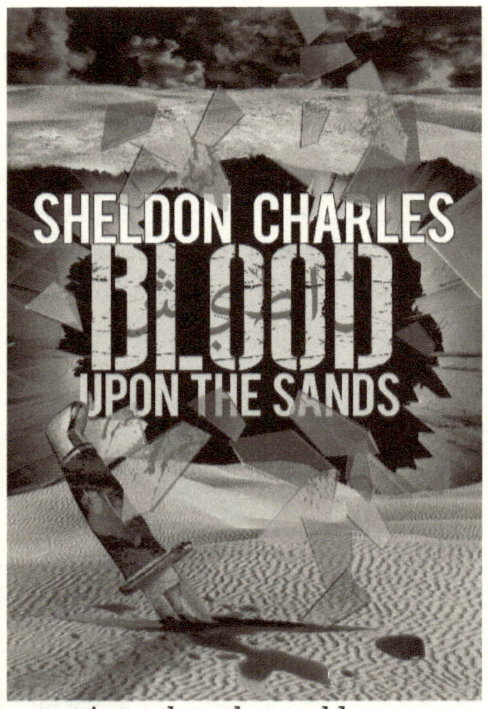

With a sinister and sociopathic ex-KGB assassin sowing hatred against the down-trodden population of stateless people and racial tensions reaching a fever pitch, events quickly spiral out of control. Evan finds himself desperately attempting to stop an insidious conspiracy, prevent further bloodshed and give a voice to a voiceless people by the power of his pen.

Blood Upon the Sands -- A suspenseful thriller that will keep you nailed to the edge of your seats, Sheldon Charles weaves a masterful tale centered on real-world history and based on the current situation of Kuwait's Bedoon population.

Now in eBook, Paperback & Audiobook